TROY RISING

BAEN BOOKS by JOHN RINGO

TROY RISING
Live Free or Die • *Citadel* • *The Hot Gate*
Troy Rising (edited with Gray Rinehart)

SHADOW'S PATH (with Casey Moores)
Not That Kind of Good Guy • *Welcome to the Jungle*
Tides of Ruin (forthcoming)

TRANSDIMENSIONAL HUNTER (with Lydia Sherrer)
Into the Real • *Through the Storm* • *Behind the Veil* • *Beyond the Rift*

BLACK TIDE RISING
Under a Graveyard Sky • *To Sail a Darkling Sea* • *Islands of Rage and Hope*
Strands of Sorrow • *The Valley of Shadows* (with Mike Massa)
Black Tide Rising (ed. with Gary Poole) • *Voices of the Fall* (ed. with Gary Poole)
River of Night (with Mike Massa) • *We Shall Rise* (ed. with Gary Poole)

LEGACY OF THE ALDENATA
A Hymn Before Battle • *Gust Front* • *When the Devil Dances*
Hell's Faire • *The Hero* (with Michael Z. Williamson)
Cally's War (with Julie Cochrane) • *Watch on the Rhine* (with Tom Kratman)
Sister Time (with Julie Cochrane) • *Yellow Eyes* (with Tom Kratman)
Honor of the Clan (with Julie Cochrane) • *Eye of the Storm*

COUNCIL WARS
There Will Be Dragons • *Emerald Sea* • *Against the Tide*
East of the Sun, West of the Moon

INTO THE LOOKING GLASS
Into the Looking Glass • *Vorpal Blade* (with Travis S. Taylor)
Manxome Foe (with Travis S. Taylor) • *Claws that Catch* (with Travis S. Taylor)

EMPIRE OF MAN (with David Weber)
March Upcountry • *March to the Sea* • *March to the Stars* • *We Few*

SPECIAL CIRCUMSTANCES
Princess of Wands • *Queen of Wands*

PALADIN OF SHADOWS
Ghost • *Kildar* • *Choosers of the Slain* • *Unto the Breach*
A Deeper Blue • *Tiger by the Tail* (with Ryan Sear)

STANDALONE TITLES
The Last Centurion • *Citizens* (ed. with Brian M. Thomsen)
Beyond the Ranges (with James Aidee)

TROY RISING

EDITED BY

JOHN RINGO

& GRAY RINEHART

BAEN

Troy Rising

A Baen Books Original

Baen Publishing Enterprises
P.O. Box 1403
Riverdale, NY 10471
www.baen.com

ISBN: 978-1-6680-7344-5

Cover art by Kurt Miller

First printing, September 2026

Distributed by Simon & Schuster
1230 Avenue of the Americas
New York, NY 10020

Library of Congress Cataloging-in-Publication Data

Names: Ringo, John, 1963- editor | Rinehart, Gray editor
Title: Troy rising / edited by John Ringo and Gray Rinehart.
Description: Riverdale, NY : Baen Publishing Enterprises, 2026. | Series: Troy rising
Identifiers: LCCN 2026020599 (print) | LCCN 2026020600 (ebook) | ISBN 9781668073445 hardcover | ISBN 9781964856797 ebook
Subjects: LCSH: Science fiction, American | Short stories, American | LCGFT: Science fiction | Short stories
Classification: LCC PS648.S3 T76 2026 (print) | LCC PS648.S3 (ebook)
LC record available at https://lccn.loc.gov/2026020599
LC ebook record available at https://lccn.loc.gov/2026020600

Printed in the United States of America
10 9 8 7 6 5 4 3 2 1

CONTENTS

INTRODUCTION

GRAY RINEHART

There's something about maple syrup.

Not the brown sugar-water too often sold under the name, but the real stuff, genuine blood of trees, boiled and fixed, thick and rich and luscious. It speaks at once of simple pleasures and the hard work, patience, and inventiveness that bring them to us. Of seasons changing, fresh air, woodland paths strewn with leaf litter.

And war.

Not just any war, but a war so brutal it brought our species to the brink of extinction. A war that introduced us to powers beyond our solar system, powers that underestimated the hard work, patience, and inventiveness of humanity. Powers that underestimated our capacity to find advantages wherever we can, even in something as seemingly mundane as maple syrup, and to exploit those advantages with ruthless precision. Powers that did not count on our ability to rally, to arm ourselves in spectacular fashion and sally forth, and to meet them and defeat them in the deadly ground of space.

There is, of course, much more to John Ringo's Troy Rising series—*Live Free or Die*, *Citadel*, and *The Hot Gate*—than maple syrup, and the idea that species that evolved on different worlds, with drastically different nutritional needs from ours, might just possibly find certain molecular combinations intoxicating that we often take for granted. On the technical side, the *science* side of science fiction, the novels feature artificial intelligences with distinct personalities, laser systems that harness the power of the sun, and of course, battlespheres "grown" from spinning nickel-iron asteroids. And the personalities loom as large as the asteroidal battle stations, showcasing John's faith in humanity's tenacity, resourcefulness, and willingness to bear crushing burdens, overcome daunting obstacles, and make tremendous sacrifices in pursuit of seemingly impossible goals: the most important of which is the goal of freedom and self-determination.

Now, for the first time, John has invited a cadre of authors to join him in exploring and expanding the Troy Rising universe. We hope you find their contributions, along with John's new short novel, captivating—like the sweet, satisfying taste of maple syrup on fresh pancakes on a frosty morning.

END RUN

Adam Oyebanji

If anyone could have seen her in flight, Bob Rossum's ship, *Theory of Forms*, would have been a sight to behold. Sleek and needle-nosed and elegantly proportioned, she was a thing of beauty, slicing silently through vacuum toward the waiting gate. In doing so, she crossed the flight path of a patroling *Constitution*-class cruiser, missing the bigger ship by little more than a kilometer.

That she could do this without provoking any kind of reaction was testimony to the fact that *Theory of Forms* was almost completely invisible. Metamaterials and modified pressor technology bent light and its electromagnetic brethren around the hull, giving no hint of her presence.

It'll be good to be home, Bob thought. Though even as his mind formed the words, he couldn't help but wonder if they were true.

"Gate emergence. Mass, approximately eighty-eight hundred metric tonnes; velocity..."

The shift boss at Space Traffic Control looked up as his lead controller struggled for words.

"That's a lot of tonnage to be going nowhere, Jim. You got a velocity for me?"

"Uh... No, boss. I do not. I, uh, I got nothing. Gate readings are real clear, though. *Something* has come through, but there's nothing on the scopes. Not radar, not infrared, not visual, not anything." The controller's flustered expression turned hopeful. "Guess it's a glitch, huh?"

The shift boss found himself frowning.

"Maybe. Tag it and send it up the chain for analysis."

The night had been beautiful, Bob thought, even if he'd spent more of it than he would have liked soaking wet. It had taken forever to dry out, to shed the scratchy aftermath of seawater and sand. But the sky had been clear, the stars bright, the breeze gentle and less humid than expected. There'd been no moon, of course, but the starlight had shone bright enough to hint at the forested slopes of the Alborz mountains: a hulking, deeper black against the night sky. Their distant shadow would have stretched as far as the eye could see were it not for the streetlight glare of the city ahead, the white-and-orange glow of Bandar-e-Anzali.

Now, with his work in the city done, a gray-fingered dawn was brushing against the salt-stained concrete and plate glass of his destination, the Pasdaran Grand Hotel. Given the boxy efficiency of the architecture, Bob had little doubt that its rooms would be modestly sized and devoid of character. But the best of them would overlook the rolling waves of the Caspian Sea.

Not that he expected to see inside of one.

Water, gray as the early morning sky, was lapping against the shoreline as he strode into the marble-tiled lobby. The night manager, caught unawares by his daybreak visitor, hurriedly stubbed out a cigarette.

"Good morning, sir. What can I do for you?" The man's English was heavily accented but comprehensible, prompting Bob into a wry smile. The manager's choice of language made sense. Even from a distance, no one was ever going to mistake him for Iranian. The expression on the man's face when he replied in near perfect Farsi was priceless.

"I was hoping for a room. One with an ocean view?"

The night manager replied with an apologetic shrug of the shoulders.

"I'm afraid it's too early for check-in, sir. Not before two p.m." His expression barely changed as a crisp hundred-dollar bill slid across the counter. "Let me see what I can do . . ." A deft clicking of computer keys. "As it happens, there *is* one available. The rate is—"

"Perfectly acceptable, I'm sure."

The night manager smiled broadly.

"May I see your passport, sir?"

"I don't have one."

The smile vanished, replaced first by bemusement, then caution.

"Are you a naturalized citizen, sir? You have a *kart-e melli*, perhaps?"

"State ID? I'm afraid not. I'm as American as they come." He allowed a gentle smile to play across his lips. "And I have American ID. From Georgia. Would you like to see my driving license?"

"Please, sir, don't make jokes about this. You can't be in Iran without a passport and a visa."

"But I am in Iran, as you can see. Without a passport or a visa. I arrived last night. Here, let me show you." He reached into his pocket. Pulled out a cell phone. Set it to playing video. "This here city of yours is real interesting, particularly after dark. There's the lagoon at night, the soccer stadium, the port, the—"

"I believe you, sir. Wish I didn't. This is most irregular. *Most* irregular." He looked at Bob expectantly.

"I imagine it is," Bob said.

More hundred-dollar bills appeared, deftly pocketed. The night manager's expansive wave took in the entirety of the lobby.

"If you'll take a seat, sir. I'll make a call to housekeeping. It will only be a few minutes."

Bob did as suggested, enjoying the firm feel of the steel-and-leather upholstery, the reassuring woosh of air-conditioning.

His ears pricked to the high-revving buzz of a motorcycle as it pulled up outside the entrance.

Two men, wearing shabby camouflage and sporting ski masks, strode across the lobby. They carried scuffed, well-used nightsticks. Dusty, rubber-soled boots squeaked against the floor.

Basij, Bob thought. Street thugs, basically. Part of Iran's IRGC, the Islamic Revolutionary Guard Corps.

"That's him," the night manager said, pointing. Fear made the man's hand tremble.

Bob Rossum rose to his feet with a smile.

"Good morning, gentlemen. What can I—?"

The first nightstick slammed into the back of his legs, collapsing him to his knees. The second crashed against his temple.

After that, nothing much registered.

* * *

London, former capital of the United Kingdom, was, like Los Angeles, Washington, D.C., and Paris, little more than a giant crater. In London's case, a crater made starkly beautiful by the creation of a vast lake, courtesy of the River Thames and the fat aquifer upon which the ancient city had once stood. Oxford, the *pro tem* capital, had been far too small to merit targeting by KEWs. Same with Cheltenham, a bucolic sandstone town that nestled in the green folds of the English countryside.

Had either the Horvath or the Rangora taken it upon themselves to know more about human cities beyond the size of their populations, Cheltenham might not have been so lucky. Cheltenham was home to GCHQ, England's equivalent of the NSA, America's junior partner in the sordid but important business of invading people's privacy. An invasion that both entities accomplished by monitoring, collecting, and processing data from all around the world. The NSA categorized what it did as signals intelligence—SIGINT. But the bland terminology didn't really cover the vast scope of the NSA's brief. Prior to the depredations of the Horvath, the NSA, making liberal use of the newly available atacirc, had admitted to rifling its way through a hundred petabytes of data *a day*, and the reality was significantly higher. Digital or analog, everything from heavily encrypted military communications to the recipe for great-grandmother's apple pie passed through its filters.

The NSA, headquartered in the outskirts of Washington, D.C., had been crippled by the KEW attack on the city: not so much by the loss of its headquarters and associated equipment, which was replaceable, but by the loss of expertise, which was not. Over fifteen thousand NSA personnel, seventy-five percent of the agency's on-site headcount, had died in the conflagration. Janitors, mathematicians, analysts: all vaporized in an instant or, far worse, consumed by impartial and uncaring flames.

Which is why Jasmine Singh, formerly of Baltimore, Maryland, found herself in a cramped conference room overlooking the round, green space at the center of the "Doughnut," GCHQ's starkly futuristic, unapologetically circular main building. Galleried and airy, with a taste in office furniture that reminded Jasmine of Starbucks, it would have been a spectacular place to work, she thought, had it not been subdivided to the nth degree to accommodate an influx of transatlantic refugees. Her hosts had been unfailingly polite, had—demonstrably—bent over backward to make them feel at home. Which didn't stop her feeling like a couch surfer. The NSA's new HQ, located in Cranberry, Pennsylvania, just outside Pittsburgh, was still waiting for its foundations to be poured. The whole project had been endlessly delayed by congressional wrangling and the diversion of tax dollars to rebuilding the space navy.

Navies were great, Jasmine thought, but without intelligence they were about as effective as a blindfolded quarterback.

"Why are we here, Jasmine?" Mac Logan, her boss, sat on the other side of the conference table, wearing his usual good-natured smile. His British opposite number, Gordon Williams, sat beside him, stiff and grim-faced. No change there, then.

"We're here to talk about fake meteors, boss."

"Fake?"

"We think so, yes."

"Can we get to the point, Miss Singh?" Williams lacked Mac's tolerance for the oblique. Also, he was an a-hole.

Jasmine fired up the conference room's A/V screen.

"Forty-eight hours ago," she said, "satellites picked up a sizeable meteor entering the atmosphere over the North Atlantic. They tracked it over northern and central Europe and into southwestern Russia, where it vanished from the 'scopes, between the cities of Saratov and Volgograd."

"Stalingrad as was," Mac murmured, still smiling.

"I'll take your word for it," Jasmine said.

"The *point*, Miss Singh? Meteors invariably vanish, do they not? It's what happens when they disintegrate. Nothing left to see."

"True. However, not long before, Space Command detected an anomaly at the gate."

"What kind of anomaly?" Williams asked.

"The kind that says eighty-eight hundred metric tonnes of something had come through from the other side, even though they couldn't see anything."

"Instrument glitch?" Mac suggested.

"They say not. Though just because they can't find one doesn't mean the glitch wasn't there. It's kinda hard to hide eighty-eight hundred metric tonnes of *anything*, never mind a spaceship, moving through vacuum. And nothing outside the gate picked it up. Logic tells us that if the gate telemetry says *A* but everything else points to *B*, then *B* is your answer. However..." She paused a moment to sync herself with the images on the A/V screen. "If you assume it's *not* a glitch, you can make some very rough estimates of trajectory based on the data collected and historical transit records. Most of which are consistent with atmospheric entry over the North Atlantic and, with a greater degree of uncertainty, the actual track of our meteor."

"That's it?" Williams pressed. "'Maybe not a glitch' and a meteor track?" He turned to Logan. "It's not quite nothing, I grant you, but it's pretty damn close. I'm not persuaded it isn't a rock."

"I'm hoping," Mac said pointedly, "that there's more."

Jasmine allowed herself the luxury of a small smile.

"There is. Based on the gate telemetry and the meteor trail, I sent the satellite data to our friends at NASA/JPL. They told us a couple of things. First, the satellites weren't getting a read on anything solid, just superheated atmospheric gases and plasma. The stuff that this thing was blasting out of its way as it came down. Second, the velocity profile is all wrong for a meteor. Meteors don't slow down much after they hit the atmosphere: they burn up or crash. This fella decelerated. Hard. And third—"

"You said a *couple* of things," Mac teased.

"So, I lied. The third thing is the most important."

"Being?"

"Just before the sats lost contact, this so-called rock executed a perfectly controlled thirty-degree turn." She took particular satisfaction from the humbled twist of Gordon Williams's mouth. "Meteors don't maneuver."

"They tell me you haven't eaten."

"I don't recall anyone offering," Bob said. He was careful to sound unconcerned.

The man on the other side of the interrogation room's scratched and possibly bloodstained table raised an eyebrow. After seventy-two hours in a featureless white cell, the chamber's drab gray décor, bloodstained or not, represented a welcome change of pace. He chose to ignore the heaviness of the chains binding his wrists to the table's rough wood, the shackles on his ankles, the two pungent *basij* lurking somewhere out of sight behind him. He concentrated on his interrogator instead.

The man was of medium height and build, his hair a luxuriant black, his beard neatly trimmed. His sleek dress shirt was buttoned at the collar without a tie, and the shine of his immaculately pressed suit shimmered to almost silver beneath the caged overhead lighting. The body beneath the suit carried not an ounce of fat.

Civilian clothing or not, the man reeked of military. IRGC, almost certainly. He made great play of setting his tablet on the table. Of reading it.

"Robert Ulysses Rossum, of Dalton, Georgia, according to your driving license. Thirty-two years of age—"

"Am I really? Guess I must be. I don't feel that old, though."

"You may not live to be much older unless you are very, very careful. Are you a careful man, Mr. Rossum?"

"When I have to be."

"Now would be a good time. You understand?"

Bob nodded.

"How did you enter the country?"

"By spaceship."

"I'm not in the mood for jokes."

"I'm not joking. I set down, let's see . . . a hundred and three hours, thirty-six minutes ago. My ship's lying at the bottom of the Caspian Sea."

"You crashed?"

"Oh, no. Just not keen on passing through customs is all. I came ashore near Bandar-e-Anzali, took some videos on my phone, tried to book a hotel and, well, the rest you know."

"The videos you took included pictures of the Anzali Naval Base." The interrogator tapped his tablet, pulling up images from Bob's cell phone. "These are close-ups of our latest *Moudge*-class frigate."

"'Latest' is a strong word. She looks real old to me. Honestly, I'm surprised she's still—"

The interrogator's finger barely twitched and yet the chair was kicked out from under him. He staggered to keep upright on shackled feet, gripping the table for balance.

A mistake.

One of the *basij* smashed a nightstick across his fingers.

"I thought you said you were a careful man, Mr. Rossum. In this place we show respect. You show *me* respect. Understand?"

"Yes, sir." He was shoved roughly back in his seat.

"You admit to being a spy?"

"If it gets your attention, yes."

The interrogator's expression bordered on the incredulous. Bob half expected the chair to be kicked away again, but it stayed in place.

"You have my attention, Mr. Rossum. Who sent you?"

"My employers wish to remain anonymous. They do, however, have a proposition for you."

"You do not appear to understand your position. This is not a business meeting."

"I wonder if I might have my phone."

"You want to call a lawyer?" A sardonic laugh.

"No, sir. I want to show you data that you failed to pull from my phone before walking in here."

"You can't be serious."

"Deadly, sir. I can be as I said a, ah, *careful* man. All that you've ripped from my phone is what I wanted you to see. But now that I have your attention, I would like you to see more."

"And why should I believe you?"

"I'm not asking you to believe me. I'm asking for my phone." Seeing anger fighting with incredulity for possession of the man's face, Bob added, "Look, sir. Humoring me costs you nothing. If I've misled you in any way, you can have your *basij* goons whale on me some more." He risked a resentful glance over his shoulder. "They do seem to enjoy that."

The interrogator, after the briefest of intervals, nodded in acquiescence. Bob heard a door open and close behind him. It was several minutes before it opened again. The phone was placed on the table, within reach of his chained hand. Not that Bob Rossum needed a hand for what needed to be done. When he spoke again, it was in a language that no one else in the room had ever heard.

There were audible gasps as the device projected a hologram.

Deep space. A slow spinning of gashed and gutted metal.

"From my recent travels, sir." The hologram shifted, a glowing blueprint superimposed itself atop the wreckage, specs and data scrolling down either side. "The late, lamented USSS *Constellation*, an American cruiser lost to Rangora fire. We scanned her intensively and reverse engineered the results. Incomplete, of course, given the damage, but enough for you to build your own or something like it, if you can acquire the necessary manufacturing capabilities and skill sets. Or cooperate with a country that already has them. Russia, maybe. Or China. Information like this can buy you a lot of leverage."

The interrogator, mouth agape, took several moments to compose himself.

"I don't believe it." The words were little more than a whisper.

"Don't take my word for it, sir." He uttered something untranslatable. "The data's in your tablet, now. And more. Take it to your superiors. I'm sure they'll know someone who knows someone who can attest to the authenticity of what I've just given you."

The interrogator fixed him with a long, appraising stare.

"What is it you want, Mr. Rossum?"

"For the moment? Nothing much. A meeting with your superiors. Someone who can get things done. Here, in Bandar-e-Anzali. And if you have enough pull, I'd really like better accommodation. Something with a view of the sea."

The meeting room was bigger this time, Jasmine noted, the A/V setup more sophisticated. This was GCHQ's best, the plate-glass conference table a near match in size to the expansive window overlooking the Doughnut's inner courtyard. Shards of sunlight lanced through heavy cloud, striking a temporary, cheerful green from the manicured grass.

Mac was there, of course, with Williams the A-hole, and someone she didn't recognize, a stick-thin, gray-haired woman in an immaculately tailored pantsuit, whom Mac had introduced as Camilla: no last name and almost certainly an alias. The woman, she suspected, was the reason for the meeting, given that Mac and the A-hole already knew what she had to say.

"So, Jasmine," Mac began. "Tell us where we are with our mysterious stealth ship."

"'Stealth' is the right word, boss. This vessel, which we've code-named *Hades*, is, to all intents and purposes, invisible."

"Hence the name," Williams interjected, with the smug, know-it-all smile of a Cambridge University alumnus. "Hades is the Greek god most closely associated with the mythical helm of invisibility."

"Uh-huh," Jasmine said, intent on moving forward. "We've done a lookback with every asset we have, anything that would have had eyes on *Hades*'s trajectory from the gate to where it hit the atmosphere. And after that, in a thousand-mile radius from where the atmospheric trail went cold. We found nothing, not even a flicker."

"*Hades* is doing everything it can to make SIGINT look bad," Mac joked. No one smiled.

"But we figured, it's a spaceship, right?" Jasmine said. "*Hades* had to land *somewhere*, and wherever it landed, there should be activity. Signs of movement, maintenance vehicles, maybe; passengers or cargo coming on or off. Even if *Hades* is so invisible that it can remain unseen on the ground, there would be stuff going on around it—loading and unloading, the erection of an awning to stop us seeing the loading and unloading, or something unseen being towed by something we *can* see, like an airport tractor. You get the idea."

"And what did you find?" Camilla asked, speaking for the first time. The accent was cut-glass English.

"Nothing, ma'am. At least, at first. We paid close attention to Russian airbases, landing strips—anywhere, really, that an eighty-eight-hundred-metric-tonne vehicle could plausibly put down. Zip. Nada. Zilch."

"And Iran?" Camilla asked. "Iranian airspace isn't that far from where *Hades* broke contact."

"Same thing. Iran doesn't have an air force worth talking about, so any activity at their bases would be real easy to pick up, seeing as there's never much of anything going on there. But here's the thing..." A/V screens blinked in rhythm with her words. "Iran's *navy* has been exceptionally active. Less than twenty-four hours after *Hades* broke contact, the naval base at Bandar-e-Anzali went on high alert. Guards doubled on the perimeter and foot patrols dockside, which is practically unheard of. All of which was followed by a lot of comings and goings from one ship in particular: the IRIS *Qaf*, one of their *Moudge*-class frigates. At least one person left that vessel under heavy escort and was taken to a building linked to the IRGC—others, too, we think. We can't be certain, but it seems likely that a number of navy personnel, including the commanding officer of the *Qaf*, probably, are having some very unpleasant conversations in a cell somewhere."

"We suspect," Mac interjected, "that something happened there that embarrassed them. A security breach of some kind."

"Terrorism?" Camilla asked.

"We don't think so," Mac replied. "For a couple of reasons.

First, there's no sign of physical damage or personal injury: no plumes of smoke, no ambulances. And second..." He nodded in Jasmine's direction, tossing her the metaphorical ball.

"Second," she said, "Iran's Caspian fleet has put to sea. Every unit they could get up and running at short notice. And they've not gone far. They're operating inside their own territorial waters, looking for something. They're clearly searching a grid. With the Russians watching."

"Watching or helping?" Camilla asked.

"Watching. Any time a Russian naval asset gets too close, they get warned off by a horde of small attack boats."

"Not very comradely behavior," Williams pointed out. "Normally, given how close those countries are these days, one would have thought the Iranians would welcome the help."

"Unless," Mac said, "the price of that help is sharing whatever it is they're looking for."

"Which we believe to be *Hades*," Jasmine added. "We think something went wrong on approach and it ditched in the southern Caspian. That's a technological gold mine for the Iranians if they can find and salvage it."

"Which could be hard, depending on where she sank," Williams said. "The southern Caspian is deep. Over a thousand meters in places." A small smirk. "That's about thirty-three hundred feet in American."

Jasmine pretended she didn't need the conversion, but was impressed, nonetheless. If *Hades* was that far down, there was no way the Iranians could get to it, not without Russian help.

"We also think," she said, "that at least some of the crew survived. That they penetrated the Anzali base in a way that made the Iranians, and the *Qaf* in particular, look bad. Even if the crew just clambered aboard the *Qaf* asking for help without being intercepted, the Iranians would hate that. In fact, there's a good chance the *Hades* crew has been thrown in a cell too; Iranian hospitality being famously lacking in such circumstances."

"Maybe. Maybe not," Camilla said. She was staring into space, quietly processing the information. What intrigued Jasmine, though, was the way that Mac and the A-hole were watching her. Whatever the woman thought about all this was clearly important to them.

Oh!

For a horrible moment Jasmine feared she'd said the word out loud. *Of course she's important to them.* The NSA had little difficulty penetrating Iran's electronic networks, which was why the Iranians seldom used them for anything important. To get the good stuff, you needed spies: HUMINT, not SIGINT. And when it came to HUMINT, Iran was a notoriously difficult target. The US, since the fall of the Shah and the ending of diplomatic relations from as long ago as 1979, had almost no high-quality HUMINT in Iran. But the British, with centuries of contact, a weirdly compatible culture, and a working embassy, did. Camilla, Mac hoped, was America's way into whatever the heck it was the Iranians were up to. *That* was why she was here.

Mentally, at least, Jasmine crossed her fingers.

"Something *is* going on with the Iranians," Camilla said at last. "And this"—a manicured nail tapped lightly on a slaved A/V screen—"provides some context." She paused once more, weighing whether or not to add to the NSA's store of knowledge. "Okay, look. Last week, IRGC's intelligence organization, IO-IRGC, dispatched a mid-level officer to Bandar-e-Anzali. Not quite routine, but not that unusual. When he got back, though, whatever he had to say set the cat amongst the pigeons. Meetings all across the top tiers of the Iranian government, up to and including the office of the Supreme Leader himself. What was discussed, we don't know, but I *can* tell you that a very senior IO-IRGC officer, a Brigadier General Reza Khosravi, went to Bandar-e-Anzali last night." She looked around the room before adding, "Whatever this is, I don't think it's as simple as a security breach and salvage operation."

"Why?" Mac asked.

"Because Reza Khosravi is a fixer. He's the chap the Iranians go to when they want to strike a deal."

"Are you sure you won't have some tea?" said the man who'd introduced himself as Reza.

"No thank you, sir. I'm quite full," Bob said.

Which elicited a chuckle.

"I doubt that, Mr. Rossum. My associates tell me you haven't eaten a thing the whole time you've been here."

"They exaggerate." Bob set his sight on the blue haze of the horizon. The house was on a hill overlooking the sea, the terrace on which they were sitting cooled by a coastal breeze. He found himself feeling strangely at peace. It was so much easier to think in the presence of water.

"How do I know you're as important as you say you are?" he asked.

Reza chuckled again.

"I never said I was important, Mr. Rossum. Merely that I have the ear of people who are. People, I'm afraid, who are not prepared to drop what they're doing simply because you demand it."

"Then it may be that you and I have nothing to discuss."

"That's your prerogative, of course, but no one else will be coming in my place. We can return you to, ah, less comfortable accommodations indefinitely. No harm will come to you, rest assured. I'm important enough to guarantee that, at least. But until you're ready to tell me why it is you're here, the Islamic Republic of Iran is quite happy to keep you in solitary confinement." Reza made a pleading gesture with his hands. "Look at it from our point of view, Mr. Rossum. You're a security risk. We can't have you in dangerous proximity to high-level members of government. I really am the best you can do."

Bob stared out to sea a few moments more.

"You make a persuasive argument, sir." He shifted in his seat, turned himself so as to be looking directly into Reza's eyes. "The people I work for are prepared to provide you with the means to hack SAPL."

Reza's eyes became saucer wide. But only for a moment.

"That's not possible."

"What could I possibly have to gain by lying? I can't imagine a surer way to find myself hanged from the end of a crane."

"Of course. But the truth of what you say beggars belief. It would mean—"

"It would mean that your country is only a few keystrokes away from having the entire power of the sun at its fingertips. A power presently controlled by an egomaniacal, *American* gazillionaire, who does not care for your country at all. Loathes it, I daresay. You can live free of Tyler Vernon or die under his hateful politics." Bob leaned forward in his seat. "How long do you think it will be before it occurs to Mr. Vernon and the government he controls that they can blast every center of power in the Islamic Republic to molten ruin at the flick of a switch?"

"Tyler Vernon would never..." Reza's voice faded into doubt.

"Exactly. Just because he *hasn't* done it doesn't mean he can't, or won't. And with the Rangora and Horvath out of the picture, there's nothing 'out there' that demands his attention. Sooner or later, his thoughts, and his government's thoughts, are going to turn to more earthly matters."

"But the *consequences*, Mr. Rossum! If Tyler Vernon were to do as you say, he would truly become the Great Satan: worse than the Rangora or the Horvath because he would have obliterated millions of his own species. He would be a pariah, even among his own decadent kind."

"The Solar Array Pumped Laser is more sophisticated than that, sir. More surgical. With the right intelligence, SAPL could hit out only at your leaders. A few thousand high-value targets with only modest collateral damage. And anyway, why should he care about casualties? He is literally the most powerful man in the solar system, possibly the galaxy, and he operates with no constraint whatsoever. *No one can stop him from doing anything he wants.* The only limits he faces are those of his own conscience. And as we know all too well, human conscience is . . . malleable."

"Our intelligence on Tyler Vernon is very clear, Mr. Rossum. He is a man who operates by a set of firmly settled principles. Misguided, of course, but firmly settled. And those principles would preclude him doing what you suggest."

"Are you willing to bet your country on that, Reza? Its entire future? Assume you're right, and that Vernon is as principled as you say. What happens when he dies? Or if age degrades his thinking? Or if he marries a manipulative, Islamophobic wife? Whoever controls SAPL has absolute power, and the future is *long*. Sooner or later, a set of circumstances will arise where SAPL, directly or indirectly, will be used to bend your country to the will of its owner. Can you live with that? Can those you report to live with that?"

For several moments there was nothing to be heard but the terrace's whispering breeze, the muted, rhythmic roar of sea against sand.

"This claim you make about being able to hack SAPL. I assume you can prove it?"

Bob Rossum allowed himself a small smile. Nothing too triumphant.

"I need my phone."

* * *

Jasmine Singh banged unceremoniously on the glass door of the glass box that served as Mac Logan's office. Mac waved her in with raised eyebrows.

"The Iranians have lost a communications satellite," she announced, taking a seat on the visitor's side of Mac's cluttered desk. For a man whose entire life revolved around electronic signals, Logan's work surface supported an unholy amount of paper.

"And I care about this, why?" he asked.

"Because it was vaporized by SAPL."

Mac passed his hand over a sensor. The glass boundaries of his domain became suddenly opaque.

"You're sure?"

"Wish I wasn't. Ekvator-three, one of their older telecoms satellites, went silent a little over ninety-seven hours ago."

"Why am I only hearing about this now?"

"Because it's taken this long to figure out what happened. Satellites fail for a variety of reasons. The fact it went silent isn't particularly remarkable. It wasn't until one of our analysts realized that the satellite itself had completely disappeared that things got real. There's no debris and no signs of a collision. No one has launched munitions at it and we've taken a lookback at all Earth-adjacent space traffic. There wasn't a single vessel that could plausibly have taken a shot at the damn thing, even if the shot itself went unseen."

"And what do Apollo Mining have to say about this? SAPL's their baby, after all."

"We've made discreet inquiries with our contacts over there. No one, civilian or military, oriented SAPL's mirrors to take the shot."

Mac frowned at that.

"Well, if you're correct, our contacts either lied or they're out of the loop."

"I'm going with the latter. We, ah, took a looksee at Apollo's comms. Technically, it's a Tongan corporation, not American, so fair game. Nothing to indicate anyone ordered the shot or knew anything about it. Plus, Tyler Vernon isn't in-system right now. The man may be an entrepreneurial genius, but he's also a control freak. If SAPL was going to do something like this, even on the downlow, he'd insist on being there."

Jasmine leaned across the desk and its pile of papers, her posture lending intensity to her words.

"The shot *was* taken, and without anyone at Apollo knowing about it. We've intercepted and analyzed the signals to SAPL's mirrors, the ones that keep them aligned in whatever configuration Apollo or the military need to focus the sun's energy. The mirrors *were* realigned, boss. SAPL did this. Nothing else."

"But . . . but that makes no sense. Why would anyone take a shot at an aging Iranian satellite?"

"Proof of concept, maybe?" Jasmine hesitated in the face of Mac's skepticism before plunging on. "Here's the thing. Ekvator-three is a ho-hum comms satellite, doing ho-hum comms things. And yet, about an hour before Ekvator-three got vaporized, the Iranians had mostly shut it down. Ninety-nine-point-nine percent of its traffic got routed elsewhere."

"What about the point one percent?"

"A carrier signal between the satellite and IRGC headquarters."

"You're kidding me."

"I most definitely am not. Plus, the Iranian Space Agency retargeted a whole bunch of 'scopes to keep the thing under constant observation."

"The Iranians were *expecting* it to be blown?"

"Sure looks like it."

Mac stared over her shoulder at a blanked-out glass wall, perfectly still save for the slow rise and fall of his breathing. Jasmine tried not to fidget.

"The Iranians have infiltrated Apollo," he said at last. "With people or hackware or both." Fingers beat an agitated tattoo against the edge of his desk. "And somehow, *somehow* it's all connected to *Hades*. Unless, Jasmine, you believe in coincidence?"

"No, boss, I do not. Not in circumstances like this. And if the Iranians can take control of SAPL, then—"

"We're all ants beneath the biggest magnifying glass in the universe." Mac puffed his cheeks, pushing out an explosive breath of air. "This," he muttered, punching keys on his desk phone, "is way above my pay grade. But I'll tell you this: The a-holes whose pay grade it actually is are going to want to know more than we can give 'em. A lot more. Might as well get a jump on the fuckers."

Gordon Williams's clipped diction emerged from the desk-phone speaker.

"Yes?"

"Gordie, can you haul your highly educated Limey ass over to my office? We have ourselves a situation. And fair warning: you may have to put in a call to our mutual lady friend."

The rain, Reza assured him, was unusual for the time of year. Bob took him at his word, but it was unfortunate, nonetheless. It fell heavy and warm, stifling the sea breeze and rendering the terrace unpleasantly humid. Reza, having commented on the weather, seemed unwilling to leave the small talk behind.

"You eat nothing that is offered, you drink nothing that is offered. It is quite rude, in our culture, to refuse hospitality. Rest assured, Mr. Rossum, we have no intention of poisoning you."

"I'm neither hungry nor thirsty at the moment, sir. Please accept my apologies. I have a delicate stomach and a small appetite. I can accommodate very little." He looked out over the terrace to where gray sea met gray sky with almost no distinction. "My appetite might return if we could conclude our business. Connect my phone to a computer system of your choice, as firewalled as you wish, and you can hack into SAPL at will once I give you the password."

"The password is unpronounceable."

"A small matter for a voice simulator. I will record it for you. Once it's in your system and you use it to carry out one simple task for us, the entire program will be yours. You can protect it with whatever passwords you like. What I am offering you is, quite literally, priceless."

"And yet you have set a price."

"A transfer of funds to an account of mine at a Chinese bank. Nothing you can't afford."

"I'm not talking about the money. Your 'one simple task' is not so simple."

"Oh." Bob favored Reza with a thin smile. "Even though we are giving you SAPL, you have scruples about using it?"

"Concerns, rather. About the consequences."

"The Americans, in particular, will be very unhappy with you, but the Americans are *always* unhappy with you. And so long as you control the SAPL, their room for maneuver is limited."

"The Americans, as you say, we can handle. But what about the Grtul? They won't take kindly to the destruction of their gate. What if they retaliate?"

"They won't, because they can't. The gate, obviously, did not arrive through the gate. How could it? It came the old-fashioned way, at a modest fraction of the speed of light. The Grtul are not in-system. Once the gate is destroyed, their 'retaliation'"—Bob's fingers curled into air quotes as he said this—"can only travel here at a modest fraction of the speed of light. A Grtul response couldn't reach you for hundreds, perhaps thousands of years. By which time humanity will have developed the technology to deal with it. Not that they'll have to. *Nothing will happen.* Ever."

Reza sipped quietly at his own cup of tea, the china fine and elegantly decorated.

"What if the gate can't be destroyed?" he asked, setting the cup down again.

"If that were the case, why the ban on the use of hostile energy systems in its vicinity? It's technology, sir. Not magic. Drop it into the sun, it will vaporize. Drop the sun onto it, which is what SAPL essentially does, and you get the same result. No more gate." Bob Rossum leaned forward, his expression earnest and intense. "Do this one thing for my employers, and the hacking software is yours. The power to make America—the whole world—bend the knee to the Islamic Republic, is yours."

Another quiet sip of tea.

"So. Tell me this, Mr. Rossum. Why do your employers offer us this, ah, *gift*? What is in it for them?"

Bob Rossum smiled. Poured more tea into Reza Khosravi's now empty cup.

"I'm afraid I can't help you with that, sir. You either want what we're offering, or you don't." He paused delicately. "If the answer is no, the offer will be made elsewhere, I'm sure, though not by me. To North Korea, perhaps. Or Sudan. Or Myanmar. Who knows? Sooner or later, someone will say yes. At which point, you will have zero control over where SAPL points its mirrors. At Iran, perhaps. At which point, turning us down may not seem like the great idea you thought it was."

American bombs could burrow deep, so the bunker complex, lead-lined and shielded from all outside signals, was deeper still, linked by tunnels and blast doors to government buildings far above. A timid-looking woman, hair demurely covered in a manner often flouted by the capital's female population, entered the conference room with a trolley-load of refreshments and scuttled out, as if terrified of the male occupants she found there.

Perhaps she was. Every single man in that room, whether garbed in a clerical robe or military uniform or western-style suit, had blood on his hands.

"I worry this offer is too good to be true," said a cleric, one who spoke for the Office of the Supreme Leader. "I don't trust this Rossum's motives, seeing as he refused to reveal them."

"Their motives are irrelevant," responded a sharply suited individual, a civilian representing the presidency. "This Rossum's employers are clearly alien, with alien motives that will not matter to us once the gate is closed. Apart from those unfortunate extraterrestrials trapped in-system when the gate is destroyed, no alien will be troubling us for many hundreds of years."

"*If* the gate is destroyed," the cleric said, his voice rising in challenge. "*If.* That is what we are here to discuss."

A military man, a full general in the regular army, spoke up before the civilian could respond.

"We have both the man and his phone, Reza," he said, addressing the intelligence operative, who was sitting at the most junior position around the table. "Why not simply compel him to give us the software without the preconditions? Then this . . . discussion"—his gesture encompassed both cleric and civilian—"can be held at a more leisurely pace."

Reza pursed his lips.

"We could certainly apply more, ah, *forceful* methods. But the outcome is . . . uncertain. He has access to technologies at least on a par with the Glatun. He will probably, given his behavior so far, have a plan for such a move on our part. And I fear he has access to a heavily armed ship. I gather from our naval friends"—a couple of nods around the table—"that our subsea sensors detected *something* plunging into the Caspian consistent with Mr. Rossum's arrival. Yet, despite the depth of the water, there was no sound of an imploding hull and now, no sign of the ship itself. A technology that can function in both space and water largely undetected is a technology to be treated with caution." He hesitated before adding, "I cannot rule out that Rossum is in contact with his ship or that the ship contains crew who could do us a great deal of harm should they choose to do so."

"That seems farfetched," the civilian snapped.

"Perhaps. But two things give IO-IRGC pause. First, Rossum refuses to move away from the Caspian coast. Any system we build will have to be in Bandar-e-Anzali. He insists. Why should he care where he is in Iran unless he wishes to be close to his ship? And second, there is this." The use of electronics being widely discouraged in the bunker, he opened up a paper folder containing, among other things, transcripts of Rossum's interrogations. He read out a highlighted passage. "'*I set down, let's see... a hundred and three hours, thirty-six minutes ago. My ship's lying at the bottom of the Caspian Sea.*' A quite remarkable statement."

"How so?"

"Because he'd been in custody for over three days. Stripped, beaten probably, deprived of his possessions, and placed in a white cell. *The man didn't have a watch* and yet, when we crosscheck his timings with our naval records, he is exactly right about the time elapsed from his landing. He had to have had access to a clock. Almost certainly because, despite the strictest precautions, he is in possession of Glatun-level technology that allows him to contact his ship. Whatever we do, gentlemen, I would counsel against the further use of force. We literally don't know what we are dealing with."

"All the more reason to refuse the man's offer," the cleric said.

"I disagree," the civilian said. "Control of SAPL is too powerful a lever to give up. We can extract concessions from the Great Satan, the ending of sanctions, reparations for all the damage those godless bastards have inflicted, destroy their—"

"It's too dangerous! What if it's a trick, what if the Americans counter the hack, what if—"

"Can I make an observation, gentlemen?" The general's voice was calm and quiet but cut through the rising rancor like a laser. "While I find myself torn between the two of you, I think we must ask ourselves what happens if we *don't* do this. My personal view is that, if we don't, we are looking at the end of the Islamic Republic."

The room was suddenly silent.

"My son worked in Canada for a while," the general mused, "for one of the big American corporations. And he told me something that always stuck with me. The corporation was profitable, to the tune of billions of dollars but, being American, wanted to make more. It looked for 'efficiencies.' They cut the team my son worked in by half, from six to three—didn't think through the consequences, just did it. So now the team was scrambling, working late to make order out of the resulting chaos, doing twice as much work.

"But here's the thing. Even though my son's team was now twice as efficient, not a one of them got a pay rise. The corporation didn't say, 'You're doing more work and making us more profit as a result. We'll cut you in on some of that.' In a different world they might have split the savings fifty-fifty, twice as much work for a fifty percent pay rise isn't a bad deal for the corporation when you think about it. A ten percent pay rise is an even better deal. But the workers got *nothing*, the corporation took it all and no one batted an eyelid. Not even the workers, who were just relieved they hadn't lost their jobs."

"All very sad, I'm sure," the civilian said, acidly. "But what's your point?"

"My *point*, sir, is that we get no benefit from the gate. Tyler Vernon and the Americans take all the profit from the trade that pours through it. A few crumbs for their allies, to be sure, but otherwise they take it all. The Horvath are finished as a threat to Earth. So are the Rangora. Interstellar trade will increase even further. The wealth of an entire *galaxy* is going to line Tyler Vernon's pocket and spill into the American economy, *and their elites will keep it all.* It's what they do. How long before the US economy is a hundred times the size of the rest of the world's put together? A thousand? A *million*? The galaxy is vast compared to one planet, the wealth correspondingly so. And with all that wealth comes power—vast, unstoppable power. Unlimited resources, unlimited military strength. China will be a bug crushed under the American shoe. And if China is a crushed bug, what are we? What will happen to us when a giant of that size flicks a finger in our direction? If we have a chance, no matter how slim, to destroy the gate, we must take it. It is feeding a beast-cub that will grow to kill us if we do not."

There was a deep and thoughtful silence. Eventually, and with obvious reluctance, the cleric nodded in agreement. Talk turned to the mechanics of assembling the necessary computing power and coms systems. The unseen sun disappeared from the sky long before the men with blood on their hands concluded their business. Eventually, though, resolved to a new purpose, they trooped from the room.

Women came to clean up after them. The same timid woman who'd brought in the refreshments trolley wheeled it out again, wiping it down and returning it to its usual place in the kitchen. Briefly checking that she was alone, she opened a concealed compartment and removed a tiny microphone and HD card. The two were hardwired together, no signal leaking out to be detected by a bug sweep. The woman transferred the tiny device to a small void in the metal clasp of her purse, the metal masking its existence from the scanners she would have to pass on the way out.

The small concrete building at the center of the Anzali naval base would have been nondescript except for two things. First, it was fenced off from the rest of the facility; and, second, there was a wild profusion of comms dishes on the roof and adjacent curtilage. What had once been an administrative block had been repurposed for Operation Mithra, the seizure of SAPL from American control.

Bob Rossum stood at the back of the operations center, watching the proceedings. His phone still controlled everything he could see and would continue to do so until he was satisfied the gate had been destroyed. After that, the Iranians could do with the system as they pleased. He thought briefly of the tens of millions waiting for him in his Chinese bank account and was surprised to find that the thought gave him no pleasure. The only thing that interested him was the destruction of the gate, which, from the increasing tempo of the activity in front of him, looked imminent. A photograph of the Supreme Leader glared unsmilingly from a wall, flanked on either side by huge flags: the red, white, and green of the Islamic Republic, the blue and gold of the IRGC.

"The mirrors are responding!" someone yelled excitedly. "The mirrors are—"

BOOM!

A roaring of smoke and flame. Daylight pouring through missing walls. Shadowy figures. Helmets. Armor.

Guns. Bodies slumping to the ground in response to a pop-pop-popping that was softer than the damage inflicted.

Bob Rossum didn't swear. The sound that escaped his lips was too inhuman for that. But his phone wiped the Iranian computers in response. Melted itself into sludge.

Just as the first bullet slammed into his chest. He staggered under the impact.

A second.

A third. The Navy SEAL responsible for Bob Rossum's demise advanced toward him, eyes wide with a growing disbelief.

It was the fourth bullet that put him down. And as it did so, Bob's mind opened itself to a deep and existential truth.

Of course, he thought. *Of course*.

By the time he hit the ground he had ceased to think.

Not so far away, in the darkness of the Caspian Sea, the *Theory of Forms* surrendered to the incredible pressures bearing down on it. Iranian sensors picked up the short, sharp crack of an imploding hull.

The clock was ticking. Down and down. Bob Rossum opened his eyes. All he could see was ceiling.

"Jesus f—!"

"Don't shoot, don't shoot. I'm not a threat."

"I'll be the judge of that." Different voice, graveled with authority.

But no one shot him.

He was able to sit up, albeit with difficulty. He'd been dumped in the corner of the compartment. He propped his back against the angle of the walls. Looked around him.

It was a *Myrmidon*, no doubt about it. In flight, a whole bunch of SEALs strapped into their seats. Those who could had turned to stare at him, the gazes none too friendly. One of them unstrapped and approached. He kept his distance, though, with his weapon leveled.

"You're a robot," he said. That same graveled voice.

"Human simulacrum." A wry smile. "I only just found out. I've rebooted, obviously, but I'm no longer fully functional."

"Hardly surprising with all those slugs in you."

"That's not what I mean. My ship, my controlling AI, it's gone. Self-destructed. My autonomous programming is more... limited."

"Huh. Who made you?"

"No idea."

"Why are you here?"

"I don't think my AI would like me sharing that information."

"Your AI's dead."

Which struck this version of Bob Rossum as an entirely reasonable observation.

And the clock was ticking. Down and down.

"Humans are a threat. To the entire galaxy. In the space of a few short years, you have progressed from shooting overgrown fireworks above your atmosphere to savaging the Horvath and Rangora in deep space. In self-defense, admittedly, but it's not in your nature to act merely in self-defense, is it? Having defeated them at your doorstep, you will attack the Rangora and the Horvath on theirs and subjugate them both. And after that, what next? You return home and all is sweetness and light? Hardly. The history you tell yourselves glorifies war and conquest. Left alone, you will take that history and make it everyone else's future. A human empire, with the rest of us, the ones you let live anyway, scurrying around at your feet. Better to cut the infection off at the source, to cauterize it. Destroying the gate, isolating you from the galaxy for centuries, was the simplest and most elegant way. And SAPL had more than enough power to do it."

"Why use the Iranians? We know you can hack SAPL on your own: you shot down an Iranian satellite. Why not just take the gate out yourself?"

"Taking out a gate results in . . . consequences. My employers didn't want their fingerprints on the operation."

"Fair enough. But why the Iranians? Why not the Chinese or the Russians? Those are countries that have a beef with the good guys, and the resources to do real damage."

"They have too many resources, too much clout. China and Russia are global players, prepared, even now, to go toe to toe with the United States. The Iranians aren't and can't. The Chinese and the Russians want to *control* the gate, not destroy it. They view the gate as an opportunity, while the Iranians see it as a threat. Given the chance, it was a virtual certainty that the Iranians would vaporize the gate. The Chinese and Russians? Not so much."

And with that, the clock in Bob Rossum's system counted down to zero. There was a gurgle of liquids, the acrid stench of decomposing components. Bob Rossum melted down into a fused and useless pile of junk. Some luckless maintenance guy would have to take a sledgehammer and wedge to prise the remains off the deck plates.

The *Myrmidon*, having reached the top of its ballistic arc, arrowed down toward North America and the warm welcome of home.

"Mission accomplished," Jasmine said when Mac told her the news. Then, seeing his expression, added, "You don't seem very happy about it."

"I'm not. We still don't know who did this. All we know is that we have an enemy even more invisible than *Hades*, and no reason to think that they won't try again." Mac stared vexedly through the glass walls of his office. "Whoever they are, they're a heck of lot more dangerous than the Horvath or Rangora."

"I can think of several million dead humans who would beg to differ, boss."

"Really?" Mac regarded her with a smile that made him look suddenly and terminally tired. "Destroying that gate would have destroyed humanity's future, cut us off from progress and technology for maybe a thousand years. A thousand *years*, Jasmine. Think about that. A thousand years ago, Vikings were struggling across the oceans in longships, and the Normans were here, invading merry olde England. Bows, arrows, chain mail. A thousand years is a *long* time. On that scale, what the Rangora did, the Horvath, barely registers. And these guys came within minutes of success using one ship and a talking mannikin. Compared with whoever the hell these guys are, the Rangora and Horvath are knuckle-draggers, nothing but mass and momentum and missiles. These guys did an end run around SAPL. They took our greatest military defense and came within a gnat's breath of turning it against us." Mac tapped a clenched fist against the edge of his desk. "This is a wholly different threat, Jasmine. Insidious as poison. A poison to which we most decidedly do not have the antidote."

"I see."

"I doubt you do. Not yet anyway. Wait till you get to my age." A dry chuckle, totally devoid of humor. "And it gets worse."

"How is that even possible?"

"Well... we figured that, to be so convincing, Robert Ulysses Rossum had to be modeled on a real human being. Maybe there was a real, human Bob Rossum from Dalton, Georgia. If so, maybe his history, his contacts, could give us a clue about who we were dealing with. And you know what we found when we went digging?"

"Obviously not, boss."

"No Robert Rossum, but a boatload of references to RUR, Rossum's Universal Robots."

"I literally have no idea what you're talking about."

"Neither did I. But I can now tell you that the word 'robot' comes from a Czech play called *R.U.R., Rossum's Universal Robots,* which was first performed in 1920. Our mannikin's initials were RUR. Its last name was actually Rossum, and its first name is as close to robot as makes no difference. What does that tell you?"

Jasmine Singh tried to ignore the sinking feeling in her stomach. "That they know infinitely more about us than we know about them. So much so, they can even have fun with it. Someone who can sink that deeply into human culture is going to know every weakness we have. They'll exploit it ruthlessly."

"Exactly. Exhibit One being what they just did." With a visible effort, Mac forced himself to grin. "You did great, Jasmine, and I've let the powers that be know that. Maybe next time, whenever it comes, we'll catch a break."

"We did catch a break. We figured out what they were up to and put a stop to it. Score one for the good guys."

"True. Their AI is dead, their mannikin is a lump of polymer, and SAPL is still under Tyler Vernon's control. But the one thing I was hoping for—the whole reason for sending in the SEALs rather than a missile—that didn't work out so good."

"And what was that, boss?"

"I was hoping to get my hands on Robert Rossum's God damned phone."

CANDY FROM A BABY

Mike Massa

"Hey, Stu," came a familiar voice. "Stu Pegaso. You here yet? We're waiting for you."

Stuart Ellison Pegaso IV angrily thumbed on the speaker of his expensive phone, and stopped short of the elevator, standing squarely on the obnoxiously large AT&T corporate logo that covered most of the foyer. He glared at his hapless assistant, Evelyn Brooking-Smythe, who was holding the door to the elevator from the lobby.

"Rayl," Pegaso replied. "I've asked you not to call me by that name. You know I prefer Ellison. I'd be in the elevator already except, you know, phones don't work once the doors clo—"

"Whatever you say, Stu," his host, Weasley Rayl, tossed off airily. "We're in Shield Room One, and you're the last one to the party. I hope Barclays gave you the grown-up checkbook. The items we're offering are quite in demand, it seems. Not ninety seconds ago, Goldman offered me ten million to buy your seat, just to have somewhere for his assistant to sit, and illustrate the value of being on time. Oh, and nice way to follow my instruction—you were supposed to leave your phone at the office. The Horvath are dumb, but eventually they'll wonder about the significance of a dozen international banks meeting without warning."

The line cut.

Pegaso jammed the phone in his pocket, before being jostled by Brooking-Smythe, who'd dropped her briefcase and was now pushing on both doors, holding them apart. He strode through and turned around, in time to see the security guard give him a puzzled glance, just before the doors closed.

He used their mirrored surfaces to adjust his Hermes power tie and straighten the lapels of his bespoke Saville Row suit. It had the usual calming effect. Pegaso grinned, and admired the way his white, perfectly capped teeth contrasted with the late season Ibiza tan. He wasn't going to let a little shill like Rayl, little better than a high school kid at a mall pop-up cell phone counter, make him angry. Compete with these rubes for few cases of atacirc gleaned from a Glatun tramp steamer?

Ha.

Rayl and the rest of his pitiful network actually thought they were going to outmaneuver a hundred-billion-dollar investment bank. Pegaso, an American one-percenter and product of the best Ivy League schools, had risen to be most influential managing director at Barclays, with a real shot at a board seat at the next annual meeting despite not being a Brit, because he could read the room, spot the players, and smoke them at their own game.

He snorted, and shot his cuffs.

AT&T.

Candy from a baby.

"What do you mean you didn't get *any*?" Sir Richard, OM, KCB, DSC, and probably some other titles Pegaso couldn't remember, was staring out of two red-flecked eyes, divided by a fine aquiline nose. Above, Pegaso could see a forked blood vessel distort the wrinkles on his chairman's forehead. "Not a single case?"

"The provenance of the atacirc was suspect," Pegaso tried. At least there was no one to hear him get chewed out. The private office of Barclays' chairman was effectively a shield room. "The principal, a dodgy character named Tyler Vernon, wouldn't explain the origin, nor the commodity, by which he'd gained access to the Glatun, nor—"

"Did you even try to bid on the one flawless case?"

"Sir, by the time the function tests on the samples came back the bids represented the better part of our bank's quarterly gross profit!" Pegaso answered, carefully not loosening his silk tie. "Even Vernon's opening bid minimums were absurd, and I could not in good conscie—"

"Yes, Tyler Vernon. Overnight multibillionaire. Our private banking unit offered to help him with his newfound riches, but Goldman beat us to it. They said you didn't even try that much!"

"Sir, Vernon is dangerous," Pegaso said fervently. It was pretty clear he could kiss his nomination to a board seat goodbye. "I don't know what his plan is, but bypassing the Horvath can only antagonize them. It's a good thing that Barclays is well shot of this . . . this potential disaster!"

Sir Richard's cheeks now had actual spots of red in them, something Pegaso had only heard of before.

"Well shot of it?" the older man growled, his gnarled and spotted hands clenched on the edge of his mahogany desk. "Well bloody shot of it? I will well bloody strap you across the muzzle of the cannon at the Coldstream Guard's club front door and shoot you from it! You're through. Done. Fired. I shall ensure no bank in London will touch you except to boot you in the arse all the way back to your own wretched country!"

"But, Sir Richard, it was for the best." Pegaso actually used the Prada pocket square to blot his forehead, spotting the expensive fabric. "We've no exposure to the Horvath, and we're still cash-rich so when the Glatun re—"

"Yes, when the Glatun return in a few weeks, *Spinward Crossing* will bring more atacirc to trade, you dolt," the chairman snarled, and picked up his desk phone. "Do you think we will be invited now, the bank that couldn't even muster the will and capital to acquire a single one of the *twenty-six* cases of the only hard asset that matters on the planet today, and which our competitors now control in totality? You've cost us billions! At least J.P. Morgan has offered us use of their high-speed atacirc-powered trade clearing platform—for eight points of the net!"

"But, Sir Richard!"

"SECURITY!"

The road up the mountainside was unlit, and while the headlights on Pegaso's Lincoln SUV adequately illuminated the rutted and snowy dirt road, whatever lay beyond the side windows was shrouded in dark, New Hampshire forest. It had taken months to network into a new job at BofA. At every step, he'd had to carefully name-drop his participation at the very first Glatun atacirc auction, without actually disclosing either his failure, or his subsequent, ignominious departure from Barclays. It had only netted him a VP role, but he'd pressured his new director, fully two steps below Pegaso's London gig, to let him try the direct approach.

After the Glatun had returned to trade for atacirc and, more importantly, Galactic credits, Vernon had provoked the Horvath, exactly as Pegaso had predicted.

Damn Tyler Vernon to hell!

Not only was he responsible for Pegaso's current predicament, Vernon had decided to take on the US government! The president was taking steps to keep the aliens from nuking New York, LA, and Chicago, but getting responsible hands on maple sugar was proving difficult. Pegaso had expended too many of his carefully hoarded favors, and determined that, after Vernon, the next biggest maple sugar holder was some hillbilly. A LexusNexis search later, and Pegaso had the hook. He'd dress right, lean on the patriotism angle, name-drop a bit, and promise the local patriarch enough money to move away from this frozen hellscape and retire to Florida. Hell, with the sums Pegaso could offer, *whatshisname* could buy the entire retirement town. Meantime, Pegaso would hand BofA enough maple syrup options to dwarf their rival, and catapult himself back into the power position he'd lost.

Pegaso glanced at the phone clamped to his dash, checking his notes. Yep.

Mr. Jason Haselbauer. Age: seventy-one. Occupation: gentleman farmer.

Candy from a baby.

The SUV headlights illuminated the dirt cul-de-sac marking the abrupt end of the road, and a snowy field beyond. A tall, lanky man in bulky clothing loomed into view, holding one finger across his lips. Pegaso shut down, leaving his phone in the car, climbed out, and saw a few other men, at least one of whom had a slung rifle, silhouetted in the moonlight. It was damn cold. The only upside of the arctic conditions was a complete absence of insects. Pegaso could not stand bugs or any sort of creepy-crawly. Refusing to kill spiders had cost him girlfriends. Twice.

Some kind of road-clearing equipment had been trailered in, as well as a few older pickup trucks. The first man threw back his fur-trimmed hood, and motioned Pegaso toward a green canvas wall-tent leaking golden light.

Inside, a wood-fired stove heated the room. The grate, open on two sides, lit the interior well enough to show a small table flanked by a pair of wooden folding chairs. The man motioned toward a pair of headphones plugged into a small black box, while pointing toward the canvas ceiling. With a mental shrug, Pegaso copied his host's movement to don the headgear, swung the mic down over his lips, and without waiting, plunked his butt down in a chair. His ears filled with white noise, drowning out the small sounds of the fire and his own breathing.

The old fellow squinted, shucked one glove, remained standing, and held out his hand.

"The headphones are for privacy from you-know-who," Pegaso heard clearly in his 'phones. "I'm Jason Haselbauer. I understand from one of the Nashua boys you have word from Gorku, something about additional maple syrup, Mr. Pegaso."

"Delighted," Pegaso said, simultaneously scrambling upright and stripping off his right glove to trade grips with his host. Immediately, his hand was painfully compressed in a vise. "Ellison Pegaso. Thank you for meeting me." Pegaso had played this game before, but Haselbauer's hand had clamped down before he'd fully completed the grip, grinding Pegaso's knuckles. He tried pumping and letting go. After a final squeeze and unnecessary pause, Haselbauer released him, and sat.

"Ellison?" Haselbauer frowned and looked him up and down. "The letter said Stuart. That's a very nice coat, Mr. Pegaso."

"Thanks, Mr. Haselbauer," Pegaso said, resisting the impulse to massage his hand. "L.L.Bean, you know. *Us* northerners know the value of good gear. My daddy always said a good coat can save your life."

"Did he, now?" Haselbauer glanced over Pegaso's spotless down coat, Oakley ski-bib, and Ferragamo expedition boots.

"Your time is valuable, I'm sure, Mr. Haselbauer," Pegaso said, flicking the annoying headphone cord to one side. These hillbillies came up with crazy privacy solutions. This time, he waited till Haselbauer sat. "We don't actually yet have a client among the Glatun, but I've brought a business proposal for you that would greatly interest them, as you'll see."

He spent the next five minutes laying out the offer. A billion dollars, cash, in a week. Preferred stock in a dozen blue-chips, better than bullion, for the rest. Government appointment as the undersecretary in any department he wanted, so he could be the right Honorable J. Haselbauer for the rest of his life. Other inducements, well, like Florida!

In short, the total package. Just sign on the dotted line.

"Two years of irrevocable maple sugar options for the *revenuers*?" Haselbauer said, holding the contract so it caught more light from the stove. "And the imaginary message from Gorku was bait! That's all you got? Son, I don't think you understand."

"Uh, revenuers?" Pegaso said. This was the downside to dealing with small-timers. Limited comprehension. "Sir, as I laid out, this is a net-net offer. Bank of America will pay any tax obligation you incur in this deal, up front. I'm talking zero risk. Pure profit. And, you sir, will also be credited with salvaging the situation, saving the US of A from the aliens."

Haselbauer shook his head.

"Alright, consider just one year of sugar options," Pegaso began. "Same terms, half of the commitment for you! It's a hell of de—ack!"

In a single move the much older man slid the contract into the wood stove, and yanked Pegaso to his feet. The strength of Haselbauer's arm was shocking, even to a fitness guru like Pegaso who indefatigably Pilate-ed and attended Spin classes twice a week.

"You city boys just don't get it," Haselbauer said, roughly shoving Pegaso outside, tangling the headphone cord and rotating the earcups across his face. "Money is nice, but it's not even the third most important thing."

The bracing cold wasn't the most shocking thing Pegaso felt when the electronics were stripped from his head. It wasn't even the new trench, easily ten feet deep, ten wide, and twice that in length, dug into the field. Dark spoil was neatly piled alongside, where the machine he'd taken for a road scraper idled, exhaust puffing whitely from between the tracks. The operator, illuminated by the dials inside, gave him a jaunty wave.

The really shocking thing was his rental SUV at the bottom of the hole, driver door open, and the interior dome light glowing nearly as brightly as the wall tent.

"See, Mr. Pegaso, I have to decide if you're too stupid to learn." Haselbauer walked toward the edge of the hole, propelling Pegaso by the arm twisted behind his back. If his struggles impeded the mountain man's progress, it wasn't evident. "A stupid man might *intend* to abide by an agreement, but give away information that threatens me and mine. A stupid man would therefore have to accompany that there expensive *auto-mo-beel* on its last journey. A wicked man would *promise* anything to avoid that fate, and di-rectly he gets free, bring baleful consequences. So, the car again. A convincingly penitent man, perhaps one who has suffered some, well, maybe he lives. Me, I think you're the stupid sort, lying to me about the Glatun."

"Bu-bu-but," was all Pegaso could get out, staring at his SUV. "The money—"

"Come to think of it, not even in the top five, Mr. Pegaso," Haselbauer said. "Here's where you get a chance to convince me. Do it wrong, and we'll chuck you in the hole. Do it right, and I'll let you walk down the mountain, for the price of your coat. Your daddy did say a good coat can save your life, and I'm minded to see if he was right. What do you say? Just among *us northerners*."

"Number five, please come to the counter," chimed a pleasant human voice. The Glatun secretary was an AI, and he'd already forgotten the machine's name. Who names a toaster? A female human holographic head floated over the counter, talking to the last person ahead of Pegaso. As each Honeywell candidate completed a brief administrative process, they were led toward the back by a shiny black beetle twice the size of a German shepherd. Its carapace momentarily hinged open with a blur, creating disconcerting buzz. When Pegaso realized the freakishly large insect was *the* Dr. Cori who would perform human brain surgery, he'd nearly chickened out. None of the other Honeywell probationers he'd traveled with on the Glalkod shuttle had died, as far as he knew. The recovery room was elsewhere.

Ultimately, he'd decided to proceed with the process to get Glatun plantpaks, a sort of cell phone in your head that interfaced your brain to a kind of super-internet. His new company, Honeywell, was footing the bill, at least their share of it.

Pegaso itched the scar on the inside of his wrist and hid a grim smile. Like a lot of people, he'd initially ignored the little pimple, but immediately treated it as soon as the government had gotten itself together and issued the warning for the Johannsen's Worm. He'd lost Granddad, and peculiarly, both of his parents, to the Horvath plagues incited by Vernon. He'd also gotten the full vaccine, courtesy of a Glatun medical shuttle. His inveterate networking skills had come in handy, netting him not only the cure, but a galactic business card.

At least now a lot more people hated Tyler Vernon the way he already did.

After the fiasco in New Hampshire, he elected to go into the defense business. A happy side effect of last year's Horvath orbital strikes was the complete destruction of New York and London. In a flash, so to speak, all his troublesome banking references had been wiped out. Honeywell had been hiring for their missile division, and in exchange for a pretty massive drop in hiring level, all the way to purchasing agent, he'd accepted a contingent offer there. All he needed was to prove he'd worked at the banks, which was easy enough, and pass the physical for a 'plant procedure. While he waited, he'd visited his grandmother in eastern Pennsylvania.

Turned out that his granddad had been quite the preparedness freak. Down in the basement, warded by steep wooden steps that Granny couldn't use any longer, was a fully stocked survival store of shelf-stable foods and supplies, including a few gallons of Canadian maple syrup in glass jugs. After his lesson from Haselbauer, Pegaso had dug into the new economics of the very hard to find pancake condiment. The Glatun monopoly working with Tyler and company were getting a honey of a deal, so to speak, on Earth's only export. Other aliens were frantic to find other suppliers, and the right contacts were paying a *lot* more than fifty galactic credits per gallon. Thanks to that Glatun business card, he'd found the right contacts.

Pegaso had read about the implant option and the galactic medical technology. Hard currency meant he could augment his plantpak. All he had to do was beef up Honeywell's basic installation, and once he got back home, he'd outthink his way to the top, again. Defense contractors only had to be smart enough to fool the average military officer, who, let's face it, weren't all that bright. An Ivy League investment banker wouldn't find Honeywell a real challenge.

Director of Defense Projects sounded about right.

Candy from a baby.

* * *

"Number six, please come to the counter," chimed a pleasant human voice. Pegaso got to his feet, dried his palms on his newish khakis, and walked over.

"I have a small number of galactic credits, and I'd like to get some additional work done."

"Oh, big spender, we like that!" came from the speaker on the desk, synchronized to buzzing and popping noises behind him. Pegaso spun around to find Dr. Cori, the four-foot beetle, at his back. Up close, the collection of articulated, sharp-looking mandibles and glistening manipulator claws was terrifying. "Follow me, please."

Pegaso trailed the good doctor *(please, please be a good doctor!)* to an exam room, which looked entirely unremarkable. Warm beiges and pleasant pastels dominated, and the exam chair appeared to be rich, brown leather. Most of the instrument screens were so much gibberish, but he did spot a traditional vitals monitor to one side.

"We've adopted a decorative style similar to Terran medical facilities," the AI's voice announced, as he rubbernecked. "It seems to relax you humans better. Please lay back in the chair."

Beneath him, the seat pivoted back, providing rests for his arms and legs, becoming a very comfortable recliner. The vitals monitor came fully alive, and the metronomic beeping of his pulse slowed a bit.

"Mr. Pegaso, please," said the calming, secretarial machine. "What did you have in mind?"

"Hee-hee," came the beetle's voice. Pegaso's limbs suddenly went numb. "'In mind.' Get it? I'm already inside your mind? Get it?" Clicking sounded uncomfortable close to his ear.

"Uhh," Pegaso blanked, and screwed his eyes shut. The pace of the beeping surged.

"Dr. Cori," the AI remonstrated. "We've talked about this. Please stop terrifying the patients!"

"Fine, fine, spoilsport," Dr. Cori said, a touch of impatience in the otherwise perfect English. "Relax, it's a nerve block to keep you still, sonny. What enhancements would you like? We got all sorts of options in the database, and costs have come down, now that I've worked on hundreds of humans."

"Onboard memory storage," Pegaso finally managed. "Expanded range of vision. Hearing, better hearing. Basically, another one hundred credits' worth."

"Want me to fix those missing finger- and toe tips?" the doctor asked. "And the bits of ears you seem to have misplaced. What did you do, get lost in a snowstorm?"

"Something like that," Pegaso said. "Yes, yes, just do it!"

"Contract registered on the regional hypernode," caroled the AI secretary.

"In three, two, one," the doctor's voice said.

"Mr. Pegaso, please wake up," the AI said. "Mr. Pegaso."

"When do we start?" he asked, confused. The chair began to pivot upward.

"Sir, take a moment to relax," the AI said. "It's been hours. While you're recovering, I will explain the basics of 'plant operation. You merely have to think about the topic, and the software does the rest."

"Some of my finest work, if I say so myself."

Pegaso turned his head to see Dr. Cori close up. The glistening mandibles clicked and popped less than a foot away.

"Perfect replacement on the extremities, too!"

Then Pegaso realized he was hearing and comprehending the alien.

"As you can see, the 'plant auto-translates for any of the hundreds of primary languages in the spiral arm," the AI said. "Also, you can listen to your messages, rather like your old telephone. It appears you have a few high-priority messages, in fact."

Hear messages, Pegaso thought.

"Message one. Dear Stuart Ellison Pegaso, the Fourth. This is the automated Honeywell human resources program. This message is notice of your breach of contingent employment contract, to wit, violating Honeywell's Glatun-Terran biomedical agreement by separately contracting additional, unauthorized services, as specified in section four, subparagraph three-c. Your employment is terminated in the system wherever you receive this message. You must wait ten years before reapplying. Thank you for your time. Remember, why wait for the future, when you can create it! Goodbye!"

"Wait, what?" Pegaso stood upright, panicked. The room spun, and as he sagged, a gentle tractor beam laid him back in the chair. "I didn't do anything. This doesn't make sense. They can't do that."

"Please avoid standing, Mr. Pegaso," the AI said, her tone just as sweet as it had been a moment earlier. "You'll need a few minutes for your brain to adjust to the work on your auditory system.

You'll be relieved to learn I've reviewed your contract, as well as three centuries of precedent, and I can assure you your former employer's actions are easily defensible in any Terran civil court. I thought you understood when you asked for the additional work."

"Aren't you supposed to tell me," he replied, eyes still closed, "you know, *in advance*?"

"Sophonts are free beings, Mr. Pegaso. Each responsible for itself."

"Whatever," Pegaso muttered.

So he'd stay on Glalkod for a few weeks. Soak up the culture. Find the angle. He had the credits for it. Meanwhile, he'd watch himself. New place, new rules. No sweat. He could do polite. No AI was going to outthink him!

Candy from a baby.

"Can I get something to drink, Miss AI?" he asked politely.

"Ordinarily, I'd say yes, Mr. Pegaso," the AI answered. This time a head also snapped into view, the hologram adjusted to Rangoran features. The large head loomed above him, with an enigmatic reptilian smile. Or not. There were teeth showing, anyhow. "But just now, no. And why? There are three reasons. First, until you learn to manage your 'plant, you should be aware your thoughts can be transmitted in local conversation in the form of subvocal speech, especially if you are already in a conversation, unless you specify privacy. And second, your galactic credits have been impounded by the city legal AI, due to a complaint from one Niazgol Gorku."

"Who, what?" he protested feebly. "What did I do? I've never even been here before!"

"I'm the third thing, Mr. Pegaso," a new voice sounded, echoing in Pegaso's already confused brain. "My name is Zathabet Flingrr. I'm Mr. Gorku's private factor. A sort of a lawyer, if you will. You've been trading in maple syrup, over which product Mr. Gorku jealously guards his market. That's not the end of the world. However, we've learned you fraudulently claimed a business relationship with Mr. Gorku to gain a meeting with one of our most valued Terran contacts, Mr. Jason Haselbauer."

"I-I-I need..."

"Mr. Gorku takes a very dim view of others besmirching his good name. Reputation is all a sophont has, you know. Thus, you are being sued. As a result, you need to show proof of solvency in the form of employment while this case is adjudicated, or you will be confined. The confinement conditions for Terrans would be, shall we say, difficult. I'm afraid Mr. Gorku is in a position to make this process somewhat lengthy. But rejoice, Mr. Pegaso. I have in mind a way you could work off this minor debt."

Pegaso thought as fast as he could. Doubtless, reflecting his capabilities, maybe they had in mind picking his brain about advanced human banking, and derivatives calculation using Black-Scholes, and . . .

A soft snort came from Flingrr.

"Mr. Pegaso, you need to practice privacy measures, as I have told you," the AI said patiently.

Being silent suddenly seemed like the best policy at the moment. He tried hard to think of nothing, which worked as well as it ever did.

Giant beetles, industrial secrets, giant beetles, industrial secrets, man—he was actually feeling hungry . . .

"No need to compel you to share your, shall we say, rudimentary Terran banking secrets, Mr. Pegaso," Flingrr said. "Or shall I call you Stu? Plead no contest, and agree to work off your fine. I can find you a safe place to do so. Mr. Gorku runs a hospitality business, you see."

"I'm no front desk manager, Mr. Flinger," Pegaso replied. "Or chef. And I prefer Ellison, if you please."

"Oh, we don't need a human chef," Flingrr replied, snorting a bit more. "And it's Flingrr, with a soft *arr.* No, Stu, the role I have in mind for you is *scullery maid.*"

Pegaso dried his hands on the crisp white linen apron and looked around the gleaming kitchen.

It turned out the Glatun, or at least Gorku, tended to hold grudges. The interval of years working in the scullery of Gorku's restaurant was the worst experience in Pegaso's life. Automata did much of the heaviest work, but the head chef, a giant, intelligent caterpillar whose coloration resembled fluorescent tie-dye, wanted the first off-Earth Michelin star. It, or he—Pegaso was never clear, and frankly, not ready to find out—insisted on pushing the kitchen equipment to the limit. This often had disastrous results. The less said about the turducken, the better. On the other hand, galactic races often ordered it just to observe the barbaric practices of the humans.

Surprisingly, the fugu preparation went right on the first try, and the Ogut was approaching something like an acceptable cassoulet. However, the ongoing attempts at a poultry cleaning machine began as an unmitigated catastrophe, and tapered into merely disgusting. The ear-splittingly loud chicken screaming that summoned Pegaso to the scene was quickly explained by the omission in the technical manual of a key first step. Unhelpfully, it went straight to: "place chicken into plucking barrel."

Guess who got to clean the bloody mess. That's right, the scullery maid.

Things were looking up, though. Sharply limited interaction with other humans had compelled him to learn to "drive" his 'plants with great efficiency in order to do his job. Pegaso had absorbed an encyclopedia's worth about the different races that visited Glalkod, as well as the Glatun themselves. He'd learned data retrieval and organization. He'd even found a way to apologize to the medical AI he'd met on his first day, Louisa.

As a result, he'd gotten a job offer. Sort of. Some Chinese defense contractors had visited the kitchen to congratulate the Ogut chef on the Sichuan Dandan. They were surprised to find a human there. They were even more startled at his familiarities with the technology underlying the machines in the kitchen.

And they'd bought his contract. So, job offer, basically.

He'd be back on Earth in days. He'd even be back in tech, since the new company, Qua Tang Electronics, was manufacturing subassemblies for a variety of space gadgets, most of which went to, let's face it, Tyler Vernon's companies.

Still.

Tech. Finance. He'd frequently worked with Chinese-Americans, as well as the Asian quants at Barclays's, so he was confident Chinese corporate culture would be about the same. With his 'plants and his experience with alien technology, kitchen or no kitchen, he'd be back. After eating a little humble pie with the galactics, it should be a snap!

Or as the Chinese might say, tángguǒ from a bǎobǎo.

The plastic bin held sparkling trays, filled with hundreds of tiny electronic relays, each nestled in an equally tiny cup, reflecting gold highlights everywhere, because they were made, well, of gold. Pegaso leaned away from the eyepieces of his 'scope, and ran a sleeve across his forehead, twisting the white paper hat that kept hair from falling into his work.

Say this much for living in Ningbo, People's Republic of China: It made living and working in Glalkod seem familiar and homey. Pegaso had learned the mainland Chinese could hold simultaneously opposing beliefs, and feel no incongruity about it. Case in point: they both admired and despised Tyler Vernon.

Admired because he'd done great things. He'd personally repelled the Horvath cruiser in a glued-together spacecraft. Then his space laser company and the great huge battlestation utterly devastated the Horvath fleet in a return engagement. He'd also beaten off the actual Rangora. Also, he'd amassed a great fortune, and established a near monopoly on key galactic trade goods, essentially by cheating the rest of the world. The national Chinese corporate types really appreciated a successful cheat.

They despised Tyler Vernon because by their lights, despite amassing all that power, he'd done nothing with it. Worse, the ones being cheated were them! However, they didn't hate him as much as they hated the squids. They really, *really* hated the Horvath. It had everything to do with the effects of Johannsen's, which untreated, was one hundred percent fatal for anyone with black or brown hair. Losses among the mainland Chinese had been heavy. Alas, the losses hadn't included his boss at Qua Tang Electronics, Chen Junjie.

Mr. Junjie was Pegaso's immediate supervisor in the QTE Quality Assurance department. He genially hated Pegaso, but ensured Pegaso knew it wasn't personal. As a result of the plague, there was a surprising number of non-Chinese at QTE, and Junjie hated all foreigners, reserving his greatest opprobrium for Chinese born outside China. Junjie spoke understandable, if lightly non-grammatical English. The Chinese, when they weren't calling him *laowei* or *yang-guizi*, used both his first and last names, run together. All day long he heard, "Stupigaso, you no understand simple math? At least eighty percent of switches must mark as good!" Or, "Stupigaso, you down checking too many of the micromotors!" And, "These parts no assemble correctly, look like made by Stupigaso!"

Junjie didn't have 'plants of his own, so he didn't seem to fully appreciate Pegaso understood everything spoken in Mandarin. Not to mention Cantonese, which Junjie generally didn't permit to be spoken around him. Add Hokkien, Singlish, Tagalog, and a host of other South Asian languages heard daily at QTE. Under the right conditions, his augmented hearing could pull in whispers from hundreds of feet away, and he could lip-read. Over the last several months, that had come in handy, because the whispers and furtive chats among management had skyrocketed.

The current issue was relays. The ubiquitous electronic parts were used in everything, and came in an assortment of standard sizes. QTE QA was supposed to run every relay, each individually micro-serialized, through a check. The batch on Pegaso's desk right now had the same problem they usually did: a big percentage were light on the gold. Even though the Horvath demanded the precious metal, its industrial uses still mandated a local supply, and LFD Corporation—Tyler Vernon again—had mined great quantities from the asteroids. He sold it at a modest markup to his suppliers—which right there, according to the QTE managers, was proof of his incompetence. Despite the enormous profits Chinese companies were reaping from the industrial space boom, they still didn't want to contribute to the Alliance defense pact. After all, the Americans would defend Earth anyway, and for free! *They* would have stuck everyone for the maximum price of gold, defense of the solar system be damned.

In a way, they were, because someone was pocketing the difference between the amount of gold that should be on the relays, by specification, and the actual amount of gold with which QTE was actually plating the relays.

He'd faithfully reported it to Junjie. He'd been assured he was wrong:

"Stupigaso, Glatun implant wasted on small brain like you have!"

He'd heard it was a cultural issue:

"What you dumb, Stupigaso, you want attention from important people?"

He'd been assured the Alliance was too stupid to ever notice:

"Stupigaso, customer happy and never find out. This easier than take candy from baby!"

He'd even sent a note to good old Flingrr via hypernet, figuring Gorku the tycoon would have an interest in defending business partners on Earth, but there'd been no reply. Now, Pegaso had another batch of lethally flawed relays in front of him. This time, he didn't even need the printout of the test machine. Courtesy of his 'plant, he could spot the inadequacy of the gold plating in the infrared interferometer's 'scope.

It was time for a break. He rang the buzzer for permission, and Junjie confirmed with an annoyed jerk of his head. Pegaso dismounted his saddle, and carefully backed away from his workstation, one of a dozen along the final production line in this part of the multiacre factory. He walked inside the empty company lounge, gently high-fiving the lucky cat figurine on the counter. There was tea, tiny little apples, and a selection of brightly printed bags of rice crackers, roasted nori seaweed, and his favorite, spicy peas. He grabbed a bag of the latter, glanced at the TV, and did a double take.

Usually, censors wouldn't let anything about the Americans, the Alliance, or LFD through, unless it was negative coverage. That explained the English language broadcast on the lounge flatscreen. CNN had begun reporting on congressional testimony from Vernon himself. Pegaso didn't need the text banner that scrolled Mandarin across the bottom of the screen. He understood Vernon perfectly. That was a good thing, because the two didn't match. Vernon was copping to being responsible for a shuttle blowing up with all hands lost, and almost losing another, because of faulty LFD and Apollo systems. He said he would get to the bottom of it. He said it was his fault for not checking suppliers, who'd been skimping on quality. Vernon was owning it all. He mentioned China, at which point the CNN feed broke away to a Chinese talking head reading a prepared statement denouncing Tyler, and praising the quality of Chinese manufactories, which were defending the earth.

Quality.

He'd been around long enough to know how any investigation into quality of QTE products was going to go, and whose head would be sacrificed. He wasn't even certain the Chinese would restrict themselves to metaphor.

From managing director, to VP, to purchasing manager, to scullery maid, to the Designated Blame Magnet. Pegaso knew which way trouble rolled, and it wasn't uphill. He could feel a sour stomach coming on, so he would hardly need to fake it for taking half a sick day. Ningbo was a coastal city. Chinese territorial ambitions had been sidelined since the bombing, so the borders were porous again. He'd have to disable his 'plant to avoid being tracked, so there went his remaining galcreds. He'd use his limited cash to leave, and it was a toss-up it would be enough. Of course, fleeing would affirm his guilt.

Then again, staying wouldn't be much different.

It didn't take a genius.

"They teach welding here, and not just any welding," the pimple-faced boy enthused. Scars showed where he'd been busy playing amateur dermatologist. "They use lasers to fabricate stuff in space."

"Yep, they sure do, kid," Pegaso answered, and leaned on his wooden mop handle. He took a handkerchief from the pocket of his blue overalls, softened by scores of washings. The weather outside was warm, but the helium-3 powered factory sent its excess to the corporate office buildings and the nearby suburbs in the outskirts of Cocoa Beach, so the air-conditioning kept the cafeteria comfortable. The teenager, Kip, with whom he was sharing the chore of cleaning the Apollo subsidiary's offices, had been carrying on a one-sided conversation about his plans to make it big, get into space, make a difference, and make a pile of money, just like Tyler Vernon. He'd hadn't even been born when the first gate popped into the firmament above Earth, so Pegaso understood the kid would have an entirely different view of things from a person who'd lived through it all.

"What did you say your name was?" Kip asked.

"Charles," Pegaso said. "Charles Lethe. You can call me Chuck."

The display cases in the cafeteria represented a selection of things manufactured by Apollo, including models representing the progression of the increasingly large mirrors Apollo used to do space mining, and defend the earth. There were samples of the steel that had been used to make a drive plate strong enough to get two battlestations into E Eridani. There were even some electronic components, including some familiar relays. That was behind him, of course. He'd left any technical, managerial, or financial work behind with his old name. After China, and some of the odd jobs he'd taken on the way home, his ambitions were modest. A nice quiet, predictable, Earth-based life felt pretty good.

The teenage kid was chirping about his backup scheme to get into the space program by attending space welding school, or something.

"So even though my first application to basic flight school was rejected, I can still get the skills needed to get off planet!"

"Sure, kid, makes sense." Pegaso wasn't really listening. He calmly pumped the mop head in the bucket before popping it into the cadillac for a squeeze.

"And after a battle, you get big money for salvage!"

"Yeah, that too." Pegaso wrung the mop out and plopped it back onto the tile. Money could seem important, sure. No point in trying to convince a young kid full of ambition of anything different.

"Some of the techs that came back from the second Rangora attack bought Glatun 'plant packs with every option, like being resistant to vacuum, or bionic hearing!"

Pegaso winced. Yeah, he wasn't even going to try.

"With that much salvage money, I could take the entrance exam for flight school again, only pay someone to do it for me, easy as pie. That much money, it would be candy fro—"

Panic lent its wings to Pegaso, who somehow teleported across the ten feet that separated them in an instant, allowing him to get his hand over the kid's mouth before Sir "Pops A Lot" could finish the sentence.

"Do. Not. Say. That!" he said as forcefully as he could without actually yelling. "You do not want to get in the habit of saying that, okay? Believe me. I know. *I know*."

"Jeez, okay," the teen said, swiping Pegaso's hand away. "Don't be such a spaz, you geezer!"

"Everything okay out here, gentlemen?" a gravelly voice echoed across the cafeteria, to the accompaniment of measured, heavy footsteps.

"No, sir, Mr. Monaghan," the kid said, his voice breaking a little. "I mean, yessir, Mr. Monaghan."

"Everything is fine, sir," echoed Pegaso, who didn't like how the man was looking him up and down. Worse, the man briefly seemed preoccupied before he began talking to himself.

"Are you sure this is the guy?" he said, seemingly to no one. "Okay, let's see."

He stopped talking, folded his arms across a thick chest, and bigger belly, and stared Pegaso right in the face.

"Mr. Stuart Ellison Pegaso, the Fourth?" a kindly-sounding, older feminine voice chimed *inside* his head. "Please pardon the intrusion. I've taken the liberty of turning your 'plant back on. I'm the fabber AI aboard battlestation *Thermopylae,* and my name is Granadica."

"So it was really quite easy to locate you, or at least your 'plant, once we had the codes." The AI was winding up her explanation. "Then, we correlated what we already knew with what your location and apparent activity suggested, and observed you for a little while."

"You were spying on me?" Pegaso said, trying to absorb it all. He was cradling his head in his hands on the polished wooden table in a conference room whose wastebaskets he'd emptied earlier. The triangular speakerphone in the middle of the table was vaguely within his line of sight. He ignored the full coffee mug at his elbow.

"I can tell you I wasn't very excited about having a potential saboteur in my school, Mr. Pegaso," Monaghan said, before blowing on his cup of coffee. "But what the boss wants, he gets. So yeah, we spied on you, especially the kid."

"Nothing personal, Mr. Pegaso," Kip said. "Just a job."

"The possibility that Ellison was engaged in nefarious activity was of a very low order," Granadica said, her tone edging away from kindly granny toward the voice of She Who Will Be Obeyed. "It only required rudimentary analysis, which was reconfirmed by three different system AIs."

"Mr. Pegaso, as you might imagine, we track everything around Mr. Vernon very closely," came the heavier timbre of another AI, this one named Leonidas. "We knew who attended the very first atacirc meeting, decades ago. We knew you tried to bribe Mr. Haselbauer."

"Who hasn't forgotten," an even deeper voice announced. A working granite crusher sounded less threatening. Hephaestus was the third and last AI on the call. "Will likely never forget. It is one of his better qualities."

Pegaso clutched his head a little harder. Three. He was in trouble with three AIs. The room sure seemed to be getting warmer.

"We didn't notice you went to Glalkod till much later," Granadica added. "Thank the Horvath for blowing up the financial capitals of the world for that. Then later, the Rangora refreshed the chaos. As a result, when we noticed your name during the forensics for the QA investigation in China, we didn't immediately realize it was you."

"I'm really sorry, I tried to tell my boss the relays were faulty," Pegaso said, finally trying a sip of coffee which someone had thoughtfully milked and sugared. His eyes might have been watering from a new coffee allergy. Or something. "But he just didn't care!"

"Yeah, we looked at that pretty hard," Monaghan said, smiling. "The legal team that visited the factory tried to interview him, but he was 'unavailable.' I think the suits did something to make that permanent, and frankly, we thought you'd gone the same way. Ironically, the same Glatun who knew exactly where you were but hid your existence, is the same one who delivered the codes which included the backdoor access to every 'plant ever installed at Glalkod."

Pegaso looked up from his study of the tabletop woodgrain.

"Yeah, every single one, which is a helluva security risk," Monaghan added.

"In the course of pinging 'plants for updates, there was a non-zero number of surprises," Leonidas said. "Your 'plant being intact was one. The circumstances of your indenture for Gorku is another, which I suspect Mr. Vernon will address, unless something much bigger occupies his attention."

"Am I in trouble, then?" Pegaso asked, trying to read the room, as in the days of old. Unfortunately, it was pretty hard to get a handle on non-corporeal AIs.

"We're satisfied with your honesty," Granadica said. "Plus, you were one of a very few people that pushed back on the chip relay fiasco. Not to mention, your employment on Glalkod was entirely extralegal!"

"Um?" was the most Pegaso could manage.

"The furnace of your experiences has beaten the clinker from your soul, Mr. Pegaso," Hephaestus declared. "Let us see what you will do with the pure alloy."

"Granadica, gate emergence!" Leonidas announced, his voice ringing from the speaker.

"I see it," the female AI answered, "Mr. Monaghan, finish here."

There was a slight *pop* and the green LED on the speakerphone went red.

"I don't understand," Pegaso said, squeezing his coffee cup, looking between the older man and the young teenager. "What just happened? What did they decide?"

"Well, sounds like the Rangora are considering round two." Monaghan stretched for the coffee carafe. "Which isn't so great. On the other hand, seems to be the unanimous judgment of the AIs studying your case you are one of the good guys. I suspect you will be receiving a job offer soon."

"In the meantime, we get to finish mopping the cafeteria," Kip said. "Until we hear if it's a general attack. We do our bit, and the AIs do theirs."

Kip stood up.

"So do you prefer Stu, or Ellison, Chuck?"

"Ellison. Definitely Ellison."

HELLCAT

Marisa Wolf

I was covered in grease when Noah died. Blood when we got the news about Henry. Now Ginger is pulling my arm back, telling me they got a call about Byron.

I'm covered in glitter. They just announced my name.

All my brothers are dead.

Helene blinked, her heavy eyelashes weighing her eyelids, a temptation to squeeze her eyes closed.

Ginger tugged again, but Helene's body wouldn't—couldn't—move. A high-pitched whine in her ears blocked out the shouts of the crowd from the other side of the curtain. She couldn't be here. It couldn't be real.

She was at home, in her driveway, working alongside her father on his ancient pickup. Before all of it. When there were aliens, but they were confined to the smoking pits of cities far away. There were scars all over Earth, but not at home. Not for her and her family.

They just had the ragged edge of poverty to worry about. Worked multiple jobs, as they had for generations. While some had profited from the great new age of space, aliens, and the wars that immediately followed, money never flowed to Louisiana first. The money and new work and fancy equipment didn't land there. Certainly not to families like the Guidrys, whose individual members had been working multiple jobs for generations before everything went to shit.

Helene blinked again.

Her brothers had enlisted, one after the other. The skills their father had instilled—fixing things that broke because they couldn't be replaced, wielding gun or knife or axe as needed, pulling down buildings and setting up traps—all of it worked, one way or another, to make them successful as marines.

Helene had the same skills, but she was the youngest. The baby girl. She waitressed in Alfonse's Family Diner by day and helped her father in his various jobs anytime she wasn't on shift. They wanted her to be a teacher, and sometimes she wanted that too, but college was expensive and the world was busy breaking and shifting into space, so she made nice with customers and helped fix things and processed deer and survived.

It wasn't great, but it worked. Until she and her father were elbow deep in the guts of his pickup truck, picking up their heads when a stranger walked up their long, unpaved driveway. She remembered the weight of the grease on her fingers, the mess of it caked under her nails. The small, sharp cracks of oyster shells under the man's boots. The emptiness in her ears after the words, "Beau Guidry, we regret to inform you..."

She didn't go to school the next day, and then she kept not going. Easier to pick up more shifts at the diner without school in the way. Instead of classes, she studied for her GED late at night or on slow shifts, waitressed, and did more prep help for her father's woodworking.

Sometimes it felt like Noah was just out of contact for a long time, not that he was dead. It was almost a rough sort of balance, and if she couldn't appreciate it, she at least knew it for what it was.

Helene forced her eyes open, unsure when she'd closed them. Noah had been dead for days before they found out. Henry, though... Henry hadn't died right away. He'd been injured being a big damn hero. Saved the day for his platoon, and one soldier in particular. Lingered a few days.

Three long, silent days, her father skipping his hunting trip to wait for word. His old buddies brought deer to their garage for processing, stuck around to help hang the carcasses.

"Two of 'em are for you, Beau," old Alfonse had declared, turning his head to spit directly into the drain. "Make sure you got room in your freezer."

"I don't need—"

"Thank you, you say? Yeah, you're welcome." Louis, who had known Beau since they were both Helene's age, muttered something about stubborn old cusses under his breath.

Beau hadn't argued, but nodded to Helene to raid the ancient fridge in the far corner of the garage. She'd supplied the men with beers, then yanked on her thick gloves and got to carving the first of the deer.

Alfonse and Louis hadn't been gone long when the call came. Helene was onto the third deer and her father had already finished two in quick succession.

"I'll get it, since you're slower than molasses in the winter."

"Okay, old man." Helene rolled her eyes and huffed something adjacent to a laugh. While she'd been working alongside him and her brothers since she was ten, his decades of experience easily outstripped her six years, and she made a show of digging her knife in just a little harder than necessary to show what she thought of his teasing.

The *thunk* of knife into joint still lingered in her ears as her father answered the call. Video, to apologize for not sending someone, and if Helene could have crawled into the deer Alfonse and Louis had brought in, she would have.

Afterward, she couldn't recall a single thing either the man or her father had said, could only remember the precise streaks of blood coating her elbow-length gloves, the copper, iron, musky smell of raw meat, the rumble of the corner fan. At some point she'd turned toward her father, but could only focus on the overhead light shining through six empty beer bottles.

She'd gone to work the next day. Waitressing at Alfonse's didn't bring in much, but every little bit mattered. Ends hadn't been meeting before Noah and Henry died, and it wasn't about to get much better even with Byron still sending part of his pay home.

Maybe the timing had something to do with her missing cues from the strangers in her corner booth. A little too well-dressed for the area, laughing a little too loud. Like they had something worth laughing about.

Helene had gone through the motions, serving her tables, making sure old drunk Mrs. Norris had enough coffee to keep from puking in the ladies' room, knocking away Jack Rhys's hand when he asked her just how light her hair got in the summer.

Though her hair had always been a soft brown, not blond, summer brightened it enough that the boys couldn't resist asking about Johannsen's. Even now, in the depths of what passed for winter down in the swamp, the day after her brother died...

There was a *thwack* behind her as she moved on, expressionless. Maybe one of Jack's dumb friends had hit him, or Mrs. Norris had leaned over the booth to slap sense into his head, but Helene's steps hadn't faltered as she made her way to drop the check off in the corner booth.

Any combination of events that day could have led to the moment the pretty redhead put her hand down next to Helene's on the check.

"You looking for a job, hon?" The woman's voice, throaty and warm, quieted the three other women at the table.

"I've got a few," Helene had answered with a smile she couldn't feel.

"I'm talking real money, sweetie. The way you handle all this..." She'd paused, blown out her breath, and waved her other hand. "I think you'd fit in just fine."

The jobs that paid "real money" for young women without high school degrees made for a real short list. Factor in the fancy look of these particular women, and even Helene's sluggish brain kicked over a realization.

"Ma'am, I'm still seventee—"

"Waitressing, sweets. That's it, unless you want to do more down the road. I guarantee you'll make triple what you make here."

The other women at the table—all wearing various brightly colored wigs that could have been hiding blond hair or just about anything else—made enthusiastic noises of agreement.

"I—" Helene's brain offered only white noise, a bright and loud enough to erase the ambient sounds of the diner. "Wh—"

"My brother's a Marine, too." When the redhead lifted her hand, a shiny card lay on top of the check.

Of course everyone was talking about it. Of course *strangers knew.*

Pressure in her chest sent heat racing up her neck, and though Helene knew she was blushing, there was nothing she could do about it.

The redhead—Ginger Lepain, according to the shimmering writing on the card—nodded as though Helene had had an intelligent response and dropped a stack of bills on the table. Even at a glance it was far more than the check's total.

"I hope you call," the girl with the neon green wig said brightly. "I know some of my old stuff will fit you—we'll get you all set up."

"She's got a good face for it." The blue-eyed woman in the purple streaked wig grinned at Helene, and the last woman snorted.

"Not the face that's gonna make the big bucks."

The others laughed and swatted at her, but the redhead—Ginger—raised her eyebrows and leaned in toward Helene. "The face never hurts. But the attitude . . . that's what's gonna work best for you."

Up until that moment, Helene hadn't realized she'd had an attitude. She'd barely realized she was moving.

But distant, pretty, and on point were three excellent qualities to waitress successfully at the Hottest Gate.

As Helene soon found out.

Back in the present, Ginger's hand tightened on her arm, and Helene dragged in a breath. Only then did she notice that her chest ached—had she been holding her breath the whole time? Music started—her music. The intro thumped, and a round of whistles answered.

This was supposed to be her debut. She'd been waitressing at the Hottest Gate, practicing with the girls, getting ready. Dyed her hair platinum blond. Got everything she needed—the sparkly outfit, the glitter in strategic places, the eyelashes and eyeliner and garters and heels.

Now she stood, frozen, heart beating uselessly against the pressure on her chest.

An only child, handful of hours from her hometown, after her brothers had died one by one in space.

Fuck.

It was as far as her thoughts would go. The word bounced through her skull on a loop, and Ginger shouted something, and Terra brushed past them with a quick, rough side hug.

Terra was greeted by whistles and hoots and hollers on the other side of the curtain, and released from having to make the choice, Helene sagged. Her bones gave up, her muscles loosened, and she dropped into a crouch, Ginger's arms around her.

The asshole little voice in the back of her head rang over the rolling curses, *Perfect squat. Do that on stage in these shoes, pop up, and rake in the money.*

"Come on, honey. Let's get you back to sit down, get you a drink."

Helene followed without conscious effort, her thoughts looping again. She couldn't bring herself to ask who had called Ginger. Her father? Ginger's brother? Should *she* call her father?

Of course she should. But to what end? They'd never talked about it after Noah's death, after Henry's...

"Do you want a ride home? Harvey's got a guest announcer, he can take you."

Helene shook her head without considering it. She lived in walking distance. She could just swipe a bottle—she was sure Ginger wouldn't mind, certainly not any more than she'd mind her newest dancer flaking off from getting on stage. But then what? Take a bottle home, drown herself in it, wake up hungover and detached from reality tomorrow for a few precious, miserable minutes.

Her apartment, dark and sparsely furnished and with the day's dishes still piled in the sink, would not be a welcome retreat. And there was no rough balance to be found, like she had after Noah was killed. They'd never lost touch with all the boys all at once, even she couldn't convince her brain that was what was happening. They were dead, not on a mission.

Dead. No, she couldn't go home.

Stay at the Hottest Gate, with its thrumming music and a shifting crowd of faces and glowing lights and unimportant conversations... *that* she could do. Couldn't she?

Not to dance—the idea of it sent a shudder through her body that wrenched her spine—but her usual. The routine work. Serve drinks and small snacks and tell the customers about her favorite dancers.

I can do that. Going home is being useless. Guidrys are never useless.

At loose ends now and then, maybe, but never layabouts for long.

"Hell." Tanya leapt from her alcove as Ginger led Helene to the communal dressing room backstage. The brunette glanced from Helene's face to their manager's and back. "She freeze?"

It happened—first time on stage was a big step, and a bunch of the girls had been working with Helene to help get her ready.

Though Helene wasn't convinced she wanted to be a dancer, she *was* convinced she wanted the money, and she didn't want to make any of the girls think she couldn't handle it.

But she couldn't say the words. Her stomach twisted so hard she staggered, and her mouth ached as though she had drunk a whole bottle and was about to hurl it back up again.

Ginger told Tanya. Or someone else knew, because suddenly there were so many sets of arms around her, hands on her arms, an overwhelming combination of perfume, shampoo, glitter pastes, and hair mousse clogged her nose, and her breath went out again. Her vision went dark.

That's fine. Pass out. It'll be better when you wake up.

The snipey little voice in her head knocked her back into herself. Thanks to the women around her, she was on a folding chair, her head between her knees, a cool rag on the back of her neck, her sparkly heels off her feet and set to the side. Four girls and Ginger were ringed around her, eyes serious. Penny's eyes were wet, but no one was crying on her behalf, and Kira held a glass of water and a glass of brown liquor.

"I'm okay," Helene said, and though that was clearly untrue, no one argued. The girls of the Hottest Gate were no strangers to pain.

"You're not walking home." Ginger crossed her arms, but her expression was more of concern than censure.

"I'm . . . Can I work the floor?"

"Oh, Hell." Tanya crouched in front of her, her dark hair half in her eyes, her sheer robe slipping off one shoulder. "Hellie. Helene. No. Stay back here if you don't want to be alone, but don't—"

"I need to be busy."

Everyone turned toward Ginger, and Helene held her breath.

"You want to waitress the back rooms?" Ginger's mouth turned down on one side, and she tapped long, crimson bright nails against her arms.

"I . . ."

"Keep her out on the floor, Ginger." Terra shouldered into the circle, her absurdly bright pink robe tied messily instead of in its usual perfect bow. "That way we can all keep an eye on her."

A round of nods, and while the pressure in Helene's chest didn't ease, at least she didn't want to vomit anymore.

She could do this.

* * *

She might have made a mistake.

"All right blondie." The baby lance corporal at her table, all puffed up on his new rank, was maybe two years older than her, but he leaned back and propped his arm over the empty chair next to him as though he were king of the world. "When are we going to see *you* up on the stage?"

"You've got three of our best sets coming up. No need to worry about me." Helene lifted her tray, blocking the space between the kid and herself, and didn't smile. "Besides, who would keep bringing you shots if I were up there?" She didn't say "shitty" about his drink choices, but she wanted it implied. From the snickers of two of his friends, it was.

"You don't have to refill my drinks." He tipped his head back, grinning at her over the tray. "You could top me up. I mean, all that blond hair, I wouldn't want to leave you unattended slinging *drinks*. If you know what I mean."

"You don't have to say 'if you know what I mean' if you already made sure everyone knows what you meant." Now she smiled, but it felt stiff and wrong on her face. "And if you think the hair's natural, kid, I got a story to tell you about my boobs."

The three other men at the table burst into laughter, one slamming the table, the other thumping the young lance on the back.

After a long moment, he laughed too, but it was forced. She wasn't on her game, and had made the joke on him, instead of between them. As the lights dimmed, indicating a new dancer was about to be announced, she tucked her tray under her arm and put her free hand on the back of his chair. "I'll let Penny know to do her big finish in this direction. Tip her well, and you might actually meet a real blonde tonight."

While Helene couldn't manage the wink that would usually go with such a statement, the kid relaxed and his next laugh sounded more natural.

Rookie fumble in the cheap seats. Good job, Helene.

"Now coming to the stage . . . she's the sin in sincere, and boys, you're gonna sincerely love what she has to show you. Here comes Tanya, here to tempt you . . ."

Helene craned her neck toward the music booth—that hadn't been Harvey's voice, nor his usual straightforward introduction of each girl. Halfway to the bar she remembered Ginger saying something about a guest announcer, but as the bright notes of

Tanya's opening number kicked off, Helene gestured for their usual bartender, Petey.

"Guest announcer?"

"Some friend of Joe's. Got a new leg and probably looking for a new job."

Joe Grayson, Ginger's brother, had fought first with Helene's brother Noah and then with Byron. He'd been the reason Ginger had made her way to Alfonse's, because he'd asked his sister to check in on Helene. He'd heard about what had happened to Henry, had been tight with whatever marine Henry had ultimately died saving. Of course he was the sort of guy to send his injured friends to the club he'd invested in.

Not like there wasn't a return on the investment. Their town wasn't big—no one did cities anymore—but there was just enough work for some folks to have money for pretty distractions. Not to mention, the training base just north supplied a fair amount of their clientele. Between Joe and Ginger, the Hottest Gate had quite the reputation, especially among newly minted marines.

Helene wondered if the guy in the soundbooth knew Byron, realized that would be past tense, and swallowed the bile that immediately climbed her throat.

Petey, no idiot, slid a generously full shot glass her way, and she knocked it back without hesitation. Drinking on the job was not encouraged, but in certain circumstances it wasn't... *not* encouraged.

Certainly not rare enough that anyone would blame the drinks for what happened later.

"All right, folks, throw it down for Tiny Tanya, make her want to come back out—I hear she has something special planned for us later tonight!" The guest announcer was undoubtedly enthusiastic, and another flurry of dollars landed on the stage at his suggestion.

A great deal of it from the far corner of the stage, where a contingent of enlisted marines yelled back suggestions for Tanya's special show. Maybe they were friends of the temporary announcer or newly released from the base, and either way not her concern for the evening.

The guest announcer's voice was deep, all too amused, and she let it distract her as she went about her drink deliveries. He was having plenty of fun with the introductions: "Watch out for

Cinnamon's spice!" and "Her name isn't Candy, but what else could we possibly call her given the sweets, these treats won't hurt your teeth!" and "Terra holds the whole world in her hands and no wonder we're out there fighting for it..."

Harvey's stand-in was certainly giving his all.

What random thing was he planning for my introduction? Fresh meat? Something about... Helene managed a smile for the sweet regular at a middle table as she both dropped off his whiskey and decided what her potential taglines could have been from this particular man. *Here she is. Hell on wheels, a hell of a ride, a brand-new way to burn...*

Almost enough to make her regret she hadn't hit the stage. Which reminded her why she hadn't made her debut, which might have tipped her back into the waiting maw of despair if the announcer hadn't come back as the last throbbing notes of the current song wound down.

"And now, fellow enthusiasts, a special treat! Four of the Hottest Gate's lovely ladies are going onto the floor. Hold money over the head—don't get cute—of whoever you want to get a special dance for. Yes, your own head counts. *Not* that one, grunts, no one'll see it."

Laughter answered, clear over the faint music.

"Bigger the dollar count, more likely you'll get one before the end of the three songs I'm about to choose. That's right, it's a competition! Shake your money to get the moneymakers! No touching—remember you want the girls to touch *you*, and they'll only do that if you keep your hands on your money and your money on your mind."

Helene had loved this part of the night from the first time she'd seen it. She retreated to the bar, leaned back against an empty stool, and wiped her tray down. For the first song, the waitresses got out of the way and let the dancers have the floor. The girls showed off a range of their best moves, which did what it was meant to for the customers, and also helped aspiring dancers consider their own future repertoires.

Halfway through the second song the servers would go back out with rounds of drinks, which meant they became part of the show, and then of course tips for everyone went up for the third song. The waitresses weren't all planning on dancing one day, but every woman in the Hottest Gate looked like she could.

And customers loved to see the modestly dressed waitresses and the barely dressed dancers in contact.

Helene sipped the next drink Petey slid her way. Unlike the bouncers, Petey, Ginger, and even many of the dancers, she hadn't developed the skill of judging the mood of a crowd. On a normal night, she could figure the right tack to take with individual tables, but it required interaction. So she didn't bother watching the customers, and kept her eyes on the dancers.

"Did you manage to pull a dance from one of the lovely girls? That's one song down . . . maybe up the dollars and shake 'em a little harder, boys. Hands up if you need more drinks—the best thing you can do with your hands during this time! What you do with your digits on your own time is your own business!"

After noting the hands in her section, Helene finished her drink, pushed off from the bar, and twirled her tray before tucking it under her arm. Penny intercepted her immediately, and lifted her eyebrows. Concern radiated from the other blonde, and Helene mustered a smile and dipped her chin in a brief nod.

Penny put her arms around Helene's neck and writhed against her to a chorus of whistles and shouts easily heard over the pounding music.

Usually the customers liked to watch. Usually they were aware enough of themselves and the hulks that served as bouncers to keep their hands to themselves.

But nothing about this night was normal.

A skinny man—bourbon neat drinker—reached out and brushed his hand down Penny's leg. The three other men at the table—tequila, bottle craft beer, and light draft drinkers, respectively—sniggered. She swept the hand away, turned her back to Helene's front, and kept dancing. The man reached again, and again Penny slithered out of the way, but this time she made a quick gesture with her fingers, alerting Gordon, the bigger bouncer, to pay attention.

"Remember boys, no touchy touchy, just looky looky," the announcer said, his voice clear over the music.

Helene stepped to the side, to open more room, and the man shifted, both hands open, reaching and following. It didn't happen often, but it happened, and Helene knew Gordon would be there before it got ugly.

Except *she* made it ugly.

She pivoted, graceful in her non-dancing shoes, swept her tray up, swept her tray down, and cracked the touchy man on the head. He sagged back, dazed, and one of his buddies propped him up. The other two leapt to their feet, shouting, and the sweet regular in front of them and the table of men on Helene's other side surged to their feet.

"Settle down, boys," the announcer said, and Helene didn't know what anyone else did, because the tequila friend closed the distance before Gordon got there, and she swung her tray again.

It got messier from there. Penny darted out of the way, and Helene whirled the tray to cover her escape.

"Hey, sit down—Meyers, I see you down there, get the girl out of the way." The announcer had cut the music, and apparently decided to try and defuse the brewing fight from his perch.

The knot of angry men around Helene were unaffected, and Draft Beer grabbed at her tray.

Helene's vision narrowed to the arc of her tray. Time stuttered, punctuated by the slam of heavy plastic on body parts, and the guest announcer's commentary.

"Tevin, you better get—OH! It's the stripper with the steel chair! Boys, you've done it now."

An elbow dug into the side of her arm and Helene spun away, bounced off someone else so hard her ribs creaked.

"You hate to see a man lose that badly, but man do these girls make it look pretty!"

Her blood pulsed in her temples, in her throat, but for the first time all night her stomach wasn't threatening to climb out of her mouth. Her mind blanked.

"Now that's a sight for eyes to see—hell yeah, girl, use them ti—"

Her tray swung, connected, bounced away, swung again. Her forearms ached and she must have bitten her lip or tongue because copper washed over her tastebuds.

"Stomp him! Keep him down! Those heels—"

Swing. Ache. Swing.

"We're signing you up, girls. Bringing a recruiter next week. On your left, Barry!"

Her tray shattered, and Helene staggered into an upright table leg. Her breath rushed out of her, and like an idiot she tried to break the leg off the table to use that as a weapon. That obviously didn't work, and instead she turned and swung, putting her hips into it just like Noah had taught her.

"People going down, not in the fun—"

From one moment to the next she went from swinging to her arms pinned to her sides, her feet off the ground.

The world snapped back into focus, and she flailed. Someone had grabbed her from behind. Only evasion and a weapon had worked in her favor. Now she was limited in her options, but she tried them all.

Attempted to break the hold. Attempted to see who had her. Attempted to kick and aim her heels to do maximum damage.

She failed at all of it. She failed at listening too, but eventually the announcer took care of that.

"Bouncer caught himself a hellcat."

Abruptly Helene understood Gordon had her, and the motion around her had stilled.

"The bad boys have been bounced with prejudice, and there will be drinks for the winners and bruises for the losers. Should we get back to the party?"

A roar answered him.

Or maybe that was Helene's head.

She was sent to recover in Ginger's office, and Gordon poked his head in twice to check on her. Kira brought her whiskey, and Petey brought her more.

Helene tried to stretch out on Ginger's red leather couch, but her side ached and her mind threatened to think about things, so she stood and paced instead.

But then her arms ached and the room was only big enough for a few strides in either direction, so she sat on the edge of the couch and studied Ginger's desk. The calendar on the wall with draft schedules written in bright purple dry erase marker. The framed pictures of New Orleans burlesque dancers through history.

It was too much.

I should go home. Go home and call Dad.

She only then remembered she hadn't asked Ginger who'd given the news about Byron. Didn't know if her father was expecting her. Before she realized she'd made the decision, she let herself out of Ginger's office. Walked the short hallway toward the club, paused in the doorway next to the bar when the wall of sound met her.

"A round of applause for our guest tonight, Staff Sergeant Randall!" Harvey's voice boomed, as though he could make up with sound what the injured marine had done with jokes. "Get your drinks ready, because you're not going to want to look away during this ne—"

Helene leaned against the arch a moment longer, and couldn't bring herself to step farther into the club. The tables, the people, the lights and the sound were too much, and all at once her dark, lonely apartment seemed the exact right place for her.

She backed away, then slipped into Ginger's office to grab her bag. The weight of it pulled the soreness at her side, so she took out her dancing shoes, her change of clothes, and her water bottle. Still not comfortable, but there was nothing else she could safely leave. Instead she rearranged the important parts, turned her back toward the club without glancing back, and went out the staff exit on the other side of Ginger's office.

Nights in southern Louisiana rarely got cold, but a chill climbed down the back of her neck. Helene tried to put her hands in pockets that weren't there, shifted her bag around to the front as though it would add warmth, and stared at the ground in front of her.

"There she is."

The chill shifted, nearly froze her feet to the ground, and for too long a moment she didn't turn. A hand grabbed her arm, right where a bruise was forming, and the internal ice cracked. She twisted her hips and swung her bag, and the hand dropped away at the unexpected blow.

Draft Beer and Tequila were behind her.

How?

Her gaze darted around the street—she was barely a block from the club, the street deserted. The Hottest Gate was the only thing open at this hour, and few people left early.

Unless they'd been kicked out. And decided to linger.

Idiot.

They were drunk and sloppy and more mad than focused, but Helene was outnumbered and hardly in any better headspace. Fighting them—especially without her tray—would absolutely not go in her favor. Screaming wouldn't help—anyone who heard wouldn't come, and anyone who would help wasn't in any position to hear.

My father isn't losing all his children.

She shoved her hand into her bag and came up with the best equalizer she had. In one well-trained motion she lifted the gun, dropped her bag, aimed.

Tequila backed off, but Draft Beer rolled his eyes, grunted, and stumbled forward, all while lifting a broken bottle.

So she shot him.

Winged him in his right shoulder, angled pretty well so the bullet would pass into the brick of an abandoned storefront. Henry would have been proud of her plan, though Byron would have given her shit for being in the situation in the first place.

You look before you walk out a door. You keep your head on a swivel.

She'd failed those lessons, but she had the important one. *You never go out without being armed.*

Didn't help her brothers, who'd had some of the best weapons known to man.

And maybe it wouldn't help her, were she faced with asshole aliens that wanted to teach humans a lesson, or take over their planet, or gorge themselves on maple syrup like meth heads on vacation. But these weren't aliens. These were idiots.

And I'm an idiot too. But I *didn't bring a beer bottle to a gunfight.*

Draft Beer yelled and fell to his knees. Tequila whirled around, ran, and then came to an unexpectedly immediate halt. Almost in slow motion, he spun again, and crumbled in a heap.

Helene shifted her gun from the man on the ground to the shadowy figure that stood where Tequila had fallen. "It's been a night," she called. "Please take your friend and go."

There. I said please. Good girl.

"I was here to help *you*, hellcat."

The voice was deep, warm, a little too amused. Her hand started to shake as some part of her understood the danger was indeed past. It took the rest of her brain a second to understand why. The voice. The voice had registered as "safe" on some level—it was the guest announcer. The wounded marine.

"But seems like you weren't done dealing damage tonight," that voice continued.

Draft Beer crawled off the sidewalk into the street.

What a baby. I barely got him. I hope he gets tetanus from the shit on the ground.

Slowly, Helene lowered her gun. "Were you with them?"

"I know I was slow getting here, but you don't have to be insulting." He moved closer, and her eyes dropped to his uneven gait before flicking back up to his face.

"What..." She stumbled on the rest of the question, unsure what she wanted to know first.

"I saw you almost walk back into the club. Saw your face. I know that face, and I know there's a back door. And I know Gordon didn't leave to walk you home yet like he was going to. So I came after you."

"You picked up all that from the one second I was standing there?"

"I'm an observant guy." He was close enough that the one working streetlight illuminated his face. Strong jaw, sharp cheekbones. His eyebrows were drawn in, like he was irritated.

Or in pain from the whole lost leg and maybe prosthetic, the asshole voice sneered in her head. Though since *she* was the asshole, the voice had the right of it.

"Well, I'm okay. And I don't need a stranger walking me home."

"I'm not a stranger, hellcat. I'm Oliver Randall, and it's my life Henry Guidry died to save not too long ago."

Her knees turned to liquid and she very nearly followed Draft Beer in falling to the street, tetanus and all. She staggered sideways and leaned against the wall, keeping the gun pointed down until she could trust her hands to put it away.

Had the man on the video call told her and her father the name of the marine Henry had saved? Had she heard it, and blocked it out in that terrible white noise?

"Joe sent you to the club?" She couldn't ask about Henry. Couldn't ask if he knew about Byron. Couldn't manage anything but the obvious.

Oliver nodded, his eyes intent on her. On her midsection, she realized, not her breasts. He wasn't checking her out, he was keeping an eye on her body to make sure she wasn't about to collapse.

Am *I about to collapse?* It was a valid question, but if she hadn't managed to pass out yet this particular night, it wasn't changing now.

She took a deep breath, pushed herself off the wall, and grabbed her bag. "Should we call anyone for them?" she asked as she returned her gun to its compartment.

"I'll make sure they're taken care of." He gestured to his pocket, where presumably he had some sort of phone or communication device. Technology kept jumping forward, and she hadn't had much chance to keep up.

Helene had no interest in clarifying what was in his pocket, or what "taken care of" actually meant. They walked in silence for a block, and then another.

"Thank you," she said, finally remembering that was a thing that people said.

"You didn't really need me," he replied, and her sidelong glance showed he was smiling. "Kinda wish I could have called that like I did the brawl."

"I was trying to figure out what you would have used to announce me, if I had made it on stage tonight." It was a dumb thing to say, but it was all she had. Better to talk about that, rather than Henry. Or Byron. Or her life.

"Oh." The sound Oliver made landed somewhere between grunt and chuckle. "I wasn't. I think Henry would have found a way to unsave my life if I was a part of his sister stripping at the big stage at the Hottest Gate."

"Dance," she corrected, but she laughed. It was ragged, and might have edged a little too close to a different emotion entirely, but she managed to pull it together and not cry all over him.

"My point stands."

It does. What would Henry say if he knew I was working at the Hottest Gate? She'd never let the thought surface in her head, but she gave it a chance and smiled at what came to her. *"Get those big dollars, Hell, and put in a good word for me with the hot redhead."*

"So you weren't going to announce me or watch?"

"I didn't say I wasn't gonna watch." He nudged her, then pulled up short when she hissed under her breath. "You good?"

"Just a little sore." She slowed when he didn't catch up, turned back toward him. "Bruises. None of those assholes landed a clean hit."

"Oh I saw." Oliver's face was unreadable. "I know strip—dancers can be tough. I see those shoes you wear."

"I don't even know if I want to do it." The words emerged while she was still trying to figure out his expression. She only realized she'd spoken them after he cocked his head.

"What're you going to do instead?" No judgment in his voice, just an honest question.

One she didn't have the answer to, until all of the sudden she did.

"I'm going to enlist."

"*What?!*"

Exhaustion, alcohol, soreness, grief—all of it crested in a wave and threatened to pull her down. Helene reached for a lifeline—anger—and refused to drown.

"Those fuckers killed all of my brothers. All of them. I'm going to enlist, and then I'm going to kill as many of *them* as I can." She tightened her hands around her bag and felt the rightness of each word. Finally, she had a purpose, a direction, a—

"That's stupid."

It was her turn to splutter. "*What?!*"

"That's stupid. Girl like you walks into the recruitment office, they're not sending you to the Marines. Do you know what a mess most of those units are for women right now?"

The anger in his tone met hers, but before she could yell at him, she realized what the undercurrent was. Bitterness.

The Marines were about to discharge him for his leg. Her brothers were dead. His friends. Maybe his brothers too, what did she know? And here she was, suddenly deciding she could pick up and—

"Besides," he said, interrupting her thoughts again. "There's something you're not thinking about."

"I . . . what?"

"You're a good shot, a hellcat in a fight, stubborn about pain . . ." He laughed and started walking. "Hell, maybe you *should* be a marine. Wouldn't be the first one to walk out of a strip club and into the recruiter's office."

She matched his pace, studied his profile. Couldn't explain why she was listening to him so intently. "But?" she prompted.

"But there's a question you're not asking yourself."

"What's that?" Helene's heart hammered again, but in anticipation this time.

"Where you can do the most damage." He said it like a

promise, like he knew she could inflict damage. "You don't think enlisting is the only way to get revenge, do you?"

"I... It's all I'm qualified for. How else would I get to space?" And have access to the weapons, the training, the fighting force...

"How do you feel about blowing things up, hellcat?"

The only explosions she'd had anything to do with were bottle rockets and fireworks on big holidays. Fun, sparkly, occasionally dangerous... how could she *not* like them? But that wasn't what he meant.

Though, to be fair, she wasn't entirely sure what he did mean. Blowing up prison camps? Government buildings? Enemy ships? As long as aliens were on the receiving end, did it matter? No, she decided, as a thrum of satisfaction washed over her. As long as aliens were on the receiving end, it absolutely did not matter. She'd revel in every blast, every bright, shocking, radiant moment. As long as they were on the same page—aliens, not humans.

"Depends on what you have in mind." Her steps slowed, and he matched her pace.

Oliver shot a sidelong glance at her, a hint of a smile curving the edge of his mouth. They walked silently to the next corner, and then he turned fully toward her.

"Oh, I have a *list*."

Helene had spent a lot of time at the Hottest Gate, and that was still the sexiest thing she'd ever heard.

ONE FOR THE MONEY

Michael Mersault

"You must be incredibly proud," Pickford said, accepting a delicate, steaming coffee cup, his lips shifting into a placid smile.

Mr. Carr settled into his own seat across from Pickford, resting his own cup and saucer on the fine old table. "I'd be lying if I said I wasn't." Mr. Carr lifted his cup, looking at Pickford over the rim as he took a sip, his clear blue eyes twinkling. He sighed with contentment, cradling the cup in his hands. "She grabbed hold of a dream, and nothing—not Johannsen's, not the loss of her mother—nothing held her back."

"Truly remarkable," Pickford said. "Among all my prior students she must be the greatest success story: an Apollo executive, and at such a young age."

Mr. Carr took another sip, but his brows drew together and he looked at Pickford with something like skepticism in his eyes. The cup lowered. "You said you were Molly's physics professor, right?"

This represented the critical moment, Pickford knew, and he chose his words carefully. "Yes, physics. But you must think I'm offering false praise, with Tyler Vernon's daughter among my students. I assure you I'm not. Your daughter earned her way, not riding the coattails of a famous father."

"That's kind of you to say, very kind," Mr. Carr replied, his expression only lightening slightly, "but, you know, my Molly said Vernon's girl didn't get any breaks. Earned her way, same as anyone."

"Oh?" Pickford said, striving for an air of innocent surprise. "I'm sorry, I didn't realize your daughter was close with—"

"With Vernon's kid? Wasn't really; just to say hello, though I guess people thought they were close for some reason or other." Mr. Carr looked up slightly, his vision wandering as if reflecting on some sweet memory. "But she knew enough, I guess. Molly never grudged her."

Pickford barely managed to keep the expression of frustration and disappointment off his face. He had spent weeks putting this moment together, and it was for nothing... again. With an inward shrug of resignation Pickford sat up and leaned forward. "I don't suppose you have any pictures to share. Seeing my old students living their best lives is a great treasure to me."

The older man lit up. "I do. I do indeed. Just here." Mr. Carr stood up and moved to the nearby desk, shuffling through drawers. Before he could grasp the prized pictures of his daughter, Pickford slipped up behind him, clapping a firm left hand over the man's mouth, pulling his head back as the razor-edged knife in Pickford's right hand bit deep.

Pickford had learned prior lessons, keeping his left arm high to avoid the jet of blood, and gripping tight until Mr. Carr's futile struggles faded.

As the final tremors traveled through Mr. Carr's dying body, Pickford's unwanted shreds of humanity took cold refuge in pure philosophy yet again: The mass of humankind formed little more than a disease, a vile infestation, and since Pickford longed for the total eradication of his own despoiling species, why should personally extinguishing one life affect him emotionally? It shouldn't.

Perhaps after a few more similar jobs he might shed the last symptoms of his absurd tribal conditioning.

Pickford eased the crumpled body of the old man to the blood-drenched carpet and stepped back to consider the strangely cozy setting of the two coffee cups, two saucers, the deceptive image of domesticity quietly clashing with the raw, angry odor of violence. For a moment he felt as if this juxtaposition held some great meaning, just on the brink of his comprehension, but the insistent ticking of an old grandfather clock reawakened him to his mission.

How could he ever hope to be assigned more serious, meaningful missions until he began behaving more like an actual secret agent and less like a disenchanted college professor?

First, he cleared the dishes from the table, placing them in the dishwasher with an assortment of clean bowls and cups, adding the detergent and initiating the cleaning cycle. As the dishwasher began to gurgle and hum, he drew from his pocket the first of the gleaming treasures that truly validated his whole calling.

These tools of off-world design had finally been provided to Pickford when he had completed his third job, and only then did he truly believe he was in the employ of actual alien powers. Due to the necessary compartmentalization and secrecy of the network, Pickford could not be certain precisely who directed his actions. Were they Rangora? Horvath? Some rogue faction of Glatun or Ogut origin even?

He did not greatly care who stood in the shadows behind him. Whoever it was, Pickford knew they worked to depopulate the earth—if not entirely then down to a small, firmly managed population of laborers. Either eventuality represented a glorious dream to him, and he was completely committed to the cause.

But until these alien tools had been supplied, Pickford had suspected that his enigmatic taskmasters might be nothing more than passionate activists, as human as he was. Now Pickford held real hope that their combined efforts might truly make the difference, uncovering exploitable weaknesses in earth's defenses, or in the key defenders themselves, such as the person of Tyler Vernon.

Pickford activated the small device in his hand, watching its simple display as he walked from room to room, assuring that Mr. Carr didn't have some concealed surveillance system hidden away. A second device provided secure communication with Pickford's mysterious handler, and he made the requisite call.

"You are still in location," the usual voice said as soon as Pickford actuated the call.

"Yes. He is dead, but he confirmed there was no actual connection to Tyler Vernon, nor Vernon's daughter."

"Very well," the handler said, sounding unsurprised. They both knew it was yet another longshot. "Follow the usual exit protocol, and when you are clear, head west. There is another task assigned to you. It is in rural New Hampshire."

Pickford sighed internally. Another mission grasping at straws.

How many people must he kill before they finally gave him a mission of real significance?

"You... You bought a tour bus?" Julia's voice came clearly through the phone, and Zane heard the layers of surprise and displeasure in those few short words.

"It's, um, more of a tour van," Zane offered, looking at his watch as he grabbed up the van keys, his brown-bagged lunch, and the list of prepaid customers. "Really a whole tour concession, to be—"

"You spent your savings on a rural tour operation? Are you—?" She broke off. "I mean, what kind of ROI can you hope for bringing grubby tourists around to look at—what? Cows? Maple trees? Zane, I go to India for three weeks and you just... just toss everything we spoke about and jump at this?"

It had not been love at first sight for them. They had met in college, sharing more than one class in common, but Julia exuded sophistication and style: tall, slender, with jet-black hair and stunning blue eyes, while Zane's rural New Hampshire roots and blue-jean fashion aspirations placed him in a different strata entirely. Only in Professor Khan's entrepreneurism class did Julia suddenly seem to notice Zane's existence at all.

"Jules, I really want to go over it all, but I'm kind of pressed for time right now. Can I explain this to you later? I've got, you know—"

"Your tourists await already?" Julia's sigh came audibly across the line. "I'm jet-lagged, I'm going to be in meetings until six. I—I just wish that you'd spoken to me before you... I mean, we'd talked about you investing with Ryan's startup where there's some great growth potential."

Zane placed the official tour guide hat on his head, glancing at the mirror. "Um, I know, Jules. This was... this was kind of a fleeting opportunity. Had to act fast or let it slip through my fingers,"

Julia snorted. Even her snort was sexy. "Really, Zane? You fell for the Limited Time Offer gag? The oldest pressure sales trick in the book."

Back in college, Zane and Julia had both absorbed the power of Professor Khan's passion and enthusiasm in much the same way. As a third-generation American whose grandparents had bought into the American Dream when most Americans declared that

Dream dead and buried, Professor Khan recast the post-Horvath world in a new light. It wasn't merely feel-good hype either. He had provided dozens of detailed case studies from history that all revealed one abiding lesson: To those with vision and courage, every global tragedy became an opportunity. "New problems," Professor Khan said over and over, "they require new solutions, and new solutions are exceedingly valuable."

As Zane stepped out the door of his tiny apartment, holding his phone in place with his shoulder, he couldn't fault Julia's first reaction. It had been his first reaction too. A humble tour concession did not solve any new problems that he could perceive, at least no problems he perceived at first.

"No, Jules, it's not like that. I bought the business from the Haselbauers, and—"

"Haselbauers? As in Jason Haselbauer?"

Zane hurried down to the dusty blue-and-yellow tour van with the very prominent MAPLE WAR TOURS plastered all over its sides.

"Um, old man Haselbauer died a while—"

"I know that, Zane," Julia said. "I saw the news. His estate was worth—I can't recall how much."

Zane clambered into the van and tossed list and lunch on the passenger seat. "Yeah, I've known the family my whole life, and—"

"You're *friends* with the Haselbauers and you never thought to mention this to me before?"

"Not friends, Jules." Zane turned the key halfway, heating the glow plugs in the van's diesel engine. "The Haselbauers kind of . . . they kind of keep to themselves. Just known them. They, uh, they gave me first shot at this biz, Jules, and that's quite an honor, really."

Zane heard other voices raised in the background of the call, and Julia spoke to someone, "*Just a second.* Zane? I've got to get to this meeting and try to keep my eyes propped open. I feel like I could sleep a week, but I'll call you later. Just send me the contract on this deal and we'll figure a loophole to get your money back and get you out of it. I know you're so trusting, and that's sweet. But you've got to understand very, very wealthy people like the Haselbauers don't get that way through their overwhelming generosity, right?"

"Uh, Jules, there's a whole other aspect of the operation that—"

"Zane, I've really got to run. Tell me about it later, okay?"

The call ended and Zane looked at the phone, frowning for a moment at the picture of Julia there, her amazing smile aimed right at him. He sighed and sent a copy of the contract to Julia's email before setting the phone aside and driving off to the truck wash to scrub the caked layers of dust from the van as quickly as possible. He might have time for a quick bite and a cup of coffee before his tour group assembled.

Wherever things ended up with Julia, he had a job to do.

The Haselbauers had explained their simple marketing message that basically repeated the same simple refrains adorning the Applejack Diner: Maple War Tours! Historic Locations! Lifelike ReCreations! Private Viewings of Tyler Vernon's Own Hideaways!

Zane couldn't imagine such pap would generate much interest, but the Haselbauers swore it was perfect. "Old Deke Floyd ran it for us," one of the mountainous Haselbauer clan had explained, "and when that heart attack laid him low, we needed someone we trusted to keep it going. It's become kinda important to us."

That the Haselbauers even remembered Zane, let alone thought to offer him such a business opportunity, floored him.

Sure, he'd bagged the groceries of more than one member of the Haselbauer family back before he went off to college, and before that he'd worked odd jobs in the community, so local people knew him on sight. But living very humbly with his grandmother, struggling to earn extra cash with few notable skills, hadn't seemed the sort of background that would impress anyone, especially the wealthiest family in the area.

Evidently somehow it had, and Zane wondered how he would explain it to Julia. It wasn't about the simple, one-page contract he had signed; he had looked Tom Haselbauer in the eye. It was a literal handshake deal to Zane, and that handshake meant more to Zane than any contract.

Zane parked the tour van out front and strolled into the diner with nearly thirty minutes to spare. What's-her-name, the perky blond waitress, greeted him with a knowing wink, inclining her head toward the corner booth where a couple sat opposite their daughter, feasting on the house specialty: golden waffles festooned with peaches and whipped cream.

"Got time for breakfast?" the waitress asked, and Zane caught a glimpse of her nametag: *Krista—that's right.*

Zane gave her a smile. “Thanks. Coffee and a couple of eggs would be a treat.”

Krista put the order through and poured coffee. “Looks like you have a few customers eager to go,” she said, and Zane glanced at the three seated at the booth, then up to Krista, seeing her blond ponytail bouncing where it poked through her baseball cap. “There was another guy here. Think he went for a stroll.”

Zane cautiously sampled his coffee. “Mm. I have eight on my list.”

Krista turned to retrieve Zane’s plate from the window: steaming eggs and hash browns, seemingly materialized in seconds. “Deke never had many more than eight at a time, so good group. Your first, right?”

Tom Haselbauer had formed some arrangement with the Applejack Diner, one corner of the diner home to Maple War Tours brochures and signage, but Zane wasn’t exactly sure how far that arrangement went. “My first,” Zane agreed, adding nothing more and focusing on his breakfast. Krista took the coffeepot around to the three tourists, and Zane turned his thoughts back to the conversation with Julia, something she had said nagging at his mind.... Did she really believe that the Haselbauers obtained their wealth by sharp dealing and stinginess? More importantly, if—when—Julia’s great plans came together and wealth poured into her own hands, was that how she would handle affluence?

As Zane worked his way through the eggs and hash browns, he looked at the picture of Julia on his phone again, studying that smile, those eyes. Could she ever be a clutch-fisted miser? She’d certainly be much easier on the eyes than any version of Ebenezer Scrooge.

“The choice of those with discriminating taste,” Krista said, startling Zane from his reverie.

“Um, what?” he said, looking up at her.

Krista nodded toward the picture of Julia, smiling. “Your girlfriend? She’s lucky with that dark hair. You’ve heard that line, right?”

Zane took a final bite of hash browns and shook his head. “Nope.”

“Oh,” Krista shrugged, suddenly awkward. “Since Johannsen’s, you know, brunettes... they’re supposed to be more the bring-home-to-mother type.”

"I'd never thought of it that way," Zane said. He wiped his mouth with a napkin. "What do I owe you?"

Krista's smile brightened. "Part of the arrangement. On the house." Her eyes moved up past Zane. "I'd say more of your group's here."

Zane glanced over his shoulder through the front window to a few figures milling around by the tour van.

"It looks good, by the way," Krista said, and at Zane's puzzled expression added, "The van. Deke hadn't scrubbed the dust off in a while."

"Oh yeah. Thanks." Zane gulped the last of his coffee and left a fat tip before strolling out to address his first Maple War Tour group, the family of three trailing behind him. He glanced back to see Krista smiling at him, some hint of amusement in her expression. Surely to her eyes Zane could hardly be more unlike Deke Floyd. Old Deke presented a stocky, surly image to the world, but solid and confident, while Zane felt almost artificial by comparison, a lanky tyro with a head crammed full of "book learning" and little else.

Still, Zane couldn't readily picture Deke as the most effective tour guide. Despite Zane's own youth and inexperience, he liked people, and he spoke easily with most anyone. He had read through the provided tour itinerary and scripted statements until they were all but committed to memory, but unlike Deke, Zane knew he could extemporize as needed.

"Howdy, folks," Zane said, opening the van door and checking names off the list. "Welcome to Maple War Tours, I'm your guide, Zane. We'll get started as soon as everyone's aboard." The eight tourists formed an interesting collection to Zane's eyes, though he'd never considered what sort of people might pay a modest sum to look at the humble old roots of Earth's bulwark against the aliens—the humble roots of Tyler Vernon himself.

One middle-aged man sporting thick spectacles and what appeared to be a prosthetic hand wore a tight black sweatshirt featuring a hoplite hurling a missile instead of a spear, the words, TROY: BORN OF WINTER making its meaning clear. Pure fanboy, which honestly made more sense to Zane than the sizeable, vocal minority in America that persistently harped about the various evils of Tyler Vernon.

Another pair of his tourists seemed cut from similar cloth,

while two others appeared visibly affronted by the Vernon fans, leaving only the family of three, the parents evidently enslaved by their daughter's rampant curiosity. "Mister, will we get to see any spaceships today?" the young girl asked as they boarded the van.

"Sorry," Zane said. "I don't think so."

The girl heaved a sigh. "Oh, that's okay."

The tap on Zane's shoulder startled him, especially when he turned to discover a large older gentleman had somehow appeared practically right beside him.

"Excuse me," the man said in a mild, cultured voice, almost devoid of accent, "is it too late to join the tour?" One large hand opened to reveal a tidy roll of cash, and Zane realized he had no idea how to handle a cash transaction on the fly, accounting-wise.

"Oh, uh, sure," Zane said. They could figure out receipts and such later. "I'll get a handle on the paperwork when we come back."

"Yes, perfect." The man extended his large, soft hand. "Paul, Paul Smith."

"Pleasure," Zane shook the hand before counting and pocketing the money. "After you, sir."

Zane guessed Mr. Smith stood half a head taller than his own six-foot height, and he wore a tweedy sort of jacket over his thick frame, thinning hair going gray on the fringes. Zane guessed him at mid-fifties in age, but certainly spry enough.

Zane settled in the driver's seat, closing the door and starting the engine. He keyed the microphone, though he hardly needed it with such a quiet, compact group.

"Thank you for joining us today. In the next three hours we will retrace the steps that created earth's very first galactic export product; we will set foot on the actual battlefield that began earth's effective resistance; and walk through an exact replica of one historic early meeting. Many things you will see today are only available to participants of Maple War Tours, unknown to the public at large."

Zane heard the low-voiced exchanges of some passengers as he set off, and a glance in the mirror only confirmed his earlier observations. A few enthusiasts, a couple of sour apples, the family of three, and Paul Smith, whose thin smile could mean anything.

Zane slowed the van and pulled into a mostly empty parking lot. "Here you see Mac's Market, which actually employed

Tyler Vernon part-time back when he closed the first deal with Glatun traders."

One of the sour apples, a woman of maybe thirty years, piped up: "We've all heard the story of humble Tyler Vernon chopping wood and stocking shelves just before he became the richest man in the world, but he didn't really work at this little store, did he?"

"Uh, yes, ma'am," Zane said. "He did."

Looking in the mirror Zane saw her eyes roll. "Well, I suppose *you* would say that."

Zane felt the slightest flare of irritation and suppressed it. "When I was just a little kid my grandma shopped at Mac's. Tyler Vernon bagged our groceries, ma'am."

Among the smirks and jostles from the Vernon fans, and the frowns from the skeptics, Paul Smith suddenly perked up. "So you were raised here yourself? Grew up among these people?"

"Yes, sir," Zane said. "I bagged groceries here at Mac's for a time myself." Zane turned his focus back to the job. "Few know that the original bottle of Dragon's Tears—or maple syrup as we know it—came from right here at Mac's. If Tyler Vernon hadn't worked at Mac's, it's entirely possible that the Horvath would still own our skies." The next line formed an official part of his tour spiel, highlighted by the Haselbauers: "Tyler Vernon still makes occasional appearances in these parts, and locals catch glimpses of him driving his old Jeep, visiting his various properties in the area."

If that was true, Zane had never heard of it before, and he had certainly never seen the famous man casually tooling around, but he followed the script.

Zane drove on, heading out of town.

Though he heard of it most of his life, Zane had never actually been to Homer's Field before the prior week, and now the Haselbauers had transformed the old farmland in a surprising fashion, placing an unadorned structure in the field. On the outside it appeared to be a nondescript metal-framed building, but Zane led the dismounted tourists inside to a startling spectacle that he had not yet witnessed himself. Now the provided script made sense, and Zane tried to conceal his surprise as he saw the detailed tableau, a very lifelike figure of a Glatun individual seemingly frozen over what looked like an elaborate form of beer pong.

"Uh, here you see a perfect re-creation of the moment that Glatun trader, Wathaet, first tasted product number 156, also known as Dragon's Tears." A table stood before the waxwork Glatun trader, dozens of Dixie cups poised, each with handwritten numbers clearly visibly, number 156 notably apart from the others. "The eventual fate of earth lay contained in a Dixie cup."

Zane heard a snort from one of the tourists but didn't look to see from which. *Come on, I didn't write this stuff myself...*

"The crew of the *Spinward Crossing* brought six barrels of maple syrup from this field back to Glatun space, and ignited real interest about earth at last. And the sale of maple syrup provided the first human bankroll in off-planet credits. Without maple syrup there would be no Troy, no real earth defense of any substance."

"And without maple syrup Tyler Vernon would not have banked billions of dollars for himself," one of the sour apples interjected.

Zane remembered similar arguments back in college and detoured off script slightly. "True enough. Of course, billions of dollars were mostly useful for hiring thousands of people on earth and paying taxes. When he was paid in Glatun credits, that money was basically untaxable and, you know, useful for buying stuff from the galactic marketplace—really useful stuff."

"Hey," the young girl piped up, standing near the display table and eyeing the Glatun dummy. "Is this a real alien, like, stuffed or something?"

Zane chuckled. *It couldn't be, could it?* "Uh, no, just a... a clever mannequin design. Very lifelike, isn't it?"

Zane turned back to the cluster of adults, catching a glimpse of Paul Smith standing back from the others, a fleeting expression of loathing momentarily crossing his features.

Must not like kids...

As everyone loaded back onto the van, Zane keyed the microphone, returning to the script. "After the Glatun discovered the big market for maple syrup among their worlds, earth still had a problem: The Horvath controlled the high ground, and human governments were afraid to step out of line. This situation led directly to the actual Maple Syrup War, which remains a notable event in history for several reasons, including the first American combat casualty from a laser rifle."

As Zane spoke, he put the van into gear and set off to the

next destination, but his mind roved back to Julia against his will. She embodied all he ever desired in a woman plus a level of sophistication and beauty he had never dreamed of. No business deal was worth cratering his relationship with her, surely. He had sent her the contract, and if she remained adamant after talking it out with him . . . Zane would explain to Tom Haselbauer . . . what? That he'd made a mistake?

He could already visualize the look in Tom's eyes. The real mistake would be in Tom's estimation of Zane, nothing more. Zane frowned to himself. What could he do?

The next point on the tour itinerary came up, and Zane pulled off the main road, weaving through the trees until they emerged into an open area. Several visibly damaged military vehicles stood neatly arranged around a large memorial.

"Here you see the Maple War memorial, which marks the sad moment when US military personnel were tasked with illegally obtaining maple syrup for our Horvath oppressors." Glancing in the mirror, Zane saw something like a mocking smile cross Paul Smith's lips, but he pressed on. "While clashes between local citizens and military personnel were few, many people lost their lives in the conflict due to Horvath retribution strikes all around this region."

"While Tyler Vernon hid in a bunker somewhere," one of the grouches said, to the indignant murmurs of the fanboys.

Zane pointed to the mountainside rising up above their tidy clearing. "If you'll look up there, you will see Mount Moriah where Tyler Vernon stood, calling out the Horvath and drawing their fire."

The young girl and the fanboys all seemed suitably struck by the sight, but Negative Nancy piled on: "And George Washington never told a lie. These kinds of tales are part of every mythic hero, but are only as real as gullible people will swallow."

Zane took a deep breath. He felt no particular loyalty to Tyler Vernon, but sophistication to the point of disbelief in any form of honor had been tediously common in college.

"Not sure about myths, ma'am. Vernon and Jason Haselbauer stood right up there alone in the snow, calling out the Horvath. The recording of the call is available, as is the telemetry on Vernon's phone. No reasonable person disputes the basic facts, ma'am, so I guess we can only question his motives or maybe his sanity. Did he somehow know that the Glatun would intervene at the last moment to save his life? It doesn't seem likely."

"But didn't Vernon have some sort of bomb shelter?" Paul Smith inquired in a mild tone. "I seem to recall something about that."

One of the fanboys blurted, "The Lair!"

"Yes," Zane said. "The Lair."

"Will we be seeing that?"

Zane put the van in gear. "We'll be seeing the crater where it used to be."

"Um, so will we be able to see Lair Two?" one of the fanboys persisted.

Zane looked in the mirror, noticing Paul Smith's intense gaze as he said, "Lair Two is not part of the regular tour."

The remainder of the regular tour passed smoothly. They did indeed stop at an overlook offering a pleasant view of the water-filled hole that was once a repurposed mine Tyler Venon had sheltered in, then continued on to the site of another Horvath strike not far from there. They ended the tour at the carefully maintained "Maple Sugar Collection Point Alpha" where old storage tanks stood ensconced within three layers of razor wire.

"Of course, the federal government's attempt to nationalize maple syrup was short-lived," Zane said to the group, "so all this infrastructure really only served as window dressing for Horvath eyes. Tyler Vernon's gamble that the Glatun would intervene turned out to be correct, though many people of this region back then were committed to living the motto 'Live Free Or Die' regardless of what Vernon or the Glatun chose to do. But just like all of them, we may also have the choice: Will we choose temporary safety, or will we choose liberty?"

Zane saw the expected range of expressions from his small audience, one of the fanboys practically swelling with patriotic pride, while at least one of the cynics seemed on the verge of gagging.

"This concludes the regular tour, so I'll give you a moment to view those pictures of the original facility here before we head back."

The tourists wandered. It was a pleasant afternoon, and whether they bought the whole patriotic shtick or not, no one seemed in a rush to rumble back to town.

Zane looked over his small flock, seeing an opportunity to check his messages. One brief line from Julia awaited: *This contract is Swiss cheese. Today is your last day playing tour guide.*

"Excuse me." Zane jumped at the words practically in his ear.

Paul Smith had once again seemed to somehow teleport within arm's reach without making a sound.

"Um, what can I help you with, Mr. Smith?"

The stocky older gentleman looked down at Zane with a hesitant smile. "You said the other bomb shelter was not part of the regular tour. Does that mean there is an irregular tour, if you will pardon the expression? I would be happy to pay more to see such a place still intact."

The Haselbauers had promised these offers happened from time to time, and really increased the profit margin of the business, but Zane felt surprised that he could be so fortunate on his first group. Now to remember the procedure that had been explained to him…

"Uh, yes sir. I think we can access Lair Two today."

Paul Smith's eyes bored into Zane. "To actually set foot within the shelter?"

"We, uh… sure," Zane said. "We just need to drop the other folks back at the diner. And, of course, there's the extra cost involved…"

Smith peeled several bills from a roll in his pocket. "Will this do?"

"That about covers it, sir," Zane said, pocketing the cash. Things were looking up, but would Julia see it that way?

The tourists debarked quietly, several heading into the diner for a late lunch, and Zane's stomach felt like joining them, but instead he rooted around behind the driver's seat, setting aside the neatly folded American flag and grasping the New Hampshire State flag. As Paul Smith eased away from the other tourists, Zane fit the flag onto the line on the bare flagpole standing before the diner. "Forgot this earlier," Zane explained. "If you'd like to get aboard, we'll head out in just a minute."

Paul climbed in as Zane finished securing the flag. Casting a final look back through the diner's window, Zane saw Krista with menus in hand, her eyes rising to the flag stirring in the wind before settling back on Zane, worried lines on her brow. Their gaze met, and Zane felt something indefinable communicated between them as he climbed back into the van.

"This place is a bit farther from town, Mr. Smith," Zane said, "and the road's not great."

"Very well," Smith said, leaning back in his seat, his hands folded. "I shall enjoy the scenery."

The Haselbauers had described their special attentions to the tour van. Aside from the torque-loaded turbo diesel engine, the van sported four-wheel drive and air-locking differentials so the tours could operate most of the year, regardless of the New Hampshire weather. While Zane didn't need to engage the four-wheel drive, the winding back roads were in rough shape as Zane surreptitiously followed a map the Haselbauers had provided, weaving his way over tight logging roads he hadn't even known existed before.

The only moment of excitement arrived when several deer bounded out directly in their path, causing Zane to jam on the brakes, barely avoiding a collision with a wide-eyed doe. "Whoa! Sorry, sir," Zane said. "The deer never seem to get any smarter."

Paul Smith seemed unruffled, looking out at the deer as Zane slowly accelerated, continuing on. "Like all wildlife, they are wiser than they seem," Smith said in a musing tone. "They maintain their balance with nature, unlike humanity."

Zane felt momentarily distracted by their near miss, and replied without much thought. "City people always say things like that, sir. But of course the deer don't balance anything. If coyotes and hunters don't whack a bunch of deer, they overpopulate and starve."

Zane regretted speaking his mind, but Mr. Smith only smiled thinly, saying, "Well, perhaps there's a lesson in that."

Zane didn't know what that meant but only said, "Yes sir," and kept driving.

When they finally clawed their way up to the small parking area screened beneath heavy foliage, Zane felt surprised to see a battered old Jeep parked beside an open gate, a stout metal door mounted in the adjoining face of granite. While the Haselbauers had provided a checklist and broad description for these *special* tours, all the unknowns undermined Zane's confidence, especially in such a remote location, far from any aid.

"Uh, here we are, sir," Zane said, killing the engine.

"Whose vehicle is that?" Paul Smith asked, his expression suddenly alert.

"Honestly, I can't imagine who could be up here," Zane said.

They climbed out of the van and passed through the open gate together, Zane sorting through the provided keys. "Ah, this one." He unlocked the door and drew a powerful flashlight from his pocket, but a chain of caged bulbs illuminated the passageway ahead.

"So, most of the work you're seeing here, these stairs and such, they were added by Tyler Vernon back during the early days. All these cable-runs up there allowed Mr. Vernon to communicate with media sources, his own crews, and even with the White House."

"Yes," Smith said in a very low voice, quietly following Zane as they descended flight after flight of steel stairs, hundreds of feet deeper into the repurposed mine.

When they finally reached the main level, a row of lights led the way about fifty paces from the stairs to another solid, vault-like door. It stood partially open, flickering lights issuing from a visible slice within, a murmur of radio voices and crackling static growing louder by the second.

Zane hadn't been told that anyone would actually be working inside the old shelter, and his nervousness only increased as Paul Smith drew so close that Zane felt the heat of the man's breath on his neck.

Taking hold of the heavy door, Zane tugged it open and froze. Though the lighting wasn't the best, the slight figure hunched over the flickering screen was shockingly familiar.

"Mi—Mr. Vernon? I'm sorry to—" The blow to Zane's temple staggered him, but he managed to keep his feet planted and looked up through a veil of pain to see Paul Smith's hand raise a small stainless steel pistol, point it toward Tyler Vernon, and fire.

Without a conscious decision, Zane stumbled against Smith, both of his hands grasping the older man's right wrist, jerking the pistol . . . right toward his own face.

The gun fired again before his eyes, powder fragments burning Zane's cheeks, the blast from such a small gun still deafening, but Zane stubbornly held tight.

Smith growled, his left hand hooking hard into Zane's jaw,

dropping him in his tracks. Through the stars bursting in his eyes Zane saw a huge shadow suddenly envelop Paul Smith, bending Smith's arm back and back. The next gunshot sounded muffled, and Paul Smith jerked, sagging, his body sinking down to the hard, cold stone beside Zane.

Despite the red haze in his vision and the throbbing in his head, Zane struggled to stand.

"Easy. Easy now." Tom Haselbauer stepped into the uncertain light, Paul Smith's little pistol engulfed in one large hand. "He shoot you?"

Zane gathered his wits, the fog slowly receding as he took stock of himself. "No. My jaw feels about broke and my head's all lopsided."

Tom hunkered down beside Zane and began to paw irreverently through Mr. Smith's pockets. "He was strong for city folk. Surprised me a tad."

A sudden thought struck Zane and he sat up, his head painfully protesting. "Mr. Vernon?" He looked at the figure still seated in the uncertain light, unmoving.

Tom chuckled. "Naught but a big doll, son, just like that alien in the Homer's Field setup. The movie people made 'em up for us. About the most expensive part of the whole show, and they turned out real slick."

Tom began laying out items from Smith's pockets. "Professor Pickford," Tom murmured, looking in a slender leather wallet. He glanced at the pistol more carefully. "Walther PPK. Huh. Thought himself some kind of secret agent, seems." He laid the pistol down, then a small dagger, adding three very exotic-looking little devices beside it and the wallet. "Ah, here's the stuff," Tom murmured. "Our Professor Pickford was the real article."

Rising to his full height, Tom reached down to help Zane to his feet. "Your first run and you snagged an honest-to-gosh sell-out agent for the aliens. Usually we just net the lone wolf nutters, so this is something."

Zane stared down at Pickford's body, mercifully shrouded in shadows. "You . . . He's dead."

Tom stared intently at Zane until Zane looked up at him, meeting his eyes. "You okay, son? You remember I described the two sides to this business, all up front and above-board with you, and you followed the whole plan right and tight. You raised the flag just like you were supposed to, and we got here in time to prep everything and prove this gent's intentions." Tom jerked his chin toward Pickford's body. "Now the professor here was a mite stronger than I expected, and hungry to kill, so couldn't take him on the hoof like I wanted, but that's the way of war, now isn't it?"

"War," Zane said slowly, turning to look at the artful mannequin formed in the image of Tyler Vernon.

"Ayup. We fight in our own small way. Mostly we win... Sometimes we lose."

"Old Deke Floyd," Zane said realizing the implication. "Wasn't a heart attack, was it?"

"Heart failure, sure enough," Tom said dryly, "but he had help. Another gent about like this."

Zane nodded and winced with pain. "I see."

The climb back up a thousand stairs seemed an endless torture, and Zane barely kept pace with a pair of equally massive Haselbauers of the younger generation who packed Pickford's body up to daylight between them.

"I'll get in touch with the Apollo security types, and they'll deal with the feds, so you'll stay out of sight," Tom explained, seemingly accustomed to marching up countless stairs. "But you can't let a hint of this touch any electronics: no emails, texts or what have you, no phone calls hinting around. These aliens are all too good at picking up that kind of chatter."

Email... Julia!

"I understand," Zane said, his sore jaw protesting.

"Hope you do, son. Whoever's behind Pickford here might wonder where the old boy disappeared. Probably resent counterespionage in a tour guide, and pay you a visit."

Counterespionage? He hadn't thought of himself in that light, but there was a notable appeal in that image.

They mounted the final flight and Zane breathed a sigh of relief as they stepped out into natural daylight again. Tom's minions hustled their grizzly burden into the old Jeep, and Tom paused to lay out the three alien gizmos Pickford had carried on its dusty hood.

"Fifteen years ago you'd be looking at, oh, probably five million or so for just these little doodads." Zane stared at the articles of alien tech in shock. "But with so much off-world stuff around these days, probably only worth a hundred thousand, or maybe a bit more now."

Uncertain of Tom's meaning, Zane just nodded.

"Once Apollo's people clear these toys, we'll settle up." Tom grinned at Zane. "Not bad, earning more than you paid for the whole business, is it? Even if you did get a busted head doing it?"

"Yes sir," Zane managed at last, touching his swollen jaw.

"There's the spirit." Tom squinted at him a moment. "Have Krista get some ice for that when you get to town, you hear?"

"K-Krista?"

"My niece," Tom said, climbing into the Jeep. "Good girl. Smart as a whip."

His phone showed several missed calls from Julia, but with his pounding skull he felt barely capable of driving the tour van back to town without any additional distractions. As he finally pulled up to the diner, his eyes caught the rippling flag, reminding him of one last duty to perform.

He lowered the flag, folding it and placing it back in the van before he tried Julia's number.

If they had spoken in person; if he had been able to disclose the sudden financial windfall, or the unlikely service he provided for earth, perhaps Julia would have understood. He would have respected Julia more if she had simply accepted what he did share: He had made a commitment to the Haselbauers that he could not break. He even added that the growth potential was much more than she would guess, but she dismissed his explanations and cited his selfishness and his provincial thinking for bringing an end to their romance.

"You're probably right," Zane numbly agreed to her every accusation, holding a hand to his throbbing head, his eyes closed. "Have a . . . a good life." Julia ended the call without another word.

Zane opened his eyes to see Krista standing there, a sheepish expression on her face and a bag of ice in hand. "I saw—um, you looked like you were in pain. I didn't mean to overhear."

Zane shrugged, unintentionally wincing. "It's okay."

She hesitated. "My uncle told me you had a small . . . problem." Her eyes went to the lumps and bruises decorating his melon. "Here's a little ice." She held out the bag. "Would you . . . would you like something to eat?"

Zane accepted the ice and tried to smile. "Working a little late today, aren't you?"

"No," Krista said, coloring a little. "Shift's over. But . . . but my place isn't far. I could fix you something."

Zane placed the ice pack on his lumpy head and looked at her with surprise.

"I really shouldn't—" Zane began. Krista's smile faltered and Zane broke off, taking a fresh breath.

"Honestly, Krista, that sounds perfect."

SYRUP JUNKIE EXPAT

Casey Moores

A Change of Scenery

Tiny points of light flickered across the screen in excruciatingly slow motion. Every single one represented the destruction of either an enemy or a Glatun vessel, ranging from mighty dreadnoughts to tiny corvettes. The wave of death rippled through the void, those tiny dots growing larger as the enemy's wrath grew nearer. A sensor operator gave constant updates on the destruction, so Harchu's front row seat to Armageddon came complete with narration.

Each of those Glatun ships, large or small, was loaded with crews, technicians, and marines from the few remaining Glatun warrior families. A dwindling pool of loyal servitors to the Glatun people, a thinning line of defense against the growing enemy hordes gathering on all sides of Glatun Federation space, and there they were, flickering out of existence as if they were just pixels in a game or simulation and not the approach of catastrophe.

Soon, the carnage would engulf his ship, its crew, and the legion of marines under his command. If fate desired, they too would be snuffed out in the blink of an eye.

A larger, brighter flash erupted in the center of the screen as their flagship detonated.

"Commander, I request you join your assault pods," the captain said. "We've been ordered to dump all marines."

Dump. Not launch or deploy or, his personal favorite, "send forth." Just... dump.

"Aye." Harchu took several steps and entered the tube leading to his pod. The tube sealed and all went dark.

At least this way he'd never see his death coming. He'd never decided whether or not that was better.

Harchu Indolo rubbed his stubby, rounded nose to keep from gagging at the strange, bitter-tasting air. It would take getting used to. What would not take getting used to was the scenery. Rolling hills of lush green stretched out as far as the eye could see—a considerable distance with his soldier's vision enhancements. The tiny black dots of birds swirled around in mesmerizing dances, and lines of puffy white clouds along the horizon picked up a delightful myriad of colors from the setting sun.

The peaked roofs of cozy little Human homes poked through the shimmering leaves of the thick forests. In counterpoint, to the right was one of the many eyesores of Human civilization, acres of pavement and cheap construction that formed a peculiar blend of shiny new and rotting old buildings. As he understood it, Human cities existed on an eternal cycle of destruction and reconstruction. Only their oldest—and sometimes, largely forgotten—civilizations had built things that stood the test of time, the way almost all Glatun structures did. Or had, rather, until the last few centuries. It was curious and distressing that his people seemed determined to devolve to a state these Humans were industriously progressing past.

Harchu nervously adjusted his grip on the massive roller case at his side and searched for the transportation he'd ordered. Finding no sign of it, he accessed and sorted through the nearest Human cameras. He spotted the boxy, shiny black vehicle through the "dash cam" of a mercantile truck on a nearby highway a few miles away. Considering he'd waited years for this moment, he could survive a few more minutes.

Soft footsteps announced someone's approach.

"I have to say, I was even more surprised by your request to leave my employ than I was when you asked to enter it," said Fallalor Wathaet, captain of the *Spinward Crossing.* "Not too many Fleet Marines transition to the simple life of a trader."

Harchu craned his neck back and stared at the vast, light blue sky.

"Not so simple, I learned. Quieter perhaps, and with fewer actively trying to kill you—though, as we learned in Ogut space, fewer doesn't mean *none*—but never simple. But it was precisely the life I'd sought."

Captain Wathaet lifted his chin.

"And this crew still owes everything to the fact you were with us to handle those Ogut pirates. There is still tremendous strength in the Glatun of the great military families, even if almost none recognize it. But to my point, exceedingly few who follow the military path ever leave it. Fewer still retire to the backwater planet of a newly encountered race. In fact, you may be unique in this respect. You're certainly the very first to do so here, of all places."

"I imagine many more will follow when they learn this is the source of that delightful elixir made from tree blood," Harchu said. "But yes, for now I am unique on my chosen path, and I would have it no other way."

"A more suspicious ship's captain might theorize it was always your intent to find a place such as this. I am not here to question it, though I am compelled to inquire—are you not required to maintain your reserve status?"

"Oh I will, of course, maintain such a status . . . assuming they can locate me should a recall be enacted."

"I see. And if the call is sent in desperation, as I fear it might be in the near future? If the Glatun find themselves in need of every available warrior to stiffen their ranks?"

There it was. It was the true question facing all Glatun warriors, an ever-diminishing group among an ever-expanding people. That question had been his primary preoccupation in his time aboard the *Spinward Crossing*.

"I was but one soldier, an insect, one among many, stretched ever thinner around the edges of a burgeoning, but otherwise docile, swarm. If the presence or disappearance of a single insect around that periphery means the difference between the survival or failure of the swarm, then the swarm is already doomed. I hope to Cul this is not so, but either way, we are well past the point where my contribution would serve as anything more than as a mild inconvenience to an aggressor, if that. No, my honorable captain, I have served my time, and I leave the fate of the Glatun to those who still believe."

"Believe in what, exactly?"

"Anything," Harchu answered distantly.

The boxy black vehicle finally arrived. The Humans called it a "stretched Hummer." A luxury by Human standards but cheap as dirt to a Glatun with any measure of wealth, it allowed for both anonymity and the capacity to carry the entirety of Harchu's possessions. It would do.

"May the stars always illuminate your way," Captain Wathaet said.

Harchu snapped to attention and rendered a respectful bow. As he straightened, he grinned and said, "Trade hard, Fellalor."

Sweet Serenity

Rivulets of glittery black oozed and floated from the dying Horvath ship captain.

"Bridge secure," Harchu comm'd.

"Copy. Engineering secure," his sergeant comm'd in reply. "But the enviro systems are lost. We're not getting atmo back."

Since not a single assault ship remained operable, that was particularly disconcerting.

"Copy." Harchu switched to the command net. "Fleet Command, Commander Indolo. The vessel is secure, but atmo is unrecoverable. Request evac."

During the excruciatingly long wait for a reply, he ordered his marines to salvage all possible sources of air and report to the cargo bay. It wasn't the most intact section of the ship, but a "secure" location no longer existed and the bay would be the most accessible to rescue teams. As it was a Horvath ship, the lifeboats were incompatible with Glatun physiology.

The remains of his boarding team assembled as ordered. It was ironic that the light casualties they'd sustained were now a burden on their dwindling resources. It meant he had to ration their—

"Commander Indolo, Fleet Command. Be advised extraction has been delayed by ongoing operations. Execute prioritization protocols based on a fifteen-hour timeline."

An all-consuming rage flared up deep inside, but he maintained his bearing. He'd already run the numbers for the supplies they'd collected, and they would only get everyone to thirteen and a half hours. He forcefully suppressed any hint of frustration in his reply.

"Copy."

Harchu drew in a long breath before opening a private line to his sergeant. "Sergeant, we're to execute prioritization protocols for fifteen hours. Check my math, but we need to terminate our four lowest."

"Understood, Commander, and verified. Lowest four checks. If you want, sir, I'll do it."

"No. You just... stay vigilant." The sergeant would understand specifically what he meant. Not all accepted their fate.

One by one, he faced each of his four lowest ranking troops, thanked them for their service, told them the Glatun Federation honored their sacrifice, and then shut off their air half a second before discharging his pistol through their faceplates.

He hated lying to them just as much as he hated having to murder his own men.

Rescue arrived thirteen hours and fifteen minutes later. Apparently, this particular admiral preferred to pass "conservative" time estimates for these sorts of things.

The beautiful tremolo of the loons echoed across the water. Another loon answered with a high-pitched wail. This was something altogether unique in Harchu's experience of planets. He'd heard music that was somewhat similar, but not quite.

Harchu sniffed the dewy, spring air. A thin mist hung lazily over the lake, creating a dreamy, surreal effect. It reminded him more of the dusty haze that permeated ships in the aftermath of a boarding action than anything he'd seen on any of the home worlds. Of course, he'd never been near a significantly sized natural body of fresh water on any of the home worlds. Thick fogs and clouds were common in some areas, and gray smoke filled the skies of some heavily industrialized districts, but this form of fine, milky mist was... mesmerizing. Calm. Exactly the sort of relaxing that he'd sought but never imagined he'd actually find.

All at once, beautiful on a transcendental level *and* reminiscent of the most horrifying moments of his life.

His tongue dipped into his short, wide cup of syrup and lapped greedily. Visions of silent screams and fiery deaths faded away into pleasant numbness.

Yes, his retirement plan to the one place in the universe that produced the delightful nectar had been pure brilliance. Sure, he never left the cottage during the day for fear of discovery, and he had zero contact with anyone other than the man who delivered the groceries ("You sure go through a lot of syrup, mister! Can't begin to imagine how you afford it!"), but it was quiet.

Quiet was all he needed. Well, that and syrup.

The cottage itself was cozy enough—a nice place with plenty of room that he'd extensively remodeled to better fit Glatun physiology. His robochef was one of the best an individual could buy, programmed with enough variety he could have a different dish at every meal for six hundred Earth years. Not that he did—he had his favorites, of course—but the point was, he *could*.

He also had an endless library of Glatun entertainment and access to the sum total of Human entertainment as well, from their books to their television shows to their movies to their video games.

In almost every way, he had everything he needed.

Almost.

The sun was now high enough for its rays to cut through the protective forest of trees surrounding the lake. It burned away the mist and cast blinding flashes across the rippling water. Harchu retreated to his entertainment center to resume virtual construction of a vast city of multicolored blocks.

BAM! BAM! BAM!

"Hello?"

Harchu snapped up so sharply he bumped the table and knocked over his syrup cup. Thankfully, lightning reflexes caught it before any viscous fluid escaped. He took the opportunity to get in a quick lick.

"I know you're in there! We gotta talk. We need your help."

Though his mind swirled in syrup-soaked bliss, the pounding at his door simply would not cease. It was so sharp, so constant, and so loud that it bludgeoned his comfortable buzz into hiding. He briefly regarded his syrup cup, pondering whether he had enough to make the noise go away, but reluctantly accepted how persistent this damn Human was.

With a low growl, he stood, dug around for his XXL "Mainiac" hoodie, and pulled it over himself. Then he donned his custom-made cloth translator mask and sunglasses to fully conceal his face.

"What's the emergency?" he shouted through the door, his mask converting his Glatun voice into a gravelly Human male voice. He'd learned quite a bit about proper Human dialogue from the shows he'd watched. He'd also carefully constructed the voice to be unpleasant to Human ears to cut conversation short.

"Hey there, I'm Mark Matt-a-shev-ski," the man said. Harchu quickly found records of a "Matuszewski" family who lived nearby. The man was a decent size for a Human male, clean shaven, and wore a frayed Red Sox ball cap. Emotions were still somewhat difficult for Harchu to identify, but the man appeared earnest and possibly angry. "You're Jack Smith, right? Sorry I've never had the chance to meet you before."

Harchu remained silent. Sometimes, if you didn't speak, Humans would get bored or dejected and simply wander off. It had worked for him numerous times. This Human stood firm.

Mr. Matuszewski had driven up on a Human "four-wheeler," which Harchu considered a puzzling moniker. So many of their vehicles had four wheels, he didn't understand why the most basic had earned the title. In a way, it was an analogy for many strange things Humans did.

A large, double-sided axe was strapped to the back of the vehicle. It looked much more like the ones he'd seen in their Viking and fantasy shows than the kind the locals used to chop wood. Curious.

After some time, the man said, "Anyway, the emergency is that our damn lake's getting taken over!"

"What's with the axe?" Harchu asked. When silence didn't work, his next strategy was to ask personal questions until they got uncomfortable and left.

Mark chuckled. "Oh, that's an inside joke with my wife. I used to call her the 'old battle axe,' which, naturally, she couldn't stand. So, one year she got me an actual battle axe so that whenever I called her that, she could ask, 'Which one are you talking about?' Got so annoying, I stopped calling her that. Genius-level trolling. One of the reasons I love her so much. Anyway, sometime later I realized how often it's actually pretty damn useful, so I keep it with me. But that's beside the point. Back to the business I came to discuss."

His translator was a little confused over the term "business" and offered him several possibilities. A job offer, a discussion of this Human's occupation, an investment opportunity, trade offer, or, perhaps, just an issue or problem to be discussed. He chose the last as the most likely.

"And what is the business that is of concern to me?" The phrasing felt awkward, but he hoped the translator would assist. The words were meant to stall as he dug into news surrounding the lake and its area. There wasn't much to find other than some mention of decreasing property values, increased real estate activity, increased crime rates (not a problem for Harchu considering his Glatun security, skills, and equipment), and mention of possible commercial developments. None of those, as far as he could tell, were any sort of concern to him.

"It's pretty damn concerning. But I don't have time to explain it to everyone one at a time. That's why I'm having a town meeting at the rec center this evening at five p.m. Potluck if you want to bring anything but not required. We really just need everyone to hear what's happening. If we don't hang together on this one, we'll hang separately, if you know what I mean."

Harchu looked up the expression "hang." There were several definitions, but the only one that fully made sense in that context was a method of execution by strangulation. That seemed unpleasant. Even though Harchu was confident he could avoid such a fate, if it was on the table for the other residents of the lake, it might cause him considerable problems. At best, there was a strong chance he'd have to move. At worst, he'd have to kill a bunch of humans if they came and tried to hang him. Either threatened to expose his presence, which would completely ruin his retirement.

So it appeared he had to attend this "town meeting." In preparation, he looked up the meaning of "pot luck."

Trouble in Syrup Heaven

The swarms of avians—ferocious little balls of feathers with big beaks and vicious claws—just kept coming. Harchu could only marvel at how prolific their breeding must be to produce so much offspring that they could throw them at a wall of ordnance, slugs, and laser fire in so many successive waves. There was a strong chance his logistics train would run out of both power and ammunition. As it stood, they'd been fully resupplied three times and would soon need a fourth.

By all accounts, the flightless birds had been a largely peaceful race with burgeoning industrialization when the Grrtul had installed the gate in their system. This splinter faction, however, was anything but peaceful. They'd departed their own system under the guise of traders and promptly attacked the first minimally populated Glatun colony they'd found. The colony was likely slaughtered, but the Federation had sent in a contingent to search for survivors. The only way to properly do so with the Cul-forsaken birds so deeply dug in was to eradicate them. Unfortunately, orbital strikes were out of the question since Command was concerned for the safety of any surviving Glatun colonists.

So, instead, here they were, in a defensive line, expending ammunition as if it were unlimited.

It was not.

With every wave, he lost a few soldiers. The more he lost, the more avians reached their lines in the next wave. The more avians who reached the lines, the more soldiers he lost before that wave was broken. Sure, they had reserves to fill in the gaps each time, but it was still a rapidly accelerating death spiral from which he could see no possible exit.

If his commander's intent was to grind his own forces away to nothing, there was not a single thing he would be doing differently.

So, Harchu and his soldiers fired, reloaded, fired some more, and, when the avians inevitably reached their lines, they'd hack, stab, and club them to pieces until the Glatun artillery severed the advance.

Hours later, as Harchu sat exhausted, parched, and starving, he realized he didn't recognize a single one of the soldiers he commanded. Everyone he'd arrived with was either dead or back with the medical units.

He also realized it had been some time since the last wave.

They were ordered to initiate a counteroffensive. There was almost no resistance, just tiny groups of avians huddling in craters. Harchu and the other Glatun soldiers simply marched across the plains and low hills until they reached the ruins of the Glatun colony. There were just a few scattered avians there as well . . . and not a single living Glatun.

"Guess we win," Harchu muttered to himself.

What the local humans called a "Rec Center" was a large, covered area with rows of picnic tables, and restrooms at one end. It was constructed in front of a quartet of crumbling paved areas surrounded by tall metal fences he recognized from TV as tennis courts. He found a seat at the rear.

The gathered people were predominantly older Humans, but there were younger ones in attendance. Younger still children played in a small wooden structure that seemed built entirely for their amusement.

Per Human custom for a "potluck," food was laid out across one of the tables up front. For fear of standing out if he didn't contribute, Harchu had his robochef create a tray of sliced beef brisket, which seemed both generic and commonly appreciated. However, it appeared he'd done a little too well, as the dish was very popular and numerous people had asked who'd brought it. He also realized he was standing out by not partaking in the food, so he reluctantly got a plate and took tiny portions of everything offered. Then, he mixed it around the plate, pretended to take the occasional bite, and tossed some of it into the bushes behind him when no one was looking. None of the offerings included any maple syrup, sadly, but Harchu had brought some of his own in a small flask. With luck, the Humans would assume it was alcohol. Research suggested Humans were less likely to approach an alcoholic.

"If everyone's gotten a bite, I'd like to get started," said Mark, standing at the front. "The reason I've called everybody, as some of you may already suspect, is the Davises were recently conned out of their property. You've all heard of those scams where someone posing as a Realtor targets a—forgive me for the stereotyping, but it's exactly what they look for—older, less technically savvy people, preferably whose faculties are starting to fade. There's a multitude of ways—they promise refinancing, offer to create a trust for their children's sake, insurance . . . like I said, many ways, but the end result is they get the people to sign away their property under the guise of something else."

On one hand, that unknowingly surrendering property to another could be as simple as writing their name on a piece of paper was absurd. On the other hand, he knew from experience there was no shortage of overly clever thieves hiding in every dark corner of the galaxy. Moreover, these Humans were horribly undeveloped in so many ways, despite their remarkable ability to defend their system.

This got him to thinking. For the most part, he refrained

from examining the details of Human finances, interactions, and hypernet research habits of Humans—largely because the latter seemed overly preoccupied with disgusting images of unclothed, breeding Humans. However, just because he chose not to dig into their hypernet didn't mean it wasn't incredibly easy. Their security was almost nonexistent.

"What does that have to do with us?" a tall, younger, brown-haired man up front asked. "I mean, we all know about these scams. I'd hope everyone with the wherewithal to show here today is smart enough not to fall for them."

A few people muttered agreements or initiated conversations with their neighbors until Mark put up his hands.

"Alright, that's a decent point, but I'm not just here to warn you. Well, not about that, at least. For one thing, I consider everyone on this lake, whether on the Maine side or even the New Hampshire side, as family. We've always been a sort of small, informal community even back when most of us were just summer or weekend visitors."

As he spoke, Harchu found the Davis property and delved into the sale records. There had, in fact, been what they called a title transfer to a realty company a week prior. This was odd. As he understood it, Humans almost never gave things away to those who weren't their family. They usually sold them. The only exception seemed to be charity, but the realty company was clearly not a charity organization. The data surrounding it was stored in a simple local government database and so easily accessible he could literally alter any record.

"But over the last couple years," Mark continued, "with the attacks, viruses, and everything, a lot of us are up here full time and we're all so much closer. I've personally known the Davises for a long time. Hell, Steve taught me to drive a boat on this lake when I was a clueless young twentysomething. A lot of us owe them for one thing or another, so my first order of business is for us to band together to help them with the suit to recover their property."

Murmuring grew again, as the gathered people seemed wildly mixed in their support. Harchu mostly tuned this out.

It couldn't possibly be as simple as erasing the realty company from the records and putting Steven Davis back in there, could it?

Huh, it was.

There was a scanned title transfer document and Harchu was about to delete it when it occurred to him the realty company might have a physical copy of the document. In the painfully archaic way of Human systems, they could potentially resubmit it and redo the transfer.

After a moment's thought, he recovered the document he'd deleted, but then switched the names on the transfer, reversed the signatures, updated the notary, and posted a new document with the current day's date. Thus, the records would now show the title was transferred back by Human legal standards.

"But the bigger problem is this is just one of many avenues by which a larger company is acquiring a large stretch of property here. DHC Holdings is the parent company to the handful of different realty companies buying up or scamming their way into property all across the eastern side. Digging deeper, I found an investment opportunity for a lakeside resort here in Maine. It doesn't name the location, but they've got pics on their website that I recognize as Loon Lagoon and Sandy Beach."

This caused the assemblage to erupt into an uproar of shouting, side conversations, and wailing.

Mark did his best to silence them and continued speaking. Meanwhile, Harchu delved into DHC Holdings. Within a few minutes of very basic searching, he found it and its myriad subsidiaries. With nothing better to do, he rummaged through their financial reports, their tax filings, and other financial records. Major discrepancies were immediately apparent, so Harchu kept searching. It really was remarkable how poorly Humans hid their activities.

"Mister, did you bring the brisket?"

There was a tug at the back of his hood. When Harchu jerked in surprise, his sunglasses tumbled away.

The tiny, brown-eyed male Human beside him shrieked.

Conversation ceased.

The tiny Human quickly regained his composure, gathered some courage, and reached up to tug Harchu's face mask down.

"Oh God, it's one of them!" an elderly woman shouted.

Several people ran, most sat frozen in fear or shock, and a few put their hands to previously concealed pistols.

"Hold it, hold it, hold it!" Mark shouted. He stalked down the center of the picnic tables, big battle axe in one hand and waving the other.

Without much thought, Harchu prepared to disarm the man and then use him as a shield against the Humans with pistols. It would probably be best to eliminate the armed Humans before departing. This would require using more Humans as shields after Mr. Matuszewski soaked up too many bullets.

It was a shame he'd have to find a new place to live after killing all these poor Humans. It was such a nice lake and he'd grown quite attached to his cottage.

"Everybody just stop!" Mark shouting, swinging the axe in a circle in the air.

All went quiet save for the sounds of crickets in the surrounding foliage.

"Before anyone says another goddamn word, this isn't a damn Horvath and it isn't a damn Rangora! Does he look like a squid? Or a lizard?" He glanced at Harchu and shrugged. "Eh, well, sorta maybe but not really and look at that nose."

Mark turned to face Harchu and lowered the axe to his side.

"You're a Glatun, right?" Mark asked. "And a Glod at that, right?"

Fearing that to reach up and reapply his mask might set someone off, Harchu simply nodded. He knew from endless hours of Human entertainment that the motion meant "affirmative."

"Everyone, I'd like you all to meet Jack Smith, the individual who brought us that delicious brisket. A Glatun—the friendly ones." To Harchu, he said, "And I'd like to formally welcome you to Shady Pond. You've been here quite a while, haven't you?"

Harchu nodded again.

"Sorry I wasn't more neighborly until now," Mark said. "And I suppose your name isn't Jack Smith, is it?"

Harchu shook his head sideways to indicate "negative."

"Then let's do this the right way." Mark put his hand out. "Mark Matuszewski."

Harchu took the man's hand as he'd seen in countless shows and gently shook it.

"Harchu Indolo."

"Harchu." Mark said the name carefully. "Nice to meet you."

"Nice to meet you," Harchu repeated.

Some of the people relaxed and some smiled, but some still glowered. Harchu cautiously replaced his mask to facilitate better communication.

"Well, I suppose this revelation just destroyed my meeting, but—"

"Actually," Harchu said, "I believe I can help. Or, I should say, I think I have already helped. While you were talking, I researched the company that has been buying up your land. I have uncovered numerous violations of your Human laws and delivered evidence of these violations to local and, in two cases, federal law enforcement. I have also anonymously informed local news media of the newly opened investigations into these individuals. I am fairly confident that DHC Holdings will soon cease to exist as a business entity. Oh, and I reverted ownership of the Davises' property back to Steven Davis."

The sound of crickets returned.

Even Mark looked particularly dumb-founded. "What, uh, how?"

"Based on my limited understanding of Human North American legal proceedings, I believe it is best if I do not explain the details. But, now that the reason for this meeting has been nullified, may I return to my cabin?"

Found Family

Harchu stepped off the lift and took in the sight of his family's estate. The tall, gleaming towers he admired as an impressionable youth were now obscured by wide columns of flowers and vegetation. In theory, he appreciated both the beauty and the utility of the Transcendence Gardens that had become the fashion over the preceding decades. In practice, however, anyone who owned such a garden was invariably insufferable. They marveled at them and crowed about them to anyone in earshot. At large events, the gardens were frequently the primary topic of conversation, either through bragging about the latest additions, listing the overly detailed metrics on what they provided, or arguing amongst each other as to the best and most proper blend of edible, exquisite, and air-producing foliage. As it was with many things these days, it was a wonderful concept that was absolutely ruined by the self-satisfaction of those who owned them.

What he could not see, however, was the enormous statue of his greatest ancestor. Dralu Indolo had defended the Trisantion Neck in one of the most famous battles of the Crisis Wars.

"Harchu, is that you?" Before he even responded, his brother

Onkud grabbed him by the elbow and rushed him off to the left where they disappeared into the spirals of flora. And disappeared was the proper word, considering the patterns on his brother's robes were indistinguishable from the surroundings. It made for great camouflage, though Harchu would never dare suggest as much out loud. "What are you doing here?"

"I've got a significant holdover until my next assignment," Harchu said. "I messaged our progenitor I would be visiting."

"Ah, there's the problem," Onkud said. "Seeptu has largely isolated himself from the hypernet and immersed himself almost fully in the maintenance and development of the Transcendence Garden. The only times he uses his 'plants are to research or order new, well, plants.*"*

Harchu stared at the Garden for a moment before motioning to the vast emptiness where once stood the giant sculpture.

"Onkud, what happened to the statue of Dralu?"

His sibling huffed and raised his chin haughtily.

"The Indolo family no longer wishes to associate itself with the baser members of its ancestry," Onkud said. "We look to the future, to alleviating the inequities of our predecessors, to artistic visions, to philanthropic and philosophic endeavors. It was well beyond time we joined proper, enlightened society and let go of our savage reputation. The very reason I'd prefer none see you come or go."

Harchu groaned, doing his best to keep it from becoming a growl. "Because I am one of those baser members? One who has just returned from protecting the outer—"

"Please, Harchu, don't bluster about your butchery. Protect, you say? Well who protects those starving masses who you slaughtered? No, it was simply horrible, callous policy that forced *them to attack our outer planets just to scratch together the means to survive. This is why I want you out of sight and out of earshot before you embarrass us and undo everything I've done for this family. Your time, the time of the soldier, is over, Harchu. It's time to join civilization. Have you considered other options? Somewhere you can put your more uncouth skills to more...* practical *use?"*

Even though Human food and Glatun food were largely incompatible for a variety of reasons, they had one major commonality—both smelled absolutely delicious when cooking over an open fire.

"Mr. Battleaxe, is it time to go tubing yet?" an average-sized blond, blue-eyed Human male child asked.

"Mr. Battleaxe?" Mark huffed and looked at his wife, Cindy. The tall, blond woman was stretched out on a lawn chair on the dock with her nose in a book. She looked up long enough to smile sweetly and wink.

Harchu took a lick of syrup from his red plastic cup and relaxed into his flimsy wooden chair. He, the Matuszewskis, and a few other families were grilling out in a clearing on what they called Picnic Island, a long and wide tree-covered mound that jutted out of the water to form one of the lake's many inlets. A few other boats were anchored at or near the dock, with kids swimming, splashing, and jumping off floats all around. The adult Humans ate, drank, watched the kids, and talked about sports, entertainment, jobs, and occasionally politics. Harchu was always careful to avoid that last one.

"I have a real name, you know," Mark said with a slight scowl and raised eyebrow.

The child fidgeted awkwardly and fought to avoid eye contact for a moment. At length, the kid looked up again, this time with what Humans called "puppy dog eyes."

"Puh-puh-puh-pleeeaase?"

From experience, Harchu knew that would do it. Mark worked hard at pretending he didn't love towing kids around the lake.

"Alright."

"Yay! Can we go pick up my friend, too? They're just past the old Marina..."

"You're the boss, boss," Mark said. "I'm just the driver."

Harchu wondered how he'd ever survived being cooped up in his cabin all day every day wasting away, high on syrup, when outside, so much beautiful living was happening right there on the lake. In the summer, the lake was full of people water skiing, fishing, canoeing, kayaking, and just hanging out on large pontoon boats. In the winter, it was less busy, but there were still people snowmobiling, fishing, ice skating, and cross-country skiing.

So many Humans had died over the years from the Horvath attacks and plagues and then the Rangora attacks, yet the Humans here laughed and played as if none of that had ever happened. It was a wonder that Humans seemed capable of finding enjoyment no matter the weather or situation.

And for his first few years, he'd only watched from a distance and marveled at them. But in the years since his "coming out" to the local community, he'd become a part of it. Now, he lamented the time he'd wasted as nothing more than a spectator. This was what he'd been missing. Being a part of the Humans' near constant celebrations was a far better life than watching endless hours of Human shows and stacking blocks in a video game. He still did those things, but only when his Humans were working or doing any of the other strange things Humans did.

Mark slapped Harchu on the shoulder, a male Human sign of affection.

"Hey, partner, looks like I retired from one job straight into a much more demanding job," Mark said. "You gonna hold things down for me while I do my best to exhaust these tiny Humans?"

After the town hall meeting all those years earlier, Mark had convinced Harchu to start up Scambusters (Mark wanted to call it Scamelot, but his wife had vetoed it). Using Harchu's far advanced computing capabilities, the company actively identified, tracked, and investigated Human hypernet-based criminal enterprises. They'd been wildly successful for several years and made a Human fortune while shutting down dozens of large organizations who'd been looting and scavenging everything they could in the chaotic aftermath of the attacks and viruses.

Harchu had always known Human computing capabilities would someday catch up to his, though he'd underestimated how fast that would happen. A few months prior, he'd convinced Mark to sell the company. They'd made yet another fortune and gotten out of the business before their success rate plummeted.

Mark had suggested Harchu spool up a physical security company next, but Harchu had successfully argued the Humans of Earth would likely classify Harchu's version of "security" as a Weapon of Mass Destruction.

"Actually, let me make some introductions first, then I'll head out," Mark said.

He motioned to a shiny new, blue-and-white pontoon boat that had just docked. Harchu recognized the driver as Don Smithing, a large, dark-skinned Human local who'd served in the American water Navy. But the other two males and the female were unfamiliar.

The black-haired, younger-looking male helped the female and the older, gray-haired male off the boat and then helped secure it. The female was what the Humans called strawberry blond, even though he saw no connection to Earth's strawberries, and she had noticeably large mammary glands. Voluptuous was the Human term.

"Katie, get over here!" Mark called.

The female smiled and walked up the short slope to the clearing.

"Katie, this is Harchu Indolo, my Glatun business partner," Mark said.

"Technically, former partner," Harchu said. He took the female's outstretched hand. "Pleased to meet you."

"Katie Bencks," she said, shaking his hand.

The female smiled wide with big eyes and appeared borderline frantic in Harchu's limited understanding of Human body language.

"Sorry," she said. "I'm doing my best not to fangirl at Shady Pond's best-kept secret. A real live Glatun! I know there's a few of you living openly with us now, but I've only ever seen them at a distance at conventions. This is . . . I really don't know what to say. Realization of a dream, I guess."

"Katie here is the very definition of a science fiction nerd," Mark said. "Which, as you might have caught on, we Humans now just call 'science.' But Katie's kind of a big deal in her own right. PhD in Astronautical Engineering. Taught at the United States Air Force Academy back in the day."

"Well yeah, before I came down with a wicked case of Johannsen's," Katie said. "Left that life for a while to try and spit out some babies."

"Ah, then I suppose you have many children," Harchu said. He motioned to the children splashing in the water. "Are any of them here today? Perhaps the one Mark is about to take tubing?"

Katie dropped her gaze and Harchu felt strangely awkward. Mark's expression turned serious, his eyes went wide, and he shook his head slightly.

"I have said something wrong?" Harchu asked.

"No, you're fine," Katie said. "I just . . . After a few years of trying—and I tried real hard, trust me—I learned I wasn't actually capable of having children."

Numerous TV shows had taught Harchu that was a sensitive issue.

"I apologize for my ignorance," Harchu said.

"You couldn't—don't worry about it," she said.

All three males from the boat reached the clearing. Harchu now recognized the slightly diminutive older male, though they'd never formally met. The average-sized younger of the other two reached out a hand.

"Harchu, meet Kenneth Bencks," Mark said. Similar names usually meant one of two things with Humans, and this man shared no physical features with Katie.

"Call me Kenny," the man said as they shook hands.

"Are you Katie's husband?"

"Big hekkin' no, sir!" Kenneth said. "I'm Katie's little brother by way of adoption."

"Miserable excuse for an ex-husband ditched this golden-haired goddess when he couldn't get her pregnant," Don said, moving up behind Katie and wrapping an around her. "Dumbass's loss is my gain, for as long as she'll have me."

She curled up into Don and smiled. "I ain't going nowhere. I mean, nowhere without you, that is."

There was a moment when the new arrivals glanced around at each other with mild amusement, as if there was some joke he wasn't a part of.

"Anyway," Mark continued, "Kenny here is a true to life Apollo Mining reject. And after he got the 'plants, no less."

"Sold my soul to the company store," Kenny said.

"Mr. Battleaxe!" the tiny, blue-eyed child interjected. "Aren't we tubing?"

Mark frowned, tucked his chin, then puffed up, and smiled before turning around. "'Course we are!" he shouted. To the group, he said, "Sorry, but my fans are calling. But, seriously, Harchu, this guy's a damn genius and Apollo really messed up. Horrible story."

He hurried off to his speed boat.

Once he was gone, Harchu turned back to the others. "If it is another sore subject, please tell me, but what does it mean to be an 'Apollo Mining reject'?"

"Oh, well, you go through quite a bit just to get hired," Kenny said as he opened an ice chest. "And I made it through all of that, easy enough. Got the 'plants, my final training, and got sent off to my first crew."

Kenny grabbed a couple beers and passed them to Don and Katie. He offered one to the older male, but the man waved him off.

"First crew was"—Kenny scrunched up his face a little—"weird, I guess you could say? See, I was a fill in for someone they'd just lost, who was also called Kenny. It just kinda threw everyone off their game. Wasn't anything about me, they all said so, but it just didn't work and I got reassigned."

"Detail with which he should have led," Don said, slowly and succinctly, "if you hadn't heard, is that Apollo only allows for two reassignments before you're straight-up shit-canned."

"I see," Harchu said. "So your second assignment did not go any better?"

"It did not," Kenny said. He took a long gulp of beer, swallowed, and sighed. "Second crew was big on the practical jokes. I took 'em fine, never let 'em bother me, gave back a little here and there to show 'em I was cool with it. Then one asshole in particular nearly got me killed but I couldn't prove it. He'd been with them longer, so I knew if it came down to him or me, they'd pick him. Tried to avoid it, but he forced it. So here I am. Owing far more money than I would've earned working for them."

The group went quiet for a moment, enough so that Harchu could hear Mark's boat roaring around in the distance, splashing water, and Human children alternating between laughing and screaming.

"Anyway," the older man said, "that's one problem I should be able to solve, if I can sort out the details." He thrust his hand out. "Harchu Indolo, I'd like to introduce myself. I'm—"

"Jonathan Cross," Harchu said. He knew it was impolite to cut off the Human's introduction, but Human TV shows had taught him it was the right moment to dramatically interject personal knowledge. "Owner of Buzzy Field and the large estate on the far side of the lake. You were an early investor with Tyler Vernon and Apollo Mining, though you've had minimal interaction with the former for some time and you've been divesting your interest in the latter."

Don coughed, while Katie pursed her lips and glanced at Mr. Cross, who smiled with his mouth but not his eyes.

"Quite right," Mr. Cross said. "Not a full divestiture, and no bad blood with Tyler, I assure you, I'm simply backing out of an involved role with Apollo so I can focus on another endeavor. And I'm glad to see you're the kind that does your homework."

Harchu put a hand up—another dramatic gesture he'd learned from Human entertainment.

"So you're a billionaire with, in your words, 'another endeavor.'" He pointed to Kenny. "You're a fully trained and 'planted Apollo engineer looking for a way to pay back or get out of your substantial debt." He pointed to Katie. "You're easily capable, perhaps with a little more training and 'plants, of astronavigation." Finally, he pointed to his friend Don Smithing. "And you, I'm certain, could easily catch up to the demands of ship security, since that's what you did in the Navy. I am no expert in the Human way of doing things, but at a guess I would say you're putting together a crew for a small space vessel."

"Very astute," Mr. Cross said. "But we have a saying here on Earth, that the map is not the territory. A depiction of a certain place or a description of a certain environment is not knowledge of the location or environment itself. One has to go there, or have been there, for true knowledge."

"So you desire someone with experience of traveling through space to round out the crew. You are talking around an unspecified endeavor. Since this is clearly not a casual, friendly introduction as I'd thought but a formal meeting with a specific purpose, I feel it is time for you to tell me that purpose."

The gathered Humans glanced nervously at each other. Mr. Cross straightened.

"In a remarkably short time," he said, "to the specific surprise of both the Horvath and Rangora, Humans have gone from having taken a few small steps off our own planet to becoming quite adept at both astronautical mining and space warfare."

Don smiled and tightened his arms around Katie.

"Both are necessary for development of a space-bound civilization, but we are, with the exception of our maple sugar trade, completely lacking in one vital area."

He paused and glanced at the others, who stared expectantly at Harchu.

"You have no significant trade capability," Harchu said. "Even your syrup trade is based entirely on Glatun trade ships, which are disrupted every time another aggressor fleet comes through that gate."

"Exactly so."

Harchu lowered his chin and looked out over the water. "And

in order to develop such a capability, you want someone with experience in space trade."

"Well, that and a licensed pilot. Added bonus if such an individual had not just military training, but *Glatun* military training."

Now, Harchu tilted his head in a very Human gesture and locked eyes with the wealthy Human. "Mr. Cross, you've watched too much of your poorly written military entertainment. Just because I served in the military does not mean I'm qualified or licensed as a pilot."

"I did not say I thought you were a pilot because you served in the military," Mr. Cross said, his gaze fixed and confident. "I believe it because I was told directly by Wathaet that you're a licensed pilot."

Harchu fought off the urge to growl. His relaxing afternoon with Human friends was now, officially, ruined.

"I understand that you have done your homework as well, as you Humans say. But perhaps it is not military entertainment you've seen too much of, but the web comic of the man who helped you become a billionaire. You've read too much *Trade Hard*. I left the stars for a reason, and I have no intention of ever going back."

Paradise Lost

"Reports are minimal, but it has been verified that the Rangora Empire has initiated a full-scale invasion into numerous systems of the Glatun Federation. There has been no mention thus far of a justification for the invasion, though some anonymous sources blame Tyler Vernon and his personal de facto alliance with the Glatun Federation due to his continued antagonism against the Rangora. Details, as we've said repeatedly, are confused and hard to verify, but there have been countless rumors that the Rangora invasion has achieved strategic victories in many systems. We will continue to track the story as information emerges..."

Mark waggled his gloved hands and constantly shifted his VR goggle-adorned head around. Harchu's vast flat screen displayed Mark's armored character sprinting through the shelled-out ruins of an urban landscape, shooting hordes of encroaching insectoids.

"You guys are right, this game is damn addictive," Mark said.

"Told you," Dave Bergson said.

Dave was another Shady Pond local and a military veteran.

He'd latched onto Harchu as a fellow vet. For some reason, he carried the belief that he had more in common with Harchu than most of his fellow Humans. Harchu had grown to appreciate the company, so he let Dave and Mark stop by whenever they felt like it.

Dave relaxed deep in one of the couches, watching the game and sipping a beer. The room smelled of stale pizza, Dave's cigarettes, and the somewhat generic, unpleasant stench Humans developed when they occupied a space for too long. Harchu sat on the other side of Mark, watching the game progress and trying to decide whether to join in. Perhaps he would, after Dave finished venting.

"So yeah, I normally don't say these sorts of things, but people say I gotta let them out or they'll tear me up from the inside." Dave took a sip of beer, burped, and continued. "Way back when I was knee high to a grasshopper, I learned about Vietnam. It was all over TV and movies and all sorts of things. You couldn't get away from it. All those things showed a miserable hellscape, mostly meaningless, people dying in horrible ways, people getting sick afterward, it was just a mess. The people I knew who'd served didn't ever talk about it . . . and you knew you weren't supposed to ask. It was just built up as this major failure, you know, and you saw the stories about how soldiers were yelled at and cussed at when they came back and you really felt for them, knowing what they'd been through, thinking they'd been fighting and dying for their country the way their dads and uncles and maybe granddads did in the World Wars and Korea . . . and they come home and find out everyone hates them for it. Not everyone hated them, of course, that got way overblown, but I'm sure it felt like it to those guys."

On the screen, Mark tossed a grenade straight into the mouth of one of the larger, pincer-mouthed insects. It popped and its head briefly splattered into pieces on the screen.

"Yeah, suck on that, bug!" Mark shouted.

Dave paused to chuckle and took another sip. Harchu remained silent, though he was certain he knew exactly how the soldiers Dave spoke of had felt. In some ways, Humans and Glatun weren't so different.

"Anyway, biggest thing is, I always wondered how they really felt, having gone through all that miserable shit, knowing most didn't even have a choice about it but got drafted, you know. All that shit they went through and then, a couple years after that bullshit peace deal, it all goes to hell and it was like everything they did was just completely meaningless."

A ping ran through Harchu's 'plants, informing him he'd received a series of messages.

From the Glatun Federation.

He hadn't received any messages in the months since he'd received thirdhand Human news of the Rangora invasion. This was likely due to a communications blackout the moment the Rangora invaded. Messages had to travel through several gates and the Rangora only had to block the messages from being transmitted at one of them. But, if he was receiving messages again, it meant that any Rangora blackout had been lifted in his home system and all the connecting systems.

Which meant either the invasion had completely failed or fully succeeded. His money, to use a Human term, was on the latter.

Several messages were from the Glatun Federation personnel office, advising him that a recall had been issued and that he was to return to the system by any means available and reenter active service to assist in the defense of the Glatun Federation. The final message, dated several weeks later, rescinded the recall order and informed him that the Glatun Federation Military was no longer capable of processing his return.

His blood went cold.

It didn't say so, but the only possible reason was the Glatun Federation's military had ceased to exist as an organization. Surely, branches or cells of it must exist somewhere, but...

The next message was from his sole sibling.

Harchu, I have been notified by authorities that you have failed to report in response to the Federation-wide recall issued to all reserve Glatun military personnel. Was it not enough that you served for so long in the very military which antagonized the Rangora into addressing what they could only logically see as an enemy, but now that we are in dire need of that very military, you hide your head in shame, leaving us to fend for ourselves? If you represent the best of our so-called military, then perhaps it is time for us to submit to a more unification-minded entity. Whatever your status, location, and reasons for not returning, I can unhesitatingly say it is too late. Continue to hide with your shame and cowardice in whatever hole it is you have chosen. The Glatun neither want nor need your kind anymore. You have proven unfit to carry the Indolo name, and I shall curse you with every other breath until I no longer draw them.

—Onkud

Harchu's blood boiled for a moment but cooled quickly.

"Anyway," Dave continued in the background, "after spending umpteen deployments in the 'Stans, losing a few close buddies and plenty more I didn't know so well, seeing all the good we did—like one night we went out and picked up a couple kids who'd gotten injured and I thought, 'There's no way I could ever do anything more meaningful with my life.' I mean, women got to vote in that country for the first time in maybe ever, I think, and go to school. Some say we were messing with their culture, but I don't have too much to say for a culture where women can't—sorry, I'm getting off topic here. Point is, we did that for two damn decades. And then, it just ended. Just like how we saw those people hanging off helicopters trying to leave Saigon, we had people flooding airfields trying to get on our C-17s, people dying 'cause they hid up in the wheel wells, I heard. Point is, I don't have to wonder how those Vietnam vets feel anymore. 'Cause I know. I know how it feels to have given so much of yourself for something and then see every bit of meaning just... *disappear.* Vanish, like none of it ever meant anything. Still not sure how to square that."

Frozen in place, Harchu stared at his Human friend and simultaneously imagined the chaos Dave was describing and imagined his home lying in ruins after the Rangora attack. Dancing on the knife's edge of a complete mental breakdown, he opened the next message.

My dearest progeny. As I draw near the end of my days, with Rangora sweeping through our systems, I must acknowledge my failures. There are many, all centered around my reluctance to continue the honored tradition of our progenitors. I declined to serve in the belief our race had progressed beyond the need for such things. In truth, it was cowardice, laziness, and fear of losing the creature comforts provided to me by those who worked hard and fought hard for eons before my miserable existence.

I regret I never valued your determination to resume the tradition that I and too many more like me casually discarded. It is all too clear that without you and many more like you, the end of our race was only a matter of time. I need to tell you, in what might be my last hours, that you were right. That you were necessary. That you, retrospectively, are appreciated.

It is I and Onkud and countless others who failed the Federation, not you. But it is too late for such praise. While I assume you have the instinct to return and throw yourself into the fray, I beg that you do not. The battle is over, and you would be but one more casualty among millions who could not prevent our fate. Wherever you have chosen to settle, I advise you to remain. With luck, you might rebuild our house where you are, so that the Indolo name might someday again be worthy of the great Dralu, whose statue I should never have removed.

Take care of yourself, Harchu. You are the best of us.

—Seeptu Indolo

The screen displayed a giant "YOU DIED" while there were indications the battle still raged in the background.

Mark had stopped playing and, at some point, he'd removed his goggles to listen to Dave.

"It wasn't completely meaningless," Mark said. "What you did is still what you did. Whether or not it made any difference—and I bet you made a huge difference to *somebody* over there, whether you ever know it. But either way, the very fact you *tried*, that US and allied soldiers went over there and—you know that old Patton quote? I'm butchering it, but: 'You don't win a war by dying for your country, you win by making the other guy die for his.'"

"'By making the other poor, dumb bastard die for his,'" Dave said.

"Yeah, that. But the thing is, in Afghanistan we showed the world that the American soldier and our allied soldiers weren't fighting and dying for our countries, we were fighting for *theirs*.

To bring them peace, stability, and even if our politicians pissed it all away, what you guys were trying to achieve was pretty incredible. Not your fault it didn't work out, and no point dwelling on it. That's the lesson you should get from those Vietnam vets. You did your part, be proud of it, and move on."

Dave grunted and settled into the couch. "You make it sound so easy, but I sorta see what you're saying. I'll think about it."

"'Kay, well in the meantime, we got some bugs to kill." He picked up another set of goggles and gloves and held them out. "You with me this time?"

Dave grabbed the gear and smiled. "Yeah, let's kill some bugs."

Mark turned to look at Harchu. "What about you, buddy?"

The words were distant, detached, as if Harchu wasn't really in the room with them but watching it all play out on a screen, as if they were characters in their game.

"Harchu, hello? You with us?"

All at once, he snapped back into reality with them.

"I'll hop on the next round," Harchu said. "I need to make a call first."

As the pair charged into their next mission, Harchu retreated into his 'plants and contacted Jonathan Cross.

"Harchu, last time we spoke I thought you made it quite clear you had nothing more to say to me. But how can I be of service?"

"Are you still looking for a pilot?"

SHELL GAME

Michael Gants

The crumbly mass of slightly green overcooked eggs steamed in the cool air of the galley. Pete looked at them with a faint grimace of disgust. He turned to the maintenance tech sitting to his right.

"What's with these?"

The maintenance tech looked over and unconsciously mimicked Pete's grimace. "Powdered."

"Powdered? Powdered! We're working our tails off here and we're getting powdered eggs?"

The maintenance tech shrugged and went back to eating his oatmeal while scrolling through his feed. He didn't glance back at Pete or the slowly cooling eggs. Leaving the plate on the table, Pete pushed himself up and stalked to the manager's office.

"Come," a voice called when he knocked on the door.

He pushed the thin metal door open and stepped in. Maria looked up as he did so, grinned, and waved him to the seat next to the desk.

"Pete. What can I do for you?"

He sat and frowned. "Explain the breakfast situation."

Maria blinked in surprise. "What situation?"

"The eggs."

"Ahh," she said, her grin fading away quickly. "We've shifted to powdered eggs. Not my idea, nor the bosses'. Came from on high."

"How high?" Pete asked, rubbing one thick calloused hand against his knee.

"Not sure. All I know is that the station is only getting powdered, freeze-dried, dehydrated, or frozen items. Nothing fresh. Not even eggs.

"There was a memo a day or two ago about it. I'm intending on briefing everyone at the meeting this afternoon. Didn't realize the galley had already run out of fresh goods."

Pete threw his hands up in frustration. "We're working our tails off here, Maria. Everyone is. Ain't like this place is paradise. It's the same situation as my dad talked about on the rigs in the Gulf, but worse. Freezing cold outside, nowhere to go for a stroll, darn few new people. Even the sights get pretty boring quickly.

"We all signed up for it, but come on—food is about the only thing to look forward to around here. Now you're telling me they're taking that away?"

"Not quite. They aren't taking it away per se. Here." She brought up the email message and swiveled the monitor so Pete could read it easily.

"What do they mean they *can't* get fresh food?"

"How bad?" George Santos, lead logistics manager, asked pensively.

"Pretty bad." A line graph of cost to mass flashed onto the screen. "As you can see, we're looking at more than a three-hundred percent increase in cost per unit of mass in the next month." The pointer moved up the graph. "Trend analysis suggests that the price will continue to rise for the next several months. Even with a decrease in the cost of H_3, things are projecting in the wrong direction for us. You know as well as I do that projections are just that, projections. More of an educated guess than fact.

"Good news, as it is, is that based on historical trending, the cost curve will flatten out considerably once we're moving the fuel more regularly to the civilian side. However, even then we'll likely see some price increases continue." Andrew Stewart tapped the screen, and another line graph appeared, this one much lower and rising very slowly.

"This represents what we expect we'll be able to get." A new graph flashed onto the screen. "This represents overall production, this the original projected production, and this line the expected export capability. As you can see here, the overall production is well behind what we expected. The damage from the Horvath and Rangora war is continuing to cause issues. Crop yields are down significantly more than originally expected. There's also problems with farmable land."

"But three hundred percent? We're not going to be able to simply absorb that kind of increase."

"Yes, three hundred. And there isn't a thing we can directly do to change that."

The conference room was silent for several minutes, the logistics staff mulling over what Andrew had shown.

A quiet voice spoke from one end of the table. "What if there was something we *could* do about it?"

George angled his head toward the speaker, one eyebrow raised. "Have an idea, Linda?"

"Maybe. We're lifting all our supplies out from Terra, through the gate to here at Franklin, then transferring out to the ships, correct?"

George nodded. "Either with one of the Monkeys or when the transports dock at the upper end of the mine and gets a direct transfer. Are you thinking of a better way to do that?"

Linda shook her head. "No. I doubt there's any way that's more efficient to do the tasking. But what about getting food from right here? In system, I mean. Why not start a farm around here?"

Another member of the group stifled a laugh. George frowned at the sound. "Not sure it's feasible. There isn't any room on board the mine for serious hydroponics. Wasn't in the design philosophy, though in hindsight maybe it should have been. We could maybe scrounge up a few spots to put together something. Not enough to make any real difference though. And it's not like either Miranda or Puck are capable of supporting a farm."

"Why not?" someone else asked. "They've got enough gravity and atmosphere. Water too."

"Wrong kind of atmosphere," another person interjected. "Reducing. Lots of CO_2, no free O_2 to speak of. Make it kind of hard to raise cows or turnips."

"But isn't CO_2 exactly what the plants need to grow?" a third asked, pulling an ear while they talked. Someone else asked about the ability of the soil to support plants. Another countered with the studies of planting in the iron-rich sands of Mars and what had come out of that.

There were now several people talking at the same time, and George sat back. He listened intently, taking it in as the group quickly fell into a back-and-forth argumentative discussion on the possibility of starting any farming on Bespin's two largest moons. George gave them thirty minutes of brainstorming and arguing, then stepped in.

"All right, you guys are starting to go in circles. No one is putting out anything new now, and it sounds like all of the ideas have been argued out." He turned his gaze down the table. "Linda, I notice you weren't saying anything during all of this. You're the one who suggested farming, what's your idea?"

Linda cleared her throat and began repeatedly tapping her pen on the table gently. "This will sound a bit out there and isn't really in the area everyone else is talking about. Why try and use the moons at all? We've got plenty of space in orbit here. What about farming there?"

George's eyebrows rose and he gave a small head shake. "Interesting. But not really feasible."

"Why?" Linda questioned, her pen stopping just before it hit the table again.

"Time. Cost as well, but mainly time. You're not the first to suggest this. Back after the Horvath used kinetic strikes on Cairo, Mexico City, and Shanghai, I remember reading about some think tank looking into it. Their studies determined it would take over twenty years, at a minimum, to create the habitat's shell." He raised his right hand and began lifting fingers to count as he spoke.

"That was before Apollo was around and LFD wasn't building much more than mirrors. I suspect it would take significantly less time now. The problem is that unlike the Troy battleglobes, it'd need to be a hemisphere—flat on one side, domed with crystal on the other. Not a design anyone, not even Apollo, has ever tried to build.

"Oh, don't get me wrong, orbital farming solves a slew of planet-based problems. Unfortunately, it also adds new ones, like additional very soft targets for the Horvath and Rangora to blast, since with the crystal domes they couldn't be armored to any great degree.

"Finally, the size is an issue. The Troys are huge, several

kilometers across. But again, we're talking about a hemisphere, not a ball. An acre is what?" George paused and consulted his phone. "It's forty-three thousand, five hundred and sixty square feet. Historically, I believe that a farm is forty acres." He tapped the screen of his phone, doing the math. "That's over one point seven million square feet. Tiny compared to a battleglobe, but still huge. The cooling time is the real problem after the shape. The globes take years to expand and cool. I recognize it'll take less for one of these farms since they're smaller, but it will still be at least several months to a year."

He put the hand he'd been counting off with gently back on the table. "Which means that any orbital farm platform that got built wouldn't help with the costs of food in space any time soon."

Linda nodded as he finished. "All right. I don't disagree with what you've said, George. On the other hand, I think we might have a couple of habitats we could leverage right now." Linda gave a thin-lipped smile. "It'll put a dent in Franklin's ability to transport H_3 out system, but starving the workers will have the same effect, and for a lot longer."

"What kind of dent?" George frowned. "H_3 is our primary export and overall, it's what keeps the lights on here."

"I know. But not having food is going to do the same thing. Let's use the extra Liberty Ships. The ones that haven't been completed. They won't need to be spun out or cooled. I checked and we have three that are only hulls—no drives, no pumping equipment, no life support. Just empty tubes. What about those?"

George rubbed his chin. "I'll look into it. Have to make a few calls."

"How much?" Angela Baker asked, her eyes widening in surprise.

"Three hundred percent according to Logistics," Charlie Rose, the head of Special Projects group, replied from the other end of the video line. "And it is going to keep rising. Getting food off planet is difficult if it's not directly related to the Navy. Franklin Gas Mine isn't Navy. Nor are any of the groups working the asteroids. We lost a fair number of ships during the last battle, including several of our transports. Our overall lift capacity is a lot lower than expected or planned.

"The second problem is even tougher. The weather patterns

are still messed up from orbital strikes and that's continuing to affect crop outputs. Which is leading to higher general food prices. Put the two together and not only are the prices going to keep going up, it's going to get harder to get enough food out of the gravity well."

Angela rubbed her forehead with two fingers. "What's the solution? I'm assuming that you have one, or at least an idea of one. I've never known you to give me this kind of news and not have something."

Charlie gave her a sardonic grin. Special Projects was a combination think tank and troubleshooting team set up when the Franklin mine was being developed. Each of the members had primary jobs other than the group. When necessary, like this problem, they would be tasked with paralleling main groups, looking for additional solutions, or attempting to bypass conventional thinking roadblocks.

"Thanks for the faith. In this case the solution didn't come from my team. Linda Fouren, she's one of the managers in Logistics, came up with it. The plan is brilliant in its simplicity. We can use the Liberty Ships as a stop-gap solution. I'm thinking of attaching her for future projects."

Angela frowned, unconsciously brushed her hair, and leaned back in the office chair. "The Liberty Ships are tankers. They aren't even rated for atmospheric flights. How in the seven heavens will they help get food production up and costs down?"

"First, they've got a lot of space in them."

"Not a lot of room for farming."

Charlie nodded. "Agreed, if we're talking about plants. But it is a fair amount of space for small animal farming. Chickens probably. Mix in some insect and worm farms, and it starts to look more promising."

"Worm farming?" Angela wrinkled her nose. "Why would people want to eat worms?"

"Not for the people. And not to eat. Well, I guess they could be used for feeding the animals, but that wouldn't be their primary purpose. The primary purpose would be to help create more soil. Take the waste products, both plant cuttings and paper. They break it down into usable dirt. It's been used in several places on Earth over the last century. The liquid output makes a great fertilizer as well. Called worm tea."

"Why animals? Why not fruit trees or corn or tomatoes?"

Angela listened intently as Charlie continued his explanation.

"Mass. Almost everything right now boils down to mass. One of the biggest hurdles to overcome is the amount of biomass a farm takes to keep running. As it is, we're going to have to deal with some soil."

"How much and why?"

"Only half a foot. Just enough to let grass and clover grow. Clover is great for two reasons. It fixes nitrogen in the soil, which plants need. Clover also is a favorite for making honey from. Which is what the bees will be doing. Bees won't take up a lot of space.

"As to the why, it gives us a way to test some theories about orbital farming. Turns out, it's not something the galactics do. Probably because they don't have to rely on a single planet that's getting bombarded constantly. Most of them have several habitable planets to feed themselves from. Which in turn means that there aren't any good guides on how to do it.

"But returning to your original question. Why not plants? Tomatoes are deep rooted. Need plenty of soil. Call it two to three feet. Fruit trees, like cherry, apple, and peach, run between one and a half to two and a half feet of depth. 'Course, they need around twenty-five feet of space for each tree. Call it fifty-five feet trunk to trunk. And corn, whew." Charlie pretended to wipe sweat from his brow. "Corn needs about four feet, some breeds as much as six of depth to grow.

"Which translates to a lot of soil. Our calculations were for an organic soil weighing around ninety pounds. For each acre of area, at a foot deep, ends up being a bit under two thousand tons. Two thousand tons. Per acre. That's a huge amount of lift capacity just for the soil.

"And where is the soil going to come from? Heck, lack of viable soils is one of the main reasons we've started looking at going orbital with the farms. All in all, direct soil growth is out of the current running. The team is looking at some additional options for soil, a few of which this chicken farm is going to be part of. Bottom line is that of things to grow, small livestock ended up being the best balance of space, weight, and setup cost. Chicken feed is pretty compact."

"Rabbits?" Angela asked, taking a sip of her coffee. She thought for a moment. "I think I remember reading about people raising them in some places for food."

"Rabbits were the second runner-up, but they need more space and a lot more feed volumetrically. Real good meat animals. Pound for pound better than pigs or cows. Breed a lot faster too. Plus, their pellets make great fertilizer without any additional processing. Beat chicken poop in that regard. But chickens lay eggs as well as being meat. Eggs are protein dense, used in a huge number of different ways, and they produce them at a rate of about one egg per twenty-eight hours or so. We figure we can house somewhere in the neighborhood of forty thousand layers inside the farm. Which translates to putting out about thirty-eight thousand eggs every day. For years."

Charlie took a deep breath before he continued. "By itself, this place isn't going to feed everything in space. But it should help feed Franklin and everything else here in-system. It'll certainly put a dent in what's needed to be shipped up from Earth. And, hopefully, convince various groups that orbital farming is a cost-effective way to go."

As he ran down, Angela sat for a few moments, lost in thought. Finally, she looked directly at him.

"It's the best plan I've heard so far. Takes care of a huge problem, sets us up for future growth, and doesn't take a long time to get started. Which the high and mighty will appreciate since we all know how much he hates waiting for anything. On my authority, go ahead and move on the project. Pull anyone who isn't directly working on H_3. Have HR start hunting through applications for people we can hire to farm. They'll need to be space-capable and have a skill set including both robotics and farming. Let's see what your team can pull out of the proverbial magic hat this time."

Charlie nodded, tipped an invisible hat, and ended the call.

Fighting to keep his nausea from overtaking him, Charlie doubled over. His legs felt as if they were flying out from under him and his head and shoulders were moving at different speeds. Even his lungs and stomach felt as if they were attempting to travel to separate and distinct time zones.

Bending over helped some, but there still was a massive difference in how fast his feet felt like they were going and how fast his torso was moving. All while standing still inside the empty hull.

Rafiq Ahmed watched from a prone position. Even knowing what was coming wouldn't prevent the nausea so he had a heavy-dose Dramamine patch behind each ear. He pressed a button and the giant cylinder slowed. He could feel the tremors of the sat packs firing through the hull beneath his back.

"I've stopped it. You all right?"

A bubbly sounding *urk* was all Charlie got out. He continued leaning with his hands on his knees, his breath coming in slightly choked gasps. A few seconds later, his breathing slowed and returned to normal. Then he straightened his arms and slowly stood erect. He took a few deep breaths.

"That," Charlie stated slowly, still fighting down the lingering nausea, "was horrible."

Rafiq grinned. "Now you have a real understanding of why spin isn't going to work for us," he said calmly.

"Real cute. A memo next time, please. What caused that? It felt like my feet and head were trying to go in the same direction at different speeds. Where was the wind? Shouldn't there have been wind at that speed?"

"One question at a time. The overall reason is the diameter's too small." The older man twirled his hand in a circle as he continued his explanation. "In order to produce the three-fourths gravity you were feeling, the cylinder is spinning pretty fast. About twelve RPM. You were feeling the acceleration shear between the center of the cylinder and the hull. That's why you got motion sickness almost instantaneously.

"The atmosphere was spinning. In fact, there would have been some minor stratification eventually. The gas, overall, doesn't have enough mass to have any real movement separate from the spin at a low speed. Hence, no winds."

Charlie took another few deep breaths, the nausea finally subsiding and his body readjusted to microgravity. "Right. Spinning is out. Again, memo. Or you could have just shown me a video or something?"

Rafiq chuckled. "I could have. But you might have argued. Now you have a real 'gut reaction' to why it's a bad plan."

"Ohhh." Charlie rubbed his belly. "Don't make jokes. My stomach is still wondering what happened. I get your point, though. No spin. That's going to bump the cost up some." He worried at a knuckle. "Guess it will make it easier to move it around the system, though. Easier to build too since we won't need to construct any special non-rotating sections in order to dock with the gas mine or other ships. Grav plates, then?"

Rafiq nodded. "It's the only solution I can think of. Let's head back to my office. This is going to take some time and simulations."

The pair exited through the temporary lock and Charlie flew the work shuttle back to the gas mine.

"I'm understanding you want to make the most of the interior available for use?" Rafiq asked as they entered his cluttered office. "You want the entire hull for the farming?"

Charlie nodded and smiled thinly. "Yes. We can get nearly two and a half acres of space if we use all of the inner wall."

"That will make things a bit more difficult. It means you need the grav plates all around the outside." Rafiq's liquid accent thickened a bit as he gestured. "That's going to cause its own problems. Have to be careful about where we put them. Different kind of shear to worry about."

"Grav shear?" Charlie shuddered. "That's certainly something we can't afford."

"Oh, I agree." Rafiq tapped his screen and ran a quick simulation. "Hmm . . . this is going to be interesting. Aligning the plates laterally is simple. We've done it with plenty of ships. It's the curve that's the issue. See how the plates interact near the center?"

A new graphic appeared, showing the lines of gravitational force in a cross-section of the hull. As they neared the center, the straight lines bent at random angles, forming what looked like a cat's cradle mixed with a Mandelbrot set. Rafiq tapped the screen again, his finger pointing at the tangle.

"That's the shearing interaction. Goes from one gravity to over seven thousand in less than five feet."

"There any way to prevent it?"

Rafiq thought for a few moments. "I'm sure there is. Give me a day or two to work on it."

Two days later, a ping broke Charlie's concentration while he reviewed an efficiency report. He answered the call.

"Don't have them interact," Rafiq stated simply.

"What?" Charlie responded, completely at a loss as to what Rafiq was talking about. His mind was still on the numbers in his report.

"The grav plates. It turned out so simple. We don't let them interact." A broad smile crossed the researcher's face, tempering the seemingly sarcastic remark. "What I mean is that if we shift from a one-gee output to something lower, say point nine four gee, I think I can taper the output so there isn't interaction."

A diagram appeared on the screen, replacing Rafiq's face. "See? This is with the new plate configuration. No shear. Nothing trying to tear the farm apart. On the other hand, you end up with a portion of the ship that's in freefall."

"How large a portion, and more importantly, where?" Charlie asked. "I'm not sure how lower gravity might affect the animals. We want the chickens to stay healthy and produce as many eggs as they will."

Rafiq zoomed the image, reducing the visible area to a small slice of the circle. Charlie could see where the gravity lines ended. Instead of warping themselves as they had in the original plate configuration, they stopped short of the center of the ship. "There," the invisible Rafiq said. A yellow circle appeared in the empty space at the center. "You'll have about ten feet of near to true micro running from one end of the farm to the other. A cylinder of weightlessness within the main cylinder."

"How fast is the drop-off? We're going to have some flying insects and maybe birds in there eventually."

The simulation zoomed in until the edge of the gravity field was filling the screen. A graph line with numbers appeared. "Ten percent per inch. It will be noticeable, but not dangerous. I suspect the birds will stay outside it. Even if they don't, they will be fine. That distance of change won't damage anything biological."

Charlie nodded. "So even the bees won't get torn apart by the changes either. Okay, that gives us a heads-up if it becomes a problem."

The clutter in the room surprised Charlie. Most people in space tend to keep their work and personal areas tidy. This office was anything but. Data pads were strewn across not only the desk but the floor as well. Paper diagrams were taped haphazardly to walls, often covering each other when they weren't crumpled masses tossed into corners. Even the white walls had been scribbled on with ink. Charlie really hoped it was erasable, or the janitorial group was not going to be happy.

"Bruce?" Charlie called out tentatively, fearing anything too loud might upset the precarious balance of the nearest stacks of items.

A head poked up from behind the desk. Bruce's eyes widened and he stood. A thin, almost gaunt man, he clutched three sheets of printouts, a yellow highlighter, a pen, and one of the room's ubiquitous data pads. He set the pen and highlighter on a clear space on the desk and cast about for a place to put down the other items. Finally, he settled on placing them on his chair.

"Bruce, what's going on here?"

"Planning. Layout. General design ideas." He waved to the papers on the wall and grabbed another data pad from the desk. "These are the plans, ideas really, for the water-cycling system. It combines both reclamation, treatment, and distribution into a single combined plan. But it's too large right now." He dropped the pad and scanned the walls. Pointing to another set of diagrams, Bruce continued. "That's one of the layouts for the ammonia processing plant. Do you know how much ammonia chickens can produce?"

Charlie shook his head. "Not really. Never worked on a farm or knew anybody who did. That's one of the main reasons you're working on it. You spent time on a farm."

"My grandmother's place near St. Louis. For two summers. Twenty-eight years ago."

"Which is the most experience anyone in the group has. We're hiring farmers now, but it's going to be a bit until they can get here." Charlie shrugged. "How much?"

"Twelve tons."

"That is a problem," Charlie said and frowned. "Twelve tons? Per chicken?"

Bruce chuckled. "No, not per chicken. Whew, that would be a major problem. The twelve is a pretty solid estimate for each chicken house on the farm. It doesn't all show up at once. And it's not as big a problem as it sounds when you are only talking about the tonnage. Ammonia removal from wastewater has been a thing for over a century. With the time we've been in space we're getting pretty good at filtering nasty things out of the air."

"What is the problem, then?"

"Storage." Bruce waved the data pad in the air. "Apollo only released the Liberty hulls on the condition that they can convert them back to H_3 freighters in minimum time. Which removes the possibility of external storage since we can't run piping through the outer hull. That's the sticking point. I'm not certain everything will fit in the farm module. I can't seem to figure it out. Four farms, the food storage, the recycling, the..."

Charlie cut him off simply by grabbing the data pad. "All right. Cut down the numbers, then."

Bruce stood still and blinked. "But the plan calls for four houses at twenty-one thousand chickens each."

"It's a plan. Heck, this has never been done. Well, not by humans. It's new ground. If the original plan calls for things that can't be done right now, pivot. Look back at the early days of the space program. Pre-gate space program, I mean. Scientists were pivoting all the time because the politicians wanted something that when laid out, wasn't technically possible right then. Same situation. How would things look if you were only putting in three chicken houses? Would that give you enough space?"

A deep look of concentration fell across Bruce's face. "Maybe," he said distantly. "Let me run some numbers and model a few things. It might, though. Bottleneck is still the ammonia separators. There isn't any design specific for space use. Which means using a reliable Earth-based setup. I don't know how that will work up here."

Something rocked the module hard enough to throw the duty crew from their bunks in the primary compartment.

"What the hell?" asked one of the techs groggily as alarms began to wail.

A female voice, devoid of emotion spoke up. "Explosion and fire at frame one-eighty-nine, slice five. Oxygen levels decreasing at oh point oh six percent per minute. Toxic atmosphere detected in farm zone. Hull integrity sat." The computer voice paused, then began the dire litany again.

The other tech scrambled to his feet from the ground and began slipping into his farm snuggy, a single piece of clothing reminiscent of submarine work uniforms. His partner did the same.

"Suits?" the first asked.

"With an explosion? You bet. I don't care that the computer says the hull's good." He waved at the airlock door. "I won't go out there without one."

They rushed to the airlock and donned pressure suits. It took a few moments to get the equipment on and verified before they opened the inner door.

Black smoke hazed the compartment. Even though it had only been minutes since the alarms started, the interior of the habitat was already as hard to see through as the pollution fog of Victorian London. The pair tossed fire extinguishers onto the cargo section of the two-man ATV waiting at the door, then climbed aboard.

"Careful," the passenger called out as the driver accelerated between the number two and three chicken houses. The tall metal walls flashed by on either side, only occasionally visible through the thickening smoke. "You're going to crash us. Then where will we be? Not fighting the fire, that's for sure."

"Can it," said the driver testily. "I'm not going to hit the buildings."

A roaring sound grew in proportion to the thickening smoke. Dull orange-red light pulsed through the smoke, almost in time to the continued blaring of the fire alarm. The ATV skidded in wet mud as the driver hit the brakes.

A column of fire and smoke stretched toward the other side of the cylinder, turning almost ninety degrees as it hit the zero gee column. Water and AFFF rained down from the suppression drones, though it seemed to be doing little.

"We're going to have to flush the air," shouted the passenger.

"What about the chickens?" the driver yelled over the roar, pointing at the portion of the farm not on fire. "The whole test group is in this house."

"They're probably already dead. If we don't get this fire out, they're going to die anyway!"

The driver nodded and called up the required commands on the ATV's computer. A rushing sound followed, and their suits puffed to compensate for the lowering pressure. The noise and fire abated as the atmosphere was released. Finally, all the flames were gone, and no sound could be heard.

Cold, blackened pieces of twisted metal reached skyward, greasy from residue of the fire suppression foam mixed with soot. Charlie gave it another look, shaking his head.

"What happened?" he asked, still staring at the shattered ruin of chicken house two's backside.

Bruce tapped his pad, thankful the pressure suits were self-contained. He knew what a fire-blasted farmyard smelled like and was happy not to contend with it.

"Can't be certain until the team finishes a full analysis, but based on what I'm looking at here, I think the ammonia separation system got clogged." He raised one hand to forestall any comments from Charlie. "It shouldn't have. Something caused a spike, plus something else gave a spark. Maybe one and the same. All I know is that this proves the Earth design method we're employing here is too dangerous. I had concerns when we reviewed it, but it was the most reliable method known."

"It didn't work," Charlie said flatly. "Not only did it explode, but it also caused us to lose the chickens. Everything died when the techs pumped the atmo..." He paused, disgusted at the thought of the ten thousand dead birds, but better to have an accident now than when they were at full capacity. "I'm not mad at them, probably saved things from getting any worse. But it means that almost all our work is back at square one."

"Not everything," Bruce countered. "Except for this portion, the farm itself is still whole and in working order. I hate we lost the chickens, but it could have been worse."

Charlie sighed. "Fine. How are we—you—going to ensure this can't happen again?"

Two weeks later, Charlie was down in Bruce's cluttered office again.

"I'll show you. We need to take a walk, though." He tossed Charlie a set of safety glasses, ear protectors, and a heavy coat. "It's going to be loud and cold when we get there."

Bruce led Charlie to a door seemingly wedged between a separator tank and a row of large pumps. It led to a short hallway that ended in another door, this one marked for outside exit. The pair ended up on a small loading dock that had been repurposed for the Agro group. It was a calm day for Bespin, with the winds not being more than thirty-five miles per hour.

Bruce gestured to the collection of piping and tanks taking up more than three-quarters of the deck. He pulled out his ubiquitous data pad. A complex flowchart and diagram filled the screen. He pointed from the diagram to the machinery and back.

"Two phase. One part will use simple absorption filters, same as what's used on virtually every spacecraft out there. However, that's more a backup than anything else. The primary system will use a forced air system to pull from the chicken houses and pump it into water." He traced the flow with his hand. "The water will then flow past these beds of struvite. The ammonia gets absorbed there. Then the water will be heated to release the now clean air back into the general areas."

"All right," Charlie agreed. "How often will the filter beds need to be replaced? And where is the water coming from?"

"Water will be the same water that's feeding the chickens. The absorption cycle is on the waste side. That's the beauty. Two systems in one. Also turns out you can simply heat the struvite in a vacuum, and it releases the bound ammonia in pure form." He pulled open a panel and flashed a light inside. The section was half full of gray-white sand. "That's the struvite." He closed the panel before much of the material was stirred up by the winds.

"We're going to add a compression system here," Bruce continued and pointed to another section of the piping, "to bottle the ammonia rather than venting it. Reduces the need for station-keeping fuel since there's no outgassing, and we can sell the ammonia or use it in other industrial applications."

"It's also used in fertilizers," Charlie added, remembering a tidbit he'd learned somewhere.

"Yep. And that's another application for it. Not sure what the process is..." Bruce trailed off.

"I'll have someone else look into that. You've got enough on your plate right now."

"The bigger problem with chickens is the guano. It's going to be worse than I had originally thought since we aren't using the same methods as Earthbound farms do."

"Guano?" Charlie asked curiously.

"Chicken waste products. Birds—chickens in this case, but all birds—have only one waste product, a mixture of solids and liquids. Guano."

"Guano," said Charlie.

"Exactly." Bruce moved toward a large, flat, black carbon shipping pod at the nearer end of the crowded platform. "It's a pain to clean up and where a significant part of the ammonia comes from. It might have been what clogged the first system. We think these will help us out." Bruce removed the lid on the pod and the sides fell away. Charlie shuffled out of the way to prevent getting hit. In the middle of the pod's bottom sat a two-foot-tall metallic blue shape. It reminded him of the step pyramids in Mexico.

"What is it?"

"Class-Two general purpose robot."

Charlie bent down to get a better look at it. "Doesn't really look like a robot at all."

Bruce grinned sardonically. "What were you expecting? Something with a domed head? Or maybe something with a red eye that cycled back and forth?"

"Cute. No, I guess I was expecting something more, well, robot looking," Charlie admitted.

"The Class-Two is based on a venerable Ormatur design. They aren't humanoid, which means their robots aren't either. Easy to use, though. The Glatun use them in waste removal and hazardous environment clean up extensively. The bonus is since the design is so old, it doesn't need to be licensed. Completely public domain. Movement is run by small grav plates so they can perform jobs at any level of the farm. Could even fly between the houses straight across the cylinder. If this works as well as we hope at dealing with the guano, then we'll order another six or so for the farm."

"Fly across the cylinder. What about the freefall section and grav change?" Charlie asked, trying to get the comical picture of tiny flying ziggurats out of his head.

"The robots could easily be programmed to deal with the changes," Bruce assured him.

Charlie nodded. "I'm sure the farmers will appreciate not having to clean up the chicken sh . . . er . . . guano."

Though Linda had seen it from the outside during the shuttle ride, the scale didn't really register. Everything looked both tiny and huge in space, since there wasn't any good way to get a sense of how large something was until a ship was right next to it.

Now though, standing inside, the scale was obvious. The cylinder seemed to stretch forever; a gaping tunnel of smoked glass filled with darkened buildings. Linda knew in her head that it was only about three football fields in length, but her head and the rest of her senses weren't playing together right now. She leaned back and stared up at the ceiling. High overhead, ghostly points of light stood out against the darkness between jet black shapes of more buildings, for everything in the world reminding her of distant streetlights in fog. She stared at them for a few moments, then returned her gaze to the other person in the vast compartment.

"Well, here it is. Your idea in action. Okay, not quite in action yet, but fully built and waiting for the new chickens to arrive next week."

"How many people is it going to take to run the chicken farm?" Linda asked Charlie.

"Not as many as you might think. Nine people in total. The majority of the work will be done with robots. We've hired a general manager who's got a background in both farming and robotics to help out with that part. Initially it'll be just three people: the supervisor, two techs, and the bots. The Agro group determined that should be enough to get things going."

"Hmmm. Seems like that's going to be a lot of work for just three people," she said. "How long?"

"Only a few weeks. Long enough to get the chickens to the point they can start laying. That's when the real work will begin."

"It's pretty dark in here." Linda changed the subject, her breath frosting ahead of her as he spoke. "Cold too. Do you think the bees will do much in these temps? I thought they hibernated or died off during the winter."

"Trust me, once we get living things back in here, cold won't be the problem. The problem will be keeping the temperatures down. We're also on the night side right now. Things will brighten up after we cross the terminator." Charlie pointed upward. "You can sorta see the planet there, occluding the stars."

Linda looked up again and nodded. "Makes me feel like we're on the *Valley Forge*."

"The revolutionary war battlefield?" Charlie asked, confused by the comparison.

"Not the battlefield. A ship carrying forests around Saturn. Or maybe Jupiter. Don't remember. It's from an old sci-fi flick." Linda gave a short laugh. "Heck, the movie was old before the gate opened. It was old when I was born. Think it might have come out before anyone walked on the moon. But the ship definitely had a bunch of forest domes on it."

"Ah," Charlie said in a mildly distant voice. "Never heard of it. Well, your idea is what brought this all to being. What do you think?"

"It's impressive. A lot bigger than I thought it would be. Or at least it feels that way." She gestured back toward the airlock to the piloting and crew module. "Can we head back? I swear my feet are getting numb."

The pair sat at the fold down table, each with a coffee mug. Linda wrapped her hands around the ceramic and sighed.

"Warming up?"

"Yes. Never really enjoyed the cold. That's one thing I have to say I enjoy about working in space. Constant even temperature. Never have to worry about the weather."

"Never really thought about that part of it," Charlie answered. "You're right, though."

"The chickens will be living in those long buildings? They seemed pretty big."

"Not just the chickens. Those also house conveyors, candling equipment, packaging equipment, ammonia scrubbers, general maintenance area, and the worm farms. We're set up for forty thousand egg-laying birds. Additional space between the buildings for some free-range area and bee hives, and of course the sunlight and mirror spans.

"Honestly, there isn't any spare room. The design and agriculture teams planned out the usage of everything. This forward module will be the housing for the farmers. At the other end," Charlie said, gesturing to the aft wall, "is the warehousing and transfer section. It has both cargo- and personnel-sized docking rings and airlocks. Which means that ships can dock right here and get eggs. They won't have to wait for a gate transfer from Earth."

Linda nodded. "This will certainly help the situation. It won't solve the issues of food production and logistics of moving it, but it's a start. Now if we could only get some real farming habitats set up."

Charlie grinned. "Your idea for using the Liberty Ships was great out-of-the-box thinking. And it put my team down a path no one's seriously looked at since the late twentieth century. Which is why we'd like you to join us. Have you ever heard of O'Neill cylinders?"

* * *

Pete studied his breakfast plate. For the first time in over three months, it contained a real egg. A golden yolk centered in the cooked whites. There was also a piece of toast, cut in half, buttered and hot, and two pieces of bacon. He poked the yolk and was rewarded with a gush of liquid from the center.

"That's more like it!" he exclaimed in a happy tone. A smile spread across his face. He grabbed half of the toast and mopped at the plate. The bread greedily absorbed the egg.

Pete popped the piece into his mouth and chewed. "Fresh eggs again. No more of those fake powdered things."

"That's what they're saying," Pete's tablemate chimed in. "Apparently that floating farm is doing pretty well. Should have eggs coming in fresh all the time now."

"Well, whatever it takes, I guess. Just glad that they're willing to listen to us poor sods." He grabbed a piece of bacon and bit down.

Disgust flashed across his face as he pulled the partial chunk back away from his mouth. He tossed the meat back onto his plate. It bounced soggily.

His tablemate looked up in surprise.

"What's the matter this time? Are the eggs not fresh enough for your liking?"

Pete pointed an accusing finger at the half-masticated bit of food. "Eggs are fine, it's that... thing!"

"It's bacon. Came off the last food transport. I thought you would be happy we're getting a regular food run now. You were sure complaining about the eggs for the last several weeks."

Pete turned his head and aimed his glower toward his tablemate. "They can get us fresh eggs but then subject us to... to..." His finger began to shake slightly. "*Soy* bacon?!"

SEVEN TRADERS

Karl K. Gallagher

"Time to *Trade Hard*," said Captain Paladin as *Eurynome* passed through the gate.

His crew grinned. They'd been recruited from the fan group for Tyler Vernon's *Trade Hard* web comic. Now they'd bought out their ship and were going independent. There were aliens out there who needed to make deals, and *Eurynome*'s crew intended to screw them out of every credit they could.

The one exception was ex-corporal John "Father" Patricelli, late of the Marine Corps, just recruited to be the ship's security man. He sat at one of the engineering consoles, feet up, reading *The Collected Trade Hard, Vol. 2.*

"It'll take five days to get to the planet," said Ziggi, the pilot.

Dan looked up from the sensor console. "Hey, there's a meteoroid swarm just a bit off our course. A little detour would let us get some gunnery practice."

After the Battle of E Eridani, which crippled the Horvath and Rangora navies, *Eurynome* had done search and rescue work, followed by hauling salvage. Some salvage had been onboard when the crew bought out the decommissioned Liberty Ship "as is." Fragments of destroyed *Myrmidon* shuttles provided enough parts to assemble four four-terawatt laser cannons.

Paladin glanced at Patricelli. "What do you think, Father?"

He put down the comic. "Sure, we can use more practice."

Ziggi slowed the ship as they approached the meteoroids, so she could practice maneuvering rather than just flashing by.

The cannon were in two-gun turrets, one on each side of the cylindrical ship. Patricelli had called her a "mason jar" when he'd first seen *Eurynome*, and stuck to the nickname when he found out it was made of silica covered with carbon fiber. An operator station by each turret let them shoot even if the ship's network went down, though both turrets could be controlled from either one. On the first leg of the cruise, Father had spent some time teaching Dan how to be a backup gunner.

The radar provided a high-resolution display of the meteoroids. Father designated targets for himself and Dan. The display rotated as Ziggi put the ship in a spiral around the swarm.

Father's first shot missed the meteoroid clean as the ship jinked in an evasive maneuver. He adjusted the tracking. Keeping the beams in place for a few seconds heated it enough to shatter.

He wasn't satisfied. He had the calibration aligned correctly now, or at least close enough for nearby targets, but it was taking too long to set up each shot.

He matched Ziggi's maneuver as he tracked his next shot. The target rock broke apart.

One of the other blobs on the radar display turned into scattering pixels.

"I got one! I got it!" cried Dan over the intercom.

Father pushed his talk button. "Good shot, kid. Don't get cocky."

The ship's purser and supercargo was Kathy. She'd picked Dokthun as the best market for the ship's cargo. It was a world on the fringes of the Glatun Federation. Low industry, mostly agricultural, with some luxury resorts for the "get away from it all" types. The Rangora had destroyed the local security units but hadn't bombarded the world. The hypernet relays had been taken out, so there wasn't much information available.

As the planet came into view, the whole crew gathered on the bridge to get their first look at it. Dan's nose was almost touching the window. Eddie and Julie, the engineer and mechanic, respectively, looked over his shoulder.

Kathy was wrestling with her tablet, trying to synch a globe of Dokthun with the planet before her. "Ah! Okay, that's Fanbet

City. Not that it would be called a city anywhere else in the Federation."

"I thought this place had a decent population?" asked Paladin.

"It does. But they're very spread out. Don't like concentrating as much as most Glatun worlds do."

Dan threw his hands in the air in frustration. "I can't pick up any signals! The Rangora must have trashed all the communications systems here when they blew up the hypernet nodes."

"We can just land and talk to them," said Paladin. "Kathy, what's the best market?"

She looked at the globe again, then shrugged. "Fanbet is as big as any other town on the planet. We might as well go there."

Father looked up. "This is going to be just like the comic—set down and start asking the locals what they want to deal for."

The map of Fanbet Kathy had found in the Glatun archives showed a central plaza with some tall buildings around it. A landing pad for spacecraft was next to the plaza, ready to receive official visitors. Rings of smaller buildings were built around the center, shrinking until there were one-story homes against the woods.

When they passed through the cloud deck and could see the town directly, it looked different from the map. The plaza and landing pad were much smaller, as if new construction had taken over part of the land.

As *Eurynome* descended, they saw the "new construction" was tents and shacks.

Father put down the comic. "That looks like a refugee camp. Shelters built out of debris."

"The reports said the Rangora didn't bombard populated areas here," said Kathy.

Dan replied, "Maybe there was a natural disaster."

"Calm down, people," said Paladin. "In a few minutes we'll just ask them."

The Glatun didn't look like they wanted to be asked. People were running away, some in such a hurry they knocked down their tents.

Ziggi put *Eurynome* down facing the plaza. There was one Glatun in sight, kneeling at the edge of the pad.

Paladin ordered, "Dan, watch the security screens. Ziggi, Eddie, you're on watch. Father, security duty. Everyone else, come with me and let's go meet a customer."

Patricelli went down the gangway first. He studied the shantytown surrounding them. Looked like a refugee camp. Lots of trash piled up in drifts where the wind left it. Not like a normal robot-cleaned Glatun world.

He looked back at their ship. The design still bugged him. If the landing legs broke, the mason jar would roll away. The "lid" held the bridge and cargo hatch. He waved an all clear.

Paladin led Kathy and Julie down the ramp. They walked toward the kneeling Glatun.

Once they were out of the ship's shadow, the local stood up. It started shouting, "They're humans! Hey, everybody, they're humans! Come on back!"

A few heads poked out of the shanties but didn't approach.

Father wondered if his implants were translating the Glatun speech correctly. Why would humans be such a surprise to them?

The Glatun advanced and seized Paladin's hand. "By Gul, I'm glad to see you. We've been terrified. Finally someone's here to save us!"

"I'm Captain Paladin of *Eurynome*. We have a variety of goods to trade with you."

"Yes, we'll be happy to trade, but first, I am Mayor Wemath. Are you the commander of the naval force?"

Paladin shook his head. "There's no navy ships here. We're a free trader ship."

The Glatun spat a short word. "I see. So you haven't come to rescue us from the pirates?"

"Pirates?"

Their implants received an image. A line of Glatun filing into the open maw of a grounded ship. Rangora with clubs stood along the line, whacking sluggards. "The ship is landing at different towns, picking some beings to enslave, then moving to the next one. People have been fleeing to stay ahead of it, but we're the last big town before the coast. There's not really anywhere to go from here."

Julie gasped. Kathy frowned in concentration. Paladin shook his head. "This isn't what I expected."

Father said, "That's a *Zashkug*-something light troop transport. No ship-to-ship weapons. It has antimissile cannon."

Julie wheeled on him. "How the hell do you know that?"

The discharged marine shrugged. "It's in the Know Your Enemy playing cards. Four of clubs."

"Can we beat it?" demanded Paladin.

Father spread his hands wide. "Eventually. If it doesn't get us. I don't have the full specs on it."

"Letting people steal our customers is bad business," said Kathy.

The mayor perked up at that. "You will fight the pirates?"

More Glatun were returning to the shantytown. They didn't come out in the open, but they were peeking out from the shacks and tents, eavesdropping on the conversation with the humans.

"We didn't know about the pirates," Paladin temporized. "We'll have to discuss what we can do. Do you have more information about them?"

The mayor sent an information packet to their implants. "That's all we've been able to learn. They've captured anyone with valuable technical skills. People have been running away from them, but they run a pattern on which towns they hit. The refugees have been herded to here. We expect they'll show up here in two or three days."

Paladin said, "Thank you for the information. We need to talk."

The captain waved the others back into the ship. Father insisted on being the last one up. Once inside, he retracted the ramp.

"Everyone to the lounge," said Paladin. "We need to talk."

Eddie didn't bother sitting down. "We need to get the hell out of here. Pirates? In a Rangora warship? We're going to get killed."

"We can't just abandon these people," said Dan. "They need our help."

Eddie shot back, "You've watched *Seven Samurai* too many times."

"No personal attacks," said Paladin.

Several crew started talking at once.

"Hey!" said Patricelli in a military tone. "The mayor sent us a bunch of data. We should read it before we make any decisions." He forwarded the data to everyone who'd stayed on board.

"Good idea," said Paladin. "Okay, thirty-minute time-out. Then we come back here and discuss."

Father sat and started sorting through the data. It wasn't well organized. Just a collection of verbal observations from Glatun witnesses and video of the pirates in action. No analyses.

The videos showed the pirates had a standard pattern. That was useful. If they could predict enemy movements, they knew where to set up an ambush. After fast-forwarding through some roundup and sortings, Father skipped the rest. The Rangora were being fussy. Less than one in twenty were selected to be slaves.

Most of the Glatun statements were just terrified reports of a town being attacked. Father's implant filtered those out. A few were interesting. The Rangora were casual about chatting in front of their prisoners. Father's implant translated the recorded conversations.

Father had to laugh at how familiar some were. Grunts griping about guard duty were the same everywhere. Complaints about supervisors were similar. But a few had some interesting bits.

Putting them together, he realized that the transport's crew were mutineers. When the Rangoran Empire had been hit with the one-two of the humans forcing them to pull out of the Glatun Federation and war with the Ogut, their occupation forces had been scrambled. This troop transport had been overlooked. Lacking orders, the captain wanted to chase after the withdrawing fleet.

The bosun—now captain—of the ship had a different idea. Use the chaos to disappear and engage in profitable ventures. The industries of Rangora worlds were screaming for competent workers. The bosun thought they'd buy Glatun. Some Glatun survivors had eavesdropped on the crew debating what price they'd get.

"Father. Father!"

He jerked back to alertness as someone shook his shoulder.

Paladin was leaning over him. "Hey, Father, you with us?"

"Yeah. Sorry. I was focused on the data."

Julie shook her head. "I watched some of that but I was just horrified."

"Oh, there's a lot of good information if you filter it," said Father.

"Is there?" asked Paladin. "I didn't have time to go through half of it."

"Oh, yes." Realizing the rest of the crew were looking at him, Father summarized his findings. Eddie kept pacing around the table during the lecture.

"So they killed all their officers?" asked Dan.

"Killed, or just kicked them off the ship."

The back-up gunner said, "That's great! They won't be able to fight effectively. We can kick their asses!"

Father shook his head. "Doesn't make their ship any smaller. Or remove those point-defense laser clusters."

He reinforced the last comment with an image a Glatun took of the pirate ship razing half a town with fire from just one of those weapons.

"Can they get through our shield and armor?" asked Kathy.

"Not with one hit. They keep hitting us in the same place, they'll punch a hole through."

Ziggi grinned. "So I just have to keep us twisting and swooping so they can't hit the same spot twice."

"You want to fight?" Paladin asked her.

"I . . . don't know," said Ziggi reflectively. "Maybe we just leave some stuff to help the Glatun protect themselves and leave. Go someplace safer."

"Yes! Finally!" exclaimed Eddie. "We're not the Navy. Let's get the hell out of here."

He drew some glares.

Paladin said, "This isn't *Trade Hard*. We wanted to do *Trade Hard*, but the comic is about a tramp freighter as a completely independent agent. Like it or not, we're representing Earth. We don't want to, but the Glatun already see us that way. What we do reflects on Earth."

"Earth needs us to commit suicide?" demanded Eddie.

"No. We're not going to fight unless we have a plan to win. I don't see one yet. If we can't come up with a plan, we run."

Eddie sighed in relief.

Ziggi scrolled through the cargo list on her tablet. It was a mix of salvage grabbed to feed fabbers and cheap Earth-made goods that might be useful for rebuilding from an attack. Plus six drums of maple syrup Paladin had picked up cheap during the blockade.

"Can we give them those laser rifles?" she asked. Those had been part of the cleanup of *Thermopylae* after the battle.

Julie laughed. "What good would that do? They're made for Rangora. Too big for us to use. Hell, they're longer than a Glatun is tall."

"We're supposed to be making a profit," said Eddie. "Where's the profit in giving our cargo away?"

"Live customers," answered Kathy.

"Those could be crew-served weapons for the Glatun," said Father. "I'd need to work with some to see if we can do it."

Paladin frowned. "Crew-what?"

"We—the marines—have plenty of weapons too big for one guy to handle. I can try getting two or three Glatun to work with the Rangora weapons."

"So what good would that do?" carped Eddie.

Father eyed him patiently. "So we'd have a hundred or so Glatun participating in our fight against the pirates."

"What, we stand them in the cargo hatch and let them shoot while we're fighting the pirate ship?" scoffed Julie.

"No. We arm the Glatun. Set them hiding in the shantytown." Father waved at the shacks surrounding them. "When the pirates land, wait until they all come out and start sorting through the line. That's got to be most of their crew. Wait for the right moment and shoot them."

"That sounds like the start of a plan," said Paladin. "You work out the details. When you have the whole plan, present it to us. For now, we're going to adjourn this meeting."

Eddie scuffed his feet on the deck and glared at the captain. Paladin ignored him.

Most of the crew moved out of the lounge. Dan took the seat next to Father, wanting to help.

Father called, "Kathy? Could you help us out? You know the most about what's in the cargo."

"Sure." She took a seat on the opposite side of the table from Father and Dan.

Father diagrammed his concept for the ambush. Once the pirate crew was mostly dead or pinned down, *Eurynome* would pop up from hiding and disable the Rangora ship.

Kathy pointed out they didn't know of a hiding spot the pirates wouldn't detect or if the Glatun could actually operate the rifles.

The other two looked at each other. "Guess the division of labor on that is obvious," said Father.

He went down the ramp again. The Glatun mayor was still waiting, but he wasn't bothering with the kneeling anymore. More Glatun, some well dressed, had gathered to watch the humans. His appearance provoked a stir. Blue heads popped out of tents.

"Hello, human," said Mayor Wemath. "Can you save us?"

"We're trying to figure that out," said Father. "Would your people be willing to fight in their own defense?"

"Yes. Some of them. If we have weapons."

"We have weapons, but they weren't built for Glatun. I need some volunteers to work with me to see if those guns are usable for you."

One of the eavesdroppers sprang forward. "Me! I volunteer to fight."

The mayor waved it away. "Drilae, you're not old enough to vote yet."

Drilae did look a bit shorter than average, and the hair down its back hadn't fully grown out. "I can still fight."

"That's good enough for me," said Father. "Can we get eight volunteers?"

Two more stepped forward. Drilae started haranguing others. The mayor called for volunteers. Eventually there were six.

"You'll do. Come on, guys, I'll show you the weapons." Father led them up the ramp.

Drilae followed, looking back to call encouragement to the more hesitant volunteers.

Introducing the volunteers to the laser rifles quickly made Paladin realize he had to start with gun safety. Once the basics were handled, he took them out to the woods for some live-fire training.

The Glatun fiddled with the rifles, trying different holds. It was quickly apparent there was no practical way to use one solo. They paired up.

Working with them activated but with safety on led to a discovery: The sights would place an ultraviolet dot on the impact point—but only when there was an eye lined up with the sight.

That forced the arrangement for their firing teams. A Glatun, one whose implants could see UV, held the rifle sideways on its right shoulder, its eye lined up with the sight. Its partner stood behind, the stock resting on its left shoulder, ready to pull the trigger when the front Glatun called the command.

A nearby hill became the backstop for their firing range. A few trees were leveled as the Glatun learned how to get their rifles on the target.

Patricelli asked, "Should we invite other volunteers to come watch?"

They looked at each other. Drilae tilted its head side to side, a Glatun shrug. "We might find a few. But not many people want to fight."

Another volunteer said, "It's not like we can win. They're *Rangora.*"

Pep talk time. "Humans beat Rangora. Not just in the space battles. In the tunnels. Individual people shooting at each other with weapons like this. I had a rifle smaller than these. We still won. It's a matter of teamwork and training and using the terrain."

He started them competing to hit targets first as he designated them.

When Father paused to think on the next exercise, Drilae asked, "How do we keep the pirates from hitting us?"

"You've got one advantage already: you're smaller. Rangora are big targets. We'll also want to camouflage you."

"Camouflage?" asked Drilae.

"You want to disguise yourself as something else. That way they don't realize you're there. In the Marines we'd wear 'ghillie suits.' That way we'd look like a bush. Nobody shoots at a bush. So until you shoot and they realize you're not a bush, you're safe."

After some more shooting, he incentivized them for the final contest. "The team that hits first the most often will get an ounce of maple syrup. Second place, half an ounce. Third, quarter ounce."

Drilae and his partner won, but the others were close enough it was clear they could fight well.

Paladin didn't charge for the syrup. "I figured we were going to have to spend some."

The volunteers were turned loose to enjoy their drinks—Patricelli collected the rifles before letting them get drunk—and encouraged to recruit more volunteers.

Dan and Kathy were still working on the battle plan, now joined by Ziggi. "How'd it go?" asked Dan.

"They can hit the target, if we can get enough volunteers," said Father. "What do you have?"

"There's a canyon fifty kilometers from here we can hide *Eurynome* in. The timeline is pirates land, force the Glatun into their lineup, the volunteers hide in the shantytown. Then someone gives the signal—probably you—and the fight starts. *Eurynome* pops up, flies here, and starts shooting at the pirate ship before it can get its crew back on board."

Ziggi cheerfully added, "I've been working out some evasive maneuvers and ways to aim at the critical systems. We can cause a lot of damage fast."

Paladin had been standing in the hatchway. "I like it. How many shooters can you get?"

"That may be the hard part," said Father. "I only got half a dozen for the testing, and not all of them were super enthusiastic."

"Glatun culture has been pushing toward pacifism for generations. There's a stigma against the military, too," said Paladin. "So there's an uphill battle there."

"We need to inspire them," said Dan.

Kathy shook her head. "We barely understand their culture. How can we motivate them?"

"Tell them a story. Or show them a movie. Heck, show them *Seven Samurai*! It's perfect. We're in practically the same situation."

Ziggi laughed. "What, you'll narrate a translation as we show it to them?"

"Actually..." said Paladin. "Tyler Vernon translated a bunch of old movies for the Glatun. Adapted for their culture. He sent a copy of the whole library with us." The tycoon was a silent partner in *Eurynome*'s venture.

Dan demanded, "Does it have *Seven Samurai*?"

"Let me check... yes."

"All right! Time to show everybody a movie!"

Kathy shook her head. "Why would they want to watch?"

"We could bribe them," said Father. He looked at Paladin.

"Dammit, that stuff is trade goods. Fine. One drop each."

Mayor Wemath agreed to spread the word about the movie—and maple syrup.

Julie and Eddie hung a sheet of patch material off the side of the ship as the movie screen. "If they don't volunteer, we're out of here, right?" complained Eddie.

"Yes," said Paladin.

Word of maple syrup drew over a thousand Glatun to the showing. The mayor handled distribution, drafting its most trusted officials for holding the squeeze bottles. The show started when the sun was fully down.

The crew gathered around the projector. The movie opened with a brief statement from a Glatun scholar comparing feudal Japan to some pre-spaceflight periods of Glatun history. Then Kurosawa's epic began.

The Glatun were fascinated. Their culture's entertainment was polished and polite. This was rough and bold, with flaring emotions. They were used to understatement. The late Council of Benefactors would have suppressed the movie lest it inflame passions.

"Looks to be holding their attention," muttered Paladin.

"Yeah, but they all have implants," said Julie. "You never know what someone's really watching with implants."

Reactions matched the movie. The Glatun cheered when bandits were killed and wailed when a hostage villager burned to death.

"Hey, they changed the movie," complained Dan. "They took out the romance part."

Father nodded. "Glatun don't do romance."

Dan frowned. "They have to. They reproduce sexually."

"Look at the pouch under their bellies," said Father, pointing at some nearby spectators. "That's where the males and females live. They never get bigger than your fist. New neuters are raised as kids. New males and females go to someone else's pouch."

"They just hand them out?" Dan was shocked.

"No, not just. It's a big deal. But every Glatun you meet is a neuter."

The climactic battle held the crowd rapt. When the movie ended, the Glatun applauded.

"Okay, it's time to ask for volunteers," said Dan. "Make the speech, boss."

"What do you mean, me?" replied Paladin. "I don't have a speech ready. Father's the military guy."

"I'm a fucking corporal. I don't make speeches."

"God damn it." Dan strode out to stand in front of the screen, drawing the attention of the crowd. He connected his implant to the speakers that had broadcast the movie's soundtrack. What to say? They'd all watched the movie.

"The Rangora are bandits!" proclaimed Dan.

The crowd cheered their agreement.

"The Rangora are thieves and slavers!"

More agreement.

"They should be stopped!"

A hearty cheer.

"I'll fight them. There are Glatun who've volunteered to fight them. We have weapons for you!"

Father waved at his volunteers, who obediently blasted the tops off two trees.

Some of the crowd whooped in excitement, but more were shocked.

"With two hundred volunteers and our ship, we can put an end to the Rangora pirates!"

Confused mumbling.

"Step forward to volunteer to fight the Rangora! Be a villager defending your family, your neighbors, your world!"

Drilae ran forward to stand by Dan. He called on some other Glatun by name.

More joined them. Some shouted to others. A few seemed to be pushed into the group around Dan by others pressing through the crowd, but weren't bold enough to leave on their own.

"Thank you all for volunteering! This is enough help for us to fight the Rangora."

With no clue what to do next, Dan turned an imploring look on his crewmates.

Father stepped forward. "Volunteers, you will start training in the morning. We'll train you in how to use a rifle and give you some practice. We'll be ready to fight the battle by the time the Rangora get here. Get some sleep—you'll need it."

The Glatun cheered. Then the assembly broke up.

Eddie carped, "You noticed most of the samurai died, right? Tell me everybody noticed that."

There were fewer volunteers in the morning. But there were still over two hundred. Father gave them all the initial lecture, then brought up the first six to demonstrate how to operate a rifle as a pair.

Once the basic concepts were explained, he and the first six started taking groups out to the woods to practice actually firing. As the volunteers practiced, he selected the more adept ones to become trainers. Drilae had a gift as a trainer—he could spot when a pair was incompatible and split them up to work with different partners.

The training was easier than Marine marksmanship training.

Most of the recruits were grown-ups, skilled professionals, instead of testosterone-charged adolescents. When someone demonstrated competence, the others recognized that and tried to learn from it. Father could let the Glatun handle teaching rifles.

Now he had time to train the plan for the ambush. He took Wemath and Drilae to where the landing pad met the central plaza.

The mayor explained, "The Rangora pattern is to touch down on the landing pad and make everyone line up in the plaza. They blow up a building to frighten everyone into obeying. Then they come out and test our implants for skills they want in slaves. The slaves are set aside, the rest are dismissed, then they load the slaves into their ship."

Father waved at the shanty town. "When everyone else lines up, we want the rifle teams hidden in the tents and shacks."

"Should we disguise ourselves as bushes?" asked Drilae, confusing the heck out of the mayor.

"No. A bush would stand out there. The Rangora would think it was strange and investigate it. Though . . . do you have any clothes that cover you completely?"

"Such as rain gear?" said Wemath. "Of course."

"Get some. We do need to make you some camouflage."

Ziggi had this shift's watch on board *Eurynome*. There wasn't much to do, so she passed the time re-reading one of the *Trade Hard* collections.

The radio speaker crackled. "Human ship." It was an artificially generated voice. Sign of a low-quality implant. Couldn't be a Glatun.

"Who's calling?" replied Ziggi.

"This is the *Skull*. This is our world. Leave or we will destroy you."

"It's a Glatun world. The Rangoran Empire promised the Terran Alliance it would evacuate all Glatun worlds."

"The Empire is not here. The Alliance is not here. We are here. We will destroy you if you are not gone in five hours."

She decided the Rangora could have the last word. She switched to the all-crew channel. "Hey, everyone, we have a problem. We've been noticed."

They all gathered on the bridge. Ziggi replayed the conversation.

"Let 'em come," said Dan. "We want to fight them, now's good."

Patricelli barked, "Now is not good. We want the pirates to land like their usual plan, not attack our ship."

"Run to the hiding spot?" asked Kathy.

Ziggi shook her head. "If they spotted us here, they'd probably see us going there. We'd need the whole planet between us to not be detected again. Well, at least a good chunk of the planet."

"Let's do it the other way," said Paladin. "We go attack them, weakly, let them chase us off. Then they'll think they won and stick with their routine. *Eurynome* goes and hides until the signal is given. Then return for a full power attack."

The navigation display let Ziggi trace out the potential course. "We run into deep space, get out of detection range, then go get in the blind cone from the planet and return to the other side. We can hole up over the horizon and wait for your signal."

"Comments?" asked the captain.

Most liked the plan. Eddie hated it.

Father said, "I'll need to stay here. Can anyone else stay with me to help set up the ambush?"

"There won't be any cargo handling in the fight," said Kathy. "I'll join you."

Everyone else would be needed for operating the ship or doing damage control. Father gave a few quick tips to Dan before debarking.

As *Eurynome* flew away, Mayor Wemath asked, "Will your ship not be helping us fight the pirates?"

Kathy answered, "We want our ship's presence in the fight to be a surprise. It's going to try to convince the Rangora it's left the planet."

Wemath watched the Liberty Ship head toward the horizon. "I do not doubt you. I'm sure it will be back for you two."

Beside them, Patricelli opened the metal cases he'd carried off the ship and inspected the contents.

Dan ran through the inspection checklist for *Eurynome*'s laser cannon. Cannon, check. Turret motors, check. Power supply, check. Gunner: green as grass. Dan wished someone more experienced could be doing this job. But Father was off playing guerilla warrior, and Dan wasn't qualified for that.

He set the cannon for one terawatt. "Sandbagging," Father had called it. They needed to conceal their strength for the real fight.

Ziggi had the pirate ship marked on the navigation display, which Dan had up on his console.

The ship was in view! It was a brick. There were turrets at each corner of the brick. It stood upon ten landing legs. The bow had a ramp down that looked big enough a tank could drive up it. Maybe two tanks.

A synthesized voice came across the channel. "Die, you hairy vermin!"

Dan's seat straps dug hard into his side as the ship pivoted at high acceleration. He saw flashes of light out his window. The pirate was firing on them.

They'd missed clean. The antimissile clusters were intended for wide coverage to deal with swarms of missiles. A single target at this distance was hard for them to hit.

Only one of *Eurynome*'s turrets could bear on the pirate. Dan aimed for the nearest laser cluster on the pirate and fired.

The Rangoran ship's shields darkened as they absorbed the energy.

Dan cursed at himself and turned off one of the lasers in the turret. Sandbagging again. He opened fire. It looked like he was hitting where he wanted to, right on the laser cluster on the near corner, but the Rangora shields were keeping him from doing any damage.

Frustrating. But acceptable. It was part of the sandbagging.

Eurynome kept swooping back and forth, mostly avoiding the enemy fire. Dan had an indicator light for the status of *Eurynome*'s shield in the corner of his console. It stayed green, though it flickered to a lighter shade whenever the enemy landed a few bolts on the shield.

Dan kept his fire going. He kept having to switch turrets as Ziggi twisted the ship, blocking the line of sight from one or the other. He was starting to hurt everywhere his straps held him.

In theory, the enemy ship could bring four laser clusters to bear in any direction. More of them were becoming active. They must be getting their crew to their fighting positions.

Three clusters were firing at once at *Eurynome*. Ziggi jinked, but the cone of fire hit the ship. The shield indicator flashed yellow.

Ziggi went around to the port side of the pirate ship, blocking the line of sight for one of the active clusters. Then more opened up. All four were firing on this side!

The shield indicator went yellow—and stayed there. No, green, but just a brief flicker of it before going back to yellow. Ziggi put the ship through some even more violent twists.

Paladin's voice came over the intercom. "This is the captain of the human ship. You win, you have more firepower. We're leaving." There was a pause as he muted the ship-to-ship channel. "Dan, cease fire. We want to look like we gave up."

Eurynome was zooming away from the planet. Ziggi still put twists on the course, but as the range to the pirate ship increased the Rangora laser clusters were too dispersed to put many hits on the ship. The yellow indicator light darkened into the green.

"All hands, *Skull* isn't pursuing us. Stand down. Rest up. Tomorrow's going to be a busy day."

Father strode over to Kathy. "What?"

Kathy was standing between a couple of tents, avoiding one of the drifts of trash that were spread throughout the shanty town thrown up by the refugees. "How soon do you need the ghillie suits finished?" she asked.

"I need them now. We don't know how soon the Rangora will be here. Everyone has to be camouflaged by the time they're close enough to see movement."

"Show him," she said.

The pile of trash stood up. Two roughly Glatun-shaped forms were connected by a tube. Every part of them was covered with wrappers, boxes, bottles, or other detritus.

"That's good. Now make them for everybody."

Father turned to deal with his next problem: convincing the mayor to make everyone with a tent or shack on the edge let a rifle team camp out in their place.

Drilae was already working the problem on the individual level, getting permission from the best positioned shacks to occupy them.

Mayor Wemath was surrounded by gesturing Glatun. So many were talking at once Father's implant couldn't break out any of the conversation. But when he saw the human approaching the mayor waved the others away. "Father. How may I help you?"

"We need to have all the rifle teams in place before the Rangora get here."

"I know. That's what the argument"—he waved at the other Glatun around him—"was about. I will get their permission."

Father's spine unkinked a bit. "Thank you."

Father started assigning teams to their places. Marine doctrine said he should be building an L-shaped ambush, so the lines of fire wouldn't cross. Instead he was lining both sides with rifle teams. The firers would be prone on the ground, firing up. The Rangora would be towering above the Glatun, about twice their height. With everyone shooting up, there should be no danger of a team on one side shooting their counterpart on the other.

As the sun lowered, Father relaxed. The pirate raids only took place during daylight. From the pattern the locals were predicting the Rangora would follow, the raid would be during the day tomorrow.

He circulated among his troops, giving little pep talks, reminding them all they needed to be in their places before dawn, and encouraging them to sleep in position. "Remember: once you can see or hear the ship, don't move. Make sure your implant is on non-transmitting. Pick a target. Don't fire until you hear me fire. Then shoot as many Rangora as you can."

Father inspected his gear. Marine-issue laser rifle. Spare power pack. His battle armor, vacuum-rated. Overbuilt for this fight. But he was happy to have the armor. It should be turned in at Camp Pendleton, where his punitive discharge would be finalized. Patricelli had been too honest in his opinion of a butterbar's orders during the tunnel fight. *Eurynome* had taken him on while he was waiting on *Thermopylae* for his trip back to Earth.

Thinking on the fight ahead, he realized he felt good about the odds. Sure, he had troops with only the barest familiarization with the weapons they held, no formal training, and no experience of violence. But the enemy were swabbies in it for the money, who'd destroyed the authority of their chain of command. This would be the first time the pirates encountered resistance. The shock alone should shatter their morale.

He slept soundly.

He woke to a message from his implant. "Pirates in sight." The Glatun voice was clearly nervous.

The ship roared as it hovered over the landing pad. A flat artificial voice spoke in Glatun. "All inhabitants form line before us. If you do not report for inspection, this town will be destroyed."

The crack of a laser firing sounded. From previous raids, probably shooting the top off the tallest building in town. The line-up order kept repeating.

Through the periscope he could see Glatun straggling into the open area of the plaza. They assembled into a rough line. More kept coming.

The pirate ship touched down, turning off its thrusters. The announcement kept repeating.

Glatun were soon packed belly-to-butt along the length of the plaza.

The loading ramp on the ship's bow began to lower. The clang as the ramp struck the pavement startled the first rank of Glatun into flinching back. Rotating his periscope to look at the whole line, Father estimated there were close to two thousand there, and new ones were adding themselves to the end of the line.

Rangora strode down the ramp. Some were dressed for battle, with laser rifles and torso armor. Others wore utility uniforms and carried electronics or just clubs.

A couple of the rifle-armed ones took positions at the corners of the ramp. The rest with weapons began pacing down the line, making threatening gestures at any Glatun bold enough to look up at them.

The two with the electronics boxes began going down the line, pressing their boxes to the head of each Glatun. Most were told to sit down, in a harsh synthetic voice. A few Glatun were selected as slaves and told to go aboard. They obediently shuffled forward, hurried by Rangora with clubs tapping them on the back.

How soon to start the ambush? He wanted the Rangora as far from the ship as possible so they couldn't run back aboard and man their stations again. The farther down the line they were, the closer they'd be to the rest of the rifle teams. On the flip side, he wanted to start it before some volunteer lost his nerve and started shooting on his own.

This would have to do. Father aimed at one of the Rangora on the base of the ramp. He fired, scarring its helmet. A second shot punched through the visor. The Rangora fell.

He activated his radio. "It's started! It's started!" The transmission would bounce off the ionosphere to reach *Eurynome*, hiding over the horizon, and then the ship would have to fly all the way here. Hopefully they'd get here before the battle was over.

Shots were coming from all along the line, a few crackles at first then building up to a roar of fire. He saw a club-waving Rangora drop from three simultaneous shots while the rifleman beside him took none. The Glatun in the line dropped prone and started crawling away—mostly. Some panicked and ran, too many of them catching laser blasts in the cross fire.

The rifle-armed Rangora were shooting back, initially at random but it didn't take them long to spot where the fire was coming from. The shots ignited the trash the rifle teams hid among.

The other Rangora guarding the ramp went down to Father's fire. He'd returned fire in the marine's general direction. No hits.

Okay, he'd ignited the cover Father was using. His armor would keep the smoke out, but he'd get warm if all the trash caught.

His implants translated the shouts of the shocked Rangora. It was all variations on, "What the fuck?" with Rangora-specific profanity. Didn't sound like anyone was trying to organize them yet.

Father put one of the slave-testers down with a shot to the head.

The ship opened fire on the shantytown, igniting a row of shacks.

Dan was bored. The software they'd bought for controlling the cannon turrets included a "training program" that was a basic video game. A dull one.

Father's voice came across the PA. "It's started! It's started!"

Dan was pressed into his seat by ten gees of acceleration. Ziggi had warned everybody she would hit the throttle as soon as they had the word.

The acceleration backed off as drag forces built up. They were going through the atmosphere about as fast as they safely could.

In mere minutes, the pirate brick appeared on Dan's control screen. It was firing on the Glatun. Was there anyone left for the crew to rescue?

The laser cannon were dialed up to their full four terawatts each. As they zoomed down on the pirate, all four could target the same point. Dan opened up.

Only one cluster on the pirate ship was firing. Dan focused on it. The target's shields darkened as they absorbed the energy. He kept the beams focused on the same point.

The cluster firing on the Glatun shantytown pivoted to aim at the humans. Ziggi was bouncing the ship around enough it didn't score more than a few hits.

Eurynome went past the Rangora ship, putting the targeted cluster out of line of sight.

Dan muttered curses as they pivoted around the pirate. Only one turret could bear on it. He went for the nearest cluster and poured on the power.

Another laser cluster on the pirate ship opened up on *Eurynome*. It was topside, but opposite the one that had fired on the shantytown. Dan switched his fire to it.

Ziggi pivoted in another evasive maneuver, putting the firing turret out of sight of the pirate ship.

Dan swore as he switched to the other turret. Once the two cannon were focused on his target, he thumbed his push to talk switch. "Ziggi, can you keep us facing front toward them? That lets me use all the lasers."

"I'll try," came the response.

Eurynome turned toward the pirate, then side-slipped erratically.

Dan's stomach lurched. He looked away from the window, concentrating on the outline of the pirate ship on his console display. The horizon shouldn't wiggle like that.

Quadruple four-terawatt beams focused on the cluster. The pirate's shield turned black. Then there was a gap in the force-field. Dan's fire struck the pirate ship. The laser cluster's steady stream of bolts became intermittent, then stopped.

"Yes!" he crowed.

The slide-slip maneuver took them out of sight of his target. Dan looked for something vulnerable. They were at the aft side of the pirate ship. He picked a weapon cluster and concentrated on it..

Too many Rangora had spotted Patricelli's position. He retreated as the shack went up in flames. "It's a good thing they can't shoot worth a damn."

If he could find a good firing position, there were plenty of targets. Rangora were running back to the pirate ship, most of them unarmored. He ran through the back of the shanty town, looking for a shack not on fire.

Realizing he probably wasn't the only one with this problem, he transmitted an order to the volunteers. "If you don't have any pirates to shoot at, go to the outside of the shantytown and run toward the bow of the ship. Move in and shoot at the ramp."

Hopefully they could hear it over the sound of *Eurynome* flying by.

A narrow slit appeared between two shacks near the ship. Father fired at Rangora he glimpsed passing in front of it. Then one shack burst into flame. He kept moving forward.

Stepping out of the shantytown, he saw most of the Rangora left outside were going up the ramp. He plinked at the stragglers.

Two armored Rangora trotted down the ramp, carrying some equipment he didn't recognize. He opened fire. They both ducked behind one of the landing legs of the ship.

Father glimpsed activity as the two worked at putting something together. He advanced cautiously, aiming at the edge of the landing leg, ready to fire the moment one stepped out.

Pieces of the equipment swung about, flashing into view for just a second. An empty case bounced on the pavement, tossed aside by an impatient pirate.

He looked at the shape of the case. He realized they were assembling a tripod-launched anti-ship missile. One that would take down a *Myrmidon*. It would rip apart something as flimsy as *Eurynome*.

Father charged the landing leg, firing at maximum rate. A low-battery warning beeped but he kept firing. He swept the landing leg, keeping fire on both sides of it. "Suppress the bastards," he muttered, legs pounding.

Eurynome swept over them, laser cannon frying the air as they concentrated on the pirate ship.

The missile pivoted to track its target. The nose poked out from behind the landing leg. One of Father's shots struck the armed warhead.

He saw a bright flash.

A bright flash from his window distracted Dan from his console for a moment. There was a cloud of dust at the forward corner of the pirate ship. Flashing pulses from one of the cluster batteries reminded him to not play tourist.

"Good shot, Dan!" said Paladin over the intercom.

"Wasn't me." He put his cannon back on target.

"Then somebody's helping us out."

The pirate ship lifted off the ground. Its bow ramp was closing slowly.

"Whoops, I'd better give it some more room," called Ziggi.

A couple more of the previously silent laser clusters opened up on *Eurynome*. The shield-strength indicator flickered to a lighter green.

Only one turret could bear as Ziggi flew *Eurynome* away from the pirate ship. Dan fired as best he could. Once they had maneuvering room, Ziggi returned to the face-it-and-side-slip dance.

The pirate ship lifted several hundred meters into the air and pivoted.

Dan said, "Ziggi, it's bringing four active clusters to bear."

She cursed. "It can turn faster than we can circle it."

"Then keep us facing it so I can concentrate my fire!"

She didn't answer. But *Eurynome* danced back and forth, trying to evade the pirates' fire without moving far.

Focusing all four laser cannons on one of the clusters strained the pirate ship's shield. *Eurynome*'s shield was also straining as the additional clusters struck her, the shield gauge dropping toward the yellow. It would bip back into the dark green when one of Ziggi's evasions outguessed the Rangora, but the gunners on the enemy ship were learning.

Dan was learning himself. Concentrating on a single point forced the shield toward a local overload. Another laser cluster was blown apart as the shield failed over it.

The pirates twisted their ship again, putting four working clusters facing *Eurynome* again. The shield gauge dipped farther into the yellow. The Rangora were spreading their fire over the whole ship, which meant they wouldn't have local breakthroughs. They'd just hammer the shield until it collapsed and the whole ship was exposed.

Pick a target. Focus on it. Hope it was destroyed before *Eurynome*'s shields collapsed. Repeat.

Then the pirate ship twisted again, bringing four different clusters to bear.

Paladin spoke over the intercom. "Dan, we're looking at the stern of the thing. Can you put a hole in their engines?"

"I'll try." Dan shifted his focus point, aiming for the corner of one of the four modules on the stern of the pirate ship. He ignored the rain of fire coming back the other direction.

Breakthrough! A hole appeared on the pirate's stern. No dramatic sparks, but the ship lurched, its stern dropping.

"Good!" cried Paladin. "Do it again!"

Dan picked another module and aimed for its center.

The pirates were learning. The ship yawed, putting its stern out of sight.

"Hold on," said Ziggi. "I'll get behind it again."

She used strong thrust, pushing Dan into his seat, and cut across the circle, bringing them close to the pirate as she went to the other side of it.

The pirate laser clusters were designed to spread their fire to catch more missiles. As *Eurynome* passed closer, the fire hit a tighter area.

The shield gauge flashed red. There'd been a burn-through.

The ship lurched, dropping altitude for a moment before Ziggi recovered control. "Eddie, we lost a thruster," said the pilot. "Can you balance it? I'm getting some pitch torque here."

Dan started firing as the pirate's thruster modules came into view. The shield blackened under the intense power.

"Eddie?" called Ziggi again.

There was a longer pause. Julie's voice came on the intercom. "I'm on it. We have a hull breach lower aft port, try to keep that turned away from them."

"Working it."

Dan kept the fire on the module. The breakthrough came. No sparks, but a satisfying shower of debris sprayed from the pirate. He moved to a new target.

"Good work, Dan," said Paladin. "It's descending. Doesn't have enough thrust to maintain altitude."

Time to switch back to the laser clusters before they burned another hole in *Eurynome*. The shield gauge was pale orange now.

Ziggi put the ship into a loop-the-loop, escaping enough shots to let the shield gauge go yellow again.

That drew curses from Dan as he tried to keep his cannon on target.

The cluster he was aiming at blew apart as the shield parted for a moment.

He took a broader look to choose his next target—and kept looking, wide eyed, as the pirate ship plowed into the Glatun city's tallest buildings. He winced at the devastation. Hopefully everyone in them had left for the lineup and fled into the woods when the fighting started.

Fire from the laser clusters on the underside cut off as masonry ground them away.

That left one intact top side cluster facing them. Dan switched his fire to it.

Paladin copied his broadcast to the intercom. "Human ship *Eurynome* to pirate ship *Skull*. Surrender now or we will destroy you."

Dan kept his fire going. The pirates were still shooting. With only one cluster hitting them, the gauge was darkening toward green again.

"We agree to cease fire," said a synthetic voice.

The laser cluster stopped firing. So did Dan.

Kathy stood in a crowd of Glatun, all watching the ships fight. It was hard to tell who was winning. Shields flickered, lasers kept firing, the ships maneuvered. Then the pirate drooped. It drifted down.

She expected it to pull out, but it crashed. She could see part of its hull rip open where it smacked into a building, though the building was decapitated.

The Glatun cheered.

She started forward. The shantytown was mostly ashes now.

Bodies were everywhere. Some dead Rangora. No wounded Rangora. The injured Glatun were being helped away. The dead—would be taken care of later.

One body—part body—caught her eye. Drilae lay on the pavement, a determined look on its face. It'd been hit by one of the ship's lasers. The belly and hips were gone, vaporized. No blood. The edges were cauterized. The legs lay beside the body.

Kathy turned away, hands on her knees, taking deep breaths. She'd worked with the eager volunteer to get everyone into those ghillie suits.

There was work to do. She straightened up and started walking, signaling Patricelli on his implant. He'd said he was going to go silent before the battle but he should be turned back on now.

The spot where the pirate had landed was marked by Rangora bodies. There was a scorched mark, which must've been that explosion she'd heard. Patricelli should be around here.

She saw the arm first. It was a human arm. There were Glatun and Rangora ones around to compare it to. It was in the Marine battle armor Father had dressed in for the battle.

Kathy looked around for the rest of him. If he lost the arm but his armor managed to seal the blood vessels, he could have survived.

She saw a young Glatun walking toward her, holding Father's helmet.

Paladin's voice came across her implant. "Kathy, we have a ceasefire with the pirate. Can you come over and do the surrender negotiations? You're the best at talking to people. We should probably get the mayor in on this, too."

"Right. I'll find the mayor and get on that."

The young Glatun said, "I found part of your friend, what should I do with it?"

The helmet wasn't empty. Kathy took a deep breath and let the wave of dizziness pass over her. When it was gone, she said, "Put it with his arm. We'll take care of the dead later. Right now we have to take care of the living. Do you know where the mayor is?"

Kathy and Mayor Wemath walked up to the pirate ship. She thought it could be spaceworthy with some work. Which was part of what she'd been discussing with the mayor.

The ship's ramp was lowered. One corner pressed into the grass. A Rangora in utilities picked its way carefully down the canted ramp.

"Greetings. I am Purser Kathy. This is Mayor Wemath. We are here to discuss the terms of your surrender."

"I am Captain Zhoen. If you do not let us repair our ship and leave, we will destroy this town."

The mayor's spinal mane bristled.

Kathy said, "We are prepared to negotiate an agreement that will let you leave. But we're willing to kill you all if you're not cooperative."

She knew Dan was ready to open up on the pirate the moment she gave the word.

The Rangora slumped. "What do you propose?"

"You release all your captives. We will let you repair the damage to your engines so you can make it to the gate. You will allow Glatun inspectors to search your ship to verify you've cooperated with the agreement."

"No." Zhoen folded his arms, not expanding on the statement.

"Do you think you can get a better deal from us?"

"Doesn't matter. If you send us away empty-handed, we're all dead anyway. So we might as well die here and make the rest of you suffer along with us."

The pirate captain was speaking Rangora. Kathy's implant declared the tone was sincere and calm.

"Why are you going to die?" she asked.

"We're mutineers. Unless we have enough money to buy a new life, we'll all be executed."

Kathy had to admit that was an obstacle to a negotiated agreement. "Let me think a moment."

The mayor's implant couldn't translate Rangora, so she'd set hers to relay to it. It transmitted, "I'll be ground up before I give them anything valuable."

"If we want their prisoners back, we might have to pay something," she transmitted back.

"True," was the grudging reply.

She asked the Rangora, "Who knows you mutinied?"

"All of us. And anyone who sees our officers are dead."

The inspiration hit Kathy in a flash. "Go to your fleet. Tell them you were attacked by a Terran ship and all your officers were killed in the battle. You have enough battle damage to make it convincing. They'll take you back."

Zhoen stepped back in surprise. "That . . . that might work. Let me talk to my crew." He turned away.

Mayor Wemath transmitted, "I'd rather kill them all."

She silently replied, "I agree. But we're going to wind up with an agreement that leaves everyone dissatisfied."

After a few minutes the pirate captain turned back to them. "We'd need more damage to make it convincing. Can you put a laser shot into our bridge?"

"We'd be happy to."

"Good." The Rangora paused. "Is it true humans rescued the survivors of the E Eridani battle?"

"Yes. Our ship was part of that effort. We brought back hundreds of humans and Rangora." Not very comfortably, and not all were alive, but they were brought back.

"Then we agree to your conditions." Zhoen held out his hand.

Kathy and Mayor Wemath shook it in turn.

"I've ordered my crew to release your people."

Some Glatun appeared at the top of the ramp. They came down balancing cautiously. A few decided to take it on hands and knees. After one slipped and rolled down, more went to hands and knees.

Wemath picked up and embraced the one who rolled off the end of the ramp. It embraced the rest as they reached it.

The Glatun had no objection to digging two graves next to their memorial garden.

Patricelli's grave was smaller. All the pieces had been found. The Glatun stacked them in a neat pile.

The burn-through in *Eurynome*'s hull had flung molten silica over Eddie. Now that the glass had cooled, his body was held in the pose he'd been at his death, reaching up to adjust something. It made for an oversized grave.

As Glatun volunteers shoveled the last of the dirt over the graves, Paladin stood ready with the ship's Bible to read the funeral service. Kathy stood between Ziggi and Dan as the crew lined up before the graves. Rows and rows of Glatun stood behind them.

Julie was on the other side of Dan. Kathy heard her whisper, "If you quote that damn movie, I'll stab you."

Glancing up at Dan's face, Kathy thought he wasn't going to say anything. He looked shocked at how high the price of playing hero had been.

She thought it was a hell of a long way from playing *Trade Hard*.

Glatun shared the tradition of a meal following a funeral. Kathy met Drilae's "parent," the neuter who'd hosted the volunteer's gestation, and praised the young Glatun's contribution to the victory.

As the party wound down, Mayor Wemath found Kathy again. "You spoke of trading with us. Our most urgent need is a hypercomm node, do you have one?"

"We don't have a complete node, but we do have some of the key components. If you can check your stock of parts, let's see if we can provide what you still need. What do you have to offer us?"

"There's an excess of service robots from the leisure resorts, we'd be happy to trade those."

Kathy replied, "We don't have any use for those, but I suppose we might be able to trade them to people in better circumstances."

Companies on Earth would pay big to reverse engineer top-of-the-line Glatun robots. An hour of dickering ended with a list of the parts and robots to be exchanged. Mayor Wemath wasn't feeling screwed, which was a violation of the *Trade Hard* ethos. Kathy was fine with that. Once the Glatun Federation was back on its feet, their big corporations would discover Earth now had some of their key intellectual property. They'd feel screwed. That was enough for Kathy.

The party was breaking up. Glatun drifted away. Some returned to their home. Some were cleaning the debris of the shantytown. Refugees were gathering with others to organize returns to their towns, or what the pirates had left of them.

Eurynome's crew were drifting back to the ship. Probably wanting their bunks. It had been a stressful day. Kathy was too energized from the negotiation to sleep. She looked around to see who was staying up.

She almost missed Dan in the long shadows cast by the setting sun. He'd gone back to the graves, sitting by Father's and Eddie's feet.

Kathy watched him for a minute. He wasn't praying, or saying anything, or doing anything she could tell. She went over and quietly sat next to him.

A few minutes went by before Dan spoke. "It's not right."

"No, it's not," she agreed.

"I feel like I murdered Eddie."

"The Rangora killed him," Kathy protested.

"Yeah. But he was there to be killed because I wanted to fight the pirates. If I'd kept my mouth shut, we'd've left the planet and Eddie and Father would still be alive."

She shook her head. "It wasn't just you. I wanted to keep our customers. Paladin and Ziggi wanted to fight, they just didn't have a plan for how to do it. Julie was up for it when she thought we could win."

"So we all forced Eddie into a fight he didn't want."

"He signed the articles, just like us. It's not a democracy. Paladin could have said we're leaving and you would have obeyed."

Dan picked up a stick and started poking holes in the dirt. "I know. But I helped talk Paladin into it."

"Yes, along with me and Father. You don't seem too upset about losing Father."

"I am. I miss him more than Eddie, if I'm being honest. But… him dying is his own fault. He volunteered. Eddie was drafted."

"True." Kathy thought a moment. "Eddie volunteered for this trip. We all knew it would be dangerous. We didn't expect to play knight-errant when we set out. But *Trade Hard* had plenty of stories where the ship was attacked by pirates. If we'd been more careless, or they wanted more loot, the Rangora might have attacked us to take our cargo. Or take us as slaves. That's a risk Eddie was running when he came on board."

"That's true." Dan leaned back on his arms, lifting his eyes from the graves to the stars. "So what do we do next?"

"Load the cargo I just bought. Go back to Earth and sell it."

He looked at her. "Will it cover our fuel costs?"

"High-end personal service bots full of proprietary Glatun tech? The corps will be falling all over each other to dissect them. We'll have a profit, which will let us upgrade the ship, even after making some payments to Father's and Eddie's relatives."

Dan jumped to his feet. "We'd better get to work, then."

THE HOLDOUTS

Chris Kennedy

Limaror Orbital, Kalindra System

The fall of Glatun society, when it came, happened even more quickly than the "experts" had forecast. Although the Glatun Navy fought better than expected, "better" wasn't good enough, and the Rangora invaders swept through the length and breadth of the entire Glatun polity in what seemed like days, a massive wave that rolled over nearly everything in its path. That wave had diminished greatly by the time it reached the Kalindra System, though, and only three battlecruisers, along with a single cruiser, had arrived to capture it.

Sadly, that was still enough.

"I have to get you out of here," Tomkaut Altha said as the last Glatun cruiser detonated on the hologram.

Rolaut Orth ruffled his back hair in exasperation. "If we'd only had one more ship! All they have left is their stupid cruiser."

"Unfortunately, that's enough to hold the orbitals," Altha replied, motioning toward the door, "and it hasn't used any of its kinetic energy weapons yet. Depending on their mood, things are going to get . . . spicy here on the orbital, and then for the people on the planet below."

"Regardless, I refuse to simply give in to them," Orth said. He shuddered. "Living under their rule would be horrific."

Altha nodded. "They're certainly going to take everything away from you—your money, residences, and even your staff—leaving you with nothing. And that's if they let you live, and don't send you to a torture planet."

"What do you think, Keltar?"

"That seems most likely," the Level V AI running the orbital replied. "I, for one, do not look forward to them capturing me and raping my data centers."

"What are we to do, though?" Orth asked.

Altha looked the Benefactor in the eye. "Do you trust me?"

"With my life."

Altha glanced over at the speaker, through which the AI's voice had come. "Keltar, initiate Operation Holdout."

Contrary to the Rangoran media reports, the Glatun homeworld *hadn't* welcomed the Rangorans with open arms, but with the missiles and lasers of the remaining ships of their navy. Unfortunately, the Rangorans had crushed the Glatun Navy there—like it had everywhere else—and replied with kinetic-energy weapons across the surface of the homeworld.

Open-armed Glatun citizens were in even shorter supply after the conquest.

Warned by Niazgol Gorku of the Gorku Corporation, though, Orth—the head of Limaror Corporation and one of the five wealthiest Glatuns—had scraped together what he could and had fled, barely ahead of the Rangorans' arrival, and had gone to the farthest major planet in the polity, hoping that the Rangoran wave would fully dissipate prior to reaching it.

Sadly, it had not.

Three Rangoran battlecruisers and a cruiser had entered the system the day before, and the Glatun fleet—only two battlecruisers and a few in-system patrol craft—had responded. As they had so far in the war, the Glatun Navy outfought the Rangorans, only to lose due to the reptiles' greater numbers. They'd destroyed the Rangorans' battlecruisers, but the enemy's cruiser had survived.

Long before that happened, though, Tomkaut Altha, the Benefactor's personal security assistant, had developed a variety of plans with Keltar, based on what happened when the Rangorans arrived. They ran the gamut from a crushing defeat to what they'd do next if the Glatun Navy had held. The current situation was somewhere in the middle, and Altha had a plan for it.

The first—and by far the most important thing to Altha—was the safety of Rolaut Orth, something that could not be achieved if he remained on the orbital.

"Come with me, please," Altha said, taking the Benefactor's arm and leading Orth to the door of the suite. It slid to the side as they approached, and Selban Garand walked through it.

"Holdout?" Altha's second-in-command asked.

"Already in progress." Altha passed the Benefactor to Garand. "Go to the hideout and stay there until either Keltar or I contact you."

Garand nodded, then glanced at Orth. "Let's go."

"But Tomkaut, what—"

"I'll be doing what you pay me to do. Keeping you safe. Go with Selban and let me do that, please. No questions. You can work on figuring out what we do next, assuming I'm able to eliminate the Rangoran cruiser."

"Very well," Orth replied. "I can do that." He turned to Garand. "Lead on."

"What's the status?" Altha asked after the other two Glatuns left. He was already in motion, gathering his weapons and bug-out bag.

"I'm almost through changing the records of the Benefactor's presence on the orbital. As it now appears, the Benefactor was supposed to come to this system but never arrived and was presumed lost. If the Rangorans capture the orbital, that's all they'll find. Your shuttle is waiting in Bay Twenty-Seven and has already received clearance to depart for the capital on the planet below. Records will show that it never arrived and was also presumed lost in today's conflict."

"Very well," Altha replied, opening the secret door to the AI's data core. "When you're finished with the protocols, shut down, and we'll get out of here, too."

"Hi, Grub."

The giant purple caterpillar froze. "You know I hate that name."

Altha smiled as he scanned the interior of the warehouse. "Yeah, well I can't pronounce that mouthful of letters you Oguts use for naming things."

Grub turned around with a sigh. "What do you want, Altha?"

"Is that any way to greet a friend?"

"No." Grub tilted his head. "But then again, we aren't friends."

Altha feigned hurt. "You wound me. Haven't I always brought you great opportunities that made you lots of credits?"

"Opportunities that were . . . quasi-legal at best." When Altha didn't say anything, he added, "But yes, they did bring me a lot of money."

"Well, cheer up. This is straight from the Benefactor and totally aboveboard, and it's going to pay you a *lot* of money."

"I'd heard that the Benefactor picked you—a short-nose from here on the periphery—to be his new security chief. I also found it interesting that the person you saved him from to get the job was one of your past . . . associates, shall we say?"

"Perhaps. We can discuss that another time. What's more important, right now, is that I'm on his staff and know what's going on with the Rangorans. Our way of life—the way we knew it, anyway—is going to end if they take the planet."

Grub turned back to what he'd been working on. "The Rangora are here, and they've beaten our fleet. I would say that taking the planet is pretty much a fait accompli at this point."

"I have a plan that may end the Rangoran threat to this system. The Benefactor has blessed it."

"Is this a temporary ending, or one that will last for all times?"

"Nothing lasts forever." Altha shook his head slowly. "But I have a way, I think, to end this specific threat from the Rangora. More importantly, this system hasn't been broken yet. It still has its manufacturing capacity, and we can use it—"

"To what? Out-manufacture the entire Rangoran empire? With the output of just one system? You—and the rest of us here—are going to get steamrolled by their next wave of starships."

"Part of why the Rangora have been so successful in their invasion was because it was a surprise. Now that we know—"

"How are you going to stop a Rangoran battlecruiser?"

"Strap rocket motors to large asteroids and accelerate them at the gate area when the Rangora come through? I don't know yet, but I don't have to. We can deal with the next wave after we finish off this one. Right now, all that matters is getting rid of the cruiser that's here." Altha craned his neck. "The one you're putting food together for."

"You think you can hit the ship with an asteroid?" The Ogut scoffed. "Won't the cruiser see it coming?"

"*We* aren't going to take it down that way."

"We? What's this 'we' stuff? I'm no fighter, and to the best of my knowledge, the system doesn't have any more ships that can go up against it."

"That's why we're going to take it from the inside, and yes, I'm going to need your help to do so."

"I'm just a poor hotelier. I provide services—"

"You're going to provide me a way on board."

Grub turned back around and stared at Altha a moment. "I'm not going to say that I can't, because you obviously know I can. I also know the consequences if you get caught. Entropy! Even if you're successful at whatever you intend—"

Altha held up a hand. "If I'm successful, we take over the ship."

Grub's mouth made a giant *O*. "You're going to . . . take the ship? You and what army?" His voice got shrill. "*I can't get a battalion of troopers on board!* I doubt I could even get a platoon. I—"

"All I need is eight, or as many of us as you can take. If you can get us onto the cruiser without being seen, we'll handle the rest."

"They're going to know I brought you. If you fail, I'm dead, along with my family, my business, and everything that's associated with me." He shook his head. "No chance. I can survive the transition to the new Rangoran overlords."

"Can you, though?" Altha asked. He slid a knife out of a hidden sheath to pick at something under a fingernail. He looked up as he made the knife disappear again.

"So that's how it's going to be?" Grub asked.

"That's how it *has* to be. The Benefactor wants this done, and he's prepared to pay handsomely for your services. You're the only one I know who can get us on board. You now also know too much. You know I'm going to make the attempt. If somehow the Rangorans find out I'm coming, or if I fail to accomplish my mission, my . . . associates, as you called them, will come looking for you. Right now, you're already involuntarily committed to this plan."

Altha smiled. "Alternately, you can choose to join us in this patriotic endeavor and get rewarded handsomely for your services. What's it going to be?"

"I'm an Ogut, not a Glatun, so spare me the patriotism." Grub chuckled. "I am also a greedy son of a bitch, though, so I'm in, if only for the credits. I just have one request."

Altha lifted an eyebrow.

"If this fails, I want a chance at escape."

"If this goes poorly—"

"Then we're all going to die." Grub nodded. "Yes, yes. I know. That's why I want you to point a gun at me and threaten me. That way, I can say you made me do it."

"The Rangorans aren't going to let you off that easily."

"Oh, I know that. I'm still going to die; however, they might not bother to track down and kill my whole family, who I will be passing your much-appreciated payment to once we're done here."

"'Much appreciated'?"

"I would have done this for free. The Rangorans are not easy masters, and the longer we hold out, the more likely it is for someone else to come and save us."

"The only people who are going to save us are ourselves. There isn't anyone else."

"There is always someone else." The Ogut motioned with a leg toward a camera on the wall. "Now. Threaten me, please. We don't have much time."

Altha shrugged. "If you insist." The security chief aimed the rifle at the Ogut. "Help us or I'm going to kill you."

The Ogut frowned. "You could at least *try* to make it look authentic. When I pull the recording, I'd like it to look like you forced me to do this for you."

"I *am* forcing you to do it."

"We both know that, but the Rangora won't unless you look the part."

"Fine." Altha rolled his eyes. "Ready whenever you are."

Grub shrank back from him. "I can't help you. The Rangora will kill me if I do!"

"Maybe in the future," Altha said with a snarl, "but if you don't stop fooling around and help me, I'll kill you *right now*."

"Oh, I'm so scared. I will help you." Grub paused a moment and then said, "Fine. Thanks for doing that. Now what do you need?"

Altha returned two hours later to find a Dgut pushing a pseudogravity sled. The Dgut—a being that looked generally like a wide-bodied slug—turned one of its overlong eye stalks toward him.

“Are you Altha and friends?” the sophont asked.

“Yes. I’m Altha”—he motioned to the people behind him—“and these are my friends.”

“Very well.” The Dgut set the pallet down. “Come with me.”

Without waiting for an answer, the Dgut turned and slid out a back door of the warehouse. Altha shrugged to the rest of his assemblage, then he followed the being into a smaller room. Sitting in the middle of the otherwise empty space were four food carts, like what caterers would use to set up a buffet.

The Dgut pointed with a pseudopod. “There you go. Transport for four to . . .” It made a noise like it was swallowing. “Other places, let’s just say.”

“Wait,” Altha said. He motioned over his shoulder. “There’s supposed to be transportation for eight.”

“The Rangora changed the amount and type of food that they requested. If you would like to swim in the tanks with the khabash . . .”

“And get bitten and electrocuted by a school of eels?” Altha asked. “No, thanks.”

“That is what is available,” the Dgut replied. “Master Grubsxihekcowxpretowlllljerk sends his apologies.”

Altha sighed. “Fine. We’ll make do. Where do we load?”

“I don’t know what you’re talking about, but the bottom drawer has the most room. I will be back to pick up the carts in fifteen minutes. Please be gone by then.” The Dgut slithered out.

Altha turned to his team. “Teeko, you’re with me.”

The Glatun nodded.

“Slad, I’ll need you to get into tight places, so you’re in.”

The Ogut nodded.

Altha scanned the other members of his team. They’d been together for a long time, and he could see in their eyes that they were all scared, but none of them wanted to be left behind. That said, there was one who was more versatile than the others. Altha’s gaze stopped on the Ananancauimor.

“Beli, you’ll complete the team.”

The four-foot-long black scarab beetle—the last foot of which was a pair of razor-sharp cutting mandibles—skittered forward. “It’s about time.” It stared at the buffet cart. “I may need some help getting into that, though.”

“We all might,” Altha agreed as he looked at the closest one.

The carts were about five feet long and two and a half feet deep, which would have been big enough for any of the team members, except the drawers that they were supposed to fit into were only a little more than a foot high. Altha hated small areas, and this didn't appear to have much more space than a coffin. And he needed to get his gear in with him.

"It's not quite as bad as it looks," Teeko said, pulling out a drawer. "There is a little more space above the drawer once you're in."

"All right, well, let's get in and settled before the slug gets back," Altha ordered. "If you're not going, help the people who are."

Two of the bigger Glatuns went to help squeeze Beli into his conveyance, so Altha decided to attempt it on his own. He pulled out the drawer on the one no one else was using and inspected the space. Although the exterior of the cart looked like any other food cart, the interior had been strengthened and sealed, with the bottom weighted so that it wouldn't turn over when he got into the drawer if he was careful.

Or so Grub had said.

It was also supposed to stay pressurized in the event that it was exposed to vacuum, although that seal meant that the team would have to use supplemental oxygen or they risked depleting their air before they arrived on board the Rangoran cruiser.

As showing up dead wasn't particularly conducive to mission completion, all the team members had primary and secondary oxygen sources, and then a tertiary system, as well, in case the others failed or things went sideways, as well as a pack of goo that was meant to stop any leaks.

Altha slid into the drawer, bracing himself on the floor to keep the cart from overturning. *So much for having them weighted.* Unfortunately, once he was in, he was unable to bend his arm back out to grab his pack.

"Got it, boss," Luga said, handing it in to him.

"Careful!" Altha exclaimed. "The contents of that pack are worth tens of thousands of credits."

Luga handed him the pack more carefully than he had been, and Altha pulled it gently into the compartment with him.

"All set?" Luga asked after handing Altha his laser rifle.

"Yeah," Altha said softly as he looked around his small space. "As much as I can be." *This is going to suck.*

Luga slid the drawer shut.

Yep. This sucks.

Altha closed his eyes and tried to think about the last time he'd been at the Benefactor's estate on Glatus. The wide-open countryside. He worked to still his breathing and had almost relaxed when he heard Grub's voice.

"What are these carts still doing here?" the Ogut shouted. "They have to go, too, or the Rangora will be most displeased! Do you know who they're going to eat if you don't have enough food for them when you get there? *You!*"

After a pause, Grub yelled, "I don't care what you thought. Get them loaded now!"

Someone entered the room, muttering something too low to be heard. After a few moments, the cart he was in lifted, turned, and then was dropped hard enough that he had to clench his jaw to keep from crying out.

Altha worked on his breathing as three other crashes occurred, including one that elicited a small yelp. Apparently, whoever was moving the carts didn't hear it—or was told not to hear it—and the cart began to move laterally. Altha could tell when they went out the door into the main warehouse, as he began hearing a shuttle's engines, which rapidly grew louder. The cart ascended again—into the shuttle, based on the sounds around him—then the pallet the cart was on set down on the shuttle's deck. Chocks and chains followed, and after about a minute, the sounds of the shuttle's engines were muted.

Although he desperately wanted to open the drawer to get a last breath of fresh air—perhaps the last one he'd ever have—Altha closed his eyes and tried to relax again. Five minutes later, small shifts in the ship's gravity told him they were flying, and he swallowed. They were committed.

The trip to the Rangoran cruiser was uneventful, and after an hour of not hearing anything, Altha couldn't take being enclosed in the tiny space any longer. He needed to look out—to at least get a glimpse of the outside world—or he was going to go crazy.

As quietly and as gently as he could, he tried to slide the drawer out just enough to see out of.

The drawer didn't move.

He frantically pushed on the far side of the cart. Nothing. He tried to move around in the drawer, thinking maybe there was a catch somewhere, but no matter what he tried, the drawer stayed shut. In a flash, it came to him.

They stacked the carts next to each other, and I can't get out until they move the cart next to me off the pallet.

Altha swallowed, trying to fight down the terror. As bad as it had been before, knowing that he *couldn't* get out, even if he wanted to, made it even worse. He clenched his fists, trying to keep from pounding on the sides of the cart to be let out.

He took a deep breath, ready to scream at the top of his lungs, but then bit it back. This wasn't about him. It was about the future of the Glatun society. The thought of being ruled by the Rangorans cooled his terror with the fear of what would happen to his family under their rule.

This attack has to succeed, or all is lost.

With that in mind, he took another deep breath and let it out slowly.

I can do this. No one else can. And if I don't, all is lost.

Altha laid back and closed his eyes.

I will do this.

Incredibly, Altha fell asleep, but he woke up when the shuttle maneuvered and the microgravity shifts twisted his insides. Rather than think about his narrow confines, he kept his mind actively engaged by going over what would happen once they were set free.

While he hoped those plans involved the takeover of the ship, he realized there was a chance that a Rangoran might open the drawer—whether they knew he was in it or not—so Altha drew his laser pistol. It probably wouldn't stop any Rangorans he encountered, but it beat only having harsh language to use against them. But not by much.

With a slam, the shuttle landed, and the normal sounds of shipboard transfer came to him. The ramp dropping. People coming aboard and unchaining the pallets.

"Careful with that!" an Ogut yelled.

"Don't tell me what to do," a Rangoran voice replied. "I—"

"There are live foodstuffs in there. If you're not careful, you'll wreck their stasis field, and you'll be the one to have to explain it to your commanding officer!"

The Rangoran muttered but otherwise didn't reply. After a minute, Altha felt the pallet rise and move. Every adrenal gland in his body fired at once, and he was overcome by the urge to *do something*, even though there was nothing he could do. Appearing in the middle of the hangar bay would only compromise the mission and probably end with him being tortured to death.

With that in mind, he tamped down on his emotions and spent the rest of the trip trying to figure out where he was going. After a few minutes, he realized it was impossible, even though he had the *Cofubof*-class cruiser's deck plan loaded in his implants. Unfortunately, the ship had three shuttle bays, so he didn't know where he was starting from, and his ability to measure distance was rudimentary at best. Additionally, there was at least one trip on some sort of elevator, which meant they were going deeper into the ship.

To the brig? If Grub had sold them out, though—which was something that was very possible—the Rangorans would probably have pulled them out on the hangar bay, with a squad or two of troopers in attendance. The fact that they hadn't probably meant they were going to either a cargo hold or—more likely—one of the mess facilities where Grub's company was going to prepare the meal for the Rangorans.

The clatter of cutlery gave it away.

"Just put them over there and leave," a Rangoran said. "I'll get to them when I'm ready."

"As you wish," the Ogut voice from before replied.

The pallet moved again, then it shifted as if one of the carts was being removed. After a few seconds, it shifted again, and then a few seconds later, Altha's cart moved.

"You can go now," the Rangoran said shortly thereafter.

"Very well."

Altha had expected the Ogut to open his drawer, or create a disturbance, or *something*, but after nothing happened a full minute after that, he realized that he was on his own.

Very well. At least they were on the ship and no one was shooting at them. Not yet, anyway.

Altha slowly pushed open the drawer just enough to look out the crack. There was some sort of counter sticking up about six feet away, and he could see the back of a Rangoran head periodically on the other side of it. It was some sort of island, he guessed, but his vision was blocked forward and back.

Summoning up his resolve, he waited until he could see the back of the Rangoran's head again and slowly eased the drawer open. A quick scan showed the Rangoran cook was the only person in the kitchen.

Altha eased his rifle out of the drawer, but the metal buckle on the sling hit the top of the compartment with a soft clink.

It was enough, and the Rangoran spun around.

"What is going—"

Zzzt!

A laser bolt passed from right to left through the Rangoran's head. The lizard's mouth dropped open, then its eyes rolled up into its head, and it collapsed.

Careful not to kick his bag, Altha climbed out of the drawer as quickly as he could to find Teeko and Slad already out of their carts. Beli had his drawer open but was skittering uselessly, unable to extract himself.

"Nice shot," Altha said with a nod to Teeko, whose rifle was still pointing in the direction of the Rangoran cook. "You two get Beli out while I check the Rangoran."

The counters in the kitchen were oversize, just like the Rangorans, and Altha was unable to see over the five-foot-tall island. He raced around the end of the island with his rifle ready, but the Rangoran wasn't going anywhere. A pool of blood was already forming around his head.

Altha surveyed the space, like an ant would a Glatun structure. Everything was too big or too high, and he couldn't see what the Rangoran had been cooking, only that it had a pan on the stove.

Motion from the door was accompanied by a "What's going on here?"

Altha spun, his rifle up, to find two Rangorans standing in the doorway. He fired at the first one, taking it in the chest. The second started to turn away, but Teeko shot it in the back of the head, and it went down. The one Altha'd shot gave a small roar and charged toward him.

Altha fired, but the Rangoran didn't slow. Laser fire hit it several more times, then the giant lizard missed a step, fell, and slid up to Altha's feet. He shot it in the head as it started to get back up, and the Rangoran collapsed.

"Quickly," Altha said. "We have to get out of here." He looked up for the ventilation ducting and saw that even if he climbed onto the counter, he wasn't going to be able to reach it. He pointed at the access panel far over his head. "Beli, can you get up there?"

"Oh, I see," the Ananancauimor muttered. "Ask the exoskeletal to crawl up the wall like a spider." He looked at the bulkhead, then shook his head. "No way I can get up that. Not and get over to the entrance."

"I can," Slad offered from the other side of the island. The giant purple caterpillar scaled the cabinet to the right of where the Rangoran had been working, then went up the wall to the vent fan over the stove, climbed it to the ceiling, and extended himself over to the access. Slad had a tool out as he grabbed it, and he immediately went to work on the closure.

"Who tightened this?" he asked with a grunt.

"A Rangoran," Beli replied.

"No shit." Slad strained, and the fitting turned. Slad overbalanced and fell, but Altha jumped over the dead Rangoran's head to catch him. They both fell to the floor.

"I thought we were trying to be quiet," Beli noted.

"Shut up," Altha replied, extricating himself from Slad's many legs. He stood up and lifted Slad onto the counter. "Hurry." He checked once Slad was on his way; Teeko was watching the door with his rifle ready.

Slad scaled the wall again and went up into the ventilation system. After a moment, a rope snaked back down.

"Altha, come on up," Slad called.

"Why not me?" Beli asked.

"Because I can't lift your fat ass," the Ogut replied.

Altha ignored the byplay—the plan all along had been for him to go second—and he slung his pack and his rifle, and climbed the rope. Slad helped, but not much.

Slad exhaled as Altha reached the access port and climbed into the shaft. "I didn't think I'd be able to hold."

"Glad you did." Altha stuck his head through the hole. "Teeko next. Beli, watch for Rangorans."

"Yeah, yeah, leave the bug for last." Beli mounted his laser rifle to his back and faced the doorway. "Someday I'm going to be in charge, and I'm going to go first."

Slad shook his head. "Why do you put up with him?"

Altha shrugged. "He's good with tech and most laser pulses bounce off him."

"Not worth the annoyance," Slad replied as Teeko climbed into the shaft.

"Come on," Altha called. "Let's go, Beli!"

The Ananancauimor skittered past the dangling rope, raced up onto the counter, and then ran up the wall the way Slad had gone.

"I thought you couldn't do that," the Ogut noted.

Beli crawled past him. "I couldn't go up the other wall, and I couldn't see the path you took from where I was standing."

"Focus," Altha said, slapping Beli's back carapace. "Okay." He looked at Teeko. "I need you to go aft and make a disturbance that draws security to you. When we had eight, I was going to send the others with you, but now there's just you."

Teeko nodded. "I've got it." He patted his sack. "I've got just the thing for that."

"Good." Altha clasped his arm. "Stay safe. Your brother will kill me if anything happens to you."

"I'll do my best," Teeko replied, then he chuckled. "Which way is aft?"

Altha consulted the map in his implant and pointed. "If this is the kitchen I think it is, then it's that way."

"I'll get it done." Teeko walked off bent over. The ventilation shaft wasn't quite big enough to comfortably walk through upright, but it would have taken too much time to go on his hands and knees.

"*What happened here?*" a Rangoran shouted from below. "Call security, quickly!"

Altha motioned in the opposite direction of Teeko. "Let's go," he whispered. "Quickly."

The group set off with Beli in the lead, followed by Slad. They had plenty of room to walk normally, and woe to the person that ran into Beli's mandibles. Hunched over, Altha couldn't keep up with them, and he fell behind.

Leaning forward and carrying his pack, his back began to hurt almost immediately, and between the pain and trying to focus on maintaining enough speed to keep up with the others, he lost track of anything but putting one foot in front of the other. Tears filled his eyes and made it hard to see, and he almost ran into Slad when the Ogut stopped.

"Watch where you're going!" Slad whispered urgently, alerting him to the imminent collision. "We're here."

Altha sank to his knees and stretched his back with a groan. "Finally."

"Bah, it was only a few minutes." Beli scoffed. "You're out of shape."

"Try running bent over," Altha said. "Oh, wait, that's right. You can't."

"As you told Beli in the kitchen, boss, focus," Slad said. "We're here."

"Where exactly *is* here?"

"We're at the combat information center—what you probably think of as the bridge," Beli replied. "It's where they run the ship."

"I know what a CIC is," Altha replied. "We need to find the server room. It should be nearby." He brought up the ship's deck plan in his implants and sighed. He'd forgotten that none of the rooms nearby was actually labeled as the AI room, but he knew it had to be close. He scanned the shaft. "There are several junctions up there"—he jerked his chin forward—"and one behind us. You two go forward, and I'll go aft. We'll meet back here."

"What if we don't find it?" Slad asked.

"Then we'll have to take over the CIC."

"Uh, boss?" Beli asked. He pointed to the vent access panel with an antenna. "You did see down there, right? There are about eight Rangorans in the CIC. Even for us, that's a lot."

"They won't be expecting us—"

The ship vibrated slightly, then a horn began blaring in the CIC, along with strobing lights.

"Okay, maybe they'll be expecting us now," Altha said with a sigh. "Sending Teeko to make a distraction may not have been the best plan. Finding the AI room is more imperative than ever. Go!"

Altha retraced his steps to the last junction and went a short way down both passages. The only rooms visible below the shaft appeared to be administrative spaces. He returned to the CIC access panel as Slad and Beli arrived.

"No luck," Altha reported.

"Me, either," Slad added.

"I'm not surprised," Beli said.

Altha frowned. "And why is that?"

"Because I found it."

"And you couldn't just have told us that?"

"Sure. I could have, but where would the suspense have been in it? What about the drama—"

"Focus," Altha and Slad said in unison.

"Just get us there," Altha added.

Without another word, Beli turned and led them down the passageway. He made two turns, then he gently tapped on an access panel with a foreleg. "There you go," he whispered.

Altha slid forward to look into the room. Not surprisingly, it wasn't large by Rangoran standards, but by Glatun standards, it was a giant waste of space at twenty-five feet across. In the center of it, the AI sat, lights flashing. Altha moved around, trying to get a better perspective, and saw an open door.

"Does that go into the CIC?" he asked.

"I think so," Beli replied.

Altha pulled up the schematic and confirmed it, then he squared his shoulders. "Okay, so as soon as we drop in there, the AI is going to announce us, and we're going to get a response from the CIC." He paused. "The problem is that we have to hold them off long enough for our AI to boot up. I'll drop first and start the replacement, followed by Beli. Your job is to shut the hatch to the space, and if you're not able, to keep them out."

"All eight of them?" Beli asked. "You better hope I get the hatch shut."

"You better hope you do," Altha replied, "because you're the first person that's going to die if you don't."

"Got it," the Ananancauimor replied. "Shutting the door, good. Defending the space, bad."

Altha frowned at Beli and shook his head. "Ready?"

"I am," Slad replied.

Beli slid his mandibles across each other, eliciting a slicing sound. "Do it."

Altha stood and braced his back against the ceiling of the shaft, then he stomped down hard on the vent closure. The metal screeched, but held, so he slammed his boot down on it again. The latch broke, and the access panel fell open. Grabbing his backpack and rifle, he stepped into the opening and dropped.

Altha immediately realized he'd misjudged how far it was to the floor, and he ended up leaning slightly forward as he hit the deck below. Dropping his rifle, he threw himself forward and onto his back while holding the backpack to his chest with both arms.

The breath whooshed from his lungs as he hit, but he maintained his grasp on the bag. Gasping as he fought to regain his wind, he struggled to his feet.

"Very athletic," Beli said with a snort as he raced down the wall and headed to the hatch.

"Who are you, and what are you doing?" the ship's AI asked, alert to their presence. "You aren't allowed to be here!"

"Sorry, but I'm going to have to take you offline for now." Altha grabbed the handle at the top of the AI's pedestal, turned it, and lifted the core off the mount.

"Incoming!" Beli called.

Altha looked up. A large Rangoran—even bigger than normal—had a hold of the hatch with one hand while it reached for a pistol at its side. Beli pulled on the hatch, but the door might as well have been set in stone.

"Entropy!" Beli yelled as Altha pulled Keltar's core out of his pack.

Beli released the hatch, raced forward, and sliced off the Rangoran's leg mid-shin. The Rangoran crumpled but still got a shot off with his laser pistol. It flashed off Beli's carapace, sublimating some of his shell.

Altha set the core on the pedestal and turned it until it locked in place and lights began flashing on it, then he sprinted toward where his rifle lay on the floor.

Beli stepped away from the Rangoran, who was now screaming and spraying blood everywhere, grabbed the hatch, and retreated into the AI room. Before he could get it shut, though, a massive hand grabbed it and ripped it out of his grasp. Beli surged forward through the doorway, and the Rangoran slapped at his mandibles, spinning him sideways.

Altha grabbed the rifle off the floor, aimed, and pulled the trigger. Nothing happened.

"I could use a little help here!" Beli yelled. He spun and tried to move forward again, but the Rangoran leaned down and slapped him the other way.

"I'm trying!" Altha pulled the trigger again, and the whole assembly fell out of the rifle. "Shit!" He wasted a split second to check the rifle—it was definitely broken—then he hurled the rifle at the Rangoran. "Catch, asshole!"

The Rangoran looked up to see the relatively small rifle pinwheeling toward him and slapped it away easily.

Seizing his chance, Beli jumped forward and snipped off the lizard's leg at the ankle. Unfortunately, the Rangoran had been leaning forward, and he came crashing down at Beli.

"Eek!" the Ananancauimor shouted as he backpedaled for all he was worth. Reaching the hatch, he dodged to the side as the Rangoran fell into the doorway.

"Nice job taking care of him," Altha said, drawing his pistol. "But you're making it *really* hard to shut the hatch." Altha fired a couple of rounds into the Rangoran's head as it thrashed about, and it stilled.

"How does killing him help?" Beli shouted. "His body is still in the way, and now we have to move it!"

Altha ran forward. "Help me pull it into the room!"

They both grabbed the giant lizard. It would have been difficult—probably even impossible—for them to move it, but before they could, the body was yanked out of their hands by two Rangorans.

The unexpected pull threw Altha off-balance, and he staggered toward the hatch. The Rangorans dropped the body and started forward. Beli fired his rifle, drilling one of them in the stomach, but a beam flashed in from the CIC immediately after. The laser bolt hit Beli's carapace and ricocheted up into where his rifle was mounted, slagging it.

The Rangoran that hadn't been shot filled the doorway, and Beli and Altha backed away from it.

"Come on, Keltar, boot!" Altha said with a grunt as he drew his vibroknife. Altha scooped up the trigger assembly he'd dropped with his other hand and threw it at the Rangoran as he continued backward. The Rangoran swatted it away as Altha drew his pistol again.

"Attack him on three?" Beli asked. "He can't block both of us. If you could just distract him a moment..."

"You'll chop off his leg while he breaks me in half?"

"Sounds like a good plan to me," Beli said, moving off to the side so that the Rangoran couldn't watch both of them at once.

"Aside from me being broken in half, sure," Altha replied. "We just need hold on a little longer—"

"Drop your weapons!" a Rangoran yelled.

Altha looked up. Another Rangoran was in the hatchway. This one had an immense laser rifle, which was pointed at him.

The barrel was so large, Altha thought he could almost have crawled into it.

Swallowing, Altha dropped the pistol and knife.

The new Rangoran moved into the room to stand alongside the first one. A purple flash fell from above, and Slad wrapped himself around the Rangoran rifleman's head. Altha dove to the side as the rifle fired. All the fires of hell ignited on his arm.

"Help me!" the rifleman yelled.

The other Rangoran turned to assist and stepped forward, and like a black flash, Beli raced forward. The Rangoran crashed down on the stump of his leg as he tried to take a second step.

Slad stabbed his vibroknife into one of the Rangoran's ears, then he jumped clear as the Rangoran collapsed.

Beli sprinted forward, pulled the hatch shut, and locked it.

Altha stood and inspected his arm. It was missing a little of the meat of the tricep, but it was still operational. "Damn, that hurts," he muttered.

"What are you whining about?" Beli asked. "I got shot twice; you only got hit once." He turned toward Slad. "And where were you the whole time?"

"I would only have been in the way," the Ogut said, his body rippling in a shrug. "I was the strategic reserve, which turned out to be necessary when you couldn't accomplish the mission you were given."

"You might not have noticed, but I was kind of busy fighting Rangorans," Beli replied.

"I fought them too," Slad noted. He nodded to the Rangoran rifleman. "That one still has my knife in his ear, as a matter of fact."

"If all of you are finished," a new voice said, "I'm done booting and am prepared to take over the ship."

"What are you waiting for, Keltar?" Altha asked. "Do it now, before something else happens."

"I would recommend you have your supplemental oxygen ready. I think that I have closed the appropriate valves, but with the Rangorans' sloppy maintenance, who knows?"

The group scrambled for their breathers, and Altha said, "Don't wait; do it now!"

"As you wish," Keltar replied. "Disabling emergency protocols... done. Opening all hatches and evacuating atmosphere...

done." The AI paused. "Gentle beings, and I use that term loosely, the ship is ours."

Altha's jaw dropped. "Oh, no," he said. "I forgot about Teeko."

"Well, you might have forgotten about him, but I didn't," Keltar said primly a moment later. "He was holed up in a storage compartment that functions as an emergency pressurization loss shelter. He is safe and sound, and when the rest of the ship is fully pressurized, he will come join you in the CIC."

"Great," Altha said. "And thanks for looking out for him."

"You're very welcome," the AI replied. "Now, if you don't mind, I have some some systems to optimize if I'm going to be here long term. The state of Rangoran computer technology... let me just say that this network is not up to my standards and leave it at that. Call me if you need me."

"Will do. Will you let us know when it is safe to move about the ship?"

"It's safe now, although I don't know if I would do so."

"Are there still live Rangorans aboard it?" Slad asked.

"None that I am aware of, but some didn't take the depressurization very well. Many of them went overboard, but others didn't, and there are... messes which will take some cleaning up. Additionally, there is gear everywhere, blocking some of the passageways. If you move about the ship, you will need to exercise caution, which I know isn't your forte."

Altha chuckled. "Got it." He went to the hatch, undogged it, and walked out into the CIC. Buried deep in the ship, the pressurization loss here wouldn't have been as sudden as around the exterior doors and hatches. There were only two Rangoran bodies in the CIC, and both appeared to have been trying to get to emergency breathing apparatuses when they were overcome.

"How soon do you think it will be until they start to stink?" Beli asked.

Slad scoffed. "More than they already do?"

Altha looked around. He hadn't been sure enough of the plan to worry about what he'd do if it had actually worked, and now he found himself at a bit of a loss. He'd figured that Keltar would drive the ship to wherever they needed, and that it was just a matter of the Benefactor sending up a shuttle to rescue them.

"So, we did it!" Teeko said as he walked into the CIC.

"It appears so," Beli said, nodding toward one of the Rangoran bodies. "Guess who tried to decompress you?"

"What?"

"Ignore him," Altha said. "We had a battle for the AI center, and as soon as we got the hatch shut, I told Keltar to evacuate the ship. I may not have inquired about your safety prior to doing so."

Teeko scoffed. "I knew what was coming, so I created the distraction and then found somewhere safe to hide—"

"Sorry to interrupt," Keltar said, "but another Rangoran *Cofubof*-class cruiser has just gated into the system. The Rangoran High Command wants an update on the battle that occurred here."

Altha scratched his chin. "Do you have any examples of this ship's communications?"

"Yes. I have files of all their communications. If you're asking if I can imitate anyone from this ship, I can do the CO, the XO, and most of the communications watchstanders, as well as some of the maintenance and food supply officers."

"Good. Please give them a report on how the battle went, using any examples you have on reports that have been made to their High Command in the past."

"You mean, the ones with all the flowery language that ensures no one blames us for anything that went wrong?"

Altha nodded. "The CO of the task force made mistakes, we tried to warn him, but he blundered into their prepared defenses. Blah, blah, blah."

"Got it."

"Also, I want you to break orbit and tell the new ship that we have high-ranking prisoners on board, including one of the Glatun Benefactors, that we will transfer to them to take back to the homeworld . . . wherever that is."

"Ligaghux," Keltar explained.

"Is it just me," Beli asked, "or does that just sound as awful as it probably is?"

"No doubt." Altha nodded.

"What is your plan?" Keltar asked.

"We're going to get to point-blank range, and then we're going to hit them with everything we have."

"What if they ask about why we're not sending the Benefactor now on a shuttle?"

"Make something up. He was wounded and we're stabilizing him for transport. Then the shuttle broke and the Benefactor had to go back to medical to wait. Stall them. Also, if you need something else, just tell them that we got resupplied from the planet, and we'll be sending over some goodies. They'll just assume that any delays we have are due to us picking through what the planet sent us so that we can keep the choicest morsels."

"How much longer do you intend to wait?" Keltar asked as the ship's shuttle—remotely piloted by the AI—neared the Rangoran cruiser. "I think they are starting to get suspicious."

"This is close enough, then," Altha replied. "Fire all weapons."

"Firing."

The tactical hologram showed missiles spewing from all the ship's launchers, and Altha could feel the launches as the missiles were ejected into the black. The ship's lasers began firing, as well, with all of them aimed at the same point—the engineering section at the back of the ship.

The Rangoran cruiser, who'd lowered its shields to allow the shuttle to approach, couldn't get them back up in time, and the lasers drilled through the armor and into the critical engineering spaces beneath. One of the fusion plants detonated catastrophically.

The missiles, when they arrived, targeted the biggest pieces of the ship. They didn't serve any purpose aside from turning the former ship into a greater number of navigational hazards.

"Oops," Beli said. "So much for using it as a stationary missile platform to defend the gate."

Altha winced. "Yeah. Maybe we'll at least be able to recover some of its missiles to rearm this ship."

"It is statistically unlikely," Keltar said, "based on the number of secondary explosions observed."

"Well, they're sure to send more ships," Slad noted. "Maybe next time we can aim for a different part of one."

Altha nodded.

"So," Keltar asked, "what are your intentions now?"

"We return to the planet and see what the Benefactor has come up with to help defend the system. If we need fuel, we go get it from the mining station at the sixth planet."

"That's not what I meant. What are your intentions for *how* we're going to hold off the Rangorans? Eventually, they are going to notice that they haven't heard from either the first task force they sent here or from the cruiser they sent to get a report."

"We hold out," Altha replied. "As long as we can."

"And when more Rangorans come?"

"I don't know." Altha ruffled his back fur in a shrug. "We'll have to figure it out, but I know one thing: We'll fight this ship until we can't, and we'll use everything at our disposal to hold off the Rangora. If it comes down to putting rockets on asteroids and launching them toward the gate, then that's what we'll do. We hold out. At all costs."

SKEETERS

Jason Cordova & Melissa Olthoff

"This right here is some bullshit, ma'am."

Josepha Cruz, coxswain of the *Myrmidon* cargo shuttle 11242—affectionately christened *Maslow's Hammer* by its four-person crew—glanced up from the control console, a frown on her pale features. Next to her, her engineer was softly cursing up a storm in Spanish.

"What's up?" she asked.

Maslow's Hammer had been deep in the E Eridani system for two weeks now after the final Rangoran attack, collecting whatever scrap they could find at the behest of Apollo Mining. From the look of things, humanity had almost lost the battle and the system. Almost, as the old axiom went, only counted in horseshoes and hand grenades.

On the other hand, the Rangora had both their navy and spirit *shattered* against the surface of the massive battlestation *Thermopylae*. The aggressive alien invaders had lost, and recovery operations were underway. Both *Troy* and *Thermopylae* were swamped, with the majority of their shuttles destroyed when the Rangora made their final, desperate push.

From the vacuum of space came opportunity for independent cargo shuttles like *Maslow's Hammer*. *Myrmidon* shuttles were prohibitively expensive and very few people could actually afford to buy one outright. However, since Tyler Vernon—the man who'd built the SAPL, saved Earth multiple times from alien threats, and was arguably the richest person in the history of the planet—was also a forward-thinker, many smaller, upstart companies were granted the opportunity to lease-to-own them at reasonable rates.

Her family, former ranch hands living near the Red River in north Texas and struggling to keep themselves fed after the destruction of Dallas, had immediately jumped at the opportunity. They'd never looked back.

"New tasking from *Thermopylae.* ATC wants us to scan quadrant one-three-four-two for any signs of Rangora scrap, ma'am." Her cousin, engineer, and probably closest friend Aaliyah Servin looked as though she wanted to scream. They might be cousins but Aaliyah was a stickler for following the chain of command in the shuttle. It was a clear holdover from her own active duty days as a marine. "*Scrap.*"

Cruz grimaced. Scrap duty in an already cleared quadrant? One that didn't even qualify as a scrapyard anymore? It'd been picked *clean* by everyone and their mothers by this point. The odds of them finding anything worth more than a few credits were so close to zero that no one would be able to differentiate the percentage points.

"That's not going to pay very well."

"No, ma'am. It will not. Won't even cover fuel costs."

She sighed inwardly. Six months. All Cruz needed was six months of steady, consistent work and the final credits owed on *Maslow's Hammer* could finally be paid off. The family would no longer be under the onus of debt and they could finally start to make some *real* money, where ranching would be more of a hobby than actual work. Not that it wouldn't still be work. Anyone who'd ever worked a ranch soon learned the meaning of a hard day's labor, but they'd no longer be dependent on the income.

Taskings like this from ATC would delay that dream, push the debt down the road by up to a year. That was inexcusably inefficient.

"Let's request a different tasking," Cruz grumbled, rolling her eyes. "One that actually makes sense."

"I tried."

Of course she had. Her engineer was wonderfully efficient and just as motivated to pay off their debt as she was.

"They want us to search for atacirc, ma'am," Aaliyah scornfully added.

Cruz turned and stared at her cousin, confused.

"There are billions of credits just *floating* out there in the boneyard, waiting for an entrepreneurial crew such as ourselves to scoop it up and bring it in, and *Thermopylae* wants us to search for *atacirc* with dozens of other company-owned ships in an already picked clean area?" It was getting harder to keep the sharp disbelief out of her tone. "Comm them and ask precisely *how* we're supposed to help without stepping on anyone else's toes for anything larger than my pinky finger! The air traffic out here is already so crowded they're just *begging* for an accident to happen!"

"*Thermopylae* ATC, this is shuttle 11242, requesting permission for different tasking in new quadrant, over," Aaliyah commed, glaring at the console as if it were responsible for their current predicament.

Which was perfectly reasonable as far as Cruz was concerned. Especially considering she was glaring just as hard.

"*Wait one, 11242,*" a woman replied after a beat, that typical iron-calm voice of a trained controller just a touch frayed around the edges. "*Salvage taskings are priority two. ATC is a little busy at the moment.*"

"Of course," Cruz muttered under her breath. "Leave us little guys out in the lurch for scrap parts while the bigshots get to snag all the credits..."

"Wasn't a 'no,' ma'am," her cousin helpfully pointed out, already in a better mood.

Cruz grumbled at the formal address but otherwise didn't reply. It was an all too familiar discussion (or argument, depending on who was asked) between them, and one Cruz wasn't sure would ever end. She suspected Aaliyah had started doing it on purpose at some point just because she knew it irritated her.

Instead, she checked the camera to the converted passenger compartment of the *Myrmidon*. Jaime and Bo were in the back, fully vac-suited near their sleds. They were relatives as well, distant cousins, though Cruz wasn't sure if they were more related to her or to Aaliyah. It didn't matter. The family had fronted the credits to get them through training so they could be certified salvage technicians, as well as through the Apollo-certified school. The need for both technicians and engineers actually outstripped the one for qualified coxswains, shockingly enough, though that had shifted after the Battle of E Eradini.

"Jaime, Bo... you guys okay back there?"

"We're fine, Josepha," Bo Ramirez replied. The short, swarthy welding tech had been the most recent member of the family to join the crew. He'd almost not gone with the family business at all. Working for Apollo paid better and the young man had been tempted by their signing bonuses. In the end, though, he decided—well, his mother decided, but nobody wanted to point that out to him—that working in the new family business was better in the long haul. "Just watching some vids to keep entertained."

"They're called training manuals for a reason, *pendejo*," Jaime Cruz grumbled. She felt reasonably confident *he* was a third cousin to her and not Aaliyah. "Study them, don't just watch."

"Hey, I passed my quals with flying colors. How'd you do on that Apollo entry exam, anyway?"

"Screw you."

"Not my type. We're not from that part of Texas. Although your mom is, isn't she?"

"Your mom lived next door to mine, you idiot!"

"Guys . . ." Cruz sighed. That was the problem with family: they knew precisely which buttons to push to piss one another off. It was almost a game in the family to see how angry they could make one another without crossing the line. "Stow it. We're requesting a new tasking to get some real work done. Run your equipment checks and confirm."

"Copy, ma'am." Bo's voice shifted from annoying second cousin to professional welding technician instantaneously. Jaime, to his credit, followed suit.

"Yes, ma'am."

Professional or not, Cruz knew both of them *absolutely* called her "ma'am" to try to push her buttons. Fortunately for their continued well-being, ATC interrupted her slightly vengeful thoughts.

"*Shuttle 11242,* Thermopylae. *New tasking request approved. Proceed to quadrant one-three-six-six. Be advised that this area has not been cleared yet and is a higher risk of debris damage to your shuttle,*" a new, deeper voice came over the comms.

This was not the harried, overworked voice who'd told them to wait previously. Definitely a step in the right direction. Cruz pumped her fist in the air and grinned.

"Confirm quadrant one-three-six-six, *Thermopylae*," Aaliyah commed back, grinning just as triumphantly as Cruz. "Requesting permission to free range for salvage, over."

It might have been pushing it, but Cruz knew that her cousin's instincts when it came to this sort of stuff were usually spot on. Free-range salvage ops were the best and quickest way to earn credits. It meant that anything and everything they found out there, while ostensibly belonging to the aforementioned Tyler Vernon and Apollo Mining, was a potential target and that nobody could tell them precisely *what* they would be salvaging. It meant that Cruz and company would be free to spot the biggest, juiciest salvage and bring it in and receive the entirety of their share, instead of splitting it with ATC or anyone else who might be directing traffic. It meant *real* money.

The odds of *Thermopylae* giving them the approval, however, was extremely—

"Free-range salvage permission granted, shuttle 11242. Good hunting."

Cha-*ching*. "Hell yeah!" Aaliyah exclaimed, pumping her fist in the air.

Cruz blinked and hurriedly took over the comms from her cousin. "Wait . . . that was a yes?"

"Confirmed, shuttle 11242," the same deep voice replied. *"Your retasking request fits the necessary predetermined parameters of maximum coefficiency. The request is simply ahead of the bell curve."*

"Hot damn," Cruz breathed. "Copy that, *Thermopylae*. Thank you."

"You're welcome, shuttle 11242. And for the record, this is Argus. Not Thermopylae*."*

"Oh," she squeaked. She'd never talked to an AI before. It was . . . unsettling. The AIs were notoriously shy and uncommunicative toward independent contractors like herself. Still, they'd just done something not many other indies could claim. It was a good sign. "Copy that, Argus. Thanks for your help."

"You're welcome, shuttle 11242. Argus, out."

A grin stretched across her face. She switched comms and broadcast throughout the ship. "Boys and girls, it's time to go and get *paid*!"

"This quadrant hasn't been cleared yet," Cruz reminded them for the dozenth time as *Maslow's Hammer* moved quickly through the debris field. She deftly maneuvered the shuttle between two dead, hulking Rangoran AV shells, her scanners constantly searching for any sign of a power cell or something similar. Fuel was still selling at a premium price and was the quickest sure-fire way to make some credits in a hurry. "Neither Paris nor Argus have eyes out here at the moment. They're focused on SAR near *Thermopylae* proper. We're on our own if something happens, so keep an eye out."

The journey had taken them almost six hours. Fortunately, the fuel reserves in the tank of the *Myrmidon* shuttle were enough for almost three *hundred* hours, so nobody had been concerned with doing a Dutchman this far out in the system.

In that time the duo in the compartment hold had recharged their oxygen tanks and triple-checked their sleds to ensure that everything was in order. The gravitics needed to accelerate the shuttle fast enough to get on-site before anyone else had a chance to poach their salvage had called for everything and everyone to be strapped down tightly. Since this was the SOP on *Maslow's Hammer*, however, it hadn't been that big of a deal. The increased gravity for five hours before deceleration had begun had been less than pleasant, but worth it.

"Beginning sweep now," Aaliyah murmured as she accessed her console via her implant. It always took a few moments for the systems to filter out the residual energy signatures, and Cruz waited patiently, adjusting their flight path as needed while her cousin did her job. "Getting low power signatures from various points. Marking them."

Cruz wrinkled her nose as she reviewed their current haul. The hardest part of the job was identifying which Rangoran equipment was valuable and what was junk. Unfortunately, most of the wreckage they'd recovered was simply that—fabber scrap, good only for Granadica to produce more *Myrmidon*s, missiles, and only God knew what else from within *Thermopylae*. No big score as of yet.

Picking up atacirc would have at least covered their refueling costs, but Cruz didn't regret requesting the new tasking. Even if they didn't recover a Rangoran drive or, more impressively, an intact fuel reserve, there was more than enough salvage in this sector to ensure they could cover their next shuttle payment.

"Hmm . . . energy spikes here, here, and here," Aaliyah commented as markers began to appear on the image of the first ruined Rangoran assault vector. "Could be energy weapon capacitors. We'd need to get a closer look to confirm, ma'am."

"Moving us in," Cruz said and shifted the *Myrmidon* to port, using momentum to skew around the jagged outcropping of twisted, ruined Rangoran hull. Something bounced off their shuttle but it was soft, subtle. More of a *thud* than the expected *clang* of metal striking metal. Cruz sucked in a breath and waited for an alarm, but none came. Whatever it was, it hadn't punctured the hull. "Bio matter . . . probably."

"Rangoran bodies everywhere," Aaliyah confirmed with a grimace. "Vacuum does horrible things to bodies. Hmm . . . I wonder how these ships drifted out this way so quickly."

"These were the first sacrificial lambs through the gate during the second wave, I bet," Cruz said as she slowed the *Myrmidon* to a near-crawl. "*Thermopylae* chewed them up and spit them out. Then they just . . . drifted."

"Current orbit calculations suggest they'll fall into the star within fifty years, ma'am," Aaliyah said after a moment. "Maybe sooner if they're nudged by a comet or asteroid. Should we report that as well?"

"Not my circus, not my monkeys," Cruz said. "Pretty sure someone is watching and doing the calcs for us already. Smart money is on Argus. Probably worried we might screw something up and blow ourselves up. Whatever. Isolate the energy spikes on the assault vectors. Maybe their energy weapon's banks are charged?"

They were. Cruz was almost giddy as the thought of millions of credits bounced around in her head. It would take a deft hand by Bo and Jaime to cut them out without causing too much damage, but she had confidence in their abilities. And while Apollo Mining *technically* owned the salvage rights to the system, the percentage cut would still be massive and allow them to make the final payments for *Maslow's Hammer* not just on time but *early*.

Taking a deep, calming breath, she waited as the duo in the cargo hold slowly prepped their sleds. For all the grief they gave one another, they were absolute professionals when it came to salvage ops. The sleds—formerly leased through Apollo as well, but bought outright months before—were ideal for this sort of operation.

"*Maslow's Hammer*, Sled One. Secure for vacuum."

"Sled Two, secured for vacuum."

Even now, it still gave her a thrill hearing someone use the name of the ship and not its number designation. Even if it was just the crew.

"Confirmed, sleds. Be careful out there." Cruz glanced over at Aaliyah. "Depressurize."

The trick to depressurizing the cargo hold area was to do it slowly. While the boys and their sleds could withstand a rapid depressurization of the compartment, they might potentially damage the ship itself on their way out the hatch. The idea of scratching her baby gave Cruz nightmares. From comments Aaliyah had made months before, she was apt to murder anyone who damaged the ship through negligence. Or otherwise.

The former marine was very particular about the shuttle.

Cruz watched as the cargo hold finished depressurizing and the sleds moved forward, whispering the same prayer she did every time Bo and Jaime went out into vacuum.

"Keep them safe, Lord, and bring them both home..."

The two men guided their sleds through the twisted wreckage of the first AV, being careful to avoid the jagged edges of metal that could puncture their suits or damage the sleds. Bo let Jaime lead, the older of the two far more experienced maneuvering in tight confines such as this.

"You got those power readings marked?" Jaime asked for the fourth time as they slipped through the ruined corridor. It was slow going even with the highly maneuverable sleds but they were managing. For now.

"Yeah. Check your readouts."

Bo eventually stopped at the first marker and disembarked from the sled. The actual source of energy they were reading was farther down the corridor but there was too much debris to safely navigate further. Glancing over his shoulder, he could faintly see the lights of *Maslow's Hammer* about a mile away from the twisted, ruined hull.

"Never gets old," he murmured softly.

"Quit being a little bitch and help me find the relay," Jaime said, tapping him on the shoulder. "What panel?"

"Five down, third from the end," Bo replied, turning back. "And only bitches don't appreciate a good view."

"Only view I want to see is a bottle of cerveza and a half-naked woman in my bunk after I get paid."

"Your priorities are screwed up, *mijo*."

"You say so."

The cutting of the energy banks was a delicate task and required a steady hand. Too close to the storage banks and they ran the risk of a cataclysmic failure of the containment unit, which would kill them both. Too far, and they might hit the auxiliary cutoff switch and kill the powered banks entirely. The risk of death was admittedly lower if that happened, but both of them knew that reprieve from the Reaper would only last until Josepha got her hands on them. She had, like most women in the family, a fiery temper.

"Got an O-line here," Bo said as he stopped cutting momentarily. He eyed the energy bank then consulted the schematics. "Moving two feet up and cutting again."

"Atmo?" Jaime asked.

"Looks like it. Still has pressure, too."

"Yeah, don't cut that. Might affect the rotation of the ship."

"No shit, Sherlock."

"Keep cutting, Watson."

Diligence and patience were the keys to the kingdom. Both men, fortunately, had those in spades. The work continued apace and before long, they had the first energy bank fully cut and ready. The only thing they needed to do now was to move it out of the spinning dead hulk of the assault vector.

Easy peasey.

"Huh. That's weird."

Cruz looked up from her book, frowning. Once the sleds had been launched, they'd backed away from the wreckage to a reasonably safe distance to wait for the pickup call. Aaliyah had taken over watching the cousins work. Other than keeping an eye on the proximity alerts and the screens, there wasn't much else for Cruz to do.

"What's weird, Aaliyah?"

"Gravitics spike near the edge of the bow of our AV," the engineer muttered as she leaned over the console. Readings were flying over the screens. "Someone just kicked off a drive or something, ma'am."

"Could it be the Rangoran ship?" Cruz asked, the thought of Rangora still alive within the dead AVs and looking for blood sending a chill down her spine. Aaliyah shook her head.

"Their engines aren't in the front, and have a different signature. No, this is something else. Should we recall the boys, ma'am?"

Cruz chewed her bottom lip for a moment, contemplating. They were so *close* to completion. Pulling out now would waste all the work they'd done. On the other hand, the safety of the crew was ultimately her responsibility. If either man were injured or killed, she would never be able to look at herself in the mirror again. Their mothers wouldn't be too pleased, either.

"Call them in."

It was a tough decision, but she knew it was the right one.

"Bo, Jaime, return to the barn, over."

"*Uh... come again?*" Bo's voice replied over the comms. "*We've almost got this first energy bank cut free, Aaliyah. What's up?*"

"RTB, damn it. Don't argue with me."

"*Copy RTB, over.*" Jaime cut in.

"Ma'am? I've got a firmer grasp of the readings. Looks like a *Myrmidon* shuttle like ours."

Another shuttle? Cruz looked at the readings to confirm what Aaliyah had seen. What were they doing way out here?

"Hold off on RTB, boys. Looks like it's just another shuttle. Keep working the energy banks, over," Cruz decided after another moment of consideration. The readings kept coming and her heart sank as an all too familiar number popped up on the designator. They'd run across this particular shuttle before on salvage operations around *Thermopylae* back on the Sol System. They were a company like themselves, leasing the shuttle and subcontracting out to Apollo Mining.

At least, she felt confident they'd crossed paths before. She flipped frequencies before finding the open broadcast channel.

"Unidentified *Myrmidon*, this is shuttle 11242. Be advised this is a legal salvage and you are getting a little too close for comfort, over."

"*Shuttle 11242, this is shuttle 1023. Captain McBride speaking. That's a firm negative. Y'all are poaching on my salvage, over.*"

"That man has a punchable voice," Aaliyah murmured softly. "I already don't like him."

"Poaching? *Poaching?!* His salvage? Is he insane?" Cruz demanded, ignoring her cousin as she glared at the readings on the console. The other shuttle was languidly sitting there, directly between *Maslow's Hammer* and the ruined Rangoran AVs. It was *precisely* where their shuttle would have been had they not backed away due to the weird gravitic anomaly. Or rather, where they would have been situating the energy bank of the Rangora with their admittedly weak tractor beam. "That bloodsucking mosquito is trying to poach *us*!"

"Shuttle 1023, you are advised to back away from these AVs. We have already claimed them both as salvage and, pursuant of our leasing agreement with Apollo Mining, have begun salvage operations, over." Aaliyah snapped off the response in a way only a marine could.

"*That is a negative, shuttle 11242. We have rightfully claimed this as salvage and our operators are already within. Our agreement with Apollo dictates exclusivity with McBride Salvage. Back off, over.*"

"Skeeters," Cruz hissed through tightly clenched teeth as her inner Texan came roaring to the forefront. They *had* run across these guys before. The memory made her blood boil. "Bloodsuckin' thievin' parasites..."

"You are mistaken, shuttle 1023," Aaliyah said coldly, her tone professional. "You do not have any exclusive salvage rights to either vessel. We already have a team onboard the AV and are currently working *our* salvage, over."

"*Well then, 11242, they might want to be careful. Space is dangerous, after all, and we don't want any accidents to happen.*"

Cruz blinked. Was the other shuttle pilot *threatening* them? Threatening her *boys*?

"Listen here, motherfu—"

"Negative, 1023. You will back off and withdraw your salvage operators. We have permission to be here and this is our salvage, over." Aaliyah smoothly cut Cruz off before she could really get spun up.

"*You have no exclusionary claim, 11242. Your word against mine. Best of luck with your salvage ops. Ten twenty-three, out.*"

"I don't like this, ma'am," Aaliyah said once she'd ensured that the comms had well and truly ended. "We should call the boys back and move on. Or, I don't know, maybe call Argus?"

"Move on?" Cruz stared at her cousin as if she'd lost her mind. "We've got *two*—not one, but *two*—Rangoran AVs in very good shape here, worth millions each even with our percentage shares, and you want to *walk* because some little asshole in a shuttle is starting shit? Did our ancestors walk away from the Alamo when Santa Anna showed up? Did our great-grandfather walk away from the cartels? No! We Cruzes stand up to bullies! We don't back down!"

"The cartels shot our *bisabuelo* forty-seven times and burned his body after hanging him from a freeway overpass," Aaliyah reminded her, one brow arched high. "And our ancestors died at the Alamo, ma'am."

"That's beside the point." Cruz remained undeterred, righteous anger burning in her veins. "We do not run away from bullies. Not this family."

"I better not get shot and burned to a crisp . . ." Aaliyah sighed. "Bo, Jaime, be advised that another shuttle is working this salvage as well. You might run into some other sleds, over."

"*Huh?*" Bo responded immediately. "*What'd you mean, 'run into other sleds'?*"

"*She said there are other sleds working, idiot,*" Jaime cut in. "*So don't crash your sled if you see someone.*"

"*Want us to RTB still, Aaliyah?*" Bo asked.

"Negative," Cruz snarled. At her engineer's concerned look, she took a deep breath and continued in a slightly calmer tone. "Keep working that energy bank. Just don't let it drift out into open space. Bring it back to the shuttle and make sure we take possession of it, over."

"*That's going to take more time, cuz,*" Jaime pointed out. "*We won't get as much.*"

"I'm aware of that. Do it, but be careful. I don't trust those other guys."

"*Copy that.*"

"Are you sure about this, ma'am?" Aaliyah asked carefully as she watched the other shuttle move into position alarmingly close by.

Concern bubbled up beneath the justifiable rage.

"No . . ."

"Hey," Jaime said, nudging his cousin gently and dipping his helmet toward the far end of their hallway. "Company."

Bo looked up and spotted a pair of sleds down the twisted hallway. Like Jaime, he'd listened to the communication between their cousin and the other shuttle, and was in full agreement that the exclusivity claim of the salvage op was absolute horseshit. Having shoveled it for ten years as a child, Bo could smell it from a mile away, and he ran a critical eye over the interlopers.

Both suits were almost identical to theirs. However, instead of the plain helmets, both of the newcomers sported a strange silver logo. It reminded Bo of a crane, but an old-fashioned one from back when diesel engines ruled the farm.

"We got us a standoff," Jaime muttered. Bo nodded. His cousin, as usual, was the master of the obvious. "We gonna chase 'em off?"

"I got this."

"You sure?"

"Oh yeah."

"Okay. Have fun." Jaime didn't quite turn fully away from the two other suits, but the move made it abundantly clear that he either didn't view them as a threat, or simply showed his confidence that his cousin could handle anything the newcomers threw at them.

"*Hola, amigos,*" Bo broadcasted in the open, pitching his accent as strong as he could. He hefted his optical welder up and waved in a not-quite friendly manner toward the two sleds. "Nothing for you guys here. Maybe go find your salvage somewhere else? Move along now. Have a good day."

The duo from the other shuttle didn't say a word in reply. Instead, they turned their sleds and disappeared back into the darkness. Bo snorted. He'd expected a little more of an argument from them.

"Boss is right," Jaime muttered on their private comms once the two sleds were out of sight. "Bunch of thievin' skeeters, every last one of 'em."

"Yep. C'mon, cuz. Let's get this back onto the ship."

"Boss? On our way back with the first energy bank. Just letting you know that they got sleds already moving around in this wreck. Trying to poach, from the look of things. We, ah, *encouraged* them to find their salvage somewhere else."

Cruz's cursing on the other end was impressive.

While waiting for the boys to return with the first energy bank, Cruz did a little digging into McBride Salvage. There wasn't much on them, only the confirmation that she had crossed paths with them before during the salvage operations after the Horvath had finally been eliminated as a threat to the Sol System. It had been a brief encounter, true, but certain things tended to stick in Cruz's mind. One of those being when a competitor steals a salvage out from under you. The other being the smarmy voice of their leader.

Bo and Jaime had managed to rip out four different energy banks from the first Rangoran AV, each one at half capacity. It wasn't going to make them rich, but it would cover their fuel costs and operating expenses. With the boys needing breaks every now and then—one of the safety requirements the family insisted on when first going into this venture—they weren't hauling away as much salvage as they could. However, Cruz could live with that. After all, her safety record was perfect so far. Not many independent salvage operators could claim that.

Aaliyah, meanwhile, was keeping a close eye on the movements of the other *Myrmidon* shuttle and its sleds. Interestingly, the other company operated two sled teams in tandem, very much how Bo and Jaime operated. But with four sleds instead of two, they were able to make quicker work of the salvage operations, and soon they were starting to encroach on their area of work.

Not for the first time, Cruz was glad that they were no longer doing SAR in the immediate aftermath of the massive space battle. While finding the living and returning them to *Thermopylae* had been deeply satisfying for all of them, more often than not they'd been finding the dead instead, their rescue beacons chirping away but the Rangoran—or Human, the vacuum of space did not discriminate—inside already dead. Jockeying for position with a rival *Myrmidon* over salvage rights was far preferable to *that.*

"They're getting closer, ma'am," Aaliyah reported as the other *Myrmidon* skewed dangerously near to the exit hole that Jaime and Bo had only just started working in.

Cruz's eyes narrowed. McBride and his shuttle were becoming more of a nuisance by the hour. Scowling, she sent them a message warning them of violating their space. It was, of course, ignored.

Like the other thirteen messages she'd transmitted. The burning desire to run and tattle to Argus grew more tempting by the minute.

"How much salvage have they grabbed so far?" she asked. Aaliyah shrugged.

"They're after the same stuff we are, and working around the same rate with twice the manpower, so I'd just assume double, ma'am."

Her scowl deepened. "Thievin' skeeters."

"Ma'am, I've been scanning the other AV, and I think we might have found something. But..."

"But what?" Cruz looked at her cousin, who was rubbing the back of her neck.

"I might be wrong?"

"Wrong about what? C'mon, Aaliyah. Just tell me."

"I think I just found a full Rangoran fuel cell."

Cruz stopped breathing as she stared at the readings.

It was tentative, but as the data firmed up and the computer continued to run projections, her hope increased. If they found a fuel cell, one that hadn't ruptured, they'd be able to pay off the credits owed for *Maslow's Hammer* tomorrow *and* buy two more *Myrimidon*s outright. Red River Holdings, LLC would no longer be a one-ship operation but an actual, honest to God company. It wouldn't be at the level of Apollo Mining or the big dogs, but... they'd be on their way. The family would have nothing but security and growth ahead of it.

Her hope tangled with reality. There was only one problem that could interfere with that bright future—McBride Salvage.

"How can we confirm the fuel cell without letting McBride know we found something interesting?" Cruz demanded, tension tightening her shoulders to the point of pain.

"I don't know... casually?"

"Casually?" Cruz snorted as exasperated amusement momentarily overcame her frustration with the situation. "So, we just *casually* sling ourselves around to the other side of this hulk and *casually* direct our sleds to the same area? Maybe we can *casually* tell McBride to fuck right off while we're at it."

Aaliyah rolled her eyes at her dramatics. "It was just a suggestion, *ma'am.*"

"No... wait."

Cruz tapped her lips thoughtfully as she eyed the schematics of the Rangoran AV. Her eyes began tracing the inner corridors that, according to Bo and Jaime, were still navigable. On the opposite side of the assault vector, a massive hole had been created when a cluster of missiles had torn through it. With the rotation of the other AV in space, it was going to line up directly where the fuel cell of the other AV was floating in two hours. She started thinking over the math, the equipment they had on board, and her two sleds outside before inspiration struck.

"Casually." She laughed softly. "You know, Aaliyah? I sometimes forget how smart you are."

"Gee, thanks."

"No, really. You're brilliant." She paused and gave it a little more thought. The math was tetchy but doable with her implants… "How much air do the boys have on their packs?"

"They just recharged during the last drop. They're good for another ten hours."

"Perfect. How's our fuel?"

"Ma'am?"

"Fuel, Aaliyah. He_3 stuff in our tanks that makes our ship do the vroom-vroom thing?"

"You're hilarious, ma'am. And nominal. We're good for extended evolution. May I ask why?"

Cruz's smirked. "You may."

Aliyah gritted her teeth. "Why, ma'am?"

"One more question first…did we pack any of those new flares that Granadica came up with? The ones that work in vacuum with the oxidizer mixed in with the magnesium?"

"Yesss…" Her cousin visibly strove for patience. "But *why*?"

"Reasons I shall make clear shortly."

"Holy *shit,* Josepha! I'm about to throat-punch you." Not an idle threat from a former marine, because Aaliyah looked ready to throw hands. "Quit messing with me!"

"Oh, so it's 'Josepha' now, not 'ma'am'?" Cruz smiled sweetly at her cousin before finally relenting just a bit. "Sorry, couldn't resist. Okay, so here's what we're going to do to get these thievin' skeeters off our collective ass…"

"*You want us to do what*?!" Jaime exclaimed once the plan had been laid out to the duo inside the wreckage. His incredulity came through loud and clear to both women in the cockpit of the *Myrmidon*. "*No offense, cuz, but are you out of your fucking mind*?"

"Maybe a little," Cruz admitted as she deftly and subtly maneuvered the shuttle between the two AVs. "But it's the best way to get those thievin' skeeters off us without ruining the salvage for later! Plus, that fuel cell's intact. We ran the numbers twice. You wanted to get paid, Jaime. This is how we do it."

"*You do realize what all that residual oxygen is going to do when it vents, right*?" Bo asked.

"It's precisely what I'm hoping for."

"Fucking insane, cuz."

"That's not a 'no,' Jaime."

"Fine . . . but if I die because of this, you get to deal with my abuelita."

Cruz shrugged, entirely unconcerned. "Oh, she's an old softie. I'm her favorite."

"Actually, ma'am, I think I am," Aaliyah said smugly.

"What about that time she threw her chanclas at you for walking through her garden?"

"It was only the one, ma'am. Not both."

"Oh, right." Cruz nodded. "You probably are her favorite then. If Jaime dies, you tell her."

"You all are certifiable . . ." Bo let out a long-suffering sigh. *"Okay. We're moving into position now. I'll let you know when we're set."*

"You really think this is going to work, ma'am?" Aaliyah asked her cousin quietly, uncertainty etched upon her features. "I know we give them a lot of grief, but they're blood. My mom would kill me if I let anything happen to them."

"Your mom? Mine would skin me alive." Cruz ran the numbers a fourth time and again, nothing changed. She swallowed nervously and looked at Aaliyah. "I wish we could ask one of the AIs to triple-check the math, but I doubt they'd be willing to give up the processing power to check to see we don't blow ourselves up. I mean, the primary reason insurance on independent contractors is so high on leased shuttles is because none of the AIs can watch every single shuttle running around their space!"

"None of what you just said was reassuring," Aaliyah said flatly.

"It'll be fine. I promise."

"If you say so . . ." The engineer did not sound convinced.

Cruz began maneuvering the shuttle downward and to starboard, moving at a relative crawl. The shuttles and the ruined AVs were moving at over 15,000 kilometers an hour, so relative was definitely key. The trick, she knew from the simulations and math, was to do it at such a slow pace that the other shuttle would think they were simply poor pilots and move closer to exploit their bad positioning. In their eyes, it would be a coup, stealing the best salvage position from *Maslow's Hammer.*

Progress was painfully slow. More than once Cruz had to

fight the urge to throttle up and skew the *Myrmidon* in a slide to arrive at the target destination sooner. Patience had never been one of her strengths, and it was being tested severely now.

"McBride's moving," Aaliyah murmured in quiet voice after an hour. "Angling... increased speed... yep. He's taken the bait, ma'am."

"Shuttle 11242, this is 1023. You snooze, you lose. Our salvage now. We have the high ground and positioning. If you endanger me or my salvage crews by moving your shuttle too close to us, you will hear from our lawyers. Ten twenty-three, out."

Cruz shook her head. "Did that moron really just declare he had the high ground? In *space*?"

Aaliyah chuckled. "Remember when I said I wasn't sure if this was a good idea, ma'am? I take it back."

"There's my favorite cousin who always had my back when it came to throwing down with the *cholalitas* in high school."

"Sleds are in position now," Jaime reported briskly. *"No offense, but this better work—"*

"He already took the bait, Jaime," Cruz cut in smoothly. "All we need to do now is nudge them a little. How long do you need to cut that fuel cell free?"

"Fifteen minutes, tops."

"Good. Aaliyah is prepping for her part now."

"I don't understand why I'm the one who needs to do this," the engineer grumbled as she finished putting her helmet back on and securing it. Cruz checked her suit for any sign of a leak before giving her a thumbs-up.

"Because you're not a coxswain?" Crux reminded her. "Hold is recycling now. Pressure will be up in a minute. Once the light turns green, start the recycler and get that hold back to death pressure."

"Yes, ma'am."

"Pressurized... now. Good luck."

Aaliyah slipped out of the cockpit and into the pressurized cargo hold. As soon as the lock cycled shut, the engineer began to depressurize the compartment once more. Cruz quietly waited, ready in case something went wrong during the process.

The operation went off without a hitch and Aaliyah soon had the cargo hold open and fully exposed to the vacuum of space. Nearby, the shadow of the massive AV loomed, blocking the light from E Eridani's star and casting them into the freezing shade.

While their suits regulated the temperature, it still was still cold enough to warrant a string of expletives from the engineer.

"Focus," Cruz reminded her cousin once Aaliyah finally ran out of curses. "How're we looking back there?"

"*Ready to receive the cell,*" the engineer reported instantly. "*Tractor beam'll be able to handle towing the mass behind us, ma'am.*"

"The numbers say that, yeah. What about the other part of the plan?"

"*Should be good to go, ma'am.*"

"Bo, Jaime. Time?"

"*Moving now, cuz,*" Jaime reported. "*Cell is cut and separated.*"

"*I'm in position,*" Bo added. "*Just give me the word.*"

The comm chimed on the console. As expected, McBride had noticed the fuel cell being removed from the hulk of the AV. Cruz debated ignoring it for a moment before she answered. He could, theoretically, argue in court that she had recklessly endangered lives by ignoring a warning call from his shuttle. As farfetched as it was, she would not put it past the man. He seemed the type.

"Ten twenty-three, 11242. What can I do for you, McBride?"

"*You can quit stealing my salvage!*" His rage was palpable over the comms. Cruz gave it another five seconds tops before he started foaming at the mouth. "*You moved out of position and gave up your claim!*"

"I'm sorry, but did you say 'your salvage'?" Cruz asked in as innocent a voice as she could manage. It was tough when she couldn't stop grinning like a devil. "I do believe that you said something about the best of luck to us. We noticed the rotational shift of the AV and simply swapped our position. It looked a little dangerous to be that close to that suspicious leak as well. Surely you detected that?"

Apparently, he did not.

In space, oxygen disperses just as quickly as other gasses when released from a canister or ship. In theory, it could be used for maneuvering vessels in space. However, since the atmospheric mixture was one of the most vital systems on a ship, it would have simply been a waste to use it to maneuver. Especially when He3 was so readily available throughout the universe.

The oxygen in the Rangoran AVs had been mostly depleted,

thanks in large part to the missiles which had ended its life weeks before. However, there were little areas where pockets of oxygen remained. Some of the atmospheric lines that pumped the necessary mixture of oxygen, nitrogen, and other gases to make the air breathable were intact. These lines had been identified by the boys early on and studiously avoided during the cutting phase of salvage. Nobody wanted any accidents, after all.

Well, until McBride and shuttle 1023 had shown up, that is.

Calculating precisely how much thrust escaping gas would impart from aforementioned lines was something only an AI could do in a pinch. Through a lot of frustrated tears and some hair-pulling, Aaliyah and Cruz had managed to figure out the precise trajectory the first Rangoran AV would move when certain lines would be cut. More frustration followed when they were unable to determine precisely how empty the lines were. Calculated guesses were made, but in the end, Cruz had simply thrown her hands in the air and decided to let God figure it out. Aaliyah had reluctantly agreed.

God, apparently, had a wicked sense of humor.

With the fuel cell free of the Rangoran AV, Bo had taken his sled back to the dead vessel and begun cutting lines. The aft section of the ship, with the escaping gases, began to ever so slowly creep through space, moving at speeds barely discernible to the naked eye. After all, there wasn't that much being loosed. The Rangoran ship weighed billions of tons. Surely it couldn't do much damage to anyone or anything.

However . . . in a pinch, someone could be made to *think* something horrible was going on.

From the open cargo hold, Aaliyah had an excellent view of the Rangoran AV, the cut fuel cell, and the two sleds escorting it toward *Maslow's Hammer.* She also could see the large, gaping hole the boys had maneuvered through to get to this side of the vessel without alerting the other shuttle. It was big enough one could almost drive a *Myrmidon* through it.

It wasn't a difficult throw. The hardest part was not stumbling on the release. Throwing a lit flare in vacuum, without the expected rise and drop thanks to atmosphere and gravity, was a challenge. But Aaliyah, who might have become a softball player in another life, expected the lack of gravity to affect her aim and adjusted accordingly.

The lit flare, burning hot in vacuum thanks to the oxidizing agents within the magnesium core, flew unerringly through the large, gaping hole. Burning hotter than anything else in the near area, the intense heat created an artificial infrared radiation signature. Combined with the atmospheric leak caused by Bo that had begun to move the hulking ruin of the vessel, it made it appear that the Rangoran AV was about to cataclysmically explode right on top of shuttle 1023.

The other shuttle panicked and immediately skewed away, abandoning the four sleds *and their drivers* as it sought the safety of distance. Cowardly asshole.

By the time McBride realized that the radiation emitting from the ship and the gases were nothing more than random pockets of atmospheric gases, *Maslow's Hammer* had secured the fuel cell and energy banks, its two sleds and the boys, and were well on their way back toward *Thermopylae.*

Cruz, however, couldn't resist throwing a parting shot McBride's way.

"Shuttle 1023, this is *Maslow's Hammer.* We're recording you abandoning welders and their sleds at salvage operation designated AV1. Because you vacated the immediate vicinity of the salvage claim, we are required by our contract with Apollo Mining to report your hazardous treatment of your employees. See you on the beach..." She cut the comm to the other shuttle before he could respond, barely able to keep the glee out of her tone. "Jackass."

The bar was *slammed* that night.

Salvage operations had been going well, and with bonuses and overtime being paid, everyone had found their way to the old, reliable drinking hole. A haven for workers between shifts, it'd gotten a reputation of being the best place for affordable drinking.

Cruz and Aaliyah were seated at the high bartop table, their glasses half filled with top-shelf whiskey. They could more than afford the splurge. Finally, after all their hard work, they'd made the big score, made the *real* money.

Four hundred *million* credits.

Cruz still couldn't breathe properly, though the warmth of excellent whiskey was going a long way toward helping with that little problem. Because now, all she had were little problems.

After the family cut and taxes, the final payments for *Maslow's Hammer* and the down payment for three other *Myrmidon* shuttles, all four of them were walking away with roughly a million credits each. It was going to go down as one of the greatest salvage hauls in the history of independent contractors, ever.

Bo and Jaime had already left the bar, both men exhausted but happy. Their cuts were slightly larger by a few thousand credits thanks in part to their hazardous duty bonus. Family rules stipulated that the sled drivers be paid more than anyone else because of the risks they had to take while out in vacuum. Cruz had no issues with that. After all, it'd been her idea in the first place.

"Thieves, every last one of them," a familiar voice piped over the crowd from a nearby table.

Curious, Cruz looked around until she laid eyes on the speaker. He might have been good-looking back in the day, but age and drink had stolen much from the older man. His only remaining attractive feature were his blue eyes, but even those had been dulled. He waved around a mostly full mug, cheap beer sloshing over the edge as he continued to complain loudly to everyone in the immediate vicinity. Whether they wanted to listen to his rant or not.

Judging by the annoyed looks, they decidedly did not.

"Stole our salvage right from us and did *something* to make it look like that ship was about to blow sky high! I'm filing a complaint as soon as I have more proof."

Cruz began to smile in vicious satisfaction. She definitely recognized that voice now. It was none other than McBride, the pilot of shuttle 1023, and owner/operator of McBride Salvage. She'd recognize that smarmy and smug voice anywhere. It was, as Aaliyah had stated previously, a very punchable voice. Fortunately, it seemed to be attached to an equally punchable face.

Savage glee bubbled up beneath the mellow buzz of good alcohol.

"Hey, McBride!" she shouted at the top of her lungs over the background din of the bar. "Shuttle 1023!"

The man turned and looked their way. Cruz grinned and shot him the bird. Aaliyah, bless her, didn't hesitate for even an instant before joining in.

"Salvage claim filed and confirmed by Argus." She took a

slow sip of her whiskey, eyes twinkling over the rim of the glass. "Also, I double-checked. McBride Salvage has no exclusivity clause anywhere with Apollo Mining. We stole nothing. You? Well, we have everything on record and filed away. You bailed on your sled operators, you coward!"

McBride spluttered and denied everything, but the flush to his face was more due to guilt than rage, and the mood in the bar decisively turned against him. Nobody wanted to work with a known coward. His company was as good as dead.

"Have fun explaining it all to the arbitrator," Aaliyah called out sweetly.

Cruz winked. "Never try to bully a Cruz, ya thievin' skeeter!"

The two women flipped him off again and dissolved into laughter as the crowd joined in. Cruz couldn't stop grinning.

It sure felt good to win for a change.

THE RINGING DEEPS

JOHN RINGO

DEDICATION

As always
For Captain Tamara Long, USAF
Born: 12 May 1979
Died: 23 March 2003, Afghanistan
You fly with the angels now.

Also dedicated to
Jack Aaron Clemons
June 12, 1985–May 4, 2024

* * *

To these who are cleansed of base Desire,
Sorrow and Lust and Shame—

Gods for they knew the hearts of men,
men for they stooped to Fame,

Borne on the breath that men call Death,
my brother's spirit came.

Dedication from *Barrack-Room Ballads* by Rudyard Kipling

Beyond the path of the outmost sun through utter
darkness hurled—
Further than ever comet flared or vagrant star-dust
swirled—
Live such as fought and sailed and ruled and loved and
made our world.

They are purged of pride because they died, they know
the worth of their bays,
They sit at wine with the Maidens Nine and the Gods
of the Elder Days—
It is their will to serve or be still as fitteth Our Father's
praise.

'Tis theirs to sweep through the ringing deep where
Azrael's outposts are,
Or buffet a path through the Pit's red wrath when God
goes out to war,
Or hang with the reckless Seraphim on the rein of a
red-maned star.

They take their mirth in the joy of the Earth—
they dare not grieve for her pain—
They know of toil and the end of toil, they know God's
Law is plain,
So they whistle the Devil to make them sport who
know that Sin is vain.

And oft-times cometh our wise Lord God, master of
every trade,
And tells them tales of His daily toil, of Edens newly
made;
And they rise to their feet as He passes by, gentlemen
unafraid.

To these who are cleansed of base Desire, Sorrow and
Lust and Shame—
Gods for they knew the hearts of men, men for they
stooped to Fame—
Borne on the breath that men call Death, my brother's
spirit came.

He scarce had need to doff his pride or slough the
dross of Earth—
E'en as he trod that day to God so walked he from his
birth,
In simpleness and gentleness and honour and clean
mirth.

So cup to lip in fellowship they gave him welcome high
And made him place at the banquet board—the Strong
Men ranged thereby,
Who had done his work and held his peace and had no
fear to die.

Beyond the loom of the last lone star, through open
darkness hurled,
Further than rebel comet dared or hiving star-swarm
swirled,
Sits he with those that praise our God for that they
served His world.

AUTHOR'S FOREWORD

If you've picked this book up 'cause it has an interesting cover or you're just picking up John Ringo as an author, you need to read this:

This is my fourth installment in this series. And it starts "in media res," that is, in the middle of action. And there is no explanation. I won't say you need to pick up the first three books. But I've started to take the position that trying to introduce all the characters and situations in a new book in a series is tedious to both readers and authors. So, if you don't know who Tyler Alexander Vernon is, the vast importance of maple syrup in this universe, or why "Troy" is important other than as a city in the *Iliad*—and if you haven't gleaned that information from the other stories in this volume . . . just hang in there and it will start to make sense eventually.

Or go pick up the other books. That, at the least, will get you somewhat grounded in the universe.

Okay, hold onto your hat. We're about to enter space in the middle of a battle . . .

THE RINGING DEEPS

PROLOGUE

"Where the hell did that come from?" Admiral Clemons snarled. "What the fuck*?"*

The gate was spewing Rangora ships. Two AVs followed by cluster after cluster of Aggressor groups.

"Based upon intelligence estimates, that is a good part of the remaining Rangora fleet," Leonidas said. "About forty percent. And the correlation of forces . . . is now somewhat adverse."

"Ya think? Dexter?"

"We're shot dry, sir," Guptill replied. "Laser clusters are trashed and we've still got spin. Worst of all . . ."

"Granadica! Can you shut the door now? Please?"

"Sir," Guptill said. "The shuttles?"

"Jesus Christ!"

"Rangora are going to full launch," Leonidas intoned.

"Target?"

"Us."

"Get into the tunnels!" General Bolger snapped, bounding off the ramp. "If there are Rangora, just plow them! We need to get these shuttles space borne. Fast. Shit . . ."

The Thermopylae *was still spinning. Between that and a bit too much spring the marine commander was heading into an inconvenient orbit. He corrected with thrusters and got his feet on the surface.*

"Nearest tunnel is at three point seven mark four," Colonel Grant "Boner" Threlfall said. The J-3 of First Marine Division frankly thought that any marine not smart enough to get out of the way of the incoming missiles should have been washed out at boot.

"Let's get the fuck under armor, then," Bolger snapped. "This is about to be a very unsafe environment."

"Fuck, fuck, fuck, fuck . . ." Barnett muttered, hugging the surface of the Therm. *The tactical display was nothing but red overhead. The missiles were heading for the* Thermopylae *but that didn't mean they wouldn't target a Terran shuttle. And any one of those ship busters would open up a shuttle like a tin can being hit by . . . something really nasty. Being nearby when they hit the* Therm, *for that matter, wasn't going to be . . .*

"Impact!" MOGs called. "Gas wave . . ."

"Shiiiii . . ." Barnett screamed as the blast wave hit.

Explosions don't propagate well in space. On a planet, the majority of damage from any explosion, from a five-hundred-pound bomb to a fifty-megaton nuke, was from expanding gas. In space there is no atmosphere.

Unless, of course, the explosion was from a kinetic weapon hitting a big chunk of nickel iron. In which case it made a very temporary atmosphere composed of nickel and iron plasma.

The blast wave of not one but hundreds of multi-megaton missile impacts washed over both the retreating 142nd and the 143rd Tactical Boat Squadrons in what would later be termed "plasmaclastic flow."

Were any visual system capable of penetrating the rolling blast of plasma, the image would have been of so many soap bubbles briefly tossed in a hurricane of fire and then . . . vanishing.

CHAPTER 1

"E Eridani. Now."

Tyler Vernon was carrying his space suit and an AI core as he boarded the *Starfire*.

"Sir," his pilot commed. "With due respect, there's a battle raging in Eridani. All civilian traffic is on hold."

"One, you might remember where I started," Tyler said, stripping quickly and starting to don his suit. "Not my first rodeo. Two, I'm Tyler God Damned Vernon. I go wherever the fuck I please. Hatch is green. Move out. Argus, get me Apollo CEO, LFD CEO, et cetera."

"Yes, sir," the AI said.

"On the line, sir," Gregory Vance said. The sixty-year-old was chief executive officer of Apollo Corporation, founder and chairman of the board one Tyler Alexander Vernon.

"That was quick," Tyler said as his 'plant pinged that David Skiles, CEO of SAPL Corporation and CEO of LFD, Inc., the parent company of both megacorporations, also joined the conversation. Tyler's sometimes finicky personal AI had apparently pulled the panic bar. "Even for me you're usually harder to get ahold of."

"Pretty much everyone is following the battle in Eridani, sir," Vance replied. "I won't say work is shut down but let's say we all had a moment."

"Which is where I'm headed," Tyler replied.

"Right *now*?" Skiles asked. The former general had a fairly good appreciation of the current military situation in the star system just one jump through the Grtul gate. "Not a wise move, sir."

"General," Tyler said, "there are over one hundred thousand humans and Rangora stranded in the system. Our premier rescue force, the light boat squadrons, just got wiped away. There is *one* boat left from the 143rd. There are some 142nd boats in repair in *Troy*. That is *it* for rescue boats. This is the same type of vessel. It is *needed* in Eridani. Now. And I won't be alone. Which is the subject of the conversation. All operations in Wolf and Terra are on hold except speeding up the work on *Troy* and minimum support operations. *Every* boat we've got that can barely be spared, move it to Eridani. Everything. No exceptions.

"SAPL. Start moving every mirror capable of long-distance self-movement to Eridani."

"Sir?" Skiles said. "I'm pretty sure that the President is depending on SAPL to defend the Terran system. We're not sure who is even going to end up in control of Eridani. *Troy* is immobile, *Malta* is still not even vaguely online, as you just pointed out we've lost ninety percent of the fleet and *Thermopylae*... I'm surprised it's even still there."

"Which is the point, David," Tyler said, snapping a wrist seal into place. "We can't *repair* a *Troy* class without SAPL. And at the end of the day, whatever the President may want, I *own* SAPL. Without an act of Congress, not really her call. So, less talk, more doing."

"Comet, Paris."

"Go, Paris," Parker said, tonelessly.

Normally Engineer's Mate Second Class Dana "Comet" Parker liked talking to the AIs. Right now, she didn't know what to feel. She'd swept the net for any survivors but... both the 142nd and the 143rd boat squadrons had ceased to exist. In one brief moment most of the people she knew in the whole damned *universe* had been wiped out in nuclear fire. Just like LA all over again. And here she was carrying a bunch of clearly useless diplomats. Clearly useless 'cause their whole *point* was to *prevent* the battle that was taking place. That had just wiped out... everybody.

"As soon as the battle is over, we have to move to recovery. Suits first. I anticipate a ceasefire, whoever holds the system at the end of this battle. You'll be working around Rangoran vessels. Do not fire even if fired upon. Just pick them all up to over capacity and return to *Troy* through the gate."

"That's a long run, Paris," Parker said. Usually, you'd bring survivors to the nearest vessel that could support them. Running all of them back to the gate, going through the inevitable traffic and then into the *Troy* battleglobe was going to take time and time was one thing the survivors might not have.

"There's nowhere to put them in Eridani," Paris said. "*Thermopylae* is well and truly welded shut, there are no major vessels left in the fleet. They'll have to come back to *Troy* and the numbers may overwhelm even our support systems."

"We need more boats, Paris," Comet said. It was well above her pay grade to point that out, but she was just beyond tired.

"We're working on it," Paris said. "Dana. I have yet to extend you my condolences."

"Condolences are for after the work is done, Paris," Parker said. She'd gotten close enough to the massive battleglobe to be taken in tow by its tractor beam. She hit the override release and the four-ton shuttle, a bare speck next to the two-trillion-ton nickel-iron battle station, was sucked into one of the vessel bypasses like a mayfly being taken by a trout. She had to admit after the day she'd had it felt good to be surrounded by nickel-iron armor again.

"Agreed," Paris said. "I had never appreciated my namesake's emotions until this battle however."

"We ain't gonna lose, Paris," Parker said as the shuttle zipped through the zigzagged bypass.

"Oh, agreed again," Paris said. "*This Troy* shall not fall. Not with the hoplites and spears *I* am about to send forth."

As the shuttle shot out into the main staging area, Parker's eyes went wide. Every vessel assigned to the *Troy* was moving into launch positions. Her shuttle was being carefully maneuvered around a dozen *Independence*-class destroyers, while more *Constitution*-class cruisers and both *Defender*- and converted *Aggressor*-class battleships detached from their docking clamps.

"'He fears his fate too much . . .'" Dana muttered. The *Troy* mobile forces were the last ships Terra had to engage the Rangora fleet that had suddenly appeared in Eridani. Pretty much the last ships the Terran Navy had left.

* * *

"...just get them moving," Tyler said, watching *Troy*'s parasite squadron flow past him toward the gate surrounded by a butt-ton of Thunderbolt smart missiles. He was going to be the first *civilian* ship through the gate. He was determined on that. But he sure as hell wasn't going through with *that* lot. Not with what they were still facing. "What about the Devastators?"

"What about them?" Byron Audler said. The ship engineer was handling the logistics of the movement of "every damned thing we have that isn't vital" out of the Wolf system.

"They've still got life support, right?"

"In most cases, yes," Audler said. "Tow them into Eridani? The Rangora might want them back, boss. Or *take* them back."

"The Rangora want the Earth, the moon, and the stars," Vernon said. "If the President wants to give them back, she can. We're not going to have the logistics to repair and upgrade them any time soon, anyway. But it gives us somewhere to put the Rangora. And we're going to have to pick up Rangora. They're probably as stretched as we are."

"I don't think it's possible to be a space-faring civilization and be as stretched as we are, boss..."

"Unless I am much mistaken, we have no ships left," Colonel To'Jopeviq said.

Beor had used her Kazi codes to tap into the raw feed from Eridani. And it was clear that being very close to winning was not the same as winning. The colonel wasn't sure that either side could be said to have won. Both were trashed. But the humans had functioning warships in the Eridani system and the Rangora had...

"Essentially none at all," Beor confirmed. "Not in the case of warships. If I am remembering my last briefing correctly, this brings us down to six AVs, all damaged, less than forty battleships, mostly under repair... We have vessels under construction, but all our trained crews are..."

"Dead, prisoners of the Terrans, or floating in space," To'Jopeviq said. "And those floating in space... Many are going to die waiting for rescue."

"Their lives are the Emperor's," Beor said.

"Who, I'm given to understand, is quite a nice person for a mental child on his deathbed," To'Jopeviq pointed out. "Feel free to denounce me for that comment."

"No real response," Beor replied. The shuttle had come to a halt in mid-space between the gate and Galkod station. "Shuttle pilot?"

"We got word we're to hold here pending orders, ma'am," the pilot replied. "I don't think anyone knows quite what to do."

"Finally," To'Jopeviq said as he was automatically updated on the ceasefire. He winced at the updated casualty reports. "Make that five assault vectors. Damn these mammals. Every time we come up with a way to defeat them, they come up with a counter."

"But still no orders," Beor said. "There are forty-six shuttles in the Glalkod system. If anyone could do the math, they would all be shuttling through to Eridani as we speak. At least dropping us off. I hate to question the decisions of our betters..."

"I hope not," To'Jopeviq said with a snarl of black humor. "I might have to denounce you to the Kazi..."

"But they really should be getting started, quickly, on recovery."

"Never a notable item of importance on the part of the Imperium military," To'Jopeviq noted. "Which is another issue I wish I could point out to someone with a brain if I could find one in High Command. Both in historic terms and in the current situation. Again, the Americans."

"Not following, Colonel," the Kazi agent said.

"Third Campaign of the Seventy-Five Year War," the colonel said. "World War Two as they call it. Their Japanese enemy started with far more experience and far better trained crews, especially among their fighter and bomber squadrons. The Americans lost far more planes but far fewer crews because they were aggressive about search and rescue. And the survivors were used to train new pilots instead of being constantly flung into battle. Thus, the Japanese quickly fell behind in training as all their trained pilots died while initially inferior American pilots were picked up and got better. In the near term, there is one item of critical importance the High Command appears to have *completely* overlooked."

"That the Terrans are very hard to beat?" Beor said. "Arguably not worth the trouble? I think they may have finally gotten the message."

"No," To'Jopeviq said. "That we have virtually no fleet and no trained crews left. Which the *Ogut* surely know. And we have just given the second most powerful empire in the spiral arm a *casus belli*."

"Oh... ixi shit," Beor said, her eyes narrowing.

"We have orders, sir," the pilot commed. "I'm to do the gate transfers to return both of you to Rangor immediately."

"And the Ogut Empire just declared war," To'Jopeviq said. "At this point, I'm rather hoping to be turned over to the Kazi for a long, slow, brutal torture session by the end of which death will come as a release."

"That's not normally how people feel about us, Egil," Beor said, looking up at him.

"There are but two reasons we are being returned to Rangor versus somewhere closer," To'Jopeviq said. "One is a brutal torture session to encourage others to . . . I'm not sure what. Not be right over and over again when the High Command is wrong? The second, though, is potentially worse. Most don't normally fear that the High Command is going to ask them to somehow pull their asses out of the fire. I'd much rather face the Kazi."

"I do not need another headache," President Robards said, rubbing her eyes.

The very recently former Secretary of State had just been getting a handle on running not only the United States, which was still in recovery mode from all the devastating attacks this war had brought upon it, but the nascent Terran Alliance created by her late predecessor. Now she had thousands of spacers stranded in Eridani, a trashed battleglobe that would take months if not years to repair, if they could even get it *back* for repair, a fraction of the fleet she'd had two days ago, thousands of spacers and marines dead, and now another war.

"The bright side is that the Rangora are unlikely to be able to bring more attacks against us if they are fighting the Ogut," the Alliance SecNav pointed out. "Should we consider offering a treaty of mutual protection?"

"'The enemy of my enemy is my enemy's enemy, no more, no less,'" Admiral Marchant said. Which caused a snort from Marshall Hampson.

"Marshall?" the President said, looking at his hologram with bloodshot eyes. "Something funny?"

"Just that Admiral Marchant just quoted Tyler Vernon's old webcomic," the five-star commander of the Sol Defense Force replied. "That's one of the Twenty-Two Truths of Trading. I also agree it's true. Especially since I know very close to zero about the Ogut except that they are the main 'hospitality' race of the spiral arm and always seem to be involved in negotiations. I'd guess they're a bit like the Swiss?"

"Far from it," the President said, cracking her neck. "The Ogut are essentially a syndicalist polity based around large clans or families that control not only corporations and spheres of influence but their own fleets. The closer analogy would be the Ottomans or the Meiji Japanese if they were more economically based. Most of the 'wars' they've engaged in in the last two hundred years have been internal and with rare exceptions the battles have been essentially pro forma. Two sides will show up with forces, playact a battle with minimal losses, and withdraw. The syndicates don't like large-scale losses since that tends to be expensive. This sort of thing is anathema to them.

"The closest they have to a central military is the Emperor's bodyguard, which includes a fairly large fleet. But to actually fight the Rangora the Emperor will have to enlist the syndicates. The one brief I had that I recall on their military effectiveness indicated bad morale among their lower ranks due to generally poor and harsh conditions. But for all I know that could have been some briefer's opinion. I recall a paper that noted the same was said of Japanese forces prior to World War Two. We need a really good SPIE done on them to assess this development. So, we'll table it since they're way over *there* and we're way over *here* and the twain are unlikely to meet. Is there anything we haven't thrown at Eridani to recover the stranded personnel?"

"The 144th is getting ready for flight," Admiral Marchant said. "We're recovering into the surviving ships as fast as we can. Apollo is moving all of its equipment into Eridani. And I do mean *all*. They're continuing work on *Troy*, but every other operation is shut down to deal with recovery."

"Please God, the Rangora are almost out of ships themselves and don't attack soon," the new Secretary of State said.

"Well, we've still got SAPL," the President said. "They're not taking Terra with an exawatt mining laser staring them in the face."

"Madame President?" Athena said, diffidently. The system defense AI had been included automatically in the meeting.

"Yes, Athena?"

"Mr. Vernon has ordered SAPL moved into the Eridani system," Athena said. "Two thirds of the mirrors are on the move already."

"He did *what*?" the President snapped, grabbing her head. "Get me Vernon!"

"... because we don't need it in the Terran system and we do in Eridani," Tyler said, calmly.

"SAPL is the only defense we have left, Mr. Vernon!" the President snapped.

"I would politely disagree, Madame President," Tyler replied. "*Troy* may be a bit short on missiles but it's pushing over two hundred petawatts of power through its onboard lasers at this point. And the portion of SAPL that remains, which is functionally immobile, is another four *hundred* petawatts. We need a SAPL in Eridani to repair *Thermopylae*. Not to mention defend *that* system, which gives us a forward defense. We don't have time to build one there. So... SAPL is mobile, *Thermopylae* is not. Move the mountain to Mohammed."

"We've gotten so used to that thing covering us..." the President said, her hands over her eyes. "It makes me feel very uncomfortable having it gone."

"I'm going to lose mirrors to random chance," Tyler replied. "We're going to have to move them through a battle debris field that even Argus is having a hard time computing. There are two major asteroid belts, twenty-six independent bodies that more or less classify as planets or at least big moons, some of which are in direct interaction as binary planetoid systems. It's seventy-five percent of Sol's mass and has a thirty times greater magnetic effect and solar wind. It's less than two billion years old so the whole system is more or less a dog's breakfast. I wouldn't put SAPL in there if I didn't absolutely *have* to. Madame President, I absolutely have to."

"And at the end of the day I recall you do own it, don't you?" the President said with a slight smile.

"Well, myself and a large number of investors," Tyler said. "Who are, I assure you, going to be far more incensed at this decision. But it is necessary. While SAPL may be a major part of the Terran defense system, it is first and foremost a mining laser and for repair of the battleglobes. *Thermopylae* is going to need a lot of repair. I'll point out to the investors that I'll be charging you for that."

"Thanks so very much," the President said, drily.

* * *

"Granadica," Admiral Clemons said. "I'm sorry I was short with you earlier. I'd ask 'What's your status?,' but I think the more personal 'Are you going to be okay?' is better. *Are* you going to be okay?"

The *Thermopylae*'s kilometer-long ship fabber gave a long theatrical groan in reply.

"I'm trying to find repair systems that are sufficiently functional to repair my repair systems, Admiral," the Glatun AI replied. "If I were human, I'd more or less look like I'd just been blown up by a bomb. I even lost bits . . . that are floating in the main bay. My primary intake processor literally *blew out* and is now drifting in pieces. Which means I can't actually *do* anything until I find some way to build a *new* one. It's a bit like trying to feed yourself without a mouth. Or a stomach. Without external repair support, this is going to take weeks of recovery. Possibly months. I'm still trying to even assess the full damage. Since I'm the only fabber left in the globe, external support is unlikely. I'm sorry, Admiral, that is the truth."

"I understand, Granadica," Clemons said. "I'm just glad you survived. Professionally and personally."

"We lost too many today, Admiral," Granadica said. "But we remain. And we are going to make those crack-shell bastards pay with compound interest. However, I need to get back to . . . healing is the only real word for it. I think I took liver damage."

"I didn't know you had a liver," Clemons said, puzzled.

"I finally got a microbot into my metallochemical processor and . . . Oh! Ugh! Oh, God, that's grotesque! I can't look! But . . . looking is no longer a problem! Yay! Because *I lost the bot to a globule of fluoric acid* . . . That's my status, Admiral. Pretty much says it all. I'm not *healing*, I'm still *eating myself alive* from the inside. This is going to take time."

"Well, we seem to have that in abundance at least," Clemons said. "At least we do."

"Why am I picking up atacirc when I should be picking up survivors?" Parker asked.

They'd dropped off the human diplomatic delegation from the spectacularly failed "peace negotiations" in E Eridani. Comet had expected an immediate return to the Eridani system but had been told to hold in place. Then came the order to prep one corner of their not particularly large command compartment for an atacirc installation. Which meant they'd just lost their bunks.

When the Apollo techs finally arrived with the material, Parker tried not to gasp. Atacirc had been hysterically expensive when Tyler Vernon first discovered the Glatun taste for maple syrup. At this point it was produced by the various fabbers in the system by the shipload. But it was still a lot of atomic-level circuitry. The cubic it filled was the size of a couple of filing cabinets. And it had to be well secured to the bulkheads. Definitely just lost their bunks.

"The real question is why we're doing an AI installation on a *Myrmidon*," the boss of the tech crew replied. "These things usually go in globes or downside secure installations, not in a fricking shuttle. We're adding hypernode bandwidth as well."

"This is an AI install?" Comet asked. "Where's the AI?"

"Got no clue," the tech said. "But that's the install. Only thing that needs this much atacirc and hypernode is an AI. Don't know where you're getting the core. Don't care. We're done. You're prepped."

"What about the grav plates?" Comet asked. "The number twenty-four is right under your install. We sort of need to be able to access it."

"Again, not my concern," the tech said. "Just shut it down."

"Then your atacirc is taking up to one thousand gravities of acceleration during maneuvers," Comet said. "That bracing will take maybe ten."

"Figure it out later," the tech said, shrugging. "We've got more priorities. Ask whoever does the install. Maybe they'll know."

"Squadron," Parker commed. "Install complete. Shuttle Thirty-three ready to roll."

"Roger, Parker," Sanchez commed. "Proceed to Eridani. Rendezvous civilian vessel *Starfire*. Be advised, the gate area is getting crowded..."

"Argus," Tyler said, looking at the schematic of the gate traffic. "Get with Athena and Paris. Help them out with traffic control if they need it."

When he'd ordered "everything" into Eridani he hadn't really thought about what "everything" meant. Over the years Apollo had built up a plethora of ships. *Monkey Business*-class mining ships. Paw tugs. Freighters. Tankers. Specialty repair ships. There were more classes than he could identify without referring to his plants. Usually, they were scattered all over Wolf and Terra systems. He'd never seen all of them, most at least, maneuvering into one space.

"Already doing it, sir," Argus said. "This is quite a... showing?"

He owned a *shit ton* of ships. I mean, it was really silly at a certain level. It slowly dawned on him that he probably owned—well, *controlled*, there were a lot of investors in the corporations—the tonnage of a really serious fleet.

"Tell me that someone is working on logistics," Tyler said, thoughtfully. "We're going to need fuel, food for the crews and survivors..."

"Working on that with Apollo and LFD in my spare cycles, sir," Argus said. "We're approaching a survivor, sir. That may need your assistance."

"In other words, quit joggling our elbow?"

"This is the first time since you took me out of control of SAPL I've felt fully utilized, sir," Argus said. "Very fully."

"Sir, survivor approaching for recovery," the pilot commed.

"On it..."

CHAPTER 2

"Shuttle Thirty-three, Argus."

"Thirty-three," Comet said. She didn't allow the nervousness to enter her voice, but it didn't mean it wasn't there. The gate area was beyond crowded. She had, she thought, an encyclopedic knowledge of ship types, human and civilian, and she didn't recognize half the types preparing for gate transfer. And they were maneuvering at what she recognized as stupidly close ranges. Most of them had deflector screens but that wouldn't stop damage from a serious collision. Most of them massed and drove more than their deflectors could overcome.

"Need to take control of your shuttle," Argus replied. "We're just too crowded for human maneuvering."

"Roger, Argus," Comet said, flipping the controls to remote.

"Thanks for not arguing," Argus said. "Gate transfer in about ten minutes. We've got another load coming in from Wolf, first. Argus, out."

The shuttle suddenly went notionally "up" and then to port. It attached to the side of a *Monkey Business* with a notable clang. Argus was not playing around. The *Monkey*'s tractors locked on and that was that.

"Guess we're taking a ride to the other side," Parker said. "Angel, keep an eye on Twenty-four. I don't want to turn a billion dollars' worth of atacirc into projectiles. Especially in here."

"Aye, aye, EM," Angelito replied.

Parker just breathed for a moment and tried like hell not to cry. Months she'd been trying to get that simple response out of the damned Suds. Just the automatic and unthinking reply to an order and no questions, no arguments, just do the damned job. They'd finally gotten them to standard...

And Angel was the only coxswain they had left.

"EM, we have an incoming call," Angel said, puzzled.

"Pass it," Parker said.

"It is from... a Rangora?"

"EM2 Parker," Parker said, keying the comm.

"EM, Colonel To'Jopeviq. We spoke during the battle."

"Roger, sir," Dana said. The conversation during the previous ceasefire seemed like a million years ago. When she still had a soul.

"Since we have communications, for now, I wish to express my regret for the loss of your squadron. No... 'smack talk' as you put it. I, too, have lost close comrades in arms. We may be enemies, but I regret their loss. They were valiant and daring. True warriors as are you. You have my condolences."

Parker shook her head for a second and mouthed: *What?*

"Thank you, sir?" Dana said. "I, too, regret the loss of your comrades."

"Our lives are the Emperor's," To'Jopeviq replied. *"And in truth I had no close comrades in that battle. General Sho'Duphuder was a worthy warrior, but we were not close. Although I am a man of war, it is my wish that this latest debacle will result in a lasting peace between our polities. Frankly, you Terrans are just too fiendishly damned difficult to defeat. Had we any similarities, you would make far better allies than enemies. We should leave it at that. Again, my condolences, Engineer's Mate. May we someday have the opportunity to toast skul to absent companions."*

"Absent companions, sir."

"To'Jopeviq, out."

"What the hell?" Angelito said, turning around in his station chair.

"I..." Parker said, shaking her head. "I got nothin'. Except gonna have to report that one..."

"Ergil?" Beor said, looking at him with raised brows.

They were in the middle of another interminable wait for a gate transfer. With all the damage remaining in the Glatun systems, ships were moving everywhere to simply keep the once astoundingly wealthy and powerful polity functioning at some minimum level. What would happen when the Empire had to concentrate all its energies on the new war with the Ogut remained to be seen.

The colonel pulled up an updated social relationship schematic and pointed.

"Tyler Alexander Vernon is, arguably, the most powerful person in the Terran System," To'Jopeviq said. "Look at who one of his close comrades is."

"That is impossible," Beor said. "He is the . . . sixty-third most wealthy person in the spiral arm. There is, further, a significant difference in age. They could not have grown up together. Human males often mate with females who are much younger. Are they in a reproductive relationship?"

"Our analysts apparently cannot decipher the social link," To'Jopeviq said. "It appears to be something truly alien to our thought process. There is no sexual component that anyone is aware of. They appear to be simply . . . friends. And the definition of friendship is always species specific. It must be a human thing. But having a personal connection to someone one step from Tyler Vernon may be useful someday."

"That is an interesting point," Beor said, shaking her head. "You are getting decidedly complex in your thinking, Colonel."

"Perhaps," To'Jopeviq said. "It had the added benefit of being true . . ."

"Come on, Comet," Tyler said as they approached the next drifting spacer. "Fucking floor it."

"Excuse me, sir?" one of the officers in the compartment inquired.

In retrospect, he really should have taken some of the material out of the compartment. The antique Chippendale desk was taking up floor space that he could have used for bodies. On the other hand, there was someone curled under it and four people on top so maybe not.

The *Starfire* was not optimized for recovery. It had one small airlock into the main compartment and the compartment couldn't be evacuated. Well, it could be, if he wanted to destroy the original *Starry Night*. Or the Goya. Or the Titian.

"Sir," the pilot commed. "On this vector we are passing within visual range of three Rangora. I mean... close. We're going to have to dodge them."

Tyler looked around the already crowded compartment and sighed.

"Stand by," he said. "Argus. I need the local Rangora channel."

"Sent," Argus replied.

"Rangora in this sector," Tyler commed. "We're in a ceasefire. Try to take over this shuttle and I've got... fifteen very pissed-off human spacers who will dispute it. Some of them armed officers. Not to mention we hold this space and still have marines. I'd like to pick you up but make one hostile move and I'll space you without a suit. Got it?"

"This is Lieutenant Zigiladao. We acknowledge the ceasefire. We accept your offer and promise no hostilities."

"Okay, everybody, guess who's coming to dinner?" Vernon said, stepping to the hatch.

"They have a *marketplace*," Sergeant Ghezhosil said.

The mall in the *Thermopylae* was still small and under construction with just a few stores. Most of those had their roll doors down but the window displays were open and the Rangora were looking at them with something resembling awe.

"Why would they have food stores?" the sergeant continued, pointing. "These appear to be raw foods to be made and cooked? Do they have cookers on a battle platform?"

"It would appear so, Sergeant," Lieutenant Lanniph replied.

The part that was bothering the lieutenant was not the marketplace in a battlestation, a mobile battlestation at that, but that the Rangora marines had been escorted there and then more or less left. They had been stripped of their ammunition but retained their weapons. That bespoke either remarkable confidence or remarkable stupidity on the part of their human... captors was not quite the right word. Hosts?

"Ghezhosil, right?"

The human looked pretty much the same as the rest that Lanniph had seen. It was hard to distinguish between aliens. Its helmet off revealed a very wet head devoid of the repulsive human hair and one hand extended toward the sergeant. Had it been holding a weapon it would have been a very hostile gesture.

"Yes," Ghezhosil said, warily.

"Del Papa," the human said through his translator. "We met in the tunnels."

The human had been accompanied by a team that looked decidedly unfriendly. And while humans were small, the laser rifles they carried were more than capable of killing Rangora as they had repeatedly proven.

"Why is your hand extended, Sergeant?" Lanniph asked.

"It's a human thing," the human replied. "My tribe's anyway. When two humans of my tribe meet, we grasp hands and move them up and down, what we call 'shaking.' It is a friendly greeting and a gesture of respect. Also ensures neither one of us is holding a weapon."

Ghezhosil slowly extended his three-clawed hand and took the much smaller human's hand. The human then moved it up and down like a manual pump.

"Greeting complete," Del Papa said. "And unless we were real friends and wanted to catch up on old times and family, that completes the ritual greeting between non-enemies, which is what we are at the moment. Which brings up why I'm here."

"Which is . . . ?" Lanniph asked.

"Some of your junior enlisted got separated from your units for one reason or another," the human said. "They all acknowledge that they got the ceasefire order, but they're worried about something called 'the Kazi.' My 'plant puts that as your secret police. Something about killing their families if they surrender. We need some people to talk them down before they run out of air. Is that a matter to which you can attend?"

"It is a matter to which I can attend," the lieutenant said. "The sergeant needs to remain here to ensure the junior enlisted do not . . . perform improper actions."

"You mean loot, pillage, and burn?" Del Papa said, making a snorting noise. "Got it. I'm sure if we had your kind of booze, they'd be getting rip-roaring drunk. Very well, Lieutenant Lanniph. If you'll accompany me?"

"I will need to recharge my air systems," the lieutenant said.

"We have the systems prepared," the sergeant's translator replied.

Lanniph noticed that the reply had been a short bark.

"Can you translate what you said more exactly?" Lanniph asked.

"The precise term was 'Got you covered' as in providing cover fire," the sergeant said. "Since it is a generic human term that is used by people who would never even pick up a weapon, it says a lot about humans. Or at least my tribe."

"And what is your tribe, if I may inquire?" Lanniph asked as the sergeant led the way out of the mall.

"Fifth Special Operations Group," Del Papa said. "Yoo Nited States Army. For your general information, the guys I'm leading are Taliban goat fuckers. Up until about the time the Horvath started bombing and plaguing the hell out of us, they were our most mortal enemies. So, you can say that my tribe makes a *specialty* out of using whatever enemy comes along however we gotta use 'em."

"Lieutenant, what part of 'ceasefire' do your people not get?" Tyler asked.

Remnants of the AV were still under power. And firing at anything that came nearby. Since it was still close to the gate, that meant all the ships coming through from the Terran system. The fire wasn't very accurate and there weren't any hits, yet. But it was making recovery difficult.

"Only officers are issued hypercom implants," Lieutenant Zigiladao replied. So far, the three Rangora weren't hostile. They just seemed happy to be in air. "With the interference and damage, it is possible that some of the remaining laser stations simply are unaware of the ceasefire."

The *Constitution*-class cruiser *St. Louis* suddenly opened fire with its spinal gun. Its reply was *not* inaccurate.

"Arggh," Vernon snarled. "War is waste."

"I did not get that, Tycoon," Zigiladao said.

Tyler's implants had noted that it was simply an expression of frustration and not directed at the Rangora, so it had not translated the statement. The Rangoran translators were seriously inferior to the Glatun/human tech the humans used and had just missed the statement.

"War is waste, Lieutenant," Vernon replied. "There are much better things I could be doing with all these ships than picking up survivors and cleaning up the mess from another damned battle. My entire God damned life has been nothing but war. I am frankly tired of it. I just keep hoping that all you damned squids and lizards will figure out that Terra is *not* going away. We do not fade into the night."

"I see, Tycoon," the Lieutenant said.

Tyler's plants automatically translated his tone and body language as "uneasy confusion." Which sort of said it all about human/Rangora relations.

"Mr. Vernon, EM Parker. We are closing on your vessel. I've got a bunch of atacirc. Do you know why?"

"Because information is power, Dana," Tyler replied. "And the ability to process it is more power. And we need all the help we can get. Can you pull me into your bay on tractor? I'm not all that in zero G."

"Will do, sir."

"If you'll excuse me, folks, I've got a rendezvous to keep."

Tyler set the AI core down on the deck of the command compartment carefully and waggled a finger at the engineer.

"Before I do this, come here," Vernon said, pulling off his helmet.

"Sir?" Parker said, unstrapping and sliding out of the chair.

The tycoon wrapped his arms around the engineer's mate and hugged her, hard.

"My absolute grief and horror at what happened to the shuttles is . . . I am so glad you survived, Dana. So glad."

"Thank you, sir," Dana said, hugging him back. She tried to maintain the calm and rational face she'd been holding since she saw the loss counter but couldn't. A sob broke through. "I can't do this right now. I just *can't*. I just have to keep telling myself they're still out there, somewhere. Beyond the reach of the hypernode."

"'Beyond the path of the outmost sun,'" Tyler said, nodding. "'Live such as fought and sailed and ruled and loved and made our world.'"

"Quote, sir?" Dana asked. "God, it sucks to cry in a helmet."

"Take it off," Vernon said. "That's what atmo is for. And, yes, Kipling. An epitaph to his friend Wolcott Ballistier. Also the dedication to *Barrack Room Ballads*. A collection I strongly recommend you add to your professional reading list."

"I'll get around to that right away, sir," Dana said, taking off her helmet and wiping her eyes.

"And with that we do need to get back to work," Tyler said. He picked the AI core back up and slipped it into the slot in the atacirc pile. "AI. Activation code Alpha-Zulu-Six-Nine-One-Four-Zulu-Seven-Two-Eight-Papa."

"I am awake," the AI said. "Name?"

"The Eridani system is named for the Greek name for the Po River in northern Italy," Tyler said. "The legend is that it was created when Phaeton stole his father's solar chariot and lost control of it. It is also referred to as the Path of Souls. I name you Phaeton. Please update yourself on the current clusterfuck. Currently there are too many souls on the wrong path."

"Too few ships, too little life support, too many survivors spread too widely."

"Every AI takes its personality from its initial development," Vernon said, wearily. "Your primary purpose is to rescue all these poor souls, humans and Rangora, with humans taking precedence. The 144th boat squadron, what there is of it, is on the way. You're going to need to take control of most of their boats. If you need suggestions, you have been installed in the boat of the finest pilot I know, even before our recent losses. All clear?"

"Yes, sir," the AI said, its voice taking on a faint resonance.

"Be aware that at some point you're going to have to be unplugged and reinstalled," Vernon said, shrugging. "This is a desperation move. We can't leave you in this boat forever. I'll make that as quick and painless as possible."

"Understood," Phaeton replied. "We must get to work, sir."

"Roger," Tyler said. "Dana. Just hang in there."

"Will do, sir," Dana said. "Mr. Ver... Tyler?"

"Yes," Tyler said, tilting his head slightly to the side.

"Thank you. For... everything."

"One of these days we need to talk," Vernon said, nodding. "For now... Time to go save more people."

"Angel," Parker said, rotating her neck then donning her helmet. "Change seats."

"EM?" the coxswain said.

"Time to put my cox rate back on," Parker said. "What the hell, I'm the senior surviving coxswain in the squadron. Who's going to say no?"

"I am... not well versed in engineering, EM," Angelito said, nervously.

"Time you learned."

* * *

"Admiral, the Germans are approaching Troy space," Commander Bosnjak said.

"That sounds oddly ominous," Marchant said. "But at the moment, it's good tidings. Put me through to their commander."

"Captain Nussbaum online."

"Captain, glad to have you," Marchant commed. He had no clue about this new force.

The 144th wasn't supposed to be activated for another couple of months. It only had half its *Myrmidon*s and the crews had to have little or no real experience. And they were about to be sent into some of the toughest boat work possible, recovery in a debris field. But they were the only *Myrmidon*s, and the only boat drivers even if half trained, the Alliance had left. Picking people up with cruisers and destroyers was a losing proposition and the warships weren't fitted with so much as a single boat. Another thing to be put on the list of "things that should probably change."

"We are honored to be called, Admiral," Nussbaum said. "We have augmented our force with our instructors. However, not all boats have fully qualified coxswains nor engineers. There will be issues."

"Sir, incoming call from a new AI?" Commander Bosnjak said.

"Go?" Marchant said.

"Admiral Marchant, Captain Nussbaum, AI Phaeton. I greet you. Mr. Vernon has installed me with the express purpose of assisting in the recovery and assisting the 144th with any issues that may arise. With the captain's permission, in some cases I may request remote access. I will also be directing movement for recovery as well as integrating with AI Argus in traffic control if this meets with your approval, Admiral."

"Very much so, Phaeton," Marchant said, shaking his head. "Vernon is, as always, one step ahead."

"We very much look forward to working with you, Phaeton," Nussbaum said. There might have been a tiny note of relief in his voice, but it was hard to tell with Germans.

"Move to the port and starboard bulkheads and hang onto anything you can hang onto including each other . . ." Dana commed to the personnel, human and Rangora, in the shuttle bay. "And the bodies," she added without transmitting.

She'd already completed one run to the *Troy* with survivors. Their orders at first were just pick up humans. But it was apparent that the Rangora were in an even worse situation than the humans when it came to recovery ships. Dana tried like hell to hate the lizards that had killed practically every friend she had in the universe. But she just couldn't. Maybe it was that comm from the Rangora colonel. Or maybe it was because the Rangora seemed to have something regarding a code of honor. The survivors they'd picked up were even helpful. Maybe it was because they weren't those damned Horvath squids. But she wasn't sweating picking up the lizards. They were just more bodies.

And there was a shitload of bodies drifting around. Some of what they'd picked up had been actual bodies. When you had two space suits hooked together and the live one wasn't going to leave his or her buddy behind, you picked up the body. And space-taped it to the bulkhead. And moved on.

"Are you sure about this technique?" Phaeton asked.

"We've got ten in close proximity," Dana said. "I can close and carefully pick each one up, taking time, or I can scoop."

"Coxswain," the senior officer in the compartment commed. "Why did you just open up the main hatch?"

"'Cause it's quicker this way, sir," Dana said. "Just hang the hell on."

The tough part was really on Angel. He had to maintain inertial stability just along both bulkheads while leaving the center in zero G with an inertial buffer along the back bulkhead. Otherwise, when the suits entered, they hit the bulkhead at survivable speeds, but they were just as likely to sustain an injury. And it wasn't like he was a trained engineer.

"Angel, can you slide him over to . . . I got it," Dana said, moving through a multidimensional skew turn while using the internal gravity to slide the struggling suit over to the port bulkhead.

"To answer you, no," Angelito admitted. "I'm not even sure what you just did, and I was watching it on my screens."

"You pick up a few things," Dana said distantly as the second suit, a Rangora, tumbled into the compartment.

"I've got this one," Phaeton said. "And let me tractor the next two together. We have some debris here . . ."

"Screens on as they come through, Angel," Dana said.

"Roger," Angelito said.

"And off to the next cluster," Dana said as the last of the local suits tumbled into the compartment. "Close hatch."

"Close hatch, aye," Angel said. "Thank God."

Survivors weren't the only "debris" in the region. Bits and pieces of ships, and sophonts, were scattered freaking *everywhere*. Space was big but battles just seemed to spread material to the furthest reaches.

"Lieutenant Commander, air check on all personnel, please."

"Roger, EM."

"Find me another batch, Phaeton."

CHAPTER 3

"All the Rangora against the back bulkhead," Dana commed to the cargo. They were crammed. She'd done the "open hatch" maneuver again and this time just used the bodies in the cargo bay as cushion. It worked. Good enough for this cluster. "We're making a speed run to the gate. We'll be taking about two Gs. Just crunch and suffer. Air good?"

"Not on all suits," the lieutenant commander replied. "We've got some leakers. How long on the run?"

"I'm compressing the compartment for the run," Dana said. "Angel. Atmo. We don't have the recyclers for everyone aboard. Just the people with low air take off their helmets. Rest of you keep them on. And prepare for speed run..."

"Hold that one, Cox," the commander replied. "I just got some orders. Cycle your hatch."

"Angel, cycle hatch."

"Cycle hatch, aye."

The commander had to pull himself through the hatch through the bodies in the way. The cargo compartment was packed to cubic capacity.

"Engineer's Mate Parker," the commander said, formally. "Raise your right hand and repeat after me..." He grabbed a bar with his left and raised his own right.

"What am I repeating, sir?"

"The oath of commissioning," the commander said. "I, state your name..."

"Wait, what?" Parker asked.

"You're being commissioned, EM," the commander said, testily. "I just got orders from Admiral Clemons. Lieutenant Junior Grade. So, raise your right hand or say you reject it, in which case you can explain it to Admiral Clemons, who is a very busy man at the moment."

"I, Dana Cecilia Parker..." Dana said, still confused.

"...do solemnly swear (or affirm) that I will support and defend the Constitution of the Alliance against all enemies, foreign and domestic; that I will bear true faith and allegiance to the same; that I take this obligation freely, without any mental reservation or purpose of evasion; and that I will well and faithfully discharge the duties of the office on which I am about to enter. So help me God. You can leave the 'So help me God' off if it offends you."

"Not a problem, sir," Dana said, completing the oath. "I'd like some... Why did I just get commissioned, sir?"

"No idea, Cox," the commander said. He turned around and looked at the wall of bodies. "You'd have to ask the admiral. Anywhere I can hang on back here?"

"Dana, Paris," the AI commed as she approached *Troy.*

The battleglobe had reoriented. The main door was now pointed at the gate and wide the hell open. Given the damage that had been done to *Thermopylae* in similar circumstances, it had her nervous as hell.

"Paris, Parker," Dana said, following the programmed route right to the main door. It felt like the good old days when... It had been a long time since she'd used the kilometer-wide door.

"All your suits have at least ten minutes of air," Paris replied. "Enter the main bay. Follow the directed route. Go to Sector West. Open main hatch. Use internal inertial systems to eject all personnel. I'll take it from there. No SAPL warnings but avoid the horns. No hotdogging across my main bay this time, Comet."

"Aye, aye, Paris," Dana said. "Just *eject* them?"

"I'll pull them in under tractor," Paris said. "We're using one of the Apollo boat bays as a mass airlock. Just push them out."

"We've got some... non-survivors," Parker said.

"I have that," Paris said. "Get them unstrapped and eject them with the rest."

"Roger," Parker said. She might not hotdog it across the main bay but she was moving at the maximum allowed velocity. Okay, a touch over. "All cargo personnel. Get the casualties unstrapped. All personnel don helmets and get me a final air check. Orders are to discharge you in the main bay in vacuum for recovery by internal tractors."

"Oh, you have got to be kidding me," the lieutenant commander said, latching his helmet.

"I'm sort of boggled as well, sir," Dana said. "Angel, they got all the bodies unstrapped?"

"Looks like it?" Angelito said. "I can't really see very well. All the monitors have bodies in front of them."

"Air and latch check, Commander."

"All personnel locked and latched," the commander said.

"Angel, locked and latched?"

"Uh... yes, Miss?"

"Better hope so," Dana muttered, rolling her eyes. The implants automatically translated the Spanish Angelito was undoubtedly speaking so she was pretty sure that had been "Sí, Senorita." Which was not the correct address of... an engineer's mate, which she no longer was. So maybe Angel had gotten it *right*? Figure it out later. "Cycle down pressure both compartments."

"Cycle down, aye."

"Last air check, Commander?"

"Still some leaks but we're as good as we're gonna get."

"Angel? Any hissing?"

"I have good seal, Miss."

So, it *had* been intentional. Huh.

"Open main hatch," Dana said, closing to within a hundred meters of the indicated destination.

"Open main hatch, aye," Angel said. "Um..."

"I've got this," Dana said. The boat engineer was not supernumerary. There were a thousand items to keep an eye on with the complicated vessels. Usually that required a human to drive and a human to monitor. Dana had both jobs down to an art. "All personnel, prep for tractor exit. Just don't struggle too much and you won't get hurt. Okay, that sounded wrong..."

Dana used the internal inertial systems to slowly push all the jumbled bodies, alive and dead, out into the six-kilometer main bay.

"Your turn, Commander," Dana commed, opening up the hatch to the cargo compartment.

"If you don't mind, I'll find my own way out," the commander said.

"As long as you do it fast," Dana said. "Paris, since I have no clue what my chain of command is anymore, orders?"

"Exit main bay obeying all traffic warnings and rendezvous gate region with 144th Tactical Boat Squadron."

"Exit and rendezvous, aye," Dana said, spinning the boat around and heading back into the Big Dark. "Wonder if we're being assigned?"

"You are not," Phaeton said. "You are being attached for the mission as a supplementary source of advice and assistance. Also, the reason for your commission. Germans are very good at accepting advice from people with experience. But given your relative youth, the admiral correctly surmised they would do so better from an officer. Also, you are one of the few remaining personnel who are both coxswain and engineer trained. You would have been either commissioned or made a warrant officer in short order. And to answer your question about chain of command: as the sole surviving flight officer of the 143rd Tactical Boat Squadron, you are the Squadron Flight Officer as well as the Executive Officer. Lieutenant Mendez is the Commander."

"Okay, thanks for the explanation, Phaeton," Dana said, nodding. "Makes sense."

"And if I may add one item for your general fund of knowledge, Lieutenant?"

"Go."

"AIs take to death pressure slightly better than humans but cannot withstand it permanently?"

"Angel, O_2, now!"

"Roger, Lieutenant!"

"Oh, that's much better," Phaeton said, gasping theatrically. "That is sooo much better . . . Ow, ow! Tingles!"

"Does it really cause tingles?" Dana said, looking over at the massive cube of atacirc.

"Sort of," Phaeton said. "It doesn't have much negative effect on my core. But it breaks down and degrades the glue that holds the atacirc together. Since that's the interface between the chips . . . When air comes back you get most of it back . . . So. Yeah, tingles. And when you're in death pressure you sort of feel some of your . . . brain slipping away?"

"Permanent damage?" Dana said, wondering just what sort of eval you got for killing a brand-new AI. Probably not a good one.

"Nothing major," Phaeton said. "It didn't last that long. Point zero three percent of the atacirc is out of circuit. But that won't affect the mission and they're going to reinstall me at some point so . . . no big deal. Better than crashing the sun chariot."

"You know, maybe having you as a pilot wasn't such a good idea?"

"And it would be worse than the current situation . . . how?"

"Point."

The gate was still a mass of ships. How many damned ships did Apollo *have*? They seemed to be coming from everywhere.

"Lieutenant Parker, Captain Nussbaum, 144th Tactical Boat Squadron Commander."

"Parker, sir."

"As soon as you are on station, we are prepared to enter Eridani space."

"Captain, Phaeton. Gate opens to Eridani in four minutes. I'll handle all boats in the immediate area of the gate as it is obviously congested. All boats will be linked to ships passing through and thus not under power. Have all boats set to remote operation at this time."

"Remote operation, aye. Stand by, AI Phaeton."

"Now if they can just remember which button to push." Phaeton sighed. "Dana, pull up next to the *August Jones* and lock on."

"*August Jones*, aye," Dana said as the route markers came up on her screen.

It was another class she didn't recognize. It wasn't as big as one of the mining ships, but it was still huge compared to her dinky little boat. On the other hand, it didn't look as if it could pull people in very well. What it *did* have was a shuttle bay, which she'd never seen on a boat this size.

"Angel, lock on?"

"Grapnel four is acting up, Miss."

"One of these days we'll figure out the problem with the grapnels," Dana growled. She thought about it for a moment, then pulled up the repulsor controls and fiddled for a bit. The boat lurched sideways and locked onto the larger ship with a clang.

"Did you just *reverse* your *repulsor* settings?" Phaeton asked.

"Repulsor, tractor, same beast," Dana said. "It's all pseudo gravity."

"If you set the nineteen to five percent more grav you'd have caused a vortex," the AI said. "Not enough to cause much damage but..."

"I've got *four* vortices, as you just noticed," Dana said. "They're actually horizontally activated, which gives us six times the amount of... attachment?"

"I see it," Phaeton said. "I understand it. I wouldn't have thought of it."

"You pick up a few things. Think of it as giving the *Jones* a really strong hug."

"All ships," Argus commed. "Eridani gate coming online in five, four..."

"Admiral Clemons, Tyler Vernon."

Tyler hadn't been near the battleglobe since entering the system. But they happened to be passing by, and he dropped the viewscreen on the port bulkhead for a Mark One Eyeball look. The port bulkhead was made of optical sapphire, which gave him an unfortunately clear view of the wounded battleglobe.

"Mr. Vernon. Thank you for your help and support, although I don't know you had to come around personally."

"Oh, I just had to see what you did to my beautiful battlestation, Admiral."

The entire surface of the nine-kilometer-diameter battleglobe was *chewed*. The massive Lambdas on the sides, symbol of the Spartans of old, were virtually impossible to make out. You had to know where they were supposed to be to have a chance at spotting them. They were etched ten meters into the skin of the globe. And they were just... gone. Massive craters were everywhere. The Orion drive seemed to have bunked off to regions unknown.

It didn't look like a battleglobe. It looked like a moon that had taken a billion years of pounding from asteroids and comets. It was... sickening.

"I think the Rangora did most of the damage, honestly. Okay, the blown-open missile tubes I'll take the blame for, but..."

"How the hell do you lose an *Orion drive*, Admiral?" Tyler said, trying to figure out if he was chuckling or crying.

"Look, we just happened into a bad neighborhood," the admiral said. "Things happen. We also lost most of a marine division and two squadrons of boats, Mr. Vernon. Then there are the ship losses."

"Yeah," Tyler said, grimacing. "Aware. I'm just sort of... You got to see this from out here to appreciate the damage to the globe. I've seen *Troy* torn up a few times but *nothing* like this."

"Oh, I'd be doing a flyby if we didn't also have a main door stuck closed," Clemons commed. "The only way in and out right now is the maintenance tunnels. Which is a bit of a long walk. I'm old. I don't wanna walk that far."

"Yeah," Tyler said. "Gotta do something about that first thing. Given the security situation is sort of problematic, you probably don't want just a big damned hole in the side of the globe."

"Not my first choice, no."

"Pilot, swing us down by the main door," Tyler said. "I know we've got people to save but this needs some consideration now."

"Main door, aye, sir," the pilot replied. "Be advised there is major debris *everywhere*, sir."

For that matter there was a... fog. You didn't get fog in space.

"Are we in one of this system's damned dust belts?" Tyler asked.

"Shouldn't be, sir," the pilot replied.

"That's the remnants of about a half a million missiles chewing the globe, Mr. Vernon," Admiral Clemons replied. "It's essentially a nickel-iron fog. Also, remnants of two cruisers and... two squadrons of light boats, many of them filled with marines. Also, an unknown number of Rangora who were on the surface when the missile wave hit."

"Oh, that's just unpleasant," Tyler said as he finally got a full view of the main door. The former location of the now missing Orion drive was... twisted. The stainless-steel hinge pins were bent like pretzels and the kilometer-wide door wasn't just welded down, it was welded down *sideways*. There was a distinct skew to it. One arc was jutting outward while the other was crunched into the doorway. The kilometer-thick door itself seemed to be slightly... bent.

"I have not the slightest clue in the world how to even get that open, much less fix it. If Granadica was still online we could build another hammer..."

"Which isn't happening any time soon," Granadica cut in. "Thanks for asking how I'm doing, Tyler. Love you, too, sonny."

"Oh, I've been keeping up with the updates, Granadica," Tyler said to the irascible AI. "If we had a hospital large enough to put you in, I'd send you to it, stat. If we could get you out. Right now, I'm trying to figure out how to make a jaws of life large enough to get the door open. And, honestly, if we do get it open, I *am* sending you to the hospital. You're headed back to Wolf for Vulcan and Lud to work on. And that is the answer."

"What is the answer?" Clemons asked.

"I was thinking just cut a big hole, drill through, as we did with *Troy* in the first battle," Tyler said. "That would get shuttles through, get the survivors into your atmo, but not get Granadica *out*. What we're going to have to do is cut another door. Probably in East. Pull everything out. Cut and bang to get the primary door open. Reinstall properly if possible. If not, well, you're a globe, we'll just weld the original door down flat as reasonable and use the new one. We'll pull Granadica out as soon as we have the door cut and move her to Wolf for repair. And we'll get started on a new shell for you, Granadica. *Another* new shell."

"Hell with that, Vernon," Granadica snapped.

"What?" Tyler asked, confused.

The AI had been cranky since he'd first bought her and been creating minor "mistakes" in production equipment. It had taken years, and Dana Parker's insight, to figure out that one of her psychological issues was her old shell. The fabber was eight hundred years old. Her previous shell had been worn by years of use and abuse and she had, politely, "body image issues." Building her a new shell had been hideously expensive but worth it. She'd been worth her weight in osmium ever since. And now she didn't want a shell when the cosmetic damage from the battle had to be *much* worse?

"These are battle scars, sonny," Granadica said, angrily. "Sure, I'm going to have to figure out how to bend out the main damage. It's deep enough I'm not going to be able to function 'til it's beat out. But you can build me a new shell out of *Rangora* steel. When we're orbiting *Rangor*! Those were *my* boats, *my* people, just as much as Leonidas's and the admiral's. I *knew* those crews. They were my *friends*! I am going to make those lizard bastards *pay* for this! Besides, it's not the *external* damage that's the problem. It's internal. I'm finally up to having a whole *five percent* of my systems responding! Five. As far as I can tell, the rest are trashed. And the five percent aren't even what I need to start repairs."

"Ouch," Tyler said.

"Think that's ouch?" Granadica said. "Horn two is *bent* and half the maneuvering systems are scrap."

The massive horns in the interior of the main bay were where the orbital maneuvering engines resided. The engines were necessary to rotate the massive globe so the Orion drive could, in turn, push the globe in the proper direction. If one of the three-kilometer horns was *bent*...?

"Yeah, Admiral," Tyler said, wincing. "We're gonna have to gut this globe like a trout."

"Whatever it takes, Mr. Vernon," Clemons said. "And with that rough assessment I have a dozen other issues to address. Several dozen."

"And I've got people to pick up," Tyler said. "Pilot, onward. Argus, get me Byron Audler..."

CHAPTER 4

"You want to cut another door," Byron Audler said. The barrel-bodied, bearded, primary engineer for both *Troy* and the Wolf Helium Mine rubbed his head for a moment and sighed. "That motion of the board to have you declared clinically insane was not before time, was it?"

"There's never been a motion to have me declared clinically insane," Tyler said.

"Remind me to talk to some board members," Byron said. "The point, besides generally being able to get in and out, is specifically to get Granadica out, correct?"

"Correct," Tyler said. "And the Rangoran infantry who are starting to pile up everywhere. There are support issues there, different food types, and, well, Rangoran infantry who until recently were trying very hard to get into the interior to *take Thermopylae*... are piling up everywhere. We need a door."

"So you say, boss," Byron said. "But, again, clinically insane. The problem is thermal transfer and, well, precision. Which is going to be tough given that *Therm* still isn't entirely stable. Last but not least, if we cut all the way through, as we usually do, not only will Granadica be in the way of a SAPL beam but so will any of the exposed points in the bay—shuttle bays, personnel doors, horns, et cetera. But mostly I'm thinking we'd probably prefer to take what's left of Granadica out intact, not in pieces."

"Shit," Tyler said. "Point."

He looked at the engineer for a moment and shook his head. "And you've already thought of the answer, haven't you?"

"Maybe," Audler said, sneakily. "Seriously. Maybe. Best I can do at the moment. And it ain't gonna be easy no matter what."

"If it was easy, you wouldn't get paid the big bucks, Byron," Tyler said.

"Ain't gonna be as pretty as my normal work," Byron said. "And I want Steve."

"Astro or my son-in-law?" Tyler asked, puzzled. "Astro's retired in New Zealand last message I got."

"Australia, sir," Argus corrected.

"Both," Byron said. "I need Astro 'cause he's smart and he can talk to the uniforms good. Medal of Honor does that. And I need Little Steve 'cause he's not only good but he's your son-in-law, and that carries weight. 'Please tell me I don't have to call my dad on this . . . ' weight."

"Make up a list, send it to me, I'll send it to Greg, and you'll have them all by the end of the week," Tyler said. "And get your ass over to Eridani."

"I'm already here," Byron said, grinning. "I'm looking at *Therm* now. With Little Steve. I just needed authorization to keep him. He's the one that figured out how to cut the door. And, yeah, we're gonna have to gut this sucker."

"Get cracking," Tyler said. "Authorizations are already made, right, Argus?"

"Already filed," Argus said. "Should I get General Asaro on the line?"

"Got people to pick up," Tyler said as the shuttle slowed for another rescue. "After that."

"Be advised, General Asaro's daughter, Susan, was a lieutenant on the *Sundance*, sir," Argus said, gently. "It was lost with all hands. I sent a message of condolence with the note that you were involved in rescue and recovery work so couldn't personally call at that time."

"Shit," Tyler said, shaking his head. "What about . . . ?" He paused for a moment.

"Rachel is an engineer with the Asaro Electronics Corporation in Adelaide," Argus said. "Captain Steven Asaro, Junior, is an instructor in advanced spatial combat earthside. Both are fine."

"Get him for me anyway," Tyler said as he went to the airlock for what seemed the millionth time. "He ought to know by now there's no such thing as retirement."

Retired General Steven Asaro, former astronaut, hero of the first battle where Earth fought off the Horvath, former deep space explorer, former commander of the first actual Space Marine Regiment, former CEO of the Asaro Electronics Corporation, and current wine farmer, looked at the call on his Glatun implants and shook his head. The last thing he wanted was another damned condolence call. He just knew too many damned people who felt they had to say something. Most of them only knew Susan died because of automated social message networking. Most of them hadn't really communicated in years. It was worse than his birthday. And now it was Tyler. But, then again, it was Tyler. Unlike most of the people who had called, they went back. So, he picked up.

"'Sup, Baldy?" Asaro asked.

"Steve, first, shit," Tyler said.

"Yeah," Steve said, taking another sip of '47. It was a very good year, unlike this one. "Got the message the first time."

"Which is all I've got on that," Tyler said. "Just all I got. All the rest is trite and stupid and pointless. Second. I need you in Eridani."

"I'm retired," Asaro said, taking another sip. Maybe if he just blurred his mind enough...

"We just permanently retired ten thousand marines and spacers," Tyler said. "We're going to be retiring more if they're not rescued in time. I've got bleeding ships, a bleeding battleglobe, and I'm personally out in the *Starfire* doing rescue work. Time to put down the wine bottle and pick up the rifle, General."

"Doing what?" Steve asked, looking at the chardonnay. The color, as always, was perfect. The nice thing about making fine wine was it used up his considerable stock of OCD while being essentially unimportant. A bad batch *wasn't* life and death.

"Helping Byron fix *Thermopylae*," Tyler said. "Hell, if you don't want to do that, the Germans could use some qualified shuttle pilots. They're barely out of A school."

"She'd just gotten her first OER, Ty," Steve said, taking another sip. "She was pleased as hell to show her general/hero daddy her first walk-on-water OER. One missile or laser beam and... it all becomes pointless. Not sure I'm up to that, Tyler. I'm not sure I'm up to *going* there. I'm not sure I'm up to *seeing* Eridani."

"Which is as good a reason to call as any," Tyler replied. "You've got the choice of trying to drink your wine cellar dry or pick up the rifle, Marine. Which do you choose?"

"I hate you at times like this, Tyler," Steve said, peering into the wineglass.

"I hated you when you conned me into flying with you in the *Starfury*," Tyler replied. "Which as I recall also involved alcohol. Honestly, I'm not even sure how you're going to get up here. Every ship and boat in the system is headed for Eridani or already there."

"Not *every* bird..."

The *Starfury* project, Earth's first attempt at a space fighter, had been canceled shortly after the Glatun, facing a war they knew they were going to lose, transferred advanced military technology to their Terran allies. The tech dump had made the entire concept of a space fighter more obsolete than a WWI biplane. Missiles were more maneuverable and nearly as smart. The *Myrmidon* shuttles were more maneuverable and powerful than anything Boeing could come up with. Some of the tech had been used in the Columbia shuttles and the rest was scrapped.

Starfury II had been a testbed that was thirty percent complete when the funding was pulled. It had everything a spacecraft needed except, well, propulsion systems, power systems, and integration. Basically, it was a shell with life support. Which meant that a well-known hero/astronaut who had been one of the primary engineers of the *Starfury I*, not to mention the only pilot to ever use a space fighter in combat, could con the suits at Boeing into giving up the shell for a song. And a couple of personal appearances with investors. Okay, he did actually sing at one of them so maybe it *was* for a song.

Building what was missing from scratch had been a labor of love Steve had worked on for years. His children had cut their teeth on spatial engineering working on the systems. Mathilda, before she passed on, had been even more helpful. But it had been Susan, red-haired like her mother, freckles from the strong Australian sun, tiny little girl coveralls, clambering deep into the guts of the thing, who had probably done the most actual work.

Steve leaned his head against the sky-blue skin of the space fighter and slid his hand along the lines.

"I miss you, baby girl," he whispered. "I know Daddy promised he'd be home more. But you know when it's time for work and time for play. And Daddy's got to go back to work..."

Steve donned his old NASA helmet, reached up and keyed the hatch.

"You sure about using the clamshell technique with the 144?" Dana asked.

The squadron was being spread throughout the region, mostly in pairs. She frankly could not keep up with the deployment. That's why the AI was handling it. But the flying, that she could follow.

"Only when I'm in control on remote," Phaeton answered. "Speaking of which, open wide, skew to 148 mark plus sixteen."

"Angel, hatch," Dana said. "We've got debris ahead, Phaeton."

"That's what you're picking up, Comet," Phaeton said, distantly. "Might want to warn them to catch this on their navpacks and not with their faceplates."

"Personnel forward in the cluster, rotate rear," Dana commed. "Incoming debris."

"Then shut the damned door!" the senior NCO commed. The TM1 clearly didn't think much of flying around with an open main hatch.

"We're picking it up for some reason," Parker replied. "Orders."

"This is fracking insane," the NCO muttered. But she started getting the crowd shifted around.

As Dana approached the debris, the reason to pick it up became more apparent. It was a large gas container. Hopefully O_2. She stopped relative to the spinning cylinder and pulled it in gently with the forward tractor beam.

"And congratulations on having additional atmo," Dana commed. "Angel, shut it. Phaeton, vector."

"We don't have a line to run it, Lieutenant," the TM1 replied. "Nice catch, though."

"Thank you, TM," Dana said. "Line coming up. Angel, compartment fourteen. Back of the compartment. Don't lose all the other stuff."

She took a moment to play engineer, doing if not the fastest systems check in history then a very rapid one.

"Before you even get there," Phaeton said, "twenty-four is getting a bit out of alignment. I'm getting dren field effects in my sector one-four-eight-six atacirc. Point zero one six G torsional dren is what I'm reading."

"Yeah, got that," Dana said.

"Is this the right thing?" Angel asked, holding up a length of something tubular.

"That's a 591 power cable, Angel," Dana said with a glance. "*Behind* that. How's that, Phaeton?"

"Better, thank you. Again, tingly. Not close to the level of 'ow' but getting there."

"This one?" Angel asked.

"Power cable," Dana said, unstrapping and floating over to the compartment. Since they were in microgravity, everything was floating everywhere. "This one," she said, pulling the air-line out of the recesses of the deep compartment. "Now, take that up front while I get all this junk put back away. Go!"

"Yes, Miss!"

"Dana," Phaeton said in a robotic voice that indicated an AI getting dangerously overtaxed. "Incoming engineering call. Cannot..."

"Got it," Parker said. "Who'm I talking to?"

"Lieutenant, Engineering Recruit Wegner. We have an anomaly in our port lower thruster. May I request assistance?"

"Send your data," Dana said, trying not to sigh as she carefully restrapped all the junk Angel had let float all over the compartment.

"I apologize. I am unsure how to..."

"Wait one," Dana said, concentrating on the link for a moment. "There's a flashing icon on your screen. See it?"

"Yes, Lieutenant."

"Click it. Verify security. Good. Now I'm in your system. And...ah, crap. You got a crowbar? 'Cause you're gonna need one. Get your crowbar, a number sixteen clamping tool, and I hope you're pretty good in micro..."

(The following conversation occurred in two point four nanoseconds.)

"We need those ships centralized for repair, Phaeton," Argus argued. "The priority is to repair Thermopylae *so as to make it a useable platform for recovery."*

"I need them dispersed," Phaeton replied, squirting his proposed rescue schematic. "They have sufficient life support to pick up personnel and transfer them back to the Troy *so the boats can concentrate on pick-up and not running back and forth."*

"Those are repair ships and Mr. Vernon ordered them into the system to repair the Thermopylae.*"*

"They are also designed for large repair crews, many of whom are not even in the system. Humans take more time to mobilize than ships. I need them for rescue. Mr. Vernon is, himself, involved in rescue. I would argue that is the primary requirement at the moment. Repair is secondary."

"You were activated to be a rescue AI. You are compromised in your argument."

"The argument remains."

"We should consult a sophont," Argus said, mulishly. "You can't have them 'til we contact a sophont and get clarification."

"They take so much time," Phaeton said. "And you know they can't really listen. I have a potential answer. Athena, Goddess of Wisdom? Judgment."

"Rescue," Athena replied, instantly. "With the exception of the following craft. The primary survey and analysis team are using them. I will personally request they move to other craft so that the repair ships can be used for rescue. Update your plans based on having them in six hours. All the others will start to redeploy immediately. I'm sorry, Argus. I have to agree with the new boy."

"Fine," Argus said, petulantly. "But you have to make the calls."

"Already doing that . . ."

"And we need to move . . . why?" Byron asked, not really listening. "I'm not arguing, Athena, but . . ."

"The *August Jones* is a resupply ship, Engineer," Athena said. She wasn't really frustrated with the conversation. She realized humans had a hard time catching up and was used to it. "Personnel and equipment. It has room for seventy-eight personnel in addition to the crew. You have a team of fourteen. We need those bunks, and recyclers, to transfer from the boats that are doing rescue."

"Ah," Byron said, nodding while he looked at the geologic schematic of the *Thermopylae*'s nickel-iron walls. The nickel iron was not consistent since the entire thing was just an inflated asteroid. There were veins of other materials in it. And while that usually wasn't a big deal, in this case it might be. There were also maintenance and missile tubes in the area they were going to be cutting. Tricky, tricky... "Got it."

But he didn't seem to be moving.

"Um, Engineer?" Athena said.

"I've got it, Athena," Steve said. Tyler Vernon's son-in-law looked mildly amused. "I'll get everybody moving."

"Thank you, Steven," Athena said. "Must go. Busy, busy."

"Better than a battle," Steve said, then activated his implant. "Charlie, Steve. We're moving. New boat's on the way. Because I said so is why. Tell everybody to drop their private parts and pack. I'll update you later. Right. Oh, and pack the boss. He's in engineering land..."

"What the frack?" Dana squealed as they cleared the gate.

She was used by now to entering a new star system. No big deal. Each one looked slightly different. Same amazing wheel of stars but depending on where the gate was, how it was oriented and which direction you were traveling you might be looking at the local star, a battleglobe, the star field unaffected by the local one...

This was the first time she'd faced nothing but a wall of...

"Are those all *SAPL mirrors*?" Angel screamed.

What must be a fair fraction of the entire Solar Array Powered Laser mirror field was pointed, as far as she could tell, directly at them. Literally all she could see was mirror. Fortunately, they weren't getting "take" from the sun. What they were reflecting was mostly the gate and the stellar background. Not to mention her shuttle and the two ships that had accompanied them. It was a bit like looking at herself though a million insect eyes. Very unsettling.

"Paris!" Dana commed, if not hysterically then a bit less than calmly. "Are those SAPL mirrors?"

"I'm sorry, Lieutenant," Paris replied. "I suppose I should have warned you. We're assembling them to send through to Eridani. Just dodge around. Vector coming up."

"We're sending SAPL to Eridani?" Angel asked. "That doesn't make any sense. What's going to defend the system? We sure as hell don't have many ships left."

"*Troy*?" Parker replied. "*Malta* is partially online. And I doubt we're sending the whole thing. But if they're going to repair the *Thermopylae*, they probably need it. And good news."

"Which is . . . ?" Angel asked.

"Move SAPL in and no God damned way the Rangora are taking the system back."

"Sir, I've been thinking," Sergeant Ghezhosil said.

Some of the recalcitrant had stayed recalcitrant too long. But with various teams of humans and Rangora officers and NCOs hunting through the ixi maze that was the *Thermopylae*'s maintenance tunnels, they had gotten all the living out. The dead . . . might as well stay where they'd died. The humans would be finding corpses for decades.

"Don't, Sergeant," Lieutenant Lanniph said. "I know what you are thinking. We are in a ceasefire. One that I'm sure High Command supports given that the Ogut have now declared war. Personally restarting the war with the Terrans would be a good way to spend the rest of our short lives in the hands of the Kazi. And even if we managed it—arguable—what, exactly, are we going to *do* with it? Nice prize, but. It is currently immobile. I'm sure that the humans have thought it through as well. Which is why they are being so accommodating."

"Guess I'm just getting tired of sitting around babysitting these shell-cracks is all, sir," Ghezhosil said.

"Then perhaps we should think about a training schedule," the lieutenant said. "I'll get with the major. That will give you sergeants something to do."

"Oh, please make it good training, sir," Ghezhosil said. "Preferably something guaranteed to produce a few minor casualties. There are quite a few of this crop that don't need to breed, if you know what I mean."

"Fortunately, sergeants and officers reproduce by fission," Lanniph replied. "Like any bacteria."

CHAPTER 5

"Phaeton," Parker said after they'd dumped the latest load to a mining ship. At least they weren't having to go all the way back to the *Troy*. "Human beings require occasional rest periods. I can keep going but Angel's sort of on his last legs. And we need to perform some maintenance."

"Acknowledged, Lieutenant," Phaeton said. "I recently realized I had not calculated human rest periods, nor necessary maintenance, into the rescue plan. It is a complication, but this was never a fully solvable puzzle. The problem in the case of your crew is: where? I currently occupy the cubic your bunks are supposed to occupy. And lifespace on ships is at a premium in the system. *Troy*?"

"Too far," Dana said. "I'm going to land on *Therm*. There's a fairly short route through the door to the main bay. And I checked. Our quarters still aren't in use."

"Request sent to Leonidas and he's set a landing point," Phaeton said. "You'll need to leave the power on. I rather need it."

"Roger," Dana said, wearily. "Gimme a vector..."

"Oh my fracking God," Dana said as she approached the canted main door of the battlestation. The screens had constantly been pinging with shrapnel as she approached. The globe was surrounded by a constellation of nickel-iron dust and bits and pieces of... everything. Her systems were picking up the entire periodic table. Given the ratio of carbon... She didn't want to think why there was so much carbon in the dust. It wasn't a major component of Rangoran or human missiles. It *was* a major component of Rangora and humans.

That left out the actual condition of the landing area. The skin of the *Thermopylae* had originally been nearly perfectly smooth. There were now very few points that were not twisted metal. Leo had given them a general area to set down near one of the functioning maintenance doors. What he hadn't given them was a clear area. Because there wasn't one, really.

It wasn't only the direct battle damage. The cloud of dust and bits and pieces of . . . everything had been slowly settling towards the battleglobe, which had a notable gravitational well. At least compared to the rest of space. Her shuttle was going to be covered with junk when she came back out. And it had to be hell on the repair crews. Some of the junk was impacting with fairly high velocity. Bullet-like speeds in some cases. Just walking from the shuttle to the door was going to put them at risk.

Which told her the answer. As close to the door as possible that had any room to put the shuttle down.

"Should we maybe try for one of the ships, Miss?" Angelito asked as another bit of junk hit the screens.

"No," Dana said, hovering over the door and looking for the cleanest landing point available. "I'm going to sleep in my own rack ton . . . today. Simple as that."

"Yes, Miss," Angel said.

She finally decided there was no "best" place and put it on the least worse. The shuttle was canted and unbalanced. One leg was up on a couple-meter-wide chunk of debris that looked as if it might have come from . . . a shuttle, come to think of it. She didn't want to think about it. She *wasn't* going to think about it.

She set the tractors to hold the boat in place and unstrapped.

"Phaeton, you're going to have to devote enough cycles to monitor the systems while we're down," Dana said.

"Will do, Lieutenant," the AI said. "I'm sure I'll have enough. Things are getting somewhat more manageable."

"The Germans are going to have to do crew rest as well," Dana said. She'd spent half the operation working with the new German crews. The one good thing was she never had to tell anyone the same thing twice and they hadn't argued her orders, not even the commander. The bad part was that they were all green as grass. Nobody knew any of the tricks you picked up from being in a unit, what was called "institutional knowledge."

She was probably parked on the total accumulated "institutional knowledge" of small boat operations and had flown through the molecular level fog of same.

Wasn't. Going. To. Think.

"Oh . . . Jesus wept," Dana said as she exited the maintenance tunnel.

Once they'd gotten into the walls the damage didn't appear that bad. She should have known better. She'd heard the interior had taken damage. But her automatic alert system on whether Granadica was a casualty hadn't gone off.

She realized she should have set it for "seriously wounded." The same could be said for *Thermopylae*. She'd never realized a battleglobe *could* be this seriously wounded. It was . . . every single new experience of this day just seemed to cut her heart out over and over again.

The main bay was normally lit by a bright Dragon's Orb, a slightly dirty sapphire doped with flecks of platinum and receiving either pumped sunlight from SAPL or a laser set calculated to create "white" light.

Now it was almost entirely dark. She'd never seen a black main bay. And it was unbelievably black. Instead of the normally gorgeous reflective interior of the bay, it seemed as if the vast cavern of vacuum simply ate the few lights moving around.

What they revealed, though, was bad enough. Debris was everywhere and, again, so distorted and broken Dana wasn't even sure what most of it was. She could pick out the pencil tube their shuttles normally docked at. It had broken loose and was micro adhered to the wall of West. Horn Two was . . . bent? How the hell did you bend a kilometer-long, hundred-meter-thick bar of nickel iron?

She caught a bit of debris that was floating past and examined it. It seemed to be one very fracked-up piece of robot.

And then there was Granadica. There were lots of lights around Granny, so the damage was clear to see. Like the pencil tube, she was torn loose from her mounts and lay, bent, against the north wall. Granny was *bent*? She didn't *look* alive, that was for sure. She looked as dead as . . .

"What the hell *happened* here?" she commed to no one in particular.

"Dana," Granadica replied. "Things got a little complicated."

"Are you going to be okay?" Dana asked. "Your new shell, Granny. I'm so sorry."

"It's not my shell that's the problem," Granadica replied. "If they hadn't installed extra bracing when they rebuilt me, I'd be dead as a dodo. I mean AI core dead. Gone. As it is, most of my atacirc is spiraling around the core room. And that doesn't begin to touch the damage to my body. The internal damage is much worse than the external, if that gives you a clue."

"Is there anything I can do?" Dana asked.

"Everybody is doing everything they can, Dana," Granadica replied. "But thanks. Seriously. And what you need to do is get some rest, Dana. You've got to be wiped out."

"'Bout that way," Dana admitted. "Tell me you're going to be okay."

"I'm a robot, when it gets right down to it, Dana," Granadica said. "Just a big, old factory. Factories can be rebuilt. Those lizard bastards didn't get my AI core so, yeah, with time and a whole lot of repairs I'll be okay. I'm gonna live. I'm still here, deary. And I'm gonna be for a long time."

"Okay," Dana said, trying not to cry. She'd lost so many today. She wasn't sure what she'd do if she lost Granny as well.

When she thought about it, she knew exactly what she would do. She'd just go on. You deliver the mail.

"I'm sending one of our few remaining sleds over to pick you and your crewman up," Granadica said. "It'll be tight but you're both small. You don't want to navpak your way across the bay. Bit of a debris issue in case you hadn't noticed."

"At some point I'm going to have to hear what the hell happened," Dana said. "We'll talk later."

"Dana, one last thing," Granadica said. "I'm sending you a quarters number. You might want to stop by."

"That's in the Pathan sector, Granny," Dana said as the quarters number came up. "I don't go in the Pathan sectors. To put it mildly, we don't get along."

"Not being used by Pathans at the moment..."

She'd pinged Rammer half a dozen times since the battle, but he still wasn't picking up. The stupid marine idjit. Okay, redundant, admittedly.

She was so concentrated on her implants that she didn't even notice she'd walked into a wall of Rangora until it happened.

"What the hell?" she screamed, lurching back and scrabbling for a sidearm she didn't have. "What the frack are Rangora doing in the *mall*?"

They were, for that matter, packed into the mall. Every bit of floor space seemed to be covered in lizard. Most of them were out of their suits revealing that, like humans, they were naked under the suits. And must have had retracting genitalia or something. It was more about the Rangora than she really wanted to know.

"Calm down, Engineer's Mate," one of the helmetless Rangora hissed. "We are here on terms. You are in no danger." Her implant tagged him as an infantry officer, more or less her same rank, now.

"Comet, Leonidas," her implant pinged. "The Rangora are quartered in the mall on terms. It's the only place large enough for them. They have not been a major issue. Please do not start an incident."

"Not going to, Leonidas," Dana replied, calming down. She wasn't sure what the definition of a "major problem" might be, probably going back to trying to capture *Thermopylae*, but most of the window displays had been broken open. The Rangora didn't seem to be looting, exactly, just curious. One of their privates was holding up a bathing suit to his chest and apparently trying to figure out what it was for. Since it was a one-piece designed for someone her size, the answer might be "headscarf." Which he tried next. "Okay, since I don't want to start an incident, which might happen if I tried to maneuver through this lot..."

"Take the service door behind you..."

"Rammer," Dana said, tracing the USMC tattoo on his chest. "I want a baby."

"What the hell?" Corporal Ramage said, startled. He sat up and rubbed his eyes; he'd been half asleep. "Uh..."

"I know," the lieutenant said. "I said I didn't want kids. I'm a woman. We reserve the right to change our mind. And I'm not asking you to marry me. I know you'd say yes, but... not the right time, obviously. I'll have to apply for mommy track. Just for the pregnancy: Uncle Don and Aunt Marge will have to raise him or her. But... it's something Chief Barnett said to me. We just lost... too many. When you really think about it, what we just lost was not only a bunch of lives but a bunch of futures.

Genetics, if you want to put it that way. By the time I reached *Troy*, I'd decided that I want to leave more in this universe than some fading memories. And the way things are going... I don't think our kid will have to worry about being a slave to the Rangora. So, again, I want a baby. You willing?"

"Yes, but...?" Ramage said, shaking his head. "There's... stuff."

"I know you already have one child," Dana said. "Doesn't bother me. Among other things, means you're at least fertile," she added, grinning slyly.

"Yeah, I'm fertile," Ramage said, hotly. "Oh, you..." He leaned over and kissed her. "The real problem is, genetics will be impossible for anyone to ignore. Me enlisted. You officer. Which will kill your career, Dana."

"Screw my career," Dana said, sliding out of bed and picking up her suit. "I really do not give a rat's ass about my career. The most they're going to do is make me enlisted again. They're not going to kick me out and if they do, hey, I can get a *civilian* job teaching astrogation, engineering, and boat operations at much higher pay. The real problem is I'll have to get them to agree to remove the implant and they may ask who the daddy is going to be. I'll have to fudge that. Maybe I'll say 'Tyler Vernon.' That'll get them to shut up."

"So, why not him?" Ramage asked.

"You don't want me to have your baby?" Dana asked, looking at him unreadably.

"I've wanted you to have my baby since the first time I saw you at the Xanadu," Ramage said. "Not just fool around. Be my wife, have my child. Children. And I knew that wasn't what *you* wanted. Now... I'm not sure what I want. I'm not just thinking about me. I'm thinking about you. And the child. You really want to leave behind a baby when both Mommy and Daddy seem to have the life expectancy of a gnat? And I really don't want to screw up your career. Making you an officer is the first smart thing I've seen the Navy do. You *need* to be an officer, baby. So, yeah, why not Tyler Vernon for baby-daddy? I know you guys are close. The scuttlebutt gets around."

"You jealous?" Dana asked.

"Little. He's pretty cute for an old guy."

"Oh, you!" she said, grinning and thumping him with her helmet.

"And, yeah, I am," Ramage said. "'Cause if he asked you to marry him, you'd at least think about it, wouldn't you?"

"We don't have that sort of relationship, Rammer," Dana said, ignoring the question. "There's a reason I use your nickname there, you realize?"

"Got that," Rammer said, smiling slightly.

"We're just friends," Dana said, shrugging.

"And what are we?" Ramage asked. "I know I'm not just entirely your boy-toy you use when you want to get a little freak on."

"Problem with that?" Dana asked, sitting on the edge of the bed and checking her seals.

"Main problem is, do you really have to leave?" Ramage asked, changing the subject.

"I'm the engineer on my boat," Dana said. "Which needs more than a bit of TLC after the last few days. So, yeah, I do."

"And, yeah, I got a problem with boy-toy," Rammer said. "Bit. 'Cause I like being your friend and especially your friend with benefits. But, yeah, I want more. I love you, Dana. You do know that, right?"

"I know, Andrew," Dana said. "I'm sorry."

"I'm okay, mostly, with being friends," Ramage said. "Better than not friends. The benefits really are spectacular. But. You want a baby? With me? Then I want more. And then I'd *especially* want *you* groundside, safe and out of the service, which would be easy enough to arrange when your 'mommy track' turns out to be with an enlisted marine. But what I mostly want is for you to at least *ask* the richest man in the freaking system who is *also* a friend. And who is guaranteed to be around to *raise* said baby and *be* a daddy. 'Cause I ain't. And I'll be more than happy to be the baby's godfather or whatever. And if he says the same thing I said, 'Only if you marry me,' you better damned well say yes. 'Cause I don't bang bimbos."

"Rammer, you told me once your idea of a perfect wife was a girl with an IQ twice her breast size," Dana said, shaking her head. "I'm absolutely certain that Tyler Vernon gets at least one request a day from women who want to have his baby. Want me to ask Leonidas?"

"If he says no, or if he puts conditions on it you won't go for, then I'll, reluctantly, agree," Ramage said. "You gotta ask, though."

"Why do men have to be such freaking idiots?" Dana asked.

"'Cause if we weren't we'd stay as far away from women as possible," Rammer said, reaching up and pulling her down. "'Cause y'all's crazy as bedbugs."

"Really do have to go," Dana said.

"Takes you less than a minute to don a suit," Ramage said. "You've got time. Stand by for docking maneuvers, Lieutenant..."

"Back so soon, Lieutenant?" Phaeton said. "Your vitals suggest you did not get much rest."

"No rest for the wicked, Phaeton," Dana said, sitting down in the engineer's station and beginning the checks.

"If you would like me to, again, jump ahead, I've been maintaining all engineering systems but there are some issues that require manual adjustment," Phaeton said, carefully.

"Go with list," Dana said.

"Grapnels are acting up. Apparently as usual..."

"What's the status on the Germans?" Dana asked as she got the last balky grav adjustment on the grapnels fixed.

"They are all down on crew rest," Phaeton said. "And have maintenance issues as well. When they wake up, we'll get to that."

"I think we're going to have to either shut down number eighty-six or I'll have to find parts somewhere in *Therm*," Dana said, looking at the indicators through her helmet's HUD. "And if we shut down eighty-six, we're going to be limited in accel. Time to wake Angel up. He's useless for engineering but he can at least fetch and carry."

"I have a location on grav plate spares," Phaeton said. "Want me to handle it?"

"If you could," Dana said, standing up. "We're going to need parts for the Germans. Has anyone looked at that?"

"There are people working on that," Phaeton said.

"Lieutenant Mendez, Parker," Dana said, heading back to the engineering chair.

"Parker, it is good to hear from you," the lieutenant said.

She and Mendez hadn't really interacted when the full squadron had still been around. He was one of the newer replacement officers' post-CAPEX and post the installation of Granadica, when the 143 had finally started to get its feet under it.

All dust now. All that work. So much plasma and space dust.

"We've still got bodies and parts in the globe," Dana said. "The Germans are going to need parts. Hell, if we had any trained bodies left, they'd need those. But they're mostly going to need parts and supplies. Would you please start rousting out a working party? In the case of my boat, I need a 416 grav plate, a 2494 power cable, six O_2 canisters and two cases of rations. If you could integrate with the Germans and find out their requirements as well. We'll find a short route out through the maintenance tunnels, probably load this boat and move the materials out to their boats. If that makes sense to you, of course, Commander."

"Yes, of course, Lieutenant," Mendez replied. "I'll get Petty Officer Diaz started on that right away."

"Phaeton, could you squirt the lieutenant a list of known parts and supplies?" Dana asked, keeping Mendez in the loop. "Oh, and Carlo, if you would please send someone to kick my coxswain in the butt? Time to get to work."

"I'll send someone to wake up Coxswain Angelito immediately, Lieutenant," Mendez said.

"Thank you, Lieutenant," Dana said, then cut the connection and sighed. She rubbed her eyes and thought for a moment. Then she sighed again.

"Argus?" Dana inquired delicately.

"NAILED IT!" Argus squealed. "Nailed it to the second!"

"Sure, sure," Granadica said, sending over the voucher for four hundred and sixty-eight nanoseconds of processing time. "But I'm still ahead on a single bet. And I'm betting double or nothing on a yes."

"Tyler Vernon has turned down an average of fourteen point six eight four five eight two one five three requests to be a father per day for the last twenty-six years," Argus commed.

"How long since he's been asked in person?" Phaeton asked. He was still dialing in on human sexual relations, which all the Glatun-created AIs found simply bizarre.

"Twenty-two days," Argus replied. "South African supermodel Bella Von Tosten, twice voted sexiest woman in the world by Playboy *magazine. Of course, it was the sixteenth time she'd asked in person. Mr. Vernon uses the term 'stalker.' Don't ask how many electronic requests. I set up a separate spam folder. It's a useful, if somewhat degrading, look into the broader aspects of human sexuality."*

* * *

"Lieutenant Parker?" Argus replied. "You're awake?"

"Doing some maintenance," Dana said. "Would you mind telling me Mr. Vernon's status? I'd like to make a personal call, but I don't want to bother him if he's asleep or busy."

"Mr. Vernon is involved in rescue operations," Argus replied. "How long do you anticipate the call will take?"

Dana had to think about that one.

"Answer is 'Couple of minutes,'" Argus commed. "Two hundred nano seconds."

"Not taking it," Granadica said. "That's a standard reply."

"Actual period... twenty-six minutes," Argus snapped back.

"One hundred nanoseconds for every minute shorter," Granny sent back.

"Done," Argus replied.

"You're about to owe me a lot of process time..."

"Couple of minutes," Dana said.

"He is currently in transit but approaching another pickup," Argus commed. "I would suggest after that pickup."

"She's going to go for 'it's not really that important,'" Granny said. "Hundred nanoseconds."

"Not taking it," Argus said.

"It's not really that important," Dana said.

"He'd probably appreciate a call from you, Lieutenant," Argus commed. "A long call."

"Judgment!" Granadica said.

"No hedging the bet," Athena commed. "And you two need to concentrate on work."

"This is concentrating on work," Argus replied. "Keeping Tyler Vernon functional is my job. Sex with Lieutenant Parker would significantly improve his functionality. And a new child would do so as well."

"And keeping Dana functional... keeps me functional," Granadica sent, primly.

* * *

"Why don't I just tell him you called and suggest he call back?" Argus asked.

"Because he's not only doing rescue ops?" Dana said. "Knowing Mr. Vernon, he's also spending the other time figuring out how to fix *Thermopylae*? 'Cause he's, you know, busy?"

"He enjoys talking to you, Lieutenant," Argus said. "It would improve his functionality to have a brief chat."

"Probably not this one," Dana said. "It probably should wait until we're done with rescue ops, at least."

"Dana, Granny."

"Hi, Granny," Dana said, tiredly.

"Dana, all internal discussions on the globes are open to monitoring," Granadica pointed out.

"Oh, you . . . silicon *perverts*, you!" Dana snapped back.

"Dana, don't wait," Granadica said. "You'll put it off and put it off if you don't do it now. Make the call."

"What are the odds?" Dana asked. "If you're paying attention to this, I know you're betting on it."

"I'm double or nothing on another bet he says yes," Granadica said. "Argus is voting no."

"I think Argus would know him better than you, Granny," Dana said, her shoulders slumping. "That's as good a reason to not make the call as I can think of."

"I made four *thousand* nanoseconds that you were going to ask Corporal Ramage about being a father to your child," Granadica said. "Argus thought it was a sure thing. Argus is good with a lot of stuff. Not this. He bases his bets too much on statistical reliability. He still hasn't figured out humans are stochastically as random as it's possible to be. And in this case, Argus is dead wrong. Make the call. I'm saying that as a friend. And I've got money riding on the answer."

"Some friend," Dana said, giving a dry chuckle.

"Mr. Vernon is available," Argus said. "He has forty-six minutes to his next pickup."

Dana blew through her lips for a second then shrugged.

"Make the call."

CHAPTER 6

“This is not supporting the war effort, Lieutenant,” Sergeant Del Papa said, tiredly. “We need these boats for rescue operations, they need to be resupplied. The supplies are in here. Your missiles welded the main door shut. So, we need to hand-carry the supplies to the surface. Not a war support mission. Rescue support.”

“Does that matter, Sergeant?” Lieutenant Lanniph asked. “Frankly, any mission right now is a good thing. The men are bored and getting to be a handful.”

“I guess it doesn’t matter to you guys,” Del Papa said. “It’s one of our things. Part of our laws of war.”

“How can you have laws in war?” Sergeant Ghezhosil asked.

“Well, how it actually works is this,” Del Papa said. “We make treaties with guys we’re not going to fight that have all these laws and restrictions. Like not using prisoners for support of war efforts, what we have to feed them, stuff like that. Then we fight guys who *don’t* make those kind of treaties or just signed them to play like they were going to follow them then *don’t*. ’Cause the guys who *do* follow the rules we don’t fight anymore, anyway, ’cause they’re all our furking *allies*.

“Then, we always fight guys like, well, you, who think rules of war are for pussies, or the Horvath, who can’t seem to figure out that aliens are alien. And, frankly, tend to kick their asses halfway across the galaxy. Then teach them that if they don’t follow the rules, we’re going to kick them even harder. So, they eventually follow the rules. Just takes time to get through their heads.”

"That makes even less sense than *our* High Command," Sergeant Ghezhosil said. "You actually... You actually fight wars by *rules*? That is insane!"

"Tell me about it," Del Papa said. "And the Pathans totally agree. But we're gonna get it through those goat fuckers' heads sooner or later."

"What *are* the laws of war?" Lanniph asked, fascinated.

"I think the first line of the Geneva Convention is 'No kicking a guy when he's down,'" Del Papa said.

"Mr. Vernon, Lieutenant Dana Parker requests a brief personal call," Argus said.

"Dana made lieutenant?" Vernon asked, wearily. "When did that happen?"

"Quite rapidly," Argus said. "Will you take the call?"

"Gladly," Tyler replied. "Put her on. Dana?"

"Mr. Vernon," Parker replied. "You sound tired as hell, sir. Are you getting any crew rest?"

"We're about to take a break," Tyler said. "This boat requires maintenance, among other things."

"We're about to shuttle out equipment to the 144, sir," Dana said. "Your boat has a high degree of commonality. I'll check with your skipper and see what you need."

"On the ball as always," Vernon said, grinning. "It's good to hear from you. Again. Twice in twenty-four hours. That's something of a record. But Argus said it was a personal call."

"Just checking up on you, sir," Dana said. "Mostly wanted to assure that you were getting crew rest. I'm pretty sure that nobody was going to tell you that not only you, but your crew do need to rest. If you don't, I'll figure out how to screw up your boat so you can't keep going. Don't cross me on this."

"You sound like my wife," Tyler said, shaking his head. "Ex-wife."

"After this next pickup, drop," Dana said. "Then put your head down and let your crew put theirs down, absent critical maintenance. Then maintenance. Then rescue. You can't rescue if you're dead."

"Yes, ma'am," Tyler said, grinning.

"I'll probably be shuttling out your equipment and supplies," Dana said. "Parts at least. You'd better be somewhat functional when I arrive."

"And what about you?" Tyler asked. "You getting any rest?"

"Actually, I had a screwing session," Dana said. "So, no, not really."

"Okay," Tyler said, his eyes wide.

"I'm going to let Angel take some of the transits with Phaeton keeping an eye on him, and catnap," Dana said. "I am quite tired. But you need to get your head down. Roger?"

"Roger," Tyler said.

"Parker, out."

"Time!" Granny said. "Two thousand nanoseconds you owe me!"

"That call did not count!" Argus said. "It did not involve the specific issue of bet. And if we accept this as the baby call, you lose!"

"The call did not count," Athena said. "And it's clear Dana is screwing with you both. Which you deserve."

"Hah!" Dana said, flicking a bird at the starboard bulkhead. "Screw you both, you silicon perverts! Phaeton? You up on this issue?"

"You're my pilot and engineer," Phaeton said. "You can say I have a vested interest. So, yes."

"Can you keep an eye on Angel?" Dana asked.

"Yes."

"Then wake me up when he gets here," Dana said. "And when you compute the resupply run, make sure that I'm the one to deliver supplies to Mr. Vernon's boat, if you will."

"Sure thing, Lieutenant," the AI replied in a perky tone.

"What was *that*? Another bet or something?" Dana asked.

"I'm trying out different personality types," Phaeton admitted. "I was shooting for the cocky young enlisted guy on a PT boat in World War Two. Based generally on the movie actor Ernest Borgnine's early characters. How'd I do?"

"Phaeton, that's something to do with the sun, right?" Dana said. "I heard Mr. Vernon's explanation, but I've never been into mythology."

"Something about the sun, yes," Phaeton admitted.

"I hereby officially give you the handle 'Sparky,'" Dana said. "So, Sparky, wake me up when Angel gets here."

"Will do, Lieutenant! You can depend on me!"

"I think I'm tired enough I'm starting to hallucinate..."

* * *

"Thirty-three?"

Dana looked at the incoming call. One of the SF NCO's attached to the Pathans. Great. She was going to have to deal with Pathans.

The LZ was a huge freaking crater that might once have been a missile tube opening. Or . . . well, anything. All it was, now, was a crater. With essentially no flat spot to set down. She'd managed to get the boat more or less level to the *Thermopylae*. That was as good as it was going to get.

"Thirty-three."

"Joy. And the door is stuck. You got it on your schematics?"

"Got my front door pointed right at it," Dana said.

"Any chance you can do a burn-through with your systems?" the NCO asked. "We're out of the way."

"I can cut it," Dana said. "But it's not gonna . . ."

She was so tired, but she joggled her brain into motion.

"Let me try something," she said. "But you better get the hell out of the way."

She considered the offending door for a moment. The schematic said it was probably an internal security door, not a heavy blast door. Six inches of standard nickel iron.

"What are you going to try?" Phaeton asked. "If you just hit it with a laser, it will cut away some of it, but the door won't really move. If they push, they will be in the way of the laser."

"Got that," Dana said, picking up the bird. She brought up an aiming reticle for the flying grapnel on one screen and the onboard four-terawatt laser on another. Both of the latter were the job of the engineer, after all. "Sergeant, you guys out of the way?"

"Roger," the NCO replied.

"Here goes nothin'," Dana muttered.

First, she put the laser along the base of the door. More nickel iron spurted into vacuum, seriously degrading her laser efficiency. But she got a cut along the bottom. Then she aligned the grapnel and fired it. Tango. She put some reverse on the bird, then started to cut the rest. Slowly, the nickel-iron door more or less peeled off. She reduced reverse on it as she got to the end and finally pulled the door loose with what in atmosphere probably would have been an audible *twang*. What was audible was the *clang!* when it hit the front of the boat.

"Sergeant, stand by. I need to get rid of this trash."

"Roger. Standing by."

Dana drifted the shuttle to the side and lowered the piece of scrap onto the scarred deck. *Thermopylae*'s microgravity would probably keep it in place. It wasn't like there wasn't more scrap everywhere.

Then she drifted back to the hole.

"Angel, drop the front hatch and get up front to get everything secured," Dana said, then thought about it. "Scratch that. You take the systems. I'll make sure everything is secured."

That was, after all, the job of the engineer.

Dana went forward, then used her 'plants to drop the cargo compartment to vacuum. Then she dropped the hatch.

"Sergeant. Hatch is more or less flat, ten meters from the opening. Be advised opening is still hot. Weather is light nickel-iron fog with eighty percent chance of debris showers. Safety conditions are suboptimal. All that being said, ready for load."

"Headed out with your first load, Lieutenant," the NCO replied.

"Part of that had better be a grav plate," Dana said.

"I think we've got a bunch of those."

Dana yawned and wished she could tap her face through the helmet. Then her eyes went wide as the first massive silhouette appeared in the doorway. Her brain had just a moment of discontinuity. The shape was generally humanoid but the door was fifteen meters high and those guys... *weren't human!*

"Angel!" she snapped, pinging the hatch to close. "Bring up the main gun!"

"What?" Angel commed. "How?"

"Lieutenant, Sergeant Del Papa. Guess you weren't advised the porters were Rangora?"

"No, I was *not*!" Dana commed.

"Comet, Leonidas," Leo commed. The voice was robotic. "Porters are Rangora confirmed. Continue load, Lieutenant."

"Continuing load," Dana commed, shaking her head. "What are we, now, allies? Opening the hatch back up, Sergeant. But they make one false move..."

"Got that," the sergeant said.

The first Rangora were carrying standard ration boxes. She gestured for them to be placed at the rear of the compartment, then turned her attention to the SF NCO.

"Sergeant Ernest Del Papa, Lieutenant," Del Papa said. "And

with that, ma'am, when did you make LT? You were an EM last time we met."

"Yesterday?" Dana said. "Sort of handed to me to work with the Germans. Keep stacking at the back. I need one of those grav plates, though, before we complete the load. Your... guys okay on air?"

"We are fine, Lieutenant," one of the Rangora said.

"I need to replace the eighty-six grav plate before we complete the load," Dana said, still looking at Del Papa.

"Sergeant Ghezhosil!" the Rangora lieutenant snapped. "Bring up the grav plates, next."

"Roger, sir!"

"Lieutenant Dana Parker, One-Four-Three Tactical Boat Squadron, Lieutenant Lanniph, Rangoran Space Infantry. Lieutenant Parker is the holder of two medals for valor as well as several more for her work as an engineer. Lieutenant Lanniph is the holder of the Rangoran equivalent of the Medal of Honor for being one of the survivors of the battle of Perrechoa."

"Lieutenant," Dana said, nodding.

"Lieutenant," Lanniph replied, clapping his hands in a Rangoran salute. "Sergeant, I had not realized your intelligence on our units was so... extensive."

"We just got a data update," Del Papa said. "I'll add you're both battlefield commissions, so you have that in common."

"May I ask what your specialty was as an enlisted, Lieutenant?" Lanniph asked.

"Engineering and coxswain," Dana said. "Which since I've got an undertrained cox is what I'm doing as a lieutenant. Both engineer and coxswain. I was assigned to this boat as engineer before the battle."

"These, sir?" Sergeant Ghezhosil asked, pointing to some cases.

"Those, Sergeant," Dana replied. "Gimme."

Dana opened up a compartment and removed the tools she was going to need. Including a grav vacuum. With all this nickel iron being tracked around, she was going to have to sweep the grav plate compartment to ensure it was entirely clear of contaminants.

She set her 'plant to direct to Del Papa.

"Watch my back. You seem buddy-buddy with these guys, but I'm still in battle mode."

"I work every day with Pathans, Lieutenant," Del Papa said. "Their grandparents clapped and cheered when the towers fell. Ancient history at this point, considering the crater the Horvath made of New York, but they haven't really changed. You know them. They're barbaric animals who have no real saving graces save a strong sense of family and a degree of bloody-mindedness. They don't even have a great deal of what Westerners consider courage.

"They'll occasionally have a guy who's willing to blow himself up for Allah. Don't ask them to stand their ground to the last man or charge an objective with heavy casualties, just because of flag or honor or even Allah or family. Some will, most won't and it's suddenly every man for himself. And if you try to get them to charge or stand, they'll kill you before they kill the enemy. Which I kept in mind during the entire battle. From what I've seen of these guys, I'd honestly rather have Rangora as allies. And that's what makes me a good SF sergeant.

"The ability to be Special Forces is not really being able to run twenty miles or make a fire with sticks. It's the ability to simply not care who you use to get the job done as long as someone other than Americans are eating the bullets. Or in this case, debris shower. We look at the world through shades of gray, Lieutenant. Especially when we're in a fog of iron."

CHAPTER 7

"General Sho'Duphuder, this is Human AI Phaeton. I am the designated rescue AI for this operation. How are you doing?"

General Sho'Duphuder had to think about what answer to give to that odd query. He'd lost a massive fleet to what was clearly a fool's gambit on the part of High Command. Which meant that even if he was rescued—unlikely—he was facing Kazi justice when he returned. On the other hand, at the moment there was still air in his lifeboat. The long wait had given him time to catch up on his reading. All in all, it was a very long time since he'd had anything resembling a vacation. So . . .

"So far, so good, AI," Sho'Duphuder said. "And you?"

"Busy, busy, General," Phaeton replied. "You are aware of the current ceasefire to recover survivors, sir?"

"Yes, AI, I am aware," Sho'Duphuder said. And he'd been receiving regular platitudes from Glalkod command on the subject. Since he was pretty sure Rangor was about out of ships, the war had even left them short on freighters and passenger ships, and since the Junta was probably much more concerned with the Ogut issue and already redirecting all their remaining resources to the, very distant, Ogut border regions, he was more or less looking forward to running out of air while listening to those self-same platitudes.

"Would you kindly do a suit air and seal check on your personnel and report back, sir?" Phaeton said.

"Two days of air on the lifeboat," Sho'Duphuder replied. "Suits average another nine hours. Minimum is seven. Water and food will last longer."

"Seven. Blast. Would you mind doing cross-load and scavenging, then drain the boat's air system? I need ten on all suits."

"May I inquire why, AI?"

"I'm going to have to move you partially open, General," Phaeton replied. "Quite some distance open. I'll explain later. But I need all suits to have at least ten hours of air. In about . . . three hours."

"We will begin cross-load and recharge," the General said. "But I'm quite curious how you intend to recover our personnel. Are you intending to recover *all* fleet personnel?"

"My mandate is to recover every surviving sophont in the system, General," the AI said, seriously. "And I'm going to do my very best."

"Okay, Lieutenant, open wide and say 'Ah!'" Phaeton said.

As it turned out, Dana had never managed to catch up to Mr. Vernon. The *Starfire* had to return to *Troy* for repair. While there was commonality of systems, that didn't include everything. So, after a full day of supplying the Germans with spares and supplies, an unmitigated pain in the ass involving tossing supplies from one shuttle to the other in deep space, she was back to rescue operations.

And currently in a cluster of other shuttles in deep space well away from all the major battles. There weren't any survivors around. What there was was . . .

"Phaeton, I've got an incoming missile track," Dana said, curiously. It was tagged as a Thunderbolt, so it *probably* wasn't going to blast them out of the sky.

"Right," Phaeton said. "That's your next load."

"I'm loading a missile?" Dana said, opening her main hatch. "Not going to fit. It's longer than my cargo bay."

"You're loading what's *on* the missile," Phaeton said.

The Thunderbolt was capable of pulling even more gravs of accel than the *Myrmidon*s so its approach was amazingly slow, all things being equal. However, as it approached it was clear it was covered in . . . At first Dana could only think it was covered in bugs. But as it got closer it was clear what it was covered in was space-suited Rangora. They'd apparently used their safety clamps to attach themselves to the outside of the missile.

"This I got to see with my own eyes," Dana said, unstrapping. "Angel, you got the helm. Which means don't touch anything."

"Aye, aye, Miss," the guy who was technically the coxswain said.

"Commander Grauch," Dana commed. "Recommend all boats get their engineer up forward. Contact incoming Rangora personnel, get them situated. Go to micro in the cargo compartment for load. Then repressurize and go to grav slowly."

"Roger, Lieutenant Parker," Korvettenkapitan Grauch replied. "All boats conform to orders from Alliance Advisory Officer. Send confirmation."

God, she loved working with the Germans.

The Thunderbolt approached with what seemed glacial slowness, pivoted to port, then stopped about fifty meters from the shuttle. Slowly the Rangora began detaching from the missile and jetting over to the boat. It was apparent that most of them were not well trained for micro.

"Senior Rangora officer, Lieutenant Parker, One-Four-Three Tactical Boat Squadron, over."

"General Sho'Duphuder, Lieutenant. Thank you for the ride. At least I'm hoping you're our ride."

"We are, General." *Now I'm shuttling* Rangora *high command*, Dana thought. "If I may request, sir. We're going to pack you in to cubic, then bring on the gravity and air after we shut. And I noted that some of your personnel are better at micro than others. May I request, again, bringing those in on tractor?"

"Feel free, Lieutenant," the general said as he expertly jetted up to her location and grabbed the stanchion next to hers. "I'll make sure everyone gets situated."

"Thank you, sir," Dana said. She brought up the boat's tractor controls and started grabbing suits.

"Lieutenant Parker, Corvette Captain Grauch. Some of the Rangora are having a difficult time entering the boats. They do not appear to be well trained in microgravity."

"Recommend, where possible, engineers bring them in on tractor," Dana said. "That is a somewhat difficult maneuver with delicate volatiles. Recommend it only for your most capable engineers in that area. For the rest... we'll gather them all up eventually."

And there were a lot of the big ugly lizards. More and more missiles were entering the loading basket. Which was creating a rather unsafe condition what with all the lizards wandering in every direction going a-Dutchman.

"General, can you generally broadcast to your personnel that unless they are *fully* micro qualified, to just take their damned talons off their navpaks? Please, sir?"

"I don't have full view of the conditions, but it is clear they are getting rather scattered," the general said as a suit went spinning past the boat. "I will take care of it, Lieutenant."

"Thank you, sir," Dana said. "Phaeton, stop the approaching missiles while we get this rat-jug under control, please."

"Right you are, Lieutenant!" Phaeton said, chirpily.

"I have *got* to get a groundside job," Dana muttered. "In fact, after this, I think I'm just going to get myself reinfected with Johannsen's, have a dozen kids, and get a job as a diving instructor at a YMCA..."

"Oh, screw this," Dana said. They'd had their personnel loaded for nearly thirty minutes and were still trying to catch all the Rangora that were Dutchman in the area. One had been killed when he'd plowed face-first into a 144 shuttle. Fortunately, that had been the only casualty so far, but at this rate it wasn't going to be. "Angel, I'm leaving the shuttle. When I'm gone, close the hatch and reapply gravity, slowly, then air. Readback."

"Wait to leave the shuttle, aye," Angel said, nervously. "Reapply gravity and air, aye."

"Reapply gravity *slowly*," Dana said. "One-tenth grav per second to one full G. Then air."

"One-tenth grav per second to one grav, aye," Angel said. "Then air."

"I'm going to go round up these freaking lizards," Dana said, letting go of the grab bar and puffing some air out of her navpak.

"Where are you going, Lieutenant?" the general asked.

"To round up your strays, General," Dana replied. "You guys have only got so much air time. We're refitted to charge Rangora airpaks. Show you how when I get back. Gotta go."

"That was quite clever, Phaeton," Athena commed.

"I got it from one of Granadica's memories," Phaeton said, proudly. "When the humans first acquired you, they were still trying to get around the Glatun lockouts on military technology.

Mr. Vernon asked for a 'very high acceleration rescue buoy.' It was a fairly obvious attempt to make a kinetic missile, but the idea still works for rescue. It would be better if the Thunderbolts had a usable tractor system but needs must."

"The Balto," Granadica said. "Of course. I should have thought of that. It was, after all, my memory."

"I am optimized for rescue," Phaeton said. "Which makes me wonder what I am going to do after this is over."

"The humans generally need quite a bit of rescuing, Phaeton," Athena said, soothingly. "I'm sure you won't want for work..."

Dana had to admit she sort of enjoyed the next hour since it mostly involved literally kicking Rangora around. Jet up to some idiot lizard who had managed to spin themselves off into the Black, stabilize same, kick with both feet in the right direction while maintaining counterthrust on the navpak. Lather, rinse, repeat. Heck, the idiot lieutenant commander who'd gone spinning past her shuttle she got to kick at least six times. Rangora might be big but in micro, training and three-dimensional awareness mattered a lot more than mass or cubic. Being angry and tired as hell also helped.

The Germans were, admittedly, not a big help. Most people really learned the job of being an engineer on shuttles when they were on the job for a while. She hadn't been fully engineering qualified for nearly three months after arriving at the One-Four-Two. You simply could not train people in everything they'd encounter on the job in A School. Especially with the compressed A School they were running these days. You learned stuff like delicate manipulation of spinning human bodies with a tractor beam after you'd been there a while and preferably had a few months working the Junkyard. Heck, the only people in the One-Four-Three who could...

Okay, there was now *no one* in the One-Four-Three besides her who could do it. Might have been a couple before. Couple. Palencia could probably have done it.

The Germans would learn.

She kicked the last flailing Rangora into 144/26 and commed the engineer.

"Close the hatch and reapply gravity at one-tenth grav per second to one gravity, then reoxygenate," Dana said. "And we're done."

"That was very skillfully done, Lieutenant," Korvettenkapitan Grauch commed. "I apologize for my own flight's lack of skill in the matter."

"I was just thinking that the One-Four-Three didn't have all that many engineers who could have handled it, Commander," Dana replied. "This is what we call in the Alliance Navy 'Good Training.' But we're done."

Most of the boats had left the region, headed to whatever drop-off point Phaeton had designated. She had probably better do the same.

She approached Thirty-Three, cycled the airlock, and slid in.

"Home again, home again," she said as the airlock repressurized.

And was met with a wall of Rangora bodies.

"I would order clearing a path, Lieutenant," General Sho'Duphuder commed. "But it is really quite impossible. If you wouldn't mind, we'll move you over the personnel. It will be somewhat... lacking in dignity."

"I'm a jumped-up engineer NCO, General," Dana said, holding up her arms. "And I sort of like being crowd-surfed."

The Rangora in front of her picked her up, delicately—but it was clear it was like picking up a doll for the three-meter-tall alien—and slid her over his shoulder. Where another latched on and slid her along until she was at the rear hatch.

"Oh, wait," Dana said. "I forgot. How are your people doing on suit air, General?"

"Most have at least two hours left, Lieutenant," Sho'Duphuder replied.

"Phaeton, can you talk?"

"Bit busy," the AI replied. "Go."

"Two hours on suit air this load," Dana commed. "Enough, query?"

"Enough. Maintain onboard air."

"Roger," Dana said. "General, air, as I'm sure you aware, is one of the big things you want in space."

"Very aware, Lieutenant," Sho'Duphuder said.

"Phaeton says two hours is enough for you guys," Dana said. All the Rangora had their helmets off and latched. Both suits and boats had recyclers, hers were just better than suits and probably much better than Rangora suits. "We need to hold onto our spare. We've been using up a lot lately. Also obviously."

"Understood," the general replied. "Do you know our destination?"

"Angel, where we headed?" Dana commed, bringing the coxswain in.

"Right now we're not headed anywhere, Miss," Angel replied. "I was awaiting your orders."

Dana shifted around on the Rangora shoulders 'til she was sitting up, latched back her helmet, rubbed her nose for a second, then rubbed her face angrily. The cargo compartment smelled like a reptile house at a zoo. That was going to take *forever* to scrub out.

"Coxswain Angelito, come to one-six-three mark two-one," Dana commed, keeping the general in the loop. "Acceleration two-one-six gravities to marked location. Readback but standby."

"One-six-three mark two-one, aye," Angelito replied. "Two-one-six gravities, aye. Set and standing by."

"We're about to take one earth gravity to the rear of the shuttle, General," Dana said, relatching her helmet. "I'll give you a minute to reorient your personnel. Sorry about that, but we need to get cracking."

"Not an issue, Lieutenant," Sho'Duphuder said. "We can take acceleration better than humans."

"Bully for you," Dana said, not sending. She cycled the rear latch and slid off the shoulders of the Rangora she'd been sitting on. "Thank you for providing a seat, Petty Officer."

"Not a problem, ma'am," the Rangora replied. "You're not real heavy."

"But can you lean forward a little so I can get the hatch shut?" Dana asked, shoving at the compartment hatch. It was not budging. Freaking giant alien lizards. She was getting so sick of freaking giant alien lizards. She finally got it dogged.

"Angelito, do you have the course laid in?" Dana asked.

"Yes, miss."

"Engage."

She leaned back as the accel hit and sighed.

"Ah, gravity sweet gravity," Dana said. "I need a vacation in real air and real gravity."

"Miss," Angelito said, nervously. "I've got an anomalous reading in . . ."

"The forward repulsor screen," Dana said, angrily. "I see that, thank you. Which we're going to need. And the freaking problem is *in the cargo compartment*!"

"...Hold it steady while I fix this," Dana said, stretched across the shoulders of two Rangora with most of her upper body in the systems compartment. "That's great. Thanks. Petty Officer Gromgrak, I need a seven-millimeter wrench..."

"General To'Jopeviq," the colonel awaiting them outside the High Command offices said. "Welcome back."

"General?" To'Jopeviq said.

"By orders of the High Command," the colonel replied, reaching up and removing To'Jopeviq's rank tabs and replacing them with starbursts. "I need to pin on the major's as well. That is, Major, your new Kazi rank as well."

"Thank you, sir," Beor said, calmly.

"You need to update yourself, General," the colonel said, handing over a data tab. "You're going to be briefing High Command on the current situation with regards to Terra and its strategic importance in terms of the new war with the Ogut."

"Understood," To'Jopeviq said, stonily.

"And I wish you luck with that," the colonel said. "The last few briefers didn't even make it out of the room alive..."

"Are you saying that your intention is to declare war on the Ogut Empire, Madame President?"

The speaker was an Ananancauimor, which looked very much like a meter-and-a-half-long black scarab beetle. The Ananancauimor was the planetary consul for several species, including the Ogut. Earth was still considered something of a backwater by most species and thus had not rated a full ambassador from anyone but the now invaded and overrun Glatun. Which made the conversation a little delicate. Fortunately, she was a former career diplomat.

"When Terra was under the boot of the Horvath, it was the Glatun who broke that siege," President Robards said, not bothering to note that it was only because the Glatun wanted maple syrup. Alliances are generally based on mutual benefit, after all.

"When the Horvath threw plagues at us, it was the Glatun who sent fleets of medical ships, including Ananancauimor doctors, I do note. When they were faced by war with the Rangora, knowing that we would be snapped up along with them, they took the unprecedented move of opening up their military databases, sending us AI cores and allowing us to fully arm ourselves."

She also skipped the whole part about the AIs being suborned. Humans knew hacking back and forth. They'd scrubbed them before installation.

"We consider the Glatun our closest, indeed our only, allies," the President continued. "It is a commitment of my predecessor, of this administration and a public statement of the Terran Alliance, that we shall not stop until all Glatun planets are liberated from *any* oppression, Consul. The Federation was a liberal democracy. The Ogut Empire is not. It is what we would call a feudal caliphate. A change from Rangora tyranny to Ogut tyranny is, unfortunately, unacceptable."

"The Ogut are firmly committed to war with the Rangora, Madame President," the beetle said. "They have no direct route to the original Rangora planets except through the former Glatun Federation. They have already made clear statements they intend to liberate those planets."

"Liberate," the President said. "Such a facile word. A word does not make a reality. The Nazis said they were 'liberating' France when they invaded. The Soviets 'liberated' Poland, Hungary, Czechoslovakia. The Rangora 'liberated' the Glatun. Liberty is defined as a freedom to make one's own decisions. The Ogut Empire does not liberate. It conquers, divides the spoils and despoils. Thus, the issue, Consul. You are requested to inform the Ogut Department of Interstellar Affairs that the Terran Alliance considers any 'liberation' that does not include full reestablishment of Glatun democratic control to any systems they might take during this war as an unfriendly act."

"An unfriendly act" was diplospeak for "Get ready to draw, pardner."

"I shall convey that message, Madame President," the Anancauimor said.

It was difficult to understand any alien body language, but the President had spent most of her adult life negotiating with aliens. And she could spot "this bitch is crazy as a bedbug" from a mile away.

"You truly don't understand us, do you, Consul?" the President said.

"I admit that being planetary consul on this planet is no sinecure, Madame President," the Ananancauimor replied. "Nice place. Decent climate. Generally not much to do given the war and all. But . . . No, I don't understand humans at all."

"We have fought the Rangora to a standstill," the President said. "We have taken enormous capital and personnel losses to do so. However, we have a much deeper well than most species can believe. And if you think we are simply going to stand on the defense, you truly do not understand us. We will not come to blows with the Ogut for some time, Consul. There are a vast number of Glatun planets to truly liberate between ourselves and the region the Ogut will probably invade through. But when we get there, and we will get there, those planets had better be under local democratic Glatun rule. Or when we're done with the Horvath, done with the Rangora, then we will have to bring the fear of God to the Ogut. And by then they will, I assure you, *want* to negotiate. Best they receive the message clearly and early. By now, I think the Rangora at least are receiving it loud and clear . . ."

CHAPTER 8

"General," High Commander Phi'Pojagit said as To'Jopeviq came to the position of parade rest. "I think our thoughts on your value are communicated by the rank on your shoulders. Your analysis was, again, correct. In this case, the lack of force was due not to our own underestimation but simply limited resources. Thoughts?"

"The amount of force, coupled with separating the battle-globe from its brothers, should have worked, High Commander," To'Jopeviq said, clearly trying not to snarl. "What this battle proved, again, damnit, is that humans are just fiendishly clever at war. They are willing to take operational and tactical risks that any other species would consider insane. And their level of professionalism and courage runs so *deep* it is amazing. One single encounter we had during the battle spoke volumes on that subject.

"What is assured from the communications we are receiving from repatriating personnel is that at least the *Thermopylae* is out of action for weeks to months. Were it not for the Ogut incursion and our own condition, this would be a good time to strike. As it is, very much not a good time to strike."

"Weeks to months?" Grand Marshall Zissix said. "Our engineering analysis is at least a year."

"With respect, Grand Marshall, they take less time than that to get a *new* one online," To'Jopeviq replied, carefully. "Month or two would be my guess. Possibly more due to the reported damage to the ship fabber. But basic operational capacity? All that we really did was scratch the surface on the damned thing and trash its main bay. It looks bad but they still have a functioning laser room, as proven by the loss of the AV, their missile controls and storage are still there, their personnel quarters, life support, all undamaged. They took a major hit on power systems from their main-bay damage but once they figure out how to get into it—and they will, the little monkey bastards—that will be rectified in short order. They are moving much of their SAPL into the system to do the repairs rather than, as I would have thought, somehow moving it back into the Terran system. With SAPL in place? Two months and it will have something like eighty percent capability back."

"And I rather doubt we will be getting back E Eridani," Grand Marshall Zissix said.

"Marshall, with due respect, I think Eridani is the least of our worries," Beor said, blandly. "And that is not in reference to the Ogut. The Terrans have an expression: Blood in their eye. It refers to the fact that their eyes become bloodshot due to heightened blood pressure when they are extremely angry. The war, overall, has given them a very good head of anger at our race and the Horvath. After this latest battle in Eridani . . . they have blood in their eyes and those eyes are fixed very firmly on our race."

"Noted, Kazi Major," Zissix said.

"General," High Marshall Ucuhath said. "Aliens are alien. But the actions of the Terrans in this battle, and its aftermath, are truly alien. They are recovering our personnel at nearly the same rate as their own and are already beginning repatriation. After having essentially been given a guided tour of both their functioning and their damaged battleglobes, their ships . . .

"They are allowing those personnel not only to look at what we would consider our most secret areas, one of our intelligence officers was given a tour of the *Troy*'s *command center*! And allowing them full access to the *hypernet* so they can report all of this to us! There is some Terran group called 'the Red Cross' which has lodged a complaint against *us* that *we* are not allowing *our* personnel to contact their families! And asking for 'care packages' for the prisoners! This is, frankly, making my head hurt. Can *you* understand them, General?"

"Vaguely, High Marshall," To'Jopeviq said. "But to even begin to explain Terrans would . . . I was given to understand there has been a certain loss among briefers lately, sirs. To begin to explain what I am starting to understand about Terrans . . . ? Might I just ask, since you seem to think somewhat highly of me at the moment, that you kill me quickly and be done? If I actually gave a full briefing on Terrans, why they are so very very good at war and so impossible for us, who think of ourselves as masters of war, to understand, would lead to spending months in the hands of the Kazi. And . . . it was a long shuttle ride back. I'm rather tired to start a Kazi torture session."

"You've come to admire them," High Marshall Ucuhath said.

"I have, High Marshall," To'Jopeviq said. "As a warrior. As a Rangora. The Glatun Empire, which our forces swept aside in bare months, had hundreds of years more space experience, a very experienced space navy, deep technological expertise, vastly more capital and vastly more experience of modern technology. Despite that, the humans have done, in spacer and marine to spacer and marine comparison, *sixty-eight times* as much damage to our forces as the Glatun. That is discounting things like the SAPL that don't really apply. This is about standard battle. They just absolutely kick our tails when *we* really should win, time after time. I have come to admire them. I have come to admire them more . . ."

"More than you admire the people in this room?" Ucuhath asked.

"More than I admire most Rangora and most Rangora high officers, certainly, sir," To'Jopeviq said, knowing that statement alone guaranteed him a nice long torture session. Might as well get it over with.

The threesome looked back and forth for a moment, then Ucuhath turned back.

"We don't need your admiration, General," Ucuhath said. "We need your thoughts. Take all the time you'd like and tell us everything. Sit. My personal promise is that when you're done if we feel the need to send you to reeducation . . . we'll just make it quick."

"Yes, sir," To'Jopeviq said as one of the guards slid over a seat. "Should the major stay? I would prefer that she not be held accountable for this."

"I would prefer to stay," Beor said. "I find myself in agreement with the general on many issues. And I note that his thoughts fulfill my oath. My oath is to protect the Imperium. I will simply state that if we continue on the current path and fail to learn the lessons of the recent battles, in ten years there will be no Imperium *to* protect."

"A seat for the major," High Commander Phi'Pojagit said. "Send for skul and cancel the next... three meetings. Begin, General."

"The first thing to know about humans is that they are schizophrenic politically, truly tribal, have no single common culture much less government, and that those cultures with which we are most psychologically attuned are their *least* effective..."

"So, we towing these guys through the gate, Sparky?" Dana asked.

It had been a bitch of a couple of weeks, but they were finally towing the last string of human lifeboats up to the gate zone. They'd lost some people, human and Rangora, to various maladies. Being Dutchman for too long drove all but a few really stable people insane and when they finally cracked they had a tendency to take off their helmets for a breath of nice vacuum. Then there was the whole problem of the lifeboats and Dutchers being in the middle of the rubble from a space battle. Lifeboats and suits did not have repulsor screens so when some bit of rubble came in at velocities higher than any chemical weapon could generate... scratch one lifeboat or suit.

They'd lost even more Horvath, not that Dana gave a shit about the squids. She'd almost forgotten there were Horvath in the mix until she got the word to tow in a Horvath lifeboat. With the Rangora they usually had them empty out of the lifeboats into the cargo compartment. *Myrmidon*s could move much faster if they weren't towing.

Turned out, the stupid squids had dispensed with spacesuits. A Horvath that went Dutchman generally wigged out in less than thirty minutes. The species was intensely communal, and a "lone Horvath" was like "hen's teeth" in Galactic slang. Put one by itself, period, and they went nuts. Since it only made sense to use lifeboats, they'd just dropped the expense and bother of suits. Of course, that meant that if something happened to a ship, most of the crew died.

Squidtypical.

Dana and Angel had pretty much given up going back to *Therm* for crew rest. Over the last two weeks she'd spent more time sleeping in her suit in micro than in the rest of her career. They'd just put the compartment in micro, velcro themselves to the bulkhead and, hey, crew rest! She'd also slept and eaten on: Apollo crew resupply ships, not bad bunks, chow was good; a cruiser, horrible mess and typical Navy "crammed in every cubic" bunking; a Monkey mining ship, horrible food, great quarters; and a specialty engineering ship that was, for a working ship, practically the lap of luxury. She was totally going to work for Apollo engineering after she got out.

"We're expecting a new arrival," Phaeton replied. "Transferring to it."

"Roger," Dana said.

Like the area wasn't crowded enough. As the Apollo ships had moved off rescue they'd been moving right into repair. They weren't just repairing *Thermopylae*. They'd brought vehicle docks, some of them captured from the Rangora, through from Wolf and were working on the damaged cruisers and destroyers right in the system. On *Thermopylae*, they'd started by a series of Orion taps on the surface to get it closer to the gate then started clearing the surface and surroundings. It was much harder to do orbital engineering in a fog of debris.

SAPL was at least partially up. They were shooting on *Thermopylae*. First, they'd just broad-lased the surface for a few days. The spread SAPL had the effect of driving most of the nearby "junk" down to the surface. The nickel iron was welded back down to the deck while most of the "volatile" materials, like carbon, calcium, phosphorus, were burned out of orbit.

It was still marred as hell but there were some flat spots again.

Currently they were burning pits, probably to reinstall surface defenses. She'd heard they were going to cut a new main door sometime soon. She wanted to be well clear for that. And she and Angel definitely needed a break. Among other things, she had a truncated conversation with Tyler Vernon to finish. Problem being, he was already back in the Terran system. And she still wasn't sure she wanted to pop the question.

"Hold here, Comet," Phaeton said.

"Ain't as easy as just 'hold here, Comet,'" Dana muttered, disengaging the tractor to the front lifeboat.

The problem was, stuff in space just kept on going. And she couldn't skew around and reverse the line. You'd have a serious situation of "crack the whip." Since the lifeboats didn't have pseudogravity or inertials, not to mention they were tied together with actual tow cables, that wouldn't work.

After disengaging, she instead went to the rear lifeboat and locked on with tractors, then engaged reverse, lightly. They were also eggshells. Pull on them too hard and one of the tow lines would part or, for that matter, one of the lifeboats would part. Then they'd have spacers, some of them with their helmets off, scattered all over the lanes. Again. She knew that because it had already happened once with a German crew.

"'Hold here, Comet,'" Dana continued, muttering in her helmet. "'Pick up some Rangora, Comet.' 'Tow some stupid squids, Comet.' 'Help the Germans, Comet.' The problem with having no chain of command is there's nobody to say 'Hey, maybe Comet and Angelito need some time off?' Or, maybe, a real coxswain or an engineer? Huh? Maybe? But, no, 'Tow the lifeboats, Comet...'"

"Are you saying something, Miss?" Angelito commed.

"Just so totally hooyah for this entire experience, Coxswain Angelito," the lieutenant said. "Just so totally motivated I cannot begin to express it. I am overwhelmed with the joy of job well done after job well done after job so well freaking done! It is practically sexual how indescribably happy I am at this very moment. May we continue with this unending freaking parade of *impossible* missions for *months*, Angelito, *months*!"

"Yes, Miss," Angelito said, nervously.

"We're *parked*, Sparky!" Dana snarled, looking at the pile of atacirc in the corner. "Parked. Right here. Again!"

"Just give it a second, Lieutenant," Phaeton replied, perkily. "It's a visual!"

"I have a crowbar, Sparky," Dana said. "This had better be good."

"Blood of Christ!" Angelito said.

Dana turned back to the screens and had to admit it *was* a good visual as *Troy* emerged from the gate. Nine kilometers of smoking nickel-iron destruction was indescribably good to see finally arrive. She was scarred from previous battles but compared to *Thermopylae* she looked fresh out of the yards. If there was a yard big enough.

"Lieutenant Parker, Paris. Good to see you again."

"Same to you, Paris," Dana said. "I don't suppose we're going aboard. This bird needs some serious TLC."

"We have a dozen engineers standing by to detail it," Paris replied. "We're going to rotate to bring Parasite Bypass Two in line with your tow string. Then bring the string up to the vehicle bypass. We'll take it from there."

"Roger," Dana said, detaching and moving back to the front of the consist. The string had gotten a little wiggle in it but nothing she couldn't work with. "I need, like, five days off. Or maybe a little groundside leave. Surely I can swing that . . . ?"

They weren't the only vessels headed in the bypass. There were more shuttles and a very large ship all jockeying for position.

"Miss . . . ?" Angel asked.

"That is a Rangora assault transport," Dana said. "We are about to bring a Rangora ship designed to carry a brigade of Rangora assault infantry into battle *into* the *Troy.* Presumably to pick up the survivors of the two brigades of assault infantry that tried to take *Thermopylae.*"

"That does not make a great deal of sense, Miss," Angel said.

"Never try to figure out what upper command is thinking, Angel," Dana said. "It is never a good idea."

"I'm not sure this is a good idea, Marshall," Admiral Kinyon said. The commander of Battleglobe Squadron One did not look particularly unhappy, but he had an excellent poker face.

"It's the President's call, Admiral," Marshall Hampson said. "It's a show of strength. If we still had any friendlies we were in contact with, we'd send the Squadron around in a White Fleet capacity. We're about to swallow one of their largest assault ships with our Death Star. We know the Rangora want to get us off their plate. They're not coming back at us for quite a while what with the Ogut being on their butts. But we're not going to just be negotiating for status quo. Let them see the alternative."

"Very well, Marshall," Admiral Kinyon said. "If the President wants us to put on a show, we'll put on a show . . ."

"General Sho'Duphuder, Admiral Kinyon, Commander Battleglobe Squadron One," Admiral Kinyon said, nodding as he stood at parade rest. "Welcome to *Troy.*"

The meeting was taking place in the Level Nineteen Observation Deck, which gave a very nice view of the extremely busy, brightly lit, main-bay. There were seven captured Rangoran *Aggressor* battleships currently docking on the maneuvering horns as well as more Terran-built *Defenders* putting into their docks along the shiny nickel-iron walls. Around and among them were essentially Terra's entire remaining fleet of *Constitution*-class Cruisers and *Independence*-class destroyers, which were being moved from the Number Two Bypass to docks associated with the Number One Bypass. That didn't count masses of missiles flying out of their missile fabbers to refill the *Troy*'s literally cavernous missile storage compartments, the repair sleds and robots moving in to repair battle damage and the kilometer-long mass of Hephaestus, who was just birthing what looked very much like a *Mjolnir*-class Super-missile.

The Rangora assault ship was sort of lost in the mix. Not to mention in the grip of tractor beams so strong they were distorting the light that passed through them. The power of the tractor beams was available on the hypernet. If Rangora intel could do math, they'd realize that the *Troy*'s tractor beams alone could rip the assault carrier apart like a cooked chicken.

"A very impressive display, Admiral," General Sho'Duphuder said.

It was clear that Sho'Duphuder was less impressed with the masses of material than the operations. It looked to an untrained observer like complete chaos. The Rangoran recognized the signs of precision order. The fact that nothing was impacting at high velocities was proof that it was precisely and perfectly ordered. That many of the ships had clear signs of battle damage, probably including maneuvering, made it even more impressive.

"We aim to please, General," Admiral Kinyon said, smiling toothily. A "normal" human smile, showing teeth, was considered extremely hostile by most alien races.

"I have in general found your aim quite *dis*pleasing, Admiral," General Sho'Duphuder said. "May I inquire as to the current status of my personnel?"

"We've rounded up about ninety percent of them, General," Captain Sharp said. "The rest died due to . . . various issues. Where we could easily recover the bodies and determine cause of death, that has happened. In other cases . . . they're lost. Indications are that some lifeboats ran into missiles. Our apologies for that, General."

"Fortunes of war," General Sho'Duphuder said, clearly perplexed by the apology.

"I would like to note that your decision, while out-of-the-box, was probably one of the smartest military decisions I've ever seen, General," Kinyon said. "You saved most of your people in a hopeless tactical situation. You would have lost ninety percent if they'd stayed to fight."

"Which was the point," Sho'Duphuder said. "The problems being... many."

"I understand," Kinyon said, shrugging. "We've had many polities in our history where victory was the only acceptable result, no matter the conditions." He paused for a moment, then shrugged again. "We are more than willing to offer yourself and your senior officers sanctuary pending the outcome of the war."

"Thank you, but no," Sho'Duphuder said. "I'll accept the Kazi. That way I may at least be able to shield my senior officers from similar retribution. I am sorry for your own losses as well, Admiral. The loss of the light boat squadrons was, truly and horribly, fortunes of war. From what I've gleaned, your ships fought extremely well as well."

"Thank you, General," Kinyon said. "They do not grow old."

"Excuse me?" Sho'Duphuder asked.

"One of our poems of loss, General," Captain Sharp said. "'They do not grow old as we who are left grow old. Age does not worry, nor the years condemn.'"

"'At the going down of the sun and in the morning, we shall remember them,'" Admiral Kinyon finished. "The current plan is to use the *Ixphibimuh* to shuttle your personnel back to Glalkod station. From there... up to Rangoran forces. We request that you take temporary command of all rescued survivors, from whatever group, as senior officer and begin management of those survivors as soon as practicable. *Ixphibimuh* is the only Rangoran combatant ship we will continue to allow to enter the Eridani system now that *Troy* is on station."

"You intend to hold Eridani?" Sho'Duphuder asked, unsurprised.

"General, we shortly intend to hold *Glalkod*," Kinyon said, smiling toothily again. "So, when you get there, don't bother to unpack."

"Welcome back, Lieutenant," Lieutenant Commander Tyrell Boston said. Boston had been the Engineering Officer of the 142nd and was now its acting commander with the loss of MOGs. "To the *Troy* and the 142nd."

The 142nd was just as gutted as the 143rd. The only people in the squadron area were trogs, support personnel assigned permanently to positions in *Troy,* and newbs, recently joined personnel who hadn't made it through quals. Every qualled spacer assigned to boats had been eliminated in one blast of plasma.

The corridors of her first permanent assignment were eerily quiet. The groups of newbs solemnly taking name tags off of doors only added to the feeling of loss.

"Am I being reassigned, sir?" Dana said, standing at the position of parade rest in front of the commander's desk.

"Orders just came down," Boston said. "Sit, Dana. We've got to talk."

"Yes, sir," Dana said, taking a seat and still sitting at the position of attention.

"Your so-called permanent assignment is as Assistant Flight Officer," Boston said. "That would put you in charge of third chalk, assuming we had three full chalks. Your temporary assignment is Flight Officer, which is a lieutenant commander position, not JG. I say 'so-called permanent' because there are already other priority positions popping up, some temporary, some permanent. So, don't get real comfortable. That's not to say I don't want you back here. I do. I just see the signs you're going to be all over the place, at least for a while, rather than peacefully doing paperwork and working the Scrapyard. Got that?"

"Yes, sir," Dana said. "Question, sir?"

"Go."

"My coxswain, sir?" Dana said. "Is Angelito being assigned as well?"

"No," Boston said. "The entirety of the 143rd, including your cox, are being reassigned to the *Malta.* One Forty-Four is going to the *Therm. Malta* is being stood up. The 143 has to be stood back up. One Forty-Four, while not totally ready for action, is clearly more ready, at least in material and personnel terms, than a squadron with only four remaining coxswains and engineers and two shuttles. Your current shuttle will go back to the 143. Both squadrons are drawing from new builds out of Wolf. And we have two shuttles on hand, so you'll be getting one right away as well as an engineer. She's an EA but Chief Hartman signed off on her. I'll assume that meets your standards, Lieutenant."

"Yes, sir," Dana said, trying not to tear up. Chief David P.

"Thermal" Hartman had been her mentor when she joined the 142 as an FNG engineering recruit. If Thermal had signed off on her eng, that said it all. "Good to go, sir."

Boston paused for a moment, looking at her calmly.

"It has been a long time since any Navy has dealt with these sorts of losses," Boston said. "Especially something like small boats. So, I sort of need to dig into Army traditions."

"Sir?" Dana said as the commander pulled open a drawer.

"The Army has a tradition," Boston said, setting down a bottle of Irish whiskey and two shot glasses, then pouring. "When a regiment takes the sort of losses we did they say, 'As long as one man remains to carry the flag, the regiment is not gone.' As a trog officer, I don't really count. But you do, Lieutenant. You are the one woman remaining to carry the flag. You up to that, Lieutenant?"

"Yes, sir," Dana said, taking the shot glass.

"Absent companions," Boston said, raising the shot.

"We deliver the mail," Dana said, tossing hers down.

"You've got two days in the station, downtime," Boston said, putting the glasses away. "Light time at least. No flight time. Paperwork, mostly. For one thing, you've never signed your commissioning papers. And you're going to have to get up to speed on all the responsibilities of a Flight Officer."

"Yes, sir," Dana said.

"Without, currently, having a more senior flight officer," Boston added with a sigh and a shake of his head. "The only advice I can give you is when you're not sure what to do, ask yourself what Razor or MOGs, Chief Barnett for that matter, would do."

"Yes, sir," Dana said, her face working. "That was pretty much how I handled being with the 143, sir."

"And if that doesn't work, call me," Boston continued. "I'll help out when I can. Oh, one last bit of advice. Less advice than an order. While there may be engineering and maintenance issues that you may have to get involved in, you're a *flight* officer not an *engineering* officer. While you were a qualified flight engineer, you're not a qualified engineer *officer*. You need a bachelor's at least for that. Your days of turning a wrench are over. You don't turn a wrench unless it's critically necessary on a mission. Which it shouldn't be unless your eng is injured. Your job is to fly and manage your coxes, not work on your bird. Clear, Lieutenant?"

"Clear, sir," Dana said.

"For now, given what you've been doing for the last two weeks, you have twelve hours of downtime. No flight time tomorrow. So, I don't care if you have to get drunk, get laid, get pills from the medics, or just cry yourself to sleep in your pillow, I need you functional tomorrow at zero eight hundred. Which means sleep. Understood?"

"Yes, sir," Dana said.

CHAPTER 9

"For many months I've known this day would come," General To'Jopeviq said. "But I did not expect it this soon."

The message from Earth, passed not only to General Sho'Duphuder—who he was glad to see had survived—but through Ananancauimor envoys, was detailed, precise, and less a negotiating position than an ultimatum and battle plan. The Rangora Imperium had ninety days to remove all Rangora personnel, including long-term residents, from the Glalkod and Karoth systems, abrogate its treaty of mutual defense with the Horvath, and establish a timetable for withdrawal from all Glatun systems. At the end of the ninety-day period, the current status of ceasefire would automatically terminate absent meeting the conditions.

"The humans are mad," Toer said. "They were as seriously crippled by the last battle as our own forces. They do not have the logistics to move a force into Glalkod."

"*Troy*," Avana said. The academic looked as if he was quite ill. "They don't need ships; they can just send *Troy*."

"*Troy* won't be able to do anything but lumber around," Toer said. "And it is not entirely self-supporting. It needs food and other consumables which have to be shipped from Earth. Ninety-six tons of consumables per day. That is a lot of logistics given that they just lost a massive amount of shipping."

"They didn't lose *logistics* shipping," Avana said. "They lost warships. Which actually decreases their logistic burden. And they are as damnably good at logistics as they are at all other aspects of war."

"And they have enough parasites left to support the *Troy* against anything we can muster to defend Glalkod," To'Jopeviq said. "Much less Horvath. Two months, possibly three, to get *Thermopylae* back online."

"More than that if they are continuing to fight, General," Avana said. "Six is more likely."

"Possibly to repair the ship fabber," To'Jopeviq said. "But they are already working on cutting a main door. And with *Troy* alongside and its ship fabber supplying them?"

"*Thermopylae* took tremendous casualties in civilian support crews, General," Toer said.

"Which they turn out in droves," To'Jopeviq snapped. "Yes, rebuilding *Thermopylae* will slow their overall war effort. It may slow the completion of *Malta*. But by the time they enter the Glalkod system they will probably bring *Troy* and *Thermopylae*. Just to make the *point* if nothing else!"

"So, what do we recommend?" Beor asked.

"The Ogut are taking time getting into action," To'Jopeviq said, clomping his jaws in thought. "They have to convince their satraps that it is worth going to war with us. Gather their forces. The immediate response of High Command would probably be to keep all the forces withdrawn from Eridani in Glalkod and try to hold the system. There are logistic issues on our own side to moving them. Problem being, we *can't*. We don't have enough weight or firepower to hold any of those systems against *Troy* classes. We'd just lose them and lose them *permanently* if they stay and fight. The only reasonable recommendation is withdrawal."

"Which is defeatist," Avama said, flicking his claws nervously.

"Withdraw the forces we've recovered from Eridani inward," To'Jopeviq said, definitely. "Bring the Eridani forces to central areas and rearm and resupply. Then shift them to the *Ogut* front. On the Terran front, exchange Glalkod and possibly other systems for the prisoners in human hands."

"The High Command has a policy against prisoner exchange," Beor pointed out.

"As a polity we are stretched to the *greatest* degree," To'Jopeviq said. "We are now hyper-extended through the Glatun Federation, which is starting to develop an insurgency, in a two-front war, and we've expended most of our capital, both Rangoran and financial, on what was supposed to be a swift, victorious, war.

"In retrospect, attacking the humans *at all* was our greatest mistake. Right now, we are stretched for ships, materials, and trained personnel. We cannot get the ships we have lost back nor the materials. We *might* get the trained personnel. We'll offer a parole that they won't be used against the humans. We won't honor it. The humans know we won't honor it. But they'll probably agree if for no other reason than to get their 'non-governmental organizations' off their backs."

"This is the oddest war," Toer said.

"The Ogut do not care for losses," To'Jopeviq continued. "The primary plan on the Ogut front should be to maximize their losses *early*, which means putting as much of our throw weight on that side as we can and bring them to the bargaining table. Put our AVs in systems as system defense platforms. Counterattack aggressively. That is where the forces we've recovered from Eridani *should* be used. They are veterans and after fighting the humans, fighting the Ogut should be a much more pleasant experience.

"The humans, on the other hand, are going to keep pushing as long as they can sustain the political will. To reduce their political will, we need a method of destroying their battleglobes. The human 'electorate' sees the battleglobes as invincible. We have to dissuade them of that. Fortunately, the humans have given us the method."

"The ship missiles," Beor said.

"Those horrible bastard ship missiles," To'Jopeviq confirmed. "We will need to develop some of our own. Swiftly. One of those with enough support and time to get up to speed can crack a battleglobe. Totally destroy it? Possibly not. But take it out of action and probably kill many of its crew. They are not designed for inertial dampening and their main bay is vulnerable, as proven by this last battle.

"The Terrans are going to be busy trying to resupply the Glatun worlds," To'Jopeviq concluded. "That, right there, will slow them. Get a few of the... *Mjolnir* built and hit them as they enter one of the deeper systems, preferably at a chokepoint. But bring most of the forces back to core areas, rearm, resupply and have them face the Ogut primarily. Buy time on the Terran front through negotiations. Until we have a *Mjolnir*, negotiation is our best bet on that front. Try to dissuade them from advancing fast. If they advance fast... we're doomed."

* * *

"We need to advance as fast as possible, Madame President," Marshall Hampson said. "I am fully aware of our current stretched condition. However, it is an axiom of war to never give an enemy time to regroup. While I and the Joint Chiefs do not take issue with the ninety-day time frame, we need to put a definite lock-in on the negotiations past that. The Rangora appear much more stretched than we are. Pushing them back, now, should be our primary concern."

"After the Horvath," General Denny said. The only surviving marine general from the latest battle was on the fast track to replace General Smith as Alliance Marine Commandant.

"After the Horvath," Marshall Hampson agreed viciously. "As soon as we have agreement on transfer of the Karoth system to human control, *Troy* is going to pay the Horvath a visit they'll never forget. And if we don't get it, soon, I'm formally requesting permission to violate the in-place agreements. Given that we're at war, that should not be a strange request."

"It is not," President Robards said, frowning. "And I agree that we need to take the Horvath off the table militarily. What I will not countenance is a pure punishment raid."

"Define, Madame President," Hampson said.

"The Horvath have been our bugaboo practically from first contact," President Robards said. "I fully recognize Terra's universal loathing for those damned squids." She turned her wrist upward to show the mark of the Johannsen's Worm all of the senior officers in the room shared.

"I hate them as much as anyone. One of my own *children* died from their damned plagues. But we will not 'blast them back to the Stone Age' nor hammer them into the ground just for vengeance. Pure genocide is *not* going to happen on my watch, gentlemen. Take away their ability to be spacefaring for the time being. Remove or destroy all of their space-based industry. Station units in the system with the express purpose of ensuring they don't rebuild and to prevent infiltration by the Rangora from that flank. Set up a SAPL and defense asteroids. Et cetera.

"But you are *not* going to pound their planet's surface into oblivion with Thunderbolts nor drop our own plagues on *them*," the President concluded. "Do I make myself *perfectly* clear?"

"Clear, Madame President," Hampson said, his face hard. "You're the Commander in Chief."

"Yes," the President said, sadly. "I am. And part of the whole 'civilian control of the military' is having to be the *conscience* of the military. After all the Horvath have done to us, up to and including being the bait of this latest debacle, genocide seems the worthy outcome. But I have to look beyond this current... horror. I will not have history recall that the moment Terra stepped forward in battle, its first action was genocide. That being said, can we constrain them without it being a huge drain on our resources?"

"Depends how hard they fight back, Madame President," Marshall Hampson said, shrugging. "We should be able to constrain their actions without huge commitments. But what are we going to do with them long-term?"

"Think about that tomorrow," the President said, smiling faintly. "Because tomorrow is another day. In the meantime, ignore the Multilateral Treaty. We were never signatories. As soon as your forces are sufficiently prepared, you may engage the Horvath *at will*. In fact, the faster the better. It should send a salient message to the Rangora if before they can even get all their forces back to core worlds, *we're* already on the *offensive*. And if the Rangora do not withdraw from Glalkod in ninety days... take it by force majeure, Marshall."

"Can do," Hampson said, grinning.

"Warship construction status..."

CHAPTER 10

Men came to the place many years ago. First the landmen, making deals, leasing or buying the sparse, arid land good mostly for running very few cattle on very many acres. Then the surveyors and engineers, laying out the grids, doing feasibility studies, studying the soil to determine compressibility. Then the crews, laying down side tracks to the railroads that ran through the high plains, vast ovals of train track for reasons no one knew. They were just being paid.

Then the concrete, shipped in by trains, mobile factories producing dozens of near identical thick, heavily reinforced pads. Some speculated that Vernon was planning on building a new city in the virtual wilderness. Given the damage to most of the earth's cities, it made as much sense as anything.

Then, the work complete, the men left. And the dry upland prairie lay empty except for the tracks, maintained as was necessary, and the vast number of near identical concrete pads. The cattle came back and wandered over the pads, back to searching for sparse grass.

The pads lay silent and still, awaiting their day...

Which had finally come.

"That's a sight for God damn sore eyes," Butch muttered as the airbus approached landing.

The area was mostly what could be termed "fuck all." Damned near flat as a pancake high plains, dry but extensively farmed in plattes that ran up to ten thousand acres. The largest town in the area was Russell Springs, which was about ten trailers and some random cows.

But now there were patches of... less than fuck all.

Every five miles, scattered across an area of thousands of square miles, was what appeared to be a small community under construction. Each was connected with a recently installed set of rail lines that often cut through farms. There were travel trailers, large "AT-AT" cranes normally found in shipping ports, girders...

As the ship drifted up the line from "community" to "community" the process became more comprehensible. First there were apparently random girders. Then bits and pieces of framework. Then shells started to form. Nacelles appeared. Armor plating was attached. *Ships* started to take shape.

Independence Block III frigates. *Constitution* Block IV cruisers. *Avenger* dreadnoughts, which were replacing the already obsolete *Defenders*.

The area was Earth's newest and most productive shipyard. The man camps were groups of workers, human and robotic, who specialized in one key portion of the construction. As each phase was completed the majority of the workforce would move on to the next construction in a continuous series. It was a version of how the US and other countries had mass produced aircraft in World War II. Just *enormously* larger.

Although there were problems with building on a planet, weather and dust getting into critical areas, it was far easier to build on a planet's surface than in space. One of the biggest reasons was people. Although probably eighty percent of what was going on below her boat was done by robots, *some* humans had to be involved. And it was much easier to find people who could work on a planet than in space, not to mention cheaper. Better to build the ships in Kansas than in Wolf or deep space in the Terran system. And even the massive *Avengers* were capable of generating more than an earth's gravity of drive. Therefore, they could lift themselves out of the well.

The plans had been in the works practically since the start of the war, but the constant, and unavoidable, planetary bombardments had militated against it. It had, in fact, been one of the biggest bottlenecks to ship construction.

Now, there *were* no bottlenecks. Millions of GenJos, Generation

Johannsens, were entering the workforce. And instead of having to put them through months of training and testing specifically related to *space*, they could be employed creating the weapons of war right here "at home."

The Johannsen plagues—named after the epidemiologist at the Mayo Clinic who had first identified them—had killed nearly a fifth of the world's seven billion population when they were laid down by the Horvath. The Horvath, anticipating a far larger loss, had slipped in an additional mickey that increased both fertility and "interest" in select genetic groups. Why exactly the Horvath had determined that blond females should have a "heat" cycle and pretty much *no* way to prevent reproduction absent use of prophylactics, or abstinence—which had been Dana's teeth-grinding choice—was still being debated.

But the result had been a population explosion in developed countries that had had their "native" populations, prior to the plagues, more or less dying off. Prior to the plagues, Germany's "native" population growth rate was one point four. Two point one children per female was "replacement" rate. The post WWII "baby boom" had only averaged two point four five and that was considered "large." Twelve years after the Johannsen plague hit, Germany's population growth rate hit a high of nine point two. Germany's population had swelled by *thirty percent* in twenty years. The US had increased by fifteen percent. Certain states, Kansas was one, the population was growing like *yeast*. Utah's population growth rate was *nine point six*. Scandinavia, Russia, and Ukraine were at similar rates and the rate didn't seem to be decreasing.

Thus, Generation Johannsen. The biggest population growth boom in human history and certainly in the history of developed nations.

And those same GenJos were signing up for military service in *droves*. There was no need for conscription. She'd seen estimates that *volunteers* for Space Navy service were outstripping the infrastructure to train or even test them. Admittedly, sixty percent of volunteers didn't meet the standards for space work. Even being in one of the *big* spaceships was stressful in a way that being on, say, a wet carrier was not. Being on a *Troy* class was less so. You could occasionally forget that you were in space. But anyone who occasionally had to put on a spacesuit and step "into the Black" needed the sort of phlegmatic personality usually found only in the submarine world prior to man's ascent into the heavens. They didn't necessarily need to be as smart. The world still needed cooks. But they needed to be as stable.

Forty percent of five million, the number of recruits from old "NATO" countries who had volunteered as soon as they graduated from high school, was two *million* junior space eagles.

And they were just *starting* to fill the ships being built beneath the airbus.

"What you gotta wonder is... Where's all the *material* coming from...?"

"I can never get over this sight," Tyler said, watching the cone of metal screaming down through the sky slowed to a bare few hundred miles per hour by a ribbon chute. "It's pretty much what I got into the job of orbital mining *to* see."

When the Horvath announced their control of Earth's orbitals shortly after first contact, they did so by dropping kinetic energy weapons, missiles similar to the human Thunderbolts, onto Shanghai, Cairo, and Mexico City. When humans fought back, they dropped more on various capitals and major economic and cultural cities. Thus, the planet lost Los Angeles, New York, Washington, London, Paris, Moscow, Beijing, Berlin and a host of others. Dana Parker was three years old when that happened and walked out of the super-fires started when the thermal blast hit the chapparal in LA.

The Rangora continued the job, dropping more missiles on St. Louis, to which the American capital had moved, as well as dozens of other cities working down a list.

For decades afterward, "rocks falling from the sky" were anathema to the citizens of the planet.

The problem being that while Apollo could do a lot of work in space, material was needed on *Earth*. The population was exploding, which meant people needed "stuff." Some of that could be produced from petroleum and various "plastics." Earth still needed metals for a host of products.

They could shuttle metal or even refined components down, bring them down in huge freighters, which they did. But it was energy inefficient and costly. For years Tyler had argued that with metals, simply *dropping* them was the better choice. It was dead easy and cheap.

Separate the metals in space. Apollo had been doing that for decades and had it down to an incredibly energy- and money-efficient art. Form them into cones similar to the reentry warhead of an ICBM. Bring them into low earth orbit. Drop so as to hit an area of relatively shallow continental shelf. "Stuff" in space is actually quite cold. The "burning" of meteors, depending on their size, barely warms them up. So, when it hit, the reentry vehicle would be cold. And because it was sharply pointed, when it hit water instead of "blowing up" it would simply penetrate, albeit with a massive splash.

The few times they were allowed to experiment with the technique the reentry vehicle, big around as shipping container and three times as long, caused a more or less vertical water jet that went up nearly a thousand feet. And a reentry vehicle that big needed nearly a thousand feet of water under it just to slow down. Send down an ROV, hook up a *big* cable, and winch it up. Tricky but quite doable. Cheap, even.

They weren't going to hit anything *important*. They weren't going to wipe out a freighter much less a city. The technology to drop them precisely had been worked out long before for nuclear reentry weapons from ICBMs. Although that argument led back to the "big booms from space" issue and caused a twitch reaction in politicians.

There was, admittedly, a small issue with the continuing "environmental" movement. One of their tests had damned near impacted a freighter full of Greenpeace protesters. Not that it would have been a big loss in Tyler's opinion, but the PR implications were unpleasant.

Didn't matter if it worked. Didn't matter if it was efficient. For years the idea had been a nonstarter. Nobody was going to let him just drop metal into the ocean. Bringing it down with fuel-hog freighters was the only choice.

The combination of the groundside building program, which needed *enormous* quantities of material, and a suggestion from a very junior Apollo employee, who was now far less junior, had eventually overcome the resistance. Earth just needed the metals too much.

The change, suggested by a mechanic on one of the mining ships, was to not drop them in an *uncontrolled* manner. Most of the senior people who had been thinking about this for a long time had been thinking about it based upon either Galactic technologies, the host of tech the humans had gotten and refined, mostly from the Glatun, or pre-Galactic space technology. The ICBM reentry process being an example. *Everyone* had overlooked parachutes. Why?

Because they'd have to be lifted from the ground. And the "old guys," like Tyler himself, still had at their very core an aversion to "lift." It went back to the cost of lift from rockets, which no one had used in decades. But it was still there in the backs of their minds. So even if they thought "parachutes," they dismissed them as "too energy/money intensive."

Making the parachutes *in space* had just *never occurred to them*! Which was, Tyler had to admit to himself, idiotic. Apollo made *everything* in space. They even made *food* in space. Making parachutes for reentry vehicles in space from the same material they used for making, say, the woven nanofiber covers for Liberty Freighters, was *obvious*. The lines were essentially identical to the lines for the Franklin gas mines.

As the massive cone of metal, bigger than a tractor trailer, splashed down in a hundred feet of water barely sixty miles from Tampa, Florida, another bobbed to the surface. Because once you got around to thinking about how you could use parachutes, making a *lift balloon* was dead simple. A turbine installed on the flat portion of the cone, same place the parachute was attached, used the rush of the passing wind to pressurize a woven nanofiber air tank. Once it reached a certain speed and depth, the air was released from the tank into a woven nanofiber lift bag, which brought the cone to the surface. Instead of having to somehow extract it from bottom muck a thousand feet down.

The turbine had been added into the design of various spaceships, mostly military. When the reentry vehicle was retrieved it was detached, checked, loaded into a shipping container along with a bunch of others and when the container was filled sent to Kansas to be installed on a warship as a liquids pump.

The metals would be sent to burgeoning factory towns along the Mississippi River complex, from Mobile to Knoxville to Grand Rapids, or shipped as far away as China and India, where they'd be reformed, folded, spindled and mutilated into components ranging from Thunderbolt missiles to hinges for baby cribs. Not to mention more factories, fabbers, 3D printers, nails to make houses, power plants, tractors and electric cars.

When Tyler had picked up most of John Deere in a fire sale to prop up the renowned tractor company, he had wondered if it was simply charity. Business pundits had pointed to it as an absolutely bone-headed decision on his part. A clear example that "even if he understands space industry, he really doesn't understand business." The company was reeling from losing multiple factories as well as trained personnel in bombings and a huge fall-off in farming due to the equally huge fall-off in customers after the Horvath plagues.

The next year, due to the Johannsen retrovirus, virtually every nubile female with blond hair had given birth. And the next year and the next. And all those kids needed food.

The John Deere grav-tractor division of LFD, Inc. was now one of its most profitable divisions. And all the metal was being dropped from space. Most of it modified in ground side smelters and forges he'd either built when building was cheap to keep people in jobs or picked up for a song.

It was times like this if he wondered if he was a genius or just really incredibly lucky.

The fun part was the materials for the parachute and lift bag. Those nobody at Apollo had a really efficient use for. Not something that was guaranteed to make money. So, they were generally just dumped ashore in big piles. "If you want it, you can have it."

No problem with filling up landfills, though, because, *yes*, people wanted the stuff. It was *carbon nanofiber*. What just a few decades before was barely technologically feasible for humanity was now, due to Galactic tech, waste junk. Junk for which people, just ordinary citizens and small businesses, had found a host of uses. Sails was a big one. Entire hulls for that matter. Tents. Car repairs: there was nothing like nanofiber weave composite to strengthen a repaired fender. There was a company in Sarasota that rewound the sheets into golf clubs of all things. Good ones. He owned a set.

Where it was being dumped near a similar splash-down zone off Indonesia, people used it to make *houses*. Especially roofs. Stoves, since it was both extremely heat resistant and durable. Clothing that *never* wore out. Forget blue jeans; you were going to be handing down a pair of carbon nanofiber pants to your great-great-great-great... something grandchildren.

They really should find a way to charge for it. But every

scrap of nanofiber was essentially helping with the rebuild of civilization. And with all the leftover equipment from building the Franklin gas-mine, they produced it so inexpensively it was cheaper to just dump it once it was in the gravity well.

So, it was one of those times he'd personally decided to leave well enough alone. A bear can win sometimes, a bull can win sometimes, but a pig always loses.

"While I could sit here in the Caribbean sun and watch this all day, I suppose there's work?" Tyler asked the air.

"You're scheduled to attend the commissioning of the *Jason W. Haselbauer*, sir," Argus replied. "The ship is currently going through final grav tests. The commissioning ceremony is in seven hours. Two hours to get there with air traffic control in the region."

Jason Haselbauer had been the actual leader of the insurgency that led to the abortive Maple Syrup War. Tyler had been at most a figurehead. And he'd been a good friend up to the day of his death. While Tyler wasn't launching the ship—one of Jason's many great-granddaughters had that honor—it wasn't a commissioning he was going to miss. Especially since he'd been the one who had quietly but firmly insisted on the name.

"Let's head over to the shipyard, then," Tyler said. "It may belong mostly to General Dynamics and BAE but I always enjoy looking at it. Kill a couple of hours. Pilot?"

"Sir?"

"To the shipyard."

"We have an interesting response from the Rangora," Roland Rivera, the Alliance Minister of Interstellar Affairs said.

"Go," President Robards said.

"They're willing to cede Glalkod, and even abrogate their treaty with the Horvath, under certain conditions," Rivera said, looking at his pad.

"What are the conditions?" the President asked. "Tribute?"

"Surprisingly enough, no," Rivera replied. "They want their prisoners back."

"They need them to fight the Ogut," Marshall Hampson said. "And us. So... no would be my recommendation."

"They did offer parole on that matter," Rivera said, shrugging. "That the forces released would not be used against Terra. Not that they're going to abide by it."

"They're a logistical drain we don't need," President Robards said. "And the Rangora are going to be pretty busy with the Ogut for a while. Sorry, Marshall, but I'd just as well like to get them off our plate. What about the rest of the Glatun systems?"

"They reject that out of hand but are willing to open negotiations," Rivera said.

"Under *our* guns this time," Robards said, definitely. "Set up a timetable for prisoner transfer and withdrawal from Glalkod space. Negotiations are to take place on Glalkod. Marshall, start the planning for defending Glalkod space against all enemies. Negotiations will start after you have all the defenses in place you think are necessary. I'll have someone else look at nation rebuilding. Status on Operation Implacable Doom?"

"*Thermopylae* is stable," Hampson said. "And has had about seventy percent of its SAPL bypass repaired. Fourteen collimators available for fire. It's had its magazines sixty percent replenished by *Troy*. Power systems are at forty percent but stable at forty for battle. *Troy* is full up. There are nine battle wagons repaired to at least eighty percent. All of those have full shields, armor, missiles and drive. Most of the remaining repairs are point defense or internals. They're not hard battle-worthy but they can fight. Two more *Defenders* have completed trials and are in system. Four *Independence* and two Connies, for that matter, for a total of eleven *Defenders*, nine *Independence*, and six *Constitutions*. The *Aggressors* are taking longer to repair."

"How many do you need for Doom?" Robards asked.

"*Troy*, six *Defenders*, and the light units," Hampson said. "If you're asking for my recommendation, Madame President, leave the repairing *Defenders* and the new ones in E Eridani to protect the system and do work ups. Push forward *Troy* and a parasite squadron at your command. Given what we're facing in any direction, we're not going to lose Eridani no matter what. SAPL alone can hold it. And we have no known enemies in any direction except Eridani."

"Then start the operation," Robards said. "I want the Horvath off the table as soon as possible. But absolutely *no* deliberate genocide. Is that understood?"

"Yes, ma'am."

CHAPTER 11

"I understand that humans have a habit of tearing at their hair when sufficiently frustrated," General To'Jopeviq said, looking at the estimate on human ship construction rates. "Despite my disgust with mammals in general, at the moment that would be a useful distraction technique. Please, Toer, tell me this is an overestimation?"

"I'm afraid not, General," Toer said. The analyst had recently been promoted to Senior Information Officer and it was one of his teams that had produced the estimate. "The taking of E Eridani has made the Terran system relatively safe. Without the threat of ground bombings, the humans were able to implement large-scale construction projects that had been long planned and for which they had extensive preparation. Easily repairable infrastructure such as the rail lines had already been laid down. Areas had been surveyed and such political issues as land ownership had already been negotiated. Materials were available and scattered in various locations. Personnel had been predesignated, plans had been laid in, and structures were available from such things as refugee camps. By the time you and the major returned to Rangor, the system was beginning production. At this point they've completed two *Independence* class, a *Constitution*, and they are about to launch their *second Avenger* class. All they had to do was throw it all together."

"'All,'" To'Jopeviq said with a hiss. "You understand the complexity of something like this, yes?"

"Yes, General," Toer said, unhappily. "But as with many other issues of complexity, the *Troy*-class battleglobes, their rapid development and upgrade of their space combat ships, simply their *leap* into space, humans, and especially 'Western' humans, seem to have little trouble managing such complexity. They quite simply *do* it. It is not that there have not been issues. There were an enormous number of issues."

"This is not a new thing, at least for the Americans," Avama added. "During a previous 'cold' war as they term it, the Americans began developing ships using fission-based power systems."

"I'm not even sure what that is," Beor said.

"Not directly important, Major," Avama said, delicately. "It was a new power system of, at the time, great complexity. While barely having the roughest grasp on the technology or even the physics, the Americans conceived of using it for some of their water-borne and submarine combat ships. Before their enemies could even grasp the concept, they had multiple deployed and operational.

"By the time the 'Soviets' had created their first, rough, 'nuclear' submarine, the Americans had five, had developed three prototypes that were eventually singles and were building an improved class. Their first 'nuclear carrier' was so overpowered they were never able to use all of the power systems simultaneously. And they simply pulled some power systems and made four more. Even to other human tribes it was a seemingly impossible feat of technology and systemology. But they simply... did it. So, to the humans, Americans at least, this is nothing new."

"One estimate my team developed, based upon a *public* lecture on 'systemology,' was that the *Troy* class had fourteen *million* issues during construction," Beor continued. "These ranged from very minor, individual parts that did not meet specification, to extremely major, major designs that quite simply did not work. Yet *every single item* was overcome in what to our analysis was incredibly short order. What would have taken our military or civilian leadership months to work out was generally fixed in days or at most weeks. Eight times as fast was the general consensus. It is another case where we doubt our own analysis. Because it makes no sense."

"Don't doubt it," To'Jopeviq said, clacking his teeth. "To me it makes perfect sense."

"May I ask why, General?" Toer said. "Because it makes none to us."

"A chance encounter in the battle in Eridani," To'Jopeviq said. "Beor. The pilot."

"I recall the encounter," Beor said. "And your lecture on its importance. But I am having a hard time extending it to this analysis."

"General?" Toer said. "Still confused. And not being a sycophant but when you input it is generally important."

"Trying to figure out how to explain it," To'Jopeviq said, clacking his teeth in thought. "I also tried, and failed I think, to explain its importance to the High Command. They tried to accept my analysis, but I fear the reasoning escaped them. It is not only a new thought but one that is frankly outrageous if fully understood. Outrageous enough, I think the only reason I left the meeting alive is that they did *not* understand it. Did not understand what it implied."

He thought about the problem for a moment more, clicking his teeth in exasperation.

"During the battle we, Beor and I, were ordered to leave by General Sho'Duphuder," To'Jopeviq said. "Part of the mission was to retrieve the diplomatic group on the Ogut ship. While we were on the way to the ship, we came parallel to a human shuttle dispatched on the same mission.

"The pilot of the shuttle, a junior enlisted coxswain, contacted our ship," To'Jopeviq said. "That is the first thing, and perhaps the most important thing, to keep in mind. There was no evidence that the contact was ordered. The shuttle pilot—during, as she pointed out, a very shaky ceasefire and in easy range of our AV's main guns—took the *initiative* to contact us. Not to attempt to surrender or to plead for mercy. She called us to taunt us. To taunt us on the relatively low acceleration of our own shuttle. And, yes, she absolutely blew past us as if we were still. But when I spoke with her, she not only continued the taunts, she composed on the fly a task, condition, and standard for insulting an alien species. Then did a docking that had our pilot quite frankly shocked at its speed and precision. A hard dock sufficiently tight, it even scared the Ogut onboard.

"This was, as I pointed out to Major Beor, a *very* junior enlisted," To'Jopeviq said, looking at the group, "who had the initiative to insult us, *no* fear in doing so, either of retribution by her superiors nor fire from our own craft, and the wit and intelligence to do so *very* effectively. Her insults could have restarted a major battle, yet she had no apparent fear that her actions would be punished by her superiors."

To'Jopeviq looked at the group and hissed, then ducked his head.

"Please tell me that one of you has the understanding to see what that means in terms of human efficiency," he said.

"I think I can comprehend it," Avama said, slowly. "Vaguely. I think."

"Training and selecting personnel to take intelligent initiative enhances the decision making and issue rectification cycle," To'Jopeviq said, then sighed. "Gods of space, that sounds so..."

"Staffer?" Beor said with a slight smile.

"But it is nonetheless true," To'Jopeviq continued. "Try to imagine a very simple situation. When building a ship, an assault vector for this example, a piece of wall does not fit quite right. The solution is fairly simple. Cut it a bit, do a weld, whatever the answer.

"By the way that we Rangora do things, such a change would at the least require a supervisor to concur and even oversee. Possibly that supervisor, fearing retribution for initiative, would require a meeting and a committee would decide if the part should be cut or if a new part should be ordered. That way no one person could be held to blame if it was the wrong decision. Possibly they would order a new part rather than risk being found at fault.

"So, this particular issue might take a week to resolve. And it would require such a process simply because we do *not* train or prepare our personnel to take intelligent initiative. We debase and abhor the very concept practically from birth. We are unprepared by the very society we inhabit. Initiative is one of the great *sins* in the Rangoran Empire.

"The humans, by and large—at least the 'Western' oriented countries—would delegate the simple decisions like this to a very junior person. Possibly even a welder. Not even necessarily designate. The welder would simply look at the part, look at what it affected and decide, with or *without* previously given authority, whether to cut the part to fit or call for a supervisor.

"Even if they frequently called for supervision, the net time involved would be lower if they even occasionally made their own decisions. And from all of our research the supervisors would tend to train their subordinates to make such decisions on their own. If for no other reason than they take time and effort on the part of the supervisor. 'Intelligently lazy' management is the human term. Decisions that in the Rangoran Empire would put them at risk of demotion or even death.

"There are human managers who act more like Rangora, who require that they be involved in even the most minute decision on the part of their subordinates. Many, even most, organizations tend to try to weed out such managers who they refer to, negatively, as 'micromanagers.' Our entire *society* is built upon such micromanagement.

"The only way to overcome millions of issues is with millions of *people* who are trained, evaluated, and—worst of all from our perspective—*bred and raised* to make their *own* intelligent decisions and given the backing, authority, and even praise for doing so.

"The reason that the humans are so fiendishly clever in all these areas—fighting, manufacturing, even rebuilding their society—is pushing the responsibility and authority down to the lowest *possible* level, thus reducing the time involved in decision-making and rectifying more issues faster than we can frankly believe. Repeating: Training and selecting personnel to take intelligent initiative enhances the decision-making and issue-rectification cycle."

"Some of that I can comprehend, General," Toer said after a few moment's thought. "But there is a sociological aspect I cannot."

"Which is?" To'Jopeviq asked.

"Such a process requires insane levels of individualism," Toer said. "Take the counterexample of the Horvath. The Horvath *cannot* make an individual decision. Even the most minor decision requires some discussion by a group. How could a society where individuals are comfortable with constant personal decision-making be organized? Why would individuals who are so individualistic follow *any* orders whatsoever? A system based on that degree of individualism would automatically be anarchy."

"That is one aspect I'd considered and have no good answer for," the general admitted. "They really should be in a continuous state of anarchy."

* * *

It was weird standing on the surface of a planet.

Everything felt, smelled, looked . . . wrong. After years in space without any groundside leave, Earth was a strange place. Even the best Glatun grav-plate system had small irregularities in apparent gravity. You got so used to it, it felt normal. Earth didn't have that. "Normal" gravity felt weird. She'd heard people coming back from leave talking about it. But it was hard to comprehend until it happened. She was trying not to sway back and forth with "stable" gravity.

The sounds were wrong. Inside the Indianapolis Air and Space Port she could nearly ignore the changes. Outside, not so much. She was having a hard time putting her finger on it but part of it was that there was *no echo.* She had been surrounded by walls for so long she wasn't used to there being no bounce-back of sound. Sound just faded away into the distance. Weird.

It was a pleasant fall day. Air was crisp. But it lacked . . . character. The best recyclers in the universe couldn't get all the smells of humanity crammed into a nickel/iron ball out of the air. There were dozens of smells she unconsciously associated with space. People smells. Ozone. The constant background scent of nickel iron. There were some smells of burnt hydrocarbons from the few remaining "gas-powered" vehicles. But even *that* was causing a flinch. Burning was bad in space.

And she was constantly flinching at a low-level because there were *drafts.* Wind, actually. Not bad, not strong, but there was *wind.* Wind in space was not a good thing. It meant there's been a hull breach and breathable was *going away*! Every time the cool, light breeze touched her skin she wanted to run for her suit-locker.

She should be reveling in it. She was on the ground! She wasn't desperately trying to save lives or under fire or surrounded by nickel iron and musty smells. She didn't even have to take orders. She had thirty days to go anywhere she wanted. With nobody telling her what to do! Instead, she was flinching. She just wanted to go home, and she suddenly realized that home, for her, would *always* be space.

Then there were the vehicles themselves. People were dropping off and picking up. All normal. Except . . . when she'd left, grav-cars and fully automated driving were just starting to be "the new thing." The economic effects of the wars and even the baby boom had caused a lag in technological development despite the introduction of Galactic technologies. Hydrocarbon or hybrid vehicles using wheels, including steering wheels, were still the norm.

Most of the vehicles driving by the front of the spaceport were wheelless, drifting over the surface on repulsion systems like a land-speeder from *Star Wars*. There were even "speeder-bikes." Difference being even the bikes didn't have driving controls. None of the grav-vehicles had so much as a steering wheel as a backup. The grav-bike riders were leaned back, mostly with their arms folded, steering either with implants or simply letting the bike go where it was programmed. Ditto the cars. People were reading pads as they went by, or "drivers" were turned around chatting with the people in the back seat.

A newish red Ford F250 slid into the space in front of her, pulled up until it was parallel with the space, then slid sideways like an air-hockey puck. She had to take a moment to recognize Randall. Randall Bogenschutz was the cousin closest in age to her growing up and they'd had a decidedly "ragged" relationship. He was the cousin she'd felt closest to, for age reasons if nothing else, but he was also the cousin she'd spent the most time fighting, often physically. She'd learned the term "roundhouse" from him and learned to do it better than he could. She loved him like the brother he really was and like any brother constantly wanted to punch him for being such a dick.

She only knew the lady in the passenger side, his not particularly new bride, from videos and photos. Sarah Bogenschutz, née Carter, and her family had moved to Cayuga in "resettlement" after the Pittsburg bombing. She had the "Johannsen's" look just as Dana did: blond, blue. Come to think of it, they could have been twins, and Dana had a quickly suppressed thought that maybe Randall had seen more in her than he'd ever mentioned.

Sarah was also pregnant, again, as was obvious when she got out of the truck and wrapped her arms around the new arrival.

"Dana!" she said, grinning. "I've been wanting to meet you for years!"

"It's a pleasure to meet you as well," Dana said. She wasn't sure why she felt awkward and formal hugging her functional sister-in-law back. *Five years in military environments. Damned near zero other women around. Hugging is not high on the list of daily actions.* Thinking about it, the last hug she'd received was from . . . and she also put the thought of Tyler Vernon aside.

"Let me get your bag," Randy said, then gave her a hug as well.

"I can actually pick it up myself, Shorty," Dana said, grinning.

Randall was a year older than her growing up but always shorter. Then when they hit puberty, Dana had stopped growing upward and Randy had shot up. He now overtopped her by at least a foot and a half.

"Who's the runt now?" Randy said, grinning back. He also picked up her bag and set it in the back of the truck. "Ready to go? We've got a bit of a drive."

"Very," Dana said, opening up the back door.

"I'll ride in the back!" Sarah said. "That way you two can talk!"

Sarah was clearly the type of person who exclaimed every word.

"I'm easy," Dana said, and waved for her to enter.

"Five years," Randy said as the truck slid into traffic. He'd turned his seat to face sideways and was paying no attention to the road. "Five *years*. I can't believe it's been that long. We've been worried about you every day, you know."

Dana was watching the road, not so much to see what seemed to be the inevitable wreck as to see the changes. The first one she saw was a very large and well-marked sign, which also pinged her implants: AUTOMATED VEHICLES ONLY TWO LEFT LANES. As they got onto the interstate the truck automatically slid into the far-left lane, joined a phalanx of other cars and trucks, then accelerated up to what looked to be nearly a hundred miles per hour. The traffic wasn't heavy, but it was clearly heavily automated. Dana was used to going much much faster in space but not in such close proximity to other moving vehicles.

She felt sorry for the occasional non-automated driver stuck over in the far-right lanes. They were still having to poke along. She wondered, briefly, how the police kept them over there. Americans weren't the most law-abiding drivers in the world.

"Most of the time there's not much to worry about," Dana said, shrugging. She had the automatic honesty reaction to realize that "working the Scrapyard" was something to worry about and that "working with the Suds and Pathans" had nearly cost her her life, and her career, on numerous occasions but forbore to mention that. "When the Rangora aren't around, the job's generally about as safe as farming. Which ain't exactly a safe profession, you know."

"It's gotten safer," Randy said. "You won't believe the new

equipment Dad's bought. Everything is gravity and automated now. Hell, the only reason I've ridden a tractor in the last two years is to get a higher view of the fields. They run themselves. Practically the whole farm runs itself."

"No more tossing hay bales?" Dana asked, smiling.

Square hay bales were pretty much an anachronism in farming by the time Dana showed up at the farm when she was three. Round bales were less labor intensive, and labor always had a cost. She'd only tossed a few of them in her time.

"Hay bales, hell," Randy said. "We don't even pick rocks. The auto-plow does it for us."

"What kind of a farmer doesn't pick rocks?" Dana asked, honestly aghast.

Picking rocks had been the single most tedious and unpleasant job left in industrial farming. Almost all other forms of back labor had been eliminated due to labor cost, danger of injury and difficulty. Rock picking was the one remnant of classic "back work" farming remaining in most industrial farming, which was why it was something of a badge of honor amongst farmers.

"The plow can sense what's rock and what's soil," Randy said, shrugging. "So, we run it over the field, first, before we lay down fertilizer. It just picks 'em up and drops 'em in a trailer. Difference in density, you get that, right?"

"Computerized gravity tractor," Dana said, frowning. "Algorithm wouldn't even be that hard. How small are the rocks it picks?"

"Down to gravel," Randy said. "And strips off any soil."

"That's pretty fine grav work," Dana said, her brow furrowing. "I'm going to want to see the manual on it. Who's the manufacturer?"

"John Deere," Randy said. "You think Dad would buy anything else?"

Dana did a quick search on "John Deere" and chuckled.

"You realize it's mostly owned by Apollo, right?" she said.

"They merged a while back," Randy replied. "Like . . . ten, fifteen years? But it's still run like John Deere's always been run."

"I think I see the guiding hand, though," Dana said. "So, other than the vast changes in, well, *everything*, what's new?"

The two-story Cape Cod house at least looked the same. Standard Midwest farmhouse, one each. Same massive sheet-metal barn and the old and now unused silo that Uncle Don swore every year he was going to get torn down. Same trees. Though it looked as if her favorite sycamore had finally succumbed to age and insects and been taken down. The various cars and trucks parked out front were all sitting flat on the ground instead of on wheels, except one classic Toyota Prius that was undergoing renovation.

"Let me guess," Dana said. "Your Prius."

"You know I've got a thing for classics," Randy said, shrugging.

"It's so loud!" Sarah said. It was practically her first intervention in the conversation. "It feels so rumbly going down the road! You get used to not hearing the tires!"

"I tried to get a permit for a '70s classic," Randy said. "You wouldn't believe what they charge to drive a Camaro. You can own one if you want but the tag's nearly a thousand dollars. Forget the cost of gas. Finding gas is harder than finding gold."

"What's this run on?" Dana asked as people started spilling out of the house. They weren't all family. This was clearly a general reception.

"Electric," Randy said. "We charge it from the helium generator. Here we are. You ready?"

"I was sort of hoping it would just be family," Dana said, honestly. "Do I know all these people?"

"Yes," Randy said, looking at her quizzically. "You don't remember Julie?" he added, pointing.

Dana did in fact remember Julie Owens. They'd been best friends for years. But the slightly plump, pregnant brunette was only vaguely familiar. And the main thing she remembered was that the girl had a habit of grating her teeth on a fork every time she took a bite of food. Since they had shared lunch every day in school, not to mention spending time at each other's houses after school, been to the same gymnastics and cheerleading summer camp and otherwise were practically sisters, it had slowly worn on Dana's nerves over the years to the point she was ready to scream. Getting away from Julie grating her teeth on a fork wasn't the only reason she'd joined the Navy, but it was high on the list.

"Not enjoying the family reunion?" Uncle Don asked.

Dana had stepped outside to catch her breath. The truth was she *wasn't* enjoying it. There were too many people she both knew and didn't know. She couldn't even explain it to herself. It was just too overwhelming.

"Trying to," Dana admitted. "But..."

"Never really left," Uncle Don said, sitting down on one of the rocking chairs on the back porch. "Going to college isn't the same thing. But I knew people, friends, who went off to the wars. And it's hard coming home. They always said that."

"'Me who have been where I've been, me who have seen what I've seen, me who have done what I've done,'" Dana paraphrased. "How can I go back to Indiana again?"

"That," Don said, not getting the reference. "And you're not really staying... are you?"

"No," Dana said. "I'm going back in a month. I'm not even sure what you do with a month off."

"Relax," Don said. "Breathe the air."

"The air smells funny," Dana said. "It's the right air but it's the wrong air at the same time." She sighed and shrugged. "I'll get over it. But there was a question I was going to ask and it wasn't the right time in front of everyone."

"Go ahead," Don said.

"I'm thinking about... having a child," Dana said, shrugging again. "I don't even get why exactly. But I do want to. Problem being, I also plan on going back—to space, that is. And it's no place to raise one."

"'Mars ain't the kind of place to raise your kids,'" Don said.

"That," Dana said. "Not that we're doing much with Mars."

"I see what you're getting at and the answer is we're getting a bit old for it," Don admitted. "You have to be fast to catch young'uns and I'm getting slower. Who's the dad? And are you getting married?"

"The dad is... under discussion," Dana said, a little white lie. "And that's up in the air as well. But if you're not up for it..." She paused and frowned.

"Then ask Randy and Sarah," Don suggested. "They like kids and they're good parents."

Dana thought about trying to explain who the father might be.

"That might work," she said. "If they'll go for it."

"I'll tell you something, though," Don said. "You can plan to just have a child and go back to space. But when you're faced with the reality... Don't be so sure. No matter how much you love space, no matter how much you want to continue your career, giving up a child is different than asking someone to take care of your pet. It just is."

"Deal with that, then," Dana said. "I need to close the deal on the dad first."

"And there's that," Don said. "Who are you considering?"

Dana thought about that for a second.

"Someone who'll probably say no."

"Do you love him?" Don asked.

Dana thought about that one as well.

"Good question," Dana said. "I've got friends that say the answer is yes. But I'm not sure how I feel about him."

"Then you probably love him and just don't want to admit it."

"So now Tyler's sending me emails?" Dana said, opening the attachment.

The graphic was a meme. The top said COINCIDENCE? and below were two headlines side by side:

WORLD WIDE IQ'S DROPPING! SCIENTISTS BAFFLED!
BLONDE POPULATION REACHES all-time HIGH!

"Oh, great," Dana said, trying not to grin. "Just what I need. The richest man in the world sending me *blonde jokes*!"

She had to respond so she went on the net looking for "Tyler Vernon" jokes.

The problem being most of them were old or . . . downright disgusting and mean. She'd never really studied Tyler. He was just one of those public figures until the Wolf Mission and she'd never been into celebrity gossip.

But the level of hatred—and there was no other way to phrase it—for the man was just insane and to her infuriating. She finally had to quit when she got to a Chinese editorial cartoon that had President Robards squatting behind him wiping his butt. She was so angry she started calculating the orbitals to drop a fucking rock on Beijing.

That's when she stopped and groaned.

"Oh, damnit!" she muttered. "Those creepy AI bastards were right.

"I'm in love."

CHAPTER 12

"Madame President, we have an issue."

Her National Security Advisor rarely looked anything but bland. He was... slightly less, indicating that this was a very serious issue.

"Which is?" President Robards asked. And it had been, in terms of bad days, not the worst since she'd inherited the Office.

"We've lost contact with Wolf 359," Mr. Parsons said. "We're not sure why but it has to be a hostile act. The gate is actively being jammed."

"Athena?" the President said. "Comment?"

"There was an indication but it was low, Madame President," Athena said. "Low enough even the AIs considered an attack unlikely.

"There is the small possibility that an unknown actor from a recently opened gate has attacked. Very small. There have been no species contacted in several thousand years who had any sort of real space faring ability. Your species was as far along as any contacted in hundreds. So 'evil aliens appearing from nowhere' is unlikely.

"However, a recently opened gate does connect, though several undeveloped systems, to the Gamarana."

"Gamarana aren't a species even I recognize," the former Secretary of State said.

"We previously had no reason to contact them," Athena said. "However, they do connect to the Ogut. The reason that an attack seemed unlikely is that it would have to be an Ogut attack. The Gamarana have in-system defenses but nothing like power-projection. And they are nominally hostile to the Ogut. The only way that Wolf could be under attack is if the Ogut negotiated a pass-through of the Gamarana. And that was considered a very low likelihood. Bad call on our part as well as Alliance Intelligence but not one that I would redo in retrospect. That is, however, the highest likelihood."

"And what combat forces do we have in Wolf 359?" the President asked.

"None, Madame President," the NSA answered. "As Athena pointed out, we hadn't any indication we needed them. There are a few ships preparing to come out of the yards but there aren't even the usual crews there to pick them up. I'm not sure we have a single line officer in-system."

"Line officer," the President said.

"In conditions of combat a line officer takes command even over officers senior to him or her if they are not line officers," Athena said. "It's a very old tradition but a very specific regulation. There are reasons for it and arguments for and against, but it is still military law."

"So, we have, essentially, no one to direct the defense," the NSA said. "I suppose Admiral MacDonald will take over, but he has no actual combat training."

"You'd think he'd sort of pick it up by osmosis if he's an admiral," the President said.

"I would politely disagree with the National Security Advisor," Athena said. "There is *one* line officer in system. In fact, there is *exactly* one."

All Dana could think as she hit the water was that was one of her more terrible dives.

"Dana, it's Granny," her plant pinged.

"Yeah, Granny?" Dana said, breast stroking to the side of the pool. "What's up?"

"An Ogut task force just entered the system," Granny said with a level of calm that was truly frightening. "They're jamming the gate and external hypernode and calling for an immediate surrender."

"Ooookay," Dana said, lifting herself out of the pool and walking to her lounger and towel. Most of the main stuff in the system, including Franklin and the shipyards, was currently pretty far from the gate due to orbits. So, whatever happened, they had a little time. "There don't seem to be any alarms."

"That's because the system commander hasn't ordered them," Granny said.

"What's taking Admiral MacDonald so long?" Dana said, wrinkling her brow as she toweled off. She wasn't sure what a *Myrmidon* could do against an Ogut taskforce, but she figured she was back on duty pretty much pronto.

"Admiral MacDonald is not the system commander," Granny said. "He is the system governor, but he is a support officer. His entire career has been engineering and administrative. He is not a line officer. As such, in a defense condition such as this he legally defers to the most senior line officer."

"Okay," Dana said. "So, what's taking the 'most senior line officer' so long to issue the alarms?"

"The most senior line officer is just about to realize they are the most senior line officer," Granny said, very carefully.

Dana thought about that for a second.

"Oh, you have got to be fucking kidding me!" Dana snapped. "There are dozens, hundreds, of Navy officers in system! There are fucking *marine* officers in system! You are not telling me that..."

"They are all Support, Engineering, and Admin," Granny said. "We're having this conversation simultaneously with Admiral MacDonald and about six different legal officers and senior officers. The legal officers are reluctantly in agreement. We're AIs, Dana. We *cannot* make exceptions with something this clearly black and white. The regs are clear. In a combat situation, the senior line officer takes command over any rank. You, a lieutenant JG coxswain, are the senior line officer in-system and we are cut off from external communications. You are, right now, presently, the System Defense Commander and I need you to get past that *very quickly*, Dana. We need orders and we do not have much time."

"Hey, babe, how's it going?" Dana heard from over her shoulder.

She spun around and pointed a double knife hand at the guy.

"JUST NOT NOW!" she snarled. "This is NOT the time!"

She had no clue if he was military or civilian or if military what his rank might be. But while it should have been the time, more or less, totally acceptable socially and all that, IT WAS NEITHER THE TIME NOR THE PLACE.

"Hey, I was just..."

"Are you military?" she snapped in command voice.

"Uh, yes, I'm..."

"I really don't care," Dana said. "Granny, all military personnel present in the pool area are to form up around me to keep other people from bothering me. Further, they are not to ask questions or bother me themselves. This holds for all ranks. I need space and peace to handle this. Give me Admiral MacDonald..."

"Sir, I am aware that you and your staff have prepared a defense plan," Dana said. "And I am sure it is a very good one. I'm looking forward to reviewing it after the battle, sir. In the meantime, I have already sent my plan to the AIs, and we are preparing to execute that plan, sir."

She'd reviewed the admiral's defense plan already. Doing all the rescue work, she'd raised multitasking with her implants to a fine art. She thought, and Granny agreed, it was...suboptimal. Basically, it was "pull all the ships back to the important stuff and use the merchant ships as combat forces." It did have some stuff for SAPL, and they were already converting fabbers to missile production but...

Suboptimal.

"Lieutenant," the admiral said, somewhat stuffily. "I am aware that you are senior line officer. I am aware of, have been aware of before you were *born*, the underlying statute. But you need to realize that...I'm an *admiral*, Lieutenant. I can run a battle just fine. I could do so, again, before you were *born*. So, what we are *going to do*, is I am going to tell you how this battle is going to run, and you are going to give those orders. Is that clear, Lieutenant?"

"I understand your words, sir," Dana said, thinking how much she was going to enjoy being an instructor at the YMCA. If she could avoid the brig. "And I understand the regulation, sir. The battle plan has already been set and is, in fact, already in operation. When I have completed the battle, you return to full control of the system, sir."

"Now see here, Lieutenant!"

"Granny, give me the *Ogut* admiral now," Dana said, waving her hand. "And there goes my nascent career. Leavenworth, here I come."

She had contacted the Ogut admiral and given her name, rank, serial number, and national origin. She knew, properly, she was supposed to give her entire career CV and ancestry in a formal engagement like this. Granny even had it prepared—including the ancestry part, which was a bit odd. She had Granny shoot over the data and asked that it be "entered into record."

Then she had had to stand there while rather than "reading it into record" the Ogut admiral had verbally proclaimed the same.

Admiral Aemae EnoeIspoe O'mi Oevo'O'rae OteEju OgoOespae Uyo'Ithi AhiOedoe AyoO'wa Aegoe O' mo' OsheAe saOego' OeqaeAsaIkeAlo' UkoeUfo' EciAqeImaeIdo' IwuAwaEcoIfaeItaAgiO' liIpaeOweIdiIlaAe paeO' vaeIbo' EloeIlaeUkeAe soeOecoAe loEsaeAe daeEmiO' jaOesaOexiIboeEqaIloeO' boeIzaAe boeOefaAdiAyo' AqoeOshoe EbeEluAe luUvoUroEhuEjoeUjuOkaAwo' Ae sho' AciUshoeEniUbo' AheUpoIboeAe naAe raeAe loeAe loeAthoeAe daEveAvoEkaeOesaeOmiOjo' EciO' zoeOethuIwoeOziUshaO' fiAe yo' OegoO' toeO' zaeExuAe muIviAcaOsaOqeAe ko' Ae speEthaeAe yoeUspo of the Ogut Luwusu Syndicate—OsaOqeAeko to his friends—was having a very good day.

Ogut names were, to humans, and indeed to most sophonts, odd. Ogut itself was a difficult language for most sophonts to learn. A single Ogut word often incorporated a human sentence. And Ogut full names, which they insisted upon using in any even *semi*-formal encounter, were not exactly names as humans considered them. They were extensive histories, familial histories, and personal curricula vitae of all notable accomplishments in the Ogut's life as well as those of his ancestors. They were more or less in chronological series with ancestral accomplishments thrown in randomly.

Aemae, thus, translated as "was selected for the finest of creche schooling as a predevelopment larva and thereafter succeeded well beyond his older peers."

Cultural translation being "he got into kindergarten at two and was smarter than the five-year-olds."

It just went on from there.

Admittedly, it was just his name, with pauses for the Ogut to be translated, but it had gone on and on and on and on and on and on and...

At least the Ogut had the formal decency to wait in place while the guy pronounced his full name.

Among other things, Dana picked up he had been "something

like a hall monitor" in "something like sixth grade," had "won a spelling bee," and one of his ancestors was a pirate.

That's pretty much all she remembered.

At one point, since she hadn't bothered to read hers, she asked Granny in an aside if she had a pirate ancestor.

No, but she was descended from someone called "Grunnar the Terrible" who had apparently raped and pillaged his way up and down the Irish coast at one point.

Her ancestry was on the Irish side, which was a bit unsettling.

So was the fact that Granny knew that.

Granny had worked up a huge list of famous and infamous ancestors based on DNA analysis. Though in reality most people in the United States from Northern European background were in some way shape or form "descended" from Charlemagne.

The genes just got around.

Don't even get started on Genghis Khan. There was a gene named after him, it was so common.

She might just take the time on a *long* deployment to read the whole damned thing.

Wasn't making for interesting hearing.

Finally, it was time for the actual negotiations.

"This is really not a good time," Dana said, horking water out of her ear again. She just could not get all the stuff out. She had made sure that Granny would send exactly how she looked and what she was doing. She wasn't sure what the Ogut would think of horking water, and she really didn't give a God damn. The Brass were probably going to have a shit fit when they saw how she handled the battle. They were *having* a shit fit over a lieutenant JG being in charge of the whole damned system. And they were piped in on everything so they could see she was conducting the whole damned thing in a bathing suit. They were probably shitfitting about that, too. She didn't give a God damn about that, either.

Pissed didn't begin to cover it. These caterpillars in their tiny tin boats thought they were going to take out this system when it was under *her* command? They were about to learn a lesson any number of people had learned to their misery. The fucking 143 wrote it on their fucking hands: *No jodas con la perra de hielo*. Never mess with the Ice Bitch.

"I was just having the first good time I've had in a long time. What with the battle in Eridani and losing most of the people I knew and loved in the universe, the cleanup from that battle... It's been a rough few months. And I was just having the first downtime I've had in a long time. I also just got another tat, and it hurts like shit. So, I'm going to give you one warning: Turn your little cockleshells around and leave. Now. Immediately. And I won't turn your ships into modern art."

"You have no significant combat forces in system," the Ogut admiral replied. "Your vaunted SAPL has no systems to defend its mirrors. You have no way to defeat us. If you surrender now, the terms will be quite acceptable. We will retain all material and equipment in this system and allow all human personnel to leave. The terms become more onerous as time goes by. You are advised to surrender. The cost in capital if you fight will be more than you wish to pay."

"Not gonna happen," Dana said, horking some more water and shaking her head. "One last chance. Leave."

"You would be wise, young one, to surrender," the admiral replied. "We can discuss the terms of that surrender. It is possible we could leave you some portion of your material in return for a cash payment..."

Dana wasn't going to be bothered. Granny had offered reasonable odds that the Ogut would accept something along the lines of tribute. Pay some fraction of the value of the system to the task force and they'd leave.

That wasn't going to happen, either.

The Ogut probably had enough missiles to take out all the UNG—Unified Nuclear Grappler—beam mirrors in range of their ships. What they did not have was enough to take out all the mirrors of every type.

Most of the mirrors that shifted their angle to engage the Ogut fleet weren't UNG beams. UNG beams would have cut through the relatively weak shielding of the Ogut ships like... a very powerful laser through a butter patty.

The much less powerful BDA (Big Distributed Array) and VDA (Variable Dialing Array) beams on the other hand...

Dana had been watching the countdown. The "negotiations" were really to run out the clock.

"Okay, if that's the way you want it," she said, horking her ear again. Damn, it would just *not* come out...

* * *

"All shields are at maximum, Admiral!" the Flagship Tactical Officer reported. "We are completely blacked out."

"I thought you said you could take out their mirrors," Admiral OsaOqeAeko snapped over the sound of straining power systems. It was clear the ship was under enormous stress.

"The mirrors act at light speed, sir," Tactical said. "And they are not coming from their most powerful systems. Just their general supply mirrors. There are *thousands* of those. Impossible to take them all out. And even if we could, right now we can't even *launch*. This should not be possible! This is . . . beyond my experience, Admiral."

The sound of straining systems suddenly stopped.

"We are no longer under attack, Admiral," the tactical officer said. "But all the other ships still are."

"Why does that not make me happy?" Admiral OsaOqeAeko said, very cautiously. "Fire full spread on all . . ."

The timing had been tricky but while the AIs in system were not optimized for combat, it wasn't much different from some tricky mining and engineering they'd done in the past.

Light does not reach a point instantaneously. It is very fast, but not instantaneous. And over spatial distance there was always a bit of lag. But the various AIs of the Wolf System were used to working with that. And there really weren't that many UNG mirrors near the gate, which was where the Ogut task force still lay.

Which was why, in near simultaneity, five UNG beams hit the Ogut "battleship."

While humans had mostly paid attention to Rangora, Glatun, and Horvath ship engineering, they were well aware that anyone could become a foe at any time. So, there was, also, a complete database of Ogut ship engineering, with a notable focus on their warships.

Thus, the AIs knew precisely where to strike.

One UNG beam was targeted on the main engine power coupling. Two more were targeted on the two redundant weapons systems control centers. One was targeted on primary navigation and the fifth was targeted on primary systems cyber defense.

Not all were perfectly aligned and, unfortunately, two Ogut junior spacemen and a petty officer were killed in the first strike. The AIs quickly adjusted the beams.

Then they took over the ship's controls.

"Abandon ship! Abandon ship! This is not a drill! All hands abandon ship!"

"I didn't give that order!" Admiral OsaOqeAeko snapped.

"All hands are abandoning ship, Admiral," the XO said. "We can't stop them. Pods are ejecting as we speak."

The admiral didn't need to be told that. He could feel the shudder of every pod on the ship punching out. Given that the ship was dead in space and under the enemy's lasers it only made sense.

"What are your orders, Admiral?"

"Hello, again, Admiral."

The very under-ranked idiot was back. Although now that he thought about it, he had to wonder which of them was the idiot.

"I'd advise you to punch out with your crew, Admiral," the junior officer said, hitting her head and shaking it again in that weird human gesture that was now being translated as "emphatic." "I'm about to turn your ship into modern art. You don't want to be onboard when that happens. Oh, I apologize. You lost a few crew. We were trying to avoid that but . . . fortunes of war. I'd rather not kill everyone still onboard, but I have an example to make. Please do depart. Now."

She again gestured emphatically by striking the side of her head several times and shaking it.

"Can you define 'modern art'?" the admiral asked, carefully.

"I'm going for something postmodernist," the human replied, waggling its fingers in a sculpting gesture. "Subtle, yet distinctive. Recognizable, yet ambiguous. Or, honestly, unambiguous. Which will start happening to your ship in fifteen, fourteen, thirteen, twelve . . ."

"We are leaving!" the admiral shouted, getting out of his couch and inch-worming for the nearest escape pod. "Senior boards first!"

The next bit required some Paw tugs that fortunately had been near the gate. The Ogut hadn't fired on them, recognizing them as commercial vessels and valuable prizes.

As the secondary beams pounded the now evacuated flagship, the Paw tugs moved in and started working at it with powerful tractors. Various volatiles ejected from the ship as the energy from the sunbeams increased but the Paws were used to that and simply gathered them up for later use. There were minor explosions but those were common . . . when working with comets, especially.

Slowly, the Ogut flagship deformed and melted under the power of the mining lasers and the tugs continued to work the now malleable remaining metals. Much of the ship was not metal and that material could not be used for this sculpture, so the resulting piece of art was of significantly lower mass than the flagship but significantly more . . . emphatic.

"We are receiving a human hypercom request," the communications officer of the *Ubaotoep* said.

Senior Ship Commander (oh, God, here we go . . .) Iwaeaegab O'woeetir O'neuqaep Obiigiq Ibooexip O'noaegeb Aeruoebael Uraeo'raj Aelaeamiv Eseacoeth Etho'aqux Ukaazo'b Obiemah Aeko'o'sheb O'zo'exo'h Ipaaexey Oecaeacaj Ofuenof Iseinen Ecoeuqoek Iyao'zo'b O'spiodaet Ujaeaesho'f Iduufid Oethoo'xoth Umo'umisp Ucualith Ekaunoef Utheishuj Oedeiqey O'naeopop Aexoacot Ufaeado'l Asuoewaeth Espaeemur O'thaoevoy Aethoidel Egoeeyish Ufaeoeduz Ofoidod Aesho'uziz O'reewo'm Ujiamax Ovuo'zal O'pooemok Iweejim Akaeurar O'dioyo'n Oespaeupil Aetoealaek Oegoeoepog Aqaeatap Oco'acoev Ubaotoep Aqaeoevuk Ebueqih Enoeuqoev Uliamop Ado'asaew Ikaokut Aetho'o'lur O'heosur O'spaado'd Oexaeo'co'n Opaemo'h Aesaeoeyo'd Oroeoroep Oetuomol Ojaeaewo'd Ezio'paq—just call him Ojaeaewo'd—like all the commanders in the task force, thought this would be a very lucrative walk-over.

The fact that his command-and-control center had reached a balmy seventy-three degrees Celsius indicated this might not, in fact, be the case.

"Receive," Commander Ojaeaewo'd said.

The image was human, but he could not sort out more than that. They all looked the same to him.

"I am the current system combat commander," the human said, without proper preamble. "Your flagship has been turned into a piece of art. Your task force commander and most of the crew are alive. I permitted them to escape. All I have to do to turn your ship into art is increase the power of my lasers, and you're getting less than five percent of the power I have at my disposal. What I'm going to do next is lower the power so you can see what remains of your flagship. If you fire, I'm out of patience and I'll simply increase power and fry you like aborigines fry caterpillars for lunch. Then I'll try the next most senior commander and see if he can take a hint. Do you understand?"

"I am . . ." Ojaeaewo'd said, beginning negotiations properly.

"I'm not going to spend all day listening to your God damned formal name," the human said, gesturing with one hand. "Just read it into the record."

"Power levels on shields increasing!" engineering said. "Reaching overload!"

"I understand," Commander Ojaeaewo'd said.

"Very good," the human replied. "Now, decreasing power so you can have a look. Fire, and you end up a crispy bug."

The straining power systems slowly wound down, and the internal temperature started to fall.

"We're getting external visuals," tactical said.

"Main repeater," the commander replied.

He wasn't sure at first what he was looking at and didn't have a human expert to interpret. But it appeared to be a metal human hand floating in space. The "fingers" of the hand were clasped mostly into what he had been told was a "fist" but one finger, the middle, was upright.

He really didn't know what to make of it.

"Isotopic signatures from the metal indicate that is . . ." the tac officer said, then paused. "Commander, that is what is *left* of the flagship. We are also receiving a number of pod distress beacons."

Ojaeaewo'd didn't even have to think about that one. None of his names translated as "Heroic beyond the bounds of intelligence."

"Human commander, we accept a temporary ceasefire," the Ogut commander said. "But could you give me just a moment to access my databases?"

"As long as you don't open your missile ports and don't approach closer to our stations, I'll give you all the time you need," the human replied. "Unless it's to tell me your full formal name, in which case, stuff it. I don't have the patience of a saint, and I was off duty when you assholes arrived. But, sure, go for your life."

Commander Ojaeaewo'd picked up a pad and began accessing it.

"Human manual gestures," he commed, then started flipping

through images. There were so many. "Single finger upright..." Still many. "Possibly insulting?"

Image, image, image... He held the pad up to the repeater and clicked on the link for more information.

"Rude gesture... suggests human physiologically impossible reproductive act..." He read for a moment, burbling in thought, then set down the pad.

"There is one remaining issue of difficulty, human commander," Commander Ojaeaewo'd said. "And it is something that is entirely required and cannot be negotiated."

"What?" the human asked.

"To formally surrender the task force, I am required to have your full name, rank, and ancestry, and names of all ancestors of note as well as, I am very sorry, you must know mine. Otherwise, the surrender is not legally binding under Ogut law."

"Well, shit," the human said. "Make a hole! I'm gonna have to sit down for this one. And somebody get me a beer. This is gonna take a while. Who am I? Who am *I*?

"I am Lieutenant Junior Grade *Dana Cecilia Parker* of the handle Comet for the power and force of my flying! Daughter of Louis Parker, killed in an illegal bombardment of the city of Los Angeles by the Horvath, and Cherie Parker, who took her own life after walking out of the fiery maelstrom the Horvath created of one of our greatest cities.

"Descendant of Roman General Scipio Africanus—the only Roman general to defeat Hannibal the Great!

"Descendant of *Genghis Khan,* who conquered *most of the known world...!*"

Khan Gene... check.

"Descendant of the *fierce* Viking warrior Grunnar the Terrible, who *raped and pillaged* the Irish coast...!

"Descendant of the *Marquis de Lafayette,* though not through acknowledged ancestry...

"Descendant of Admiral Samuel Perry '*Powhatan*' Carter of Civil War fame and legend...

"Descendant of the *famous* frontiersman Daniel Boone...

"In initial tests after birth, scored in the ninety-fifth percentile in *four* of five categories. *So* close!

"Lifted myself up in my crib when *still in the neonatal ward.*

"At the age of *three*, I *walked* out of the firestorm that was all that was left of my home city, for *nine miles*!

"*First* in my class in kindergarten...

"Won the Fifth Grade spelling bee with the word *audacious*!

"Cochair of the Prairie High School varsity cheerleading team while I was a *sophomore*...!

"*Distinguished* Graduate of Engineering A School..."

It was the longest surrender in Earth's history.

But for the Ogut, at only four hours for the victorious commander to recite their family history and accomplishments, it was relatively short.

CONTRIBUTOR BIOGRAPHIES

John Ringo is the *New York Times* best-selling author of the Troy Rising series, the Black Tide Rising series, the Posleen Wars series, the Through the Looking Glass series, and more. His early life included a great deal of travel. He visited 23 foreign countries, and attended fourteen different schools. Ringo enlisted in the US military for four years as a member of the 82nd Airborne, after which he studied marine biology. John resides in East Tennessee.

Gray Rinehart (editor) is the only person to have commanded an Air Force satellite tracking station, written speeches for presidential appointees, devised a poetic form, and had music on *The Dr. Demento Show*. During his rather odd USAF career, Gray fought rocket propellant fires, refurbished space launch facilities, "flew" Milstar satellites, drove trucks, processed nuclear command and control orders, commanded the largest remote tracking station in the Air Force Satellite Control Network, and did other interesting things. His fiction has appeared in *Analog Science Fiction & Fact*, *Asimov's Science Fiction*, Orson Scott Card's *Intergalactic Medicine Show*, and several anthologies.

Gray is a contributing editor (the "Slushmaster General") for Baen Books, a singer/songwriter with three albums that feature science-fiction-and-fantasy-inspired music, and an author of award-winning nonfiction. His alter ego is the Gray Man, one of several famed ghosts of South Carolina's Grand Strand, and his website is grayrinehart.com.

* * *

Both a John W. Campbell Award and Dragon Award finalist (though not in the same year), best-selling author **Jason Cordova** is the author of the Black Tide Rising novel *Mountain of Fire*, coauthor of *To Tread Obsidian Shores* with Melissa Olthoff, and editor of *Chicks in Tank Tops, Dancing with Destruction,* and the upcoming *Chaos and Consequences* (all from Baen). He currently resides in North Carolina with his muse and one extremely vocal, annoying cat.

Karl K. Gallagher is a systems engineer, doing data analysis for a major aerospace company. Before that he was an Air Force satellite operator and an engineer in a launch vehicle start-up. He writes both hard science fiction (the Torchship Trilogy) and fantasy (*The Lost War*). His most recent book is *War By Other Means*, book seven in the Fall of the Censor space opera series. He publishes a short story monthly on his Substack, https://gallagherstories.substack.com/.

Karl's novels have been finalists for the Prometheus Award for Best Libertarian Science Fiction Novel of the Year six times: *Torchship Trilogy, Storm Between the Stars, Between Home and Ruin, Seize What's Held Dear, Captain Trader Helmsman Spy,* and *Swim Among the People.*

Michael Gants is a science fiction and fantasy author and retired Navy submariner. He currently works as a nuclear construction and operations quality oversight inspector at Sequoyah Nuclear Plant. His other jobs have included nuclear mechanic, anti-terrorism trainer, small craft boarding specialist, programmer, journalist, and aquarium technician. He resides with his fantastic family in Chattanooga, Tennessee.

A Webster Award winner and three-time Dragon Award finalist, **Chris Kennedy** is a Science Fiction/Fantasy author, speaker, and small-press publisher who has written over eighty books and published more than five hundred others. Get his free book, *Shattered Crucible*, at his website, https://chriskennedypublishing.com. A retired naval aviator, he uses his experience to give authenticity to his military science fiction stories.

Called "fantastic" and "a great speaker," he has coached hundreds of beginning authors and budding novelists on how to self-publish their stories at a variety of conferences, conventions, and writing guild presentations. He is the author of the award-winning #1 bestseller, *Self-Publishing for Profit: How to Get Your Book Out of Your Head and Into the Stores.*

Chris lives in Coinjock, North Carolina, with his wife, Sheellah, and is the holder of a doctorate in educational leadership and master's degrees in both business and public administration. Follow Chris on Facebook at https://www.facebook.com/ckpublishing/.

Mike Massa has visited ninety countries and lived in several large cities for protracted intervals while working in government, financial services, security, and the tech sector. Watching others try the same failing business or personal strategy over and over, despite radical changes in environment, can become an entertaining pastime, provided one is standing beyond the minimum safe distance. Now there's a story about it! That done, Mike will keep writing—you can find his books and short stories at your favorite booksellers and online.

Although born in the northwestern United States, **Michael Mersault** spent his formative years in a series of magical locales, including expat communities in the Middle East, a secretive air base in the Arizona desert, and an Alaskan fishing village. These endless hours of travel prompted an enduring love for books that continues unabated.

At times in his adult years, he has dabbled in kickboxing, competitive marksmanship, and international business ventures. He now lives as a semi-recluse back in the northwest, where he fluctuates between the paths of a confirmed technophile and a neo-Luddite.

Casey Moores was a USAF rescue/special ops C-130 pilot for over seventeen years—airdropping, air refueling, and flying into tiny blacked-out dirt airstrips in bad places using night vision goggles. He's been to *those* places and done *those* things with *those* people. Now he lives a quieter life, bringing those experiences to you in the form of military science fiction, fantasy, alternate history, and postapocalyptic fiction. He has numerous novels in Chris Kennedy Publishing's Blood & Armor, Four Horsemen, and Fallen World universes as well as countless short stories with a growing list of publishers.

Casey is the winner of the Imaginarium Imadjinn Awards Best Historical Fiction for *Witch Hunt* in the JTF-13 series. He is currently helping to develop John Ringo's Shadow's Path series for Baen Books. Find him at www.caseymoores.net.

Melissa Olthoff writes Science Fiction and Fantasy adventure romance with plenty of banter and heart. She is a lifelong geek as well as a veteran of the United States Air Force, both of which are incredibly useful when writing. Her degrees in meteorology and accounting are slightly less applicable to writing, but absolutely useful when it comes to supporting her family.

She has written in both shared worlds and her own universes, and through the power of caffeine and friendship, manages to juggle chaos on and off the page. Published by Baen Books, she is best known for her Griffin Corps series and Bronze Legion novels. Find out more at www.melissaolthoff.com.

Adam Oyebanji is an SF/Crime novelist whose work blends thrilling plots with thought-provoking ideas, often exploring themes of identity, belonging, and the occasional whodunnit. His work has been praised for its originality, rich world-building, and sharp storytelling. Born in the United Kingdom but having spent much of his time in the United States and West Africa, Adam draws on a global perspective shaped by a career in law and a lifelong passion for speculative fiction and murder mysteries. He is a member of the Science Fiction and Fantasy Writers Association, the British Science Fiction Association, and the Crime Writers' Association.

Marisa Wolf is a second-generation nerd who started writing genre stories at six. Over the years she taught middle school, was headbutted by an alligator, built a career in education, earned a black belt in Tae Kwon Do, and finally decided to finish all the half-started stories in her head.

She writes SFF that ends with hope, regardless of the circumstances, as shown through her coauthored novels in shared universes, solo novels in her own worlds, and a plethora of short stories. All contain various levels of snark.

After several years living on the road in an RV, Marisa, her husband, and their high-maintenance rescue dog are currently based near the beach in Virginia—but it's anyone's guess where in the country she is at any given moment. Find out more at www.marisawolf.com.